# IMMATURITY

BERNARD SHAW IN 1879

# IMMATURITY
## BY BERNARD SHAW

LONDON

CONSTABLE AND COMPANY

LIMITED

*First published in Limited Collected Edition in 1930, and reprinted for
this Standard Edition in 1931. Written in 1879*
*Reprinted 1950*

PRINTED IN GREAT BRITAIN
BY R. & R. CLARK, LIMITED, EDINBURGH

# PREFACE

THE scene of one of Mr Arnold Bennett's novels is laid in a certain *cul de sac* off the Brompton Road, nearly opposite the West Brompton District Post Office. He calls it Alexandra Grove; but its actual name is Victoria Grove. As he describes it, the houses now contrive a double rent to pay, as the gardens have been fitted up with studios, thus quietly modernizing London by the back-to-back housing so vehemently denounced as a relic of barbarism in Leeds. When I arrived there as an Irish emigrant of 20, this intensification of population had not occurred. The houses were semi-detached villas with plenty of air space round them (you could call it garden). On the other side of the back wall were orchards; for the huge Poor Law Infirmary which now occupies this space, with its tower on the Fulham Road, was not yet built. The land between West Brompton and Fulham and Putney, now closely packed with streets and suburban roads, had still plenty of orchard and market garden to give it a countrified air and to make it possible to live there, as I did for years, without feeling that one must flee to the country or wither in the smoke. All the parallel Groves connected the Fulham Road with King's Road, Chelsea, where Cremorne Gardens, an unlaid ghost from the eighteenth century, was desperately fighting off its final exorcism as a rendez-vous of the half world. Hence these now blameless thoroughfares were then reputed Bohemian, whilst Victoria Grove, as a blind alley, remained as respectable as Clapham.

I came to London from Dublin in the spring of 1876, and found my mother and my one surviving sister (I had no brothers) established in No. 13 Victoria Grove, trying to turn their musical accomplishments to account: my mother by teaching, my sister by singing. My father, left in Dublin, spared us a pound a week from his slender resources; and by getting into debt and occasionally extracting ourselves by drawing on a maternal inheritance of £4000 over which my mother had a power of appointment, and which therefore could be realized bit by bit as her three children came of age, we managed to keep going somehow.

Impecuniosity was necessarily chronic in the household. And here let me distinguish between this sort of poverty and that which furnishes an element of romance in the early lives of many famous men. I am almost tempted to say that it is the only sort of poverty that counts, short of the privations that make success impossible. We all know the man whose mother brought him up with nineteen brothers and sisters on an income of eighteen shillings a week earned by her own labor. The road from the log cabin to the White House, from the bench in the factory to the Treasury Bench, from the hovel to the mansion in Park Lane, if not exactly a crowded road, always has a few well fed figures at the end of it to tell us all about it. I always assure these gentlemen that they do not know what poverty and failure is. Beginning with as much as they expected or were accustomed to, they have known nothing but promotion. At each step they have had the income of the society in which they moved, and been able to afford its clothes, its food, its habits, its rents and rates. What more has any prince? If you would know what real poverty is, ask the younger son of a younger son of a younger son. To understand his plight you must start at the top without the income of the top, and curse your stars that you were not lucky enough to start at the bottom.

Our institution of primogeniture may have been a feudal necessity. It kept the baronies together; and the barons and their retainers kept the king and the country supplied with an army, a magistracy, and a network of local governments. But it took no account of the younger sons. These unhappy ones were brought up in the baronial castle. Let us represent the income of the barony by the figure 1000. Both sons and daughters were brought up to know no other mode of life than life at this figure. When the eldest took all, what was there left for the girls' dowries and the boys' allowances? Only the scrapings and leavings of the mother's dowry, and such charity as the new baron might choose (if he could afford it) to bestow on his poor relations. A younger son's figure, especially if he had many brothers, might easily be 20 or less, even to zero. What was the poor wretch to do, knowing no other way of living but the way that cost 1000? Easy to tell him that he must cut his coat according to his cloth. Impossible to do it without being trained to that measure from childhood. Impossible anyhow without dropping every relative and friend in the world, and stepping down, a mistrusted, ridiculous, incongruous stranger, into the social circle of his mother's maid and his brother's butler. Impossible often even to go into the army, where an officer cannot live on his pay unless he is a promoted ranker in a line regiment, and not even then with any ease. There is nothing for it but to live beyond one's income, to spunge, to beg, to take credit at the shops without means, to borrow without the prospect of being able to repay, and to blackmail the baron by presenting him with a choice between paying up and having his brother haled before the criminal courts for swindling. The alternative (to marry the daughter of a rich *parvenu*, American or British) is not always available. Who would be an Honorable on such terms if he could help it?

But think of his son, and of his son's son: the undisguised commoner, for whom, because it costs too much, there is not even the public school and university education of the baron's cadet, and who cannot avail himself of the public elementary and secondary schools because such a step would disclass the man of family! Think of the attempt to go into business with some pitiful little capital! think of the struggle to make the loathed occupation yield a living! think of the son for whom there is nothing but a clerkship in the office of some goodnatured business acquaintance! and bear in mind that the descent implies that every generation is, like the original younger son, brought up to a mode of life more expensive than its income can compass; so that it is condemned to pull the devil by the tail from its adolescence to its grave! My able and flourishing friend A tells me that he knows what poverty is and what drink is: was he not brought up in the Borough by a drunken mother? B, rolling in wealth, tells me that when he was a boy he had meat only twice a year. C, wallowing in fame, calls me a snob, after gleefully narrating his experiences in the kitchen of his father's small shop, and how he was enabled to study country house society by a childish privilege of visiting the servants' hall. How easily I cap these zests to success by the simple statement that my father was second cousin to a baronet, and my mother the daughter of a country gentleman whose rule was, when in difficulties, mortgage. That was my sort of poverty. The Shaws were younger sons from the beginning, as I shall shew when I reveal my full pedigree. Even the baronetcy was founded on the fortunes of a fifth son who came to Dublin and made that city his oyster. Let who will preen himself on his Mother Hubbard's bare cupboard, and play for sympathy as an upstart: I was a downstart and the son of a downstart. But for the accident of a lucrative talent I should today be poorer than Spinoza; for he at least knew how to grind lenses, whereas I could not afford to learn any art. Luckily Nature taught me one.

This social *degringolade* never stops in these islands. It produces a class which deserves a history all to itself. Do not talk of the middle class: the expression is meaningless except when it is used by an economist to denote the man of business who stands in the middle between land and capital on the one hand, and labor on the other, and organizes business for both. I sing my own class: the Shabby Genteel, the Poor Relations, the Gentlemen who are No Gentlemen. If you want to know exactly where I came in, you will get at such facts as that of my many uncles only one, the eldest, contrived to snatch a university education. The rest shifted as best they could without it (rather better than he, mostly). One distinguished himself as a civil servant. He had a gun, and went shooting. One made a fortune in business, and attained to carriage horses; but he lost the fortune in a premature attempt to develop the mineral resources of Ireland without waiting for the new railways produced by the late war. Two emigrated to Tasmania, and, like Mr Micawber, made history there. One was blind and dependent on his brothers: another became blind later, but remained independent and capable. One aunt married the rector of St Bride's (now demolished) in Dublin. The others married quite prosperously, except the eldest, whose conception of the family dignity was so prodigious (the family snobbery being unmitigated in her case by the family sense of humor) that she would have refused an earl because he was not a duke, and so died a very ancient virgin. Dead or alive, there were fourteen of them; and they all, except perhaps the eldest, must have had a very straitened time of it in their childhood after their father died, leaving my grandmother to bring up an unconscionable lot of children on very inadequate means. The baronet came to the rescue by giving her a quaint cottage, with Gothically pointed windows, to live in at Terenure (we called the place Roundtown). It stands in, or rather creeps picturesquely along, its little walled garden near the tram terminus to this day, though my grandfather's brass helmet and sword (he was in the Yeomanry or Militia as a gentleman amateur soldier) no longer hang in the hall. Professionally, he was some sort of combination of solicitor, notary public, and stockbroker that prevailed at that time. I suspect that his orphans did not always get enough to eat; for the younger ones, though invincibly healthy and long lived, were not athletic, and exhibited such a remarkable collection of squints (my father had a stupendous squint) that to this day a squint is so familiar to me that I notice it no more than a pair of spectacles or even a pair of boots.

On the whole, they held their cherished respectability in the world in spite of their lack of opportunity. They owed something perhaps, to the confidence given them by their sense of family. In Irish fashion they talked of themselves as the Shaws, as who should say the Valois, the Bourbons, the Hohenzollerns, the Hapsburgs, or the Romanoffs; and their world conceded the point to them. I had an enormous contempt for this family snobbery, as I called it, until I was completely reconciled to it by a certain Mr Alexander Mackintosh Shaw, a clansman who, instead of taking his pedigree for granted in the usual Shaw manner, hunted it up, and published 100 copies privately in 1877. Somebody sent me a copy; and my gratification was unbounded when I read the first sentence of the first chapter, which ran: "It is the general tradition, says the Rev. Lachlan Shaw [bless him!], that the Shaws are descended of McDuff, Earl of Fife." I hastily skipped to the chapter about the Irish Shaws to make sure that they were my people; and there they were, baronet and all, duly traced to the third son of that immortalized yet unborn Thane of Fife who, invulnerable to normally accouched swordsmen, laid on and slew Macbeth. It was as good as being descended from Shakespear, whom I had been unconsciously resolved to reincarnate from my cradle.

Years after this discovery I was staying on the shores of Loch Fyne, and being cooked for and housekept by a lady named McFarlane, who treated me with a consideration which I at first supposed to be due to my eminence as an author. But she undeceived me one day by telling me that the McFarlanes and the Shaws were descended from the Thanes of Fife, and that I must not make myself too cheap. She added that the McFarlanes were the elder branch.

My uncles did not trouble about Macduff: it was enough for them that they were Shaws. They had an impression that the Government should give them employment, preferably sinecure, if nothing else could be found; and I suppose this was why my father, after essaying a clerkship or two (one of them in an ironworks), at last had his position recognized by a post in the Four Courts, perhaps because his sister had married the brother of a law baron. Anyhow the office he held was so undeniably superfluous that it actually got abolished before I was born; and my father naturally demanded a pension as compensation for the outrage. Having got it, he promptly sold it, and set up in business as a merchant dealing wholesale (the family dignity made retail business impossible) in flour and its cereal concomitants. He had an office and warehouse in Jervis Street in the city; and he had a mill in Dolphin's Barn on the country side of the canal, at the end of a rather pretty little village street called Rutland Avenue. The mill has now fallen to pieces; but some relics of it are still to be seen from the field with the millpond behind Rutland House at the end of the avenue, with its two stone eagles on the gateposts. My father used to take me sometimes to this mill before breakfast (a long walk for a child); and I used to like playing about it. I do not think it had any other real use; for it never paid its way; and the bulk of my father's business was commissioned: he was a middleman. I should mention that as he knew nothing about the flour business, and as his partner, a Mr Clibborn, having been apprenticed to the cloth trade, knew if possible less, the business, purchased readymade, must have proceeded by its own momentum, and produced its results, such as they were, automatically in spite of its proprietors. They did not work the industry: it worked them. It kept alive, but did not flourish. Early in its history the bankruptcy of one of its customers dealt it such a blow that my father's partner broke down in tears, though he was fortified by a marriage with a woman of property, and could afford to regard his business as only a second string to his bow. My father, albeit ruined, found the magnitude of the catastrophe so irresistibly amusing that he had to retreat hastily from the office to an empty corner of the warehouse, and laugh until he was exhausted. The business struggled on and even supported my father until he died, enabling him to help his family a little after they had solved a desperate financial situation by emigrating to London: or, to put it in another way, by deserting him. His last years were soothed and disembarrassed by this step. He never, as far as I know, made the slightest movement towards a reunion; and none of us ever dreamt of there being any unkindness in the arrangement. In our family we did not bother about conventionalities or sentimentalities.

Our ridiculous poverty was too common in our class, and not conspicuous enough in a poor country, to account wholly for our social detachment from my father's family, a large and (for Ireland) not unprosperous one. In early days the baronet, being a bachelor, was clannishly accessible: he entertained even his second cousins at Bushy Park, and was specially attentive to my mother. I was never at Bushy Park myself except once, on the occasion of his funeral (the Shaw funerals were prodigies of black pomp); but if my father had been able to turn his social opportunities to account, I might have had a quite respectable and normal social training. My mother, socially very eligible, was made welcome in all directions. She sang very well; and the Shaws were naturally a musical family. All the women could "pick out tunes" on the piano, and support them with the chords of the tonic, subdominant, dominant, and tonic again. Even a Neapolitan sixth was not beyond them. My father played the trombone, and could vamp a bass on it to any tune that did not modulate too distractingly. My eldest uncle (Barney: I suppose I was called Bernard after him; but he himself was Uncle William) played the ophicleide, a giant keyed brass bugle, now superseded by the tuba. Berlioz has described it as a chromatic bullock; but my uncle could make it moo and bellow very melodiously. My aunt Emily played the violoncello. Aunt Shah (Charlotte), having beautiful hands, and refinements of person and character to match them, used the harp and tambourine to display them. Modern readers will laugh at the picture of an evening at Bushy Park, with the bachelor Sir Robert and his clan seated round an ottoman on which my uncle Barney stood, solemnly playing Annie Laurie on the ophicleide. The present distinguished inheritor of the title may well find it incredible. But in those days it was the fashion for guests to provide their own music and gentlemen to play wind instruments as a social accomplishment: indeed that age of brass is still remembered and regretted by the few makers of musical instruments whose traditions go back far enough.

And now you will ask why, with such unexceptional antecedents and social openings, was I not respectably brought up? Unfortunately or fortunately (it all depends on how you look at it) my father had a habit which eventually closed all doors to him, and consequently to my mother, who could not very well be invited without him. If you asked him to dinner or to a party, he was not always quite sober when he arrived; and he was invariably scandalously drunk when he left. Now a convivial drunkard may be exhilarating in convivial company. Even a quarrelsome or boastful drunkard may be found entertaining by people who are not particular. But a miserable drunkard—and my father, in theory a teetotaller, was racked with shame and remorse even in his cups—is unbearable. We were finally dropped socially. After my early childhood I cannot remember ever paying a visit at a relative's house. If my mother and father had dined out, or gone to a party, their children would have been much more astonished than if the house had caught fire.

How my mother rescued herself from this predicament by her musical talent I will tell elsewhere. My father reduced his tee-totalism from theory to practice when a mild fit, which felled him on our doorstep one Sunday afternoon, convinced him that he must stop drinking or perish. It had no worse effect; but his reform, though complete and permanent, came too late to save the social situation; and I, cut off from the social drill which puts one at one's ease in private society, grew up frightfully shy and utterly ignorant of social routine. My mother, who had been as carefully brought up as Queen Victoria, was too humane to inflict what she had suffered on any child; besides, I think she imagined that correct behavior is inborn, and that much of what she had been taught was natural to her. Anyhow, she never taught it to us, leaving us wholly to the promptings of our blood's blue-ness, with results which may be imagined.

In England, if people are reasonably goodnatured and amiable, they are forgiven any sort of eccentricity of behavior if only they are unaffected and all of one piece. If when I came to London I had been merely shy provincially, with incorrect table manners and wrong clothes; if I had eaten peas with a knife and worn a red tie with an evening suit, kind people would have taken me in hand and drilled me in spite of the infernal and very silly Irish pride which will never admit the need of such tuition. But my difficulties were not of that easily remediable kind. I was sensible enough to inform myself so exactly as to what I should do with a finger bowl when it was placed before me on a dessert plate, that I could give a lead in such matters to other novices who were hopelessly floored by that staggering problem. Clever sympathetic women might divine at a glance that I was mortally shy; but people who could not see through my skin, and who were accustomed to respect, and even veneration, from the young, may well have found me insufferable, aggressive, and impudent. When a young man has achieved nothing and is doing nothing, and when he is obviously so poor that he ought to be doing something very energetically, it is rather trying to find him assuming an authority in conversation, and an equality in terms, which only conspicuous success and distinguished ability could make becoming. Yet this is what is done, quite unconsciously, by young persons who have in them the potentiality of such success and ability. Napoleon could hardly have felt much reverence for his average French generals before the French Revolution, when he was apparently only a by-no-means irreproachable subaltern from Corsica. No such general could possibly have liked him or his manners at that time, though after Austerlitz even first rate generals blushed with gratification at the most condescending word of praise from him. It must have been intolerable in Stratford-on-Avon in 1584 for a local magnate of mature age, knight of the shire and justice of the peace, to be contemplated *de haut en bas* by a dissolute young poacher, and even to amuse him by intellectual inadequacy. I am sure Shakespear was too civil by nature to make any such demonstration consciously; but it is inconceivable that the future author of Lear, who was to die a landowning magnate, and be described in the parish register as a Gent., could have treated Sir Thomas Lucy quite as an ordinary country gentleman of mature age expects to be treated by an ordinary poacher in his teens.

The truth is that all men are in a false position in society until they have realized their possibilities, and imposed them on their neighbors. They are tormented by a continual shortcoming in themselves; yet they irritate others by a continual overweening. This discord can be resolved by acknowledged success or failure only: everyone is ill at ease until he has found his natural place, whether it be above or below his birthplace. The overrated inheritor of a position for which he has no capacity, and the underrated nobody who is a born genius, are alike shy because they are alike out of place. Besides, this finding of one's place may be made very puzzling by the fact that there is no place in ordinary society for extraordinary individuals. For the worldly wiseman, with common ambitions, the matter is simple enough: money, title, precedence, a seat in parliament, a portfolio in the cabinet, will mean success both to him and his circle. But what about people like St Francis and St Clare? Of what use to them are the means to live the life of the country house and the west end mansion? They have literally no business in them, and must necessarily cut an unhappy and ridiculous figure there. They have to make a society of Franciscans and Poor Clares for themselves before they can work or live socially. It is true that those who are called saints are not saintly all the time and in everything. In eating and drinking, lodging and sleeping, chatting and playing: in short, in everything but working out their destiny as saints, what is good enough for a ploughman is good enough for a poet, a philosopher, a saint, or a higher mathematician. But Hodge's work is not good enough for Newton, nor Falstaff's conversation holy enough for Shelley. Christ adapted himself so amiably to the fashionable life of his time in his leisure that he was reproached for being a gluttonous man and a winebibber, and for frequenting frivolous and worthless sets. But he did not work where he feasted, nor flatter the Pharisees, nor ask the Romans to buy him with a sinecure. He knew when he was being entertained, well treated, lionized: not an unpleasant adventure for once in a way; and he did not quarrel with the people who were so nice to him. Besides, to sample society is part of a prophet's business: he must sample the governing class above all, because his inborn knowledge of human nature will not explain the anomalies produced in it by Capitalism and Sacerdotalism. But he can never feel at home in it. The born Communist, before he knows what he is, and understands why, is always awkward and unhappy in plutocratic society and in the poorer societies which ape it to the extent of their little means: in short, wherever spiritual values are assessed like Income Tax. In his nonage he is imposed on by the prestige which the propertied classes have conferred on themselves and inculcated in the schools, and by the comfort and refinement and splendor of their equipment in contrast to the squalor of the proletariat. If he has been brought up to regard himself as one of the propertied classes, and has its whole equipment of false standards of worth, lacking nothing but the indispensable pecuniary equipment without which his education is utterly meaningless, his embarrassment and bewilderment are pitiable, and his isolation often complete; for he is left alone between the poor whom he regards as beneath him and the rich whose standards of expenditure are beyond his means. He is ashamed of his poverty, in continual dread of doing the wrong thing, resentfully insubordinate and seditious in a social order which he not only accepts but in which he actually claims a privileged part.

As I write, there is a craze for what is called psycho-analysis, or the cure of diseases by explaining to the patient what is the matter with him: an excellent plan if you happen to know what is the matter with him, especially when the explanation is that there is nothing the matter with him. Thus a bee, desperately trying to reach a flower bed through a window pane, concludes that he is the victim of evil spirits or that he is mad, his end being exhaustion, despair, and death. Yet, if he only knew, there is nothing wrong with him: all he has to do is go out as he came in, through open window or door. Your born Communist begins like the bee on the pane. He worries himself and everybody else until he dies of peevishness, or else is led by some propagandist pamphlet, or by his own intellectual impulses (if he has any), to investigate the economic structure of our society.

Immediately everything becomes clear to him. Property is theft: respectability founded on poverty is blasphemy: marriage founded on property is prostitution: it is easier for a camel to go through the eye of a needle than for a rich man to enter the kingdom of heaven. He now knows where he is, and where this society which has so intimidated him is. He is cured of his *mauvaise honte*, and may now be as much at his ease with the princes of this world as Caesar was with the pirates whom he intended to crucify when, as presently happened, the fortune of war made their captive their conqueror.

If he be not a born Communist, but a predatory combative man, eager to do the other fellow down, and happy in a contrast between his prosperity and the indigence of others, happy also in a robust contempt for cowards and weaklings, the very same discovery of the nature of our Capitalism will nerve him to play the Capitalist game for all it and he are worth. But for the most part men drift with the society into which they are born, and make the best of its accidents without changing its morals or understanding its principles.

As it happens, I was a born Communist and Iconoclast (or Quaker) without knowing it; and I never got on easy terms with plutocracy and snobbery until I took to the study of economics, beginning with Henry George and Karl Marx. In my twentieth year, at Victoria Grove, not being on Caesarian easy terms with the pirates or their retainers, I felt much as Caesar might have done if he had imagined the pirate ship to be the Mayflower, and was still more inclined to mistrust himself than to mistrust the crew, however little respect they might pay him. Not that my opinions were conventional. Read my preface to Back to Methuselah, and you will see me as the complete infidel of that day. I had read much poetry; but only one poet was sacred to me: Shelley. I had read his works piously from end to end, and was in my negations atheist and republican to the backbone. I say in my negations; for I had not reached any affirmative position. When, at a public meeting of the Shelley Society, I scandalized many of the members by saying that I had joined because, like Shelley, I was a Socialist, an atheist, and a vegetarian, I did not know that I could have expressed my position more accurately by simply saying that my conception of God was that insisted on in the first Article of the Church of England, then as now vehemently repudiated by all pious persons, who will have it that God is a substantial gentleman of uncertain and occasionally savage temper, and a spirit only in the sense in which an archbishop is a spirit. I had never thought of reading the Articles of the Church of England; and if I had I should still have used the word atheist as a declaration that I was on the side of Bradlaugh and Foote and others who, as avowed Secularists and Atheists, were being persecuted and imprisoned for my opinions. From my childhood

I had been accustomed to regard myself as a sceptic outside institutional religion, and therefore one to whom the conventional religious observances were fair game for scoffing. In this my manners were no better and no worse than those of my class generally. It never occurred to pious ladies and gentlemen to respect a sceptic; and it never occurred to a sceptic to respect a believer: reprobation and ostracism were considered natural and even obligatory on the one side, like derision, even to blasphemy, on the other. In Ireland Protestants and Catholics despised, insulted, and ostracized one another as a matter of course. In England Church people persecuted Dissenters; and Dissenters hated the Church with a bitterness incredible to anyone who has never known what it is to be a little village Dissenter in a Church school. I am not sure that controversial manners are any better now; but they certainly were odious then: you thought it your right and your duty to sneer at the man who was a heretic to your faith if you could not positively injure him in some way. As my manners in this respect were no better than other people's, and my satirical powers much more formidable, I can only hope that my natural civility, which led me to draw back when I found I was hurting people's feelings, may have mitigated my offensiveness in those early days when I still regarded controversy as admitting of no quarter. I lacked both cruelty and will-to-victory.

It may be asked here how I came by my heterodox opinions, seeing that my father's alcoholic neurosis, though it accounts for my not going into society, does not account for my not going to church. My reply, if put in the conventional terms of that day, would be that I was badly brought up because my mother was so well brought up. Her character reacted so strongly against her strict and loveless training that churchgoing was completely dropped in our family before I was ten years old. In my childhood I exercised my literary genius by composing my own prayers. I cannot recall the words of the final form I adopted; but I remember that it was in three movements, like a sonata, and in the best Church of Ireland style. It ended with the Lord's Prayer; and I repeated it every night in bed. I had been warned by my nurse that warm prayers were no use, and that only by kneeling by my bedside in the cold could I hope for a hearing; but I criticised this admonition unfavorably on various grounds, the real one being my preference for warmth and comfort. I did not disparage my nurse's authority in these matters because she was a Roman Catholic: I even tolerated her practice of sprinkling me with holy water occasionally. But her asceticism did not fit the essentially artistic and luxurious character of my devotional exploits. Besides, the penalty did not apply to my prayer; for it was not a petition. I had too much sense to risk my faith by begging for things I knew very well I should not get; so I did not care whether my prayers were answered or not: they were a literary performance for the entertainment and propitiation of the Almighty; and though I should not have dreamt of daring to say that if He did not like them He might lump them (perhaps I was too confident of their quality to apprehend such a rebuff), I certainly behaved as if my comfort were an indispensable condition of the performance taking place at all.

The Lord's Prayer I used once or twice as a protective spell. Thunderstorms are much less common in Ireland than in England; and the first two I remember frightened me horribly. During the second I bethought me of the Lord's Prayer, and steadied myself by repeating it.

I continued these pious habits long after the conventional compulsion to attend church and Sunday School had ceased, and I no longer regarded such customs as having anything to do with an emancipated spirit like mine. But one evening, as I was wandering through the furze bushes on Torca Hill in the dusk, I suddenly asked myself why I went on repeating my prayer every night when, as I put it, I did not believe in it. Being thus brought to book by my intellectual conscience I felt obliged in common honesty to refrain from superstitious practices; and that night, for the first time since I could speak, I did not say my prayers. I missed them so much that I asked myself another question. Why am I so uncomfortable about it? Can this be conscience? But next night the discomfort wore off so much that I hardly noticed it; and the night after I had forgotten all about my prayers as completely as if I had been born a heathen. It is worth adding that this sacrifice of the grace of God, as I had been taught it, to intellectual integrity synchronized with that dawning of moral passion in me which I have described in the first act of Man and Superman. Up to that time I had not experienced the slightest remorse in telling lies whenever they seemed likely to help me out of a difficulty: rather did I revel in the exercise of dramatic invention involved. Even when I was a good boy I was so only theatrically, because, as actors say, I saw myself in the character; and this occurred very seldom, my taste running so strongly on stage villains and stage demons (I painted the whitewashed wall in my bedroom in Dalkey with watercolor frescoes of Mephistopheles) that I must have actually bewitched myself; for, when Nature completed my countenance in 1880 or thereabouts (I had only the tenderest sprouting of hair on my face until I was 24), I found myself equipped with the upgrowing moustaches and eyebrows, and the sarcastic nostrils of the operatic fiend whose airs (by Gounod) I had sung as a child, and whose attitudes I had affected in my boyhood. Later on, as the generations moved past me, I saw the fantasies of actors and painters come to life as living men and women, and began to perceive that imaginative fiction is to life what the sketch is to the picture or the conception to the statue. The world is full of ugly little men who were taken to the theatre to see the Yellow Dwarf or Rumpelstiltskin when they were children; and we shall soon have women in all directions with the features of Movie Vamps because in childhood they were taken to the picture palaces and inspired with an ambition to be serpents of Old Nile.

My father disapproved of the detachment of his family from the conventional observances that were associated with the standing of the Shaw family. But he was in the grip of a humorous sense of anticlimax which I inherited from him and used with much effect when I became a writer of comedy. The more sacred an idea or a situation was by convention, the more irresistible was it to him as the jumping-off place for a plunge into laughter.

Thus, when I scoffed at the Bible he would instantly and quite sincerely rebuke me, telling me, with what little sternness was in his nature, that I should not speak so; that no educated man would make such a display of ignorance; that the Bible was universally recognized as a literary and historical masterpiece; and as much more to the same effect as he could muster. But when he had reached the point of feeling really impressive, a convulsion of internal chuckling would wrinkle up his eyes; and (I knowing all the time quite well what was coming) would cap his eulogy by assuring me, with an air of perfect fairness, that even the worst enemy of religion could say no worse of the Bible than that it was the damndest parcel of lies ever written. He would then rub his eyes and chuckle for quite a long time. It became an unacknow-ledged game between us that I should provoke him to exhibitions of this kind.

With such a father my condition was clearly hopeless as far as the conventions of religion were concerned. In essential matters his influence was as good as his culture permitted. One of my very earliest recollections is reading The Pilgrim's Progress to him, and being corrected by him for saying grievious instead of grievous. I never saw him, as far as I can remember, reading any-thing but the newspaper; but he had read Sir Walter Scott and other popular classics; and he always encouraged me to do the same, and to frequent the National Gallery, and to go to the theatre and the opera when I could afford it. His anticlimaxes depended for their effect on our sense of the sacredness he was re-acting against: there would have been no fun whatever in saying that the Adventures of Munchausen (known to us as Baron Mun Chawzon) were a parcel of lies. If my mother's pastors and masters had had a little of his humor, she would not simply have dropped the subject of religion with her children in silent but implacable dislike of what had helped to make her childhood miserable, and resolved that it should not do the same to them. The vacuum she left by this policy had, I think, serious disadvantages for my two sisters (the younger of whom died just before I came to London); but in my case it only made a clear space for positive beliefs later on.

My mother, I may say here, had no comedic impulses, and never uttered an epigram in her life: all my comedy is a Shavian inheritance. She had plenty of imagination, and really lived in it and on it. Her brother, my uncle Walter, who stayed with us from time to time in the intervals of his trips across the Atlantic as a surgeon on the Inman Liners, had an extraordinary command of picturesque language, partly derived by memory from the Bible and Prayer Book, and partly natural. The conversation of the navigating staffs and pursers of our ocean services was at that time (whatever it may be today) extremely Rabelaisian and profane. Falstaff himself could not have held his own with my uncle in obscene anecdotes, unprintable limericks, and fantastic profanity; and it mattered nothing to him whether his audience consisted of his messmates on board ship or his schoolboy nephew: he performed before each with equal gusto. To do him justice, he was always an artist in his obscenity and blasphemy, and therefore never sank to the level of incontinent blackguardism. His efforts were controlled, deliberate, fastidiously chosen and worded. But they were all the more effective in destroying all my inculcated childish reverence for the verbiage of religion, for its legends and personifications and parables. In view of my subsequent work in the world it seems providential that I was driven to the essentials of religion by the reduction of every factitious or fictitious element in it to the most irreverent absurdity.

It would be the greatest mistake to conclude that this shocking state of affairs was bad for my soul. In so far as the process of destroying reverence for the inessential trappings of religion was indecent, it was deplorable; and I wish my first steps to grace had been lighted by my uncle's wit and style without his obscenity. My father's comedy was entirely decent. But that the process was necessary to my salvation I have no doubt whatever. A popular book in my youth was Mark Twain's New Pilgrim's Progress, which horrified the thoughtlessly pious by making fun of what they called sacred things. Yet Mark Twain was really a religious force in the world: his Yankee at the Court of King Arthur was his nearest approach to genuine blasphemy; and that came from want of culture, not from perversity of soul. His training as a Mississippi pilot must have been, as to religion, very like my training as the nephew of a Transatlantic surgeon.

Later on, I discovered that in the Ages of Faith the sport of making fun of the accessories and legends of religion was organized and practised by the Church to such an extent that it was almost part of its ritual. The people were instructed in spiritual history and hagiology by stage plays full of comic passages which might have been written by my uncle. For instance, my uncle taught me an elaborate conversation supposed to have passed between Daniel in the lion's den and King Darius, in which each strove to outdo the other in Rabelaisian repartee. The medieval playwright, more daring than my uncle, put on the stage comical conversations between Cain and his Creator, in which Cain's language was no more respectful than that of Fielding's Squire Western, and similarly indecent. In all Catholic countries there is a hagiology that is fit for publication and a hagiology that is not. In the Middle Ages they may have condemned a story as lewd or blasphemous; but it did not occur to them that God or His Church could be shaken by it. No man with any faith worth respecting in any religion worth holding ever dreams that it can be shaken by a joke, least of all by an obscene joke. It is Messieurs Formalist and Hypocrisy who feel that religion is crumbling when the forms are not observed. The truth is, humor is one of the great purifiers of religion, even when it is itself anything but pure.

The institution of the family, which is the centre of reverence for carefully brought-up children, was just the opposite for me. In a large family there are always a few skeletons in the cupboard; and in my father's clan there were many uncles and aunts and cousins, consequently many cupboards, consequently some skeletons. Our own particular skeleton was my father's drunkenness. It was combined with a harmlessness and humaneness which made him the least formidable of men; so that it was impossible for him to impress his children in the manner that makes awe and dread almost an instinct with some children. It is much to his credit that he was incapable of deliberately practising any such impressiveness, drunk or sober; but unfortunately the drunkenness was so humiliating that it would have been unendurable if we had not taken refuge in laughter. It had to be either a family tragedy or a family joke; and it was on the whole a healthy instinct that decided us to get what ribald fun was possible out of it, which, however, was very little indeed. If Noah had made a habit of drinking, his sons would soon have worn out the pious solicitude which they displayed on the occasion of his single lapse from sobriety. A boy who has seen "the governor," with an imperfectly wrapped-up goose under one arm and a ham in the same condition under the other (both purchased under heaven knows what delusion of festivity), butting at the garden wall in the belief that he was pushing open the gate, and transforming his tall hat to a concertina in the process, and who, instead of being overwhelmed with shame and anxiety at the spectacle, has been so disabled by merriment (uproariously shared by the maternal uncle) that he has hardly been able to rush to the rescue of the hat and pilot its wearer to safety, is clearly not a boy who will make tragedies of trifles instead of making trifles of tragedies. If you cannot get rid of the family skeleton, you may as well make it dance.

Then there was my Uncle William, a most amiable man, with great natural dignity. In early manhood he was not only an inveterate smoker, but so insistent a toper that a man who made a bet that he would produce Barney Shaw sober, and knocked him up at six in the morning with that object, lost his bet. But this might have happened to any common drunkard. What gave the peculiar Shaw finish and humor to the case was that my uncle suddenly and instantly gave up smoking and drinking at one blow, and devoted himself to his accomplishment of playing the ophicleide. In this harmless and gentle pursuit he continued, a blameless old bachelor, for many years, and then, to the amazement of Dublin, renounced the ophicleide and all its works, and married a lady of distinguished social position and great piety. She declined, naturally, to have anything to do with us; and, as far as I know, treated the rest of the family in the same way. Anyhow, I never saw her, and only saw my uncle furtively by the roadside after his marriage, when he would make hopeless attempts to save me, in the pious sense of the word, not perhaps without some secret Shavian enjoyment of the irreverent pleasantries with which I scattered my path to perdition. He was reputed to sit with a Bible on his knees, and an opera glass to his eyes, watching the ladies' bathing place in Dalkey; and my sister, who was a swimmer, confirmed this gossip as far as the opera glass was concerned.

But this was only the prelude to a very singular conclusion, or rather catastrophe. The fantastic imagery of the Bible so gained on my uncle that he took off his boots, explaining that he expected to be taken up to heaven at any moment like Elijah, and that he felt that his boots would impede his celestial flight. He then went a step further, and hung his room with all the white fabrics he could lay hands on, alleging that he was the Holy Ghost. At last he became silent, and remained so to the end. His wife, warned that his harmless fancies might change into dangerous ones, had him removed to an asylum in the north of Dublin. My father thought that a musical appeal might prevail with him, and went in search of the ophicleide. But it was nowhere to be found. He took a flute to the asylum instead; for every Shaw of that generation seemed able to play any wind instrument at sight. My uncle, still obstinately mute, contemplated the flute for a while, and then played Home Sweet Home on it. My father had to be content with this small success, as nothing more could be got out of his brother. A day or two later my uncle, impatient for heaven, resolved to expedite his arrival there. Every possible weapon had been carefully removed from his reach; but his custodians reckoned without the Shavian originality. They had left him somehow within reach of a carpet bag. He put his head into it, and in a strenuous effort to decapitate or strangle himself by closing it on his neck, perished of heart failure. I should be glad to believe that, like Elijah, he got the heavenly reward he sought; for he was a fine upstanding man and a gentle creature, nobody's enemy but his own, as the saying is.

Still, what sort of gravity could a boy maintain with a family history of this kind? However, I must not imply that all my uncles were like that. They were mostly respectable normal people. I can recall only two other exceptions to this rule. One of my uncles married an elegant and brilliant lady, from whom he separated after scandalizing the family by beating her; but as Job himself would have beaten her when she lost her very unstable temper, nobody who knew her intimately ever blamed him. Though the neurosis which produced my father's joyless craving for alcohol had the same effect, with the same curious recalcitrance and final impermanence, in one or two other cases, and was perhaps connected with occasional family paroxysms of Evangelical piety, and some share of my father's comedic love of anticlimax, yet on the whole our collection of skeletons was not exceptionally large. But as, compared with similar English families, we had a power of derisive dramatization that made the bones of the Shavian skeletons rattle more loudly; and as I possessed this power in an abnormal degree, and frequently entertained my friends with stories of my uncles (so effectively, by the way, that nobody ever believed them), the family, far from being a school of reverence for me, was rather a mine from which I could dig highly amusing material without the trouble of inventing a single incident. What idle fancy of mine could have improved on the hard facts of the Life and Death of Uncle William?

Thus the immediate result of my family training in my Victoria Grove days was that I presented myself to the unprepared stranger as a most irreverent young man. My Mephistophelean moustache and eyebrows had not yet grown; and there was nothing in my aspect to break the shock of my diabolical opinions. Later on, when I had made a public reputation as an iconoclast, people who met me in private were surprised at my mildness and sociability. But I had no public reputation then: consequently expectation in my regard was normal. And I was not at all reticent of the diabolical opinions. I felt them to be advantageous, just as I felt that I was in a superior position as an Irishman, without a shadow of any justification for that patriotic arrogance. As it never occurred to me to conceal my opinions any more than my nationality, and as I had, besides, an unpleasant trick of contradicting everyone from whom I thought I could learn anything in order to draw him out and enable me to pick his brains, I think I must have impressed many amiable persons as an extremely disagreeable and undesirable young man.

And yet I was painfully shy, and was simply afraid to accept invitations, with the result that I very soon ceased to get any. I was told that if I wanted to get on, I must not flatly refuse invitations—actually dinner invitations—which were meant to help me, and the refusal of which was nothing short of a social outrage. But I knew very well that introductions could be of no use to one who had no profession and could do nothing except what any clerk could do. I knew I was useless, worthless, penniless, and that until I had qualified myself to do something, and proved it by doing it, all this business of calling on people who might perhaps do something for me, and dining out without money to pay for a cab, was silly. Fortunately for me, the realism that made me face my own position so ruthlessly also kept before me the fact that if I borrowed money I could not pay it back, and therefore might more candidly beg or steal it. I knew quite well that if I borrowed £5 from a friend and could not pay it back, I was selling a friend for £5, and that this was a foolish bargain. So I did not borrow, and therefore did not lose my friends; though some of them, who could have had no illusions about my financial capacity, hinted that they were quite willing, and indeed anxious, to call a gift a loan.

I feel bound to confess here, in reference to my neglect of the few invitations and offers of introductions that reached me, that behind the conviction that they could lead to nothing that I wanted lay the unspoken fear that they might lead to something I did not want: that is, commercial employment. I had had enough of that. No doubt it would have been a great relief to my mother if I could have earned something. No doubt I could have earned something if I had really meant to. No doubt if my father had died, and my mother been struck dumb and blind, I should have had to go back to the office desk (the doom of shabby gentility) and give up all hope of acquiring a profession; for even the literary profession, though it exacts no academic course and costly equipment, does exact all one's time and the best of one's brains. As it was, I dodged every opening instinctively. With an excellent testimonial and an unexceptionable character, I was an incorrigible Unemployable. I kept up pretences (to myself as much as to others) for some time. I answered advertisements, not too offensively. I actually took a berth in a telephone Company (then a sensational novelty) and had some difficulty in extricating myself from the Company which bought it up. I can remember an interview with a bank manager in Onslow Gardens (procured for me, to my dismay, by an officious friend with whom I *had* dined) with a view to employment in the bank. I entertained him so brilliantly (if I may use an adverb with which in later years I was much plagued by friendly critics) that we parted on the best of terms, he declaring that, though I certainly ought to get something to do without the least difficulty, he did not feel that a bank clerkship was the right job for me.

I have said that I had an excellent testimonial as an employee in a business office. I had, as a matter of fact, spent four and a half years at a desk in Dublin before I emigrated. I have already given the economic reasons why boys of my class have to do without university education, just as they have to do without horses and guns. And yet I cannot deny that clergymen no better off than my father do manage somehow to start their sons in life with a university degree. They regard it as an absolute necessity, and therefore do not consider whether they can afford it or not. They must afford it. The need for it may be an illusion; but we are subject to such illusions: one man cannot live without a grand piano, another without a boat, another without a butler, another without a horse, and so on through a whole range of psychological imperatives. I have known women set up orphanages because they could not do without children to beat. Place their necessities in any rational order, and you will find that many of them cannot afford these things. They get out of the difficulty by simply rearranging your rational order as a psychological order, and putting their fancies at the top and their needs at the bottom. It is no use telling a woman that she needs good food and plenty of it much more vitally than she needs a seven guinea hat, a bottle of hair dye, a supply of face powder and rouge, a puff and a hares-foot. She will live on tea and rashers for months rather than fore-go them. And men are just as unreasonable. To say that my father could not afford to give me a university education is like saying that he could not afford to drink, or that I could not afford to become an author. Both statements are true; but he drank and I became an author all the same. I must therefore explain, just as seriously as if my father had had fifty thousand a year, why I did not graduate at Trinity College, Dublin.

I cannot learn anything that does not interest me. My memory is not indiscriminate: it rejects and selects; and its selections are not academic. I have no competitive instinct; nor do I crave for prizes and distinctions: consequently I have no interest in com-petitive examinations: if I won, the disappointment of my com-petitors would distress me instead of gratifying me: if I lost, my self-esteem would suffer. Besides, I have far too great a sense of my own importance to feel that it could be influenced by a degree or a gold medal or what not. There is only one sort of school that could have qualified me for academic success; and that is the sort in which the teachers take care that the pupils shall be either memorizing their lessons continuously, with all the desperate strenuousness that terror can inspire, or else crying with severe physical pain. I was never in a school where the teachers cared enough about me, or about their ostensible profession, or had enough conviction and cruelty, to take any such trouble; so I learnt nothing at school, not even what I could and would have learned if any attempt had been made to interest me. I congratu-late myself on this; for I am firmly persuaded that every un-natural activity of the brain is as mischievous as any unnatural activity of the body, and that pressing people to learn things they do not want to know is as unwholesome and disastrous as feeding them on sawdust. Civilization is always wrecked by giving the governing classes what is called secondary education, which produces invincible ignorance and intellectual and moral imbecility as a result of unnatural abuse of the apprehensive faculty. No child would ever learn to walk or dress itself if its hands and feet were kept in irons and allowed to move only when and as its guardians pulled and pushed them.

I somehow knew this when I began, as a boy entering on my teens, to think about such things. I remember saying, in some discussion that arose on the subject of my education, that T.C.D. men were all alike (by which I meant all wrong), and that I did not want to go through college. I was entirely untouched by university idealism. When it reached me later on, I recognized how ignorantly I had spoken in my boyhood; but when I went still further and learnt that this idealism is never realized in our schools and universities, and operates only as a mask and a decoy for our system of impressing and enslaving children and stultifying adults, I concluded that my ignorance had been inspired, and had served me very well. I have not since changed my mind.

However that may be, I decided, at thirteen or thereabouts, that for the moment I must go into business and earn some money and begin to be a grown-up man. There was at that time, on one of the quays in Dublin, a firm of cloth merchants, by name Scott, Spain, and Rooney. A friend of ours knew Scott, and asked him to give me a start in life with some employment. I called on this gentleman by appointment. I had the vaguest notion of what would happen: all I knew was that I was "going into an office." I thought I should have preferred to interview Spain, as the name was more romantic. Scott turned out to be a smart handsome man, with moustachios; and I suppose a boy more or less in his warehouse did not matter to him when there was a friend to be obliged: at all events, he said only a few perfunctory things and was settling my employment, when, as my stars would have it, Rooney appeared. Mr Rooney was much older, not at all smart, but long, lean, grave and respectable.

The last time I saw the late Sir George Alexander (the actor) he described to me his own boyhood, spent in a cloth warehouse in

Cheapside, where they loaded him with bales, and praised him highly for his excellent conduct, even rewarding him after some years to the extent of sixteen shillings a week. Rooney saved me from the bales. He talked to me a little, and then said quite decisively that I was too young, and that the work was not suitable to me. He evidently considered that my introducer, my parents, and his young partner, had been inconsiderate; and I presently descended the stairs, reprieved and unemployed. As Mr Rooney was certainly fifty then at least, he must be a centenarian if, as I hope, he still lives. If he does, I offer him the assurance that I have not forgotten his sympathy.

A year later, or thereabouts, my uncle Frederick, an important official in the Valuation Office, whom no land agent or family solicitor in Dublin could afford to disoblige, asked a leading and terribly respectable firm of land agents, carrying on business at 15 Molesworth Street, to find a berth for me. They did so; and I became their office boy (junior clerk I called myself) at eighteen shillings a month. It was a very good opening for anyone with a future as a land agent, which in Ireland at that time was a business of professional rank. It was utterly thrown away on me. However, as the office was overstaffed with gentlemen apprentices, who had paid large fees for the privilege of singing operatic selections with me when the principals were out, there was nothing to complain of socially, even for a Shaw; and the atmosphere was as uncommercial as that of an office can be. Thus I learnt business habits without being infected with the business spirit. By the time I had attained to thirty shillings a month, the most active and responsible official in the office, the cashier, vanished; and as we were private bankers to some extent, our clients drawing cheques on us, and so forth, someone had to take his place without an hour's delay. An elder substitute grumbled at the strange job, and, though an able man in his way, could not make his cash balance. It became necessary, after a day or two of confusion, to try the office boy as a stopgap whilst the advertisements for a new cashier of appropriate age and responsibility were going forward. Immediately the machine worked again quite smoothly. I, who never knew how much money I had of my own (except when the figure was zero), proved a model of accuracy as to the money of others. I acquired my predecessor's very neat handwriting, my own being too sloped and straggly for the cash book. The efforts to fill my important place more worthily slackened. I bought a tailed coat, and was chaffed about it by the apprentices. My salary was raised to £48 a year, which was as much as I expected at sixteen and much less than the firm would have had to pay to a competent adult: in short, I made good in spite of myself, and found, to my dismay, that Business, instead of expelling me as the worthless impostor I was, was fastening upon me with no intention of letting me go.

Behold me therefore in my twentieth year, with a business training, in an occupation which I detested as cordially as any sane person lets himself detest anything he cannot escape from. In March 1876 I broke loose. I gave a month's notice. My employers naturally thought I was discontented with my salary (£84, I think, by that time), and explained to me quietly that they hoped to make my position more eligible. My only fear was that they should make it so eligible that all excuse for throwing it up would be taken from me. I thanked them and said I was resolved to go; and I had, of course, no reason in the world to give them for my resolution. They were a little hurt, and explained to my uncle that they had done their best, but that I seemed to have made up my mind. I had. After enjoying for a few days the luxury of not having to go to the office, and being, if not my own master, at least not anyone else's slave, I packed a carpet bag; boarded the North Wall boat; and left the train next morning at Euston, where, on hearing a porter cry, in an accent quite strange to me (I had hardly ever heard an h dropped before) "Ensm' faw weel?" which I rightly interpreted as "Hansom or four wheel?" I was afraid to say hansom, because I had never been in one and was not sure that I should know how to get in. So I solemnly drove in a growler through streets whose names Dickens had made familiar to me, London being at its spring best, which is its very best, to Victoria Grove, where the driver accepted four shillings as a reasonable fare for the journey.

I did not set foot in Ireland again until 1905, and not then on my own initiative. I went back to please my wife; and a curious reluctance to retrace my steps made me land in the south and enter Dublin through the backdoor from Meath rather than return as I came, through the front door on the sea. In 1876 I had had enough of Dublin. James Joyce in his Ulysses has described, with a fidelity so ruthless that the book is hardly bearable, the life that Dublin offers to its young men, or, if you prefer to put it the other way, that its young men offer to Dublin. No doubt it is much like the life of young men everywhere in modern urban civilization. A certain flippant futile derision and belittlement that confuses the noble and serious with the base and ludicrous seems to me peculiar to Dublin; but I suppose that is because my only personal experience of that phase of youth was a Dublin experience; for when I left my native city I left that phase behind me, and associated no more with men of my age until, after about eight years of solitude in this respect, I was drawn into the Socialist revival of the early eighties, among Englishmen intensely serious and burning with indignation at very real and very fundamental evils that affected all the world; so that the reaction against them bound the finer spirits of all the nations together instead of making them cherish hatred of one another as a national virtue. Thus, when I left Dublin I left (a few private friendships apart) no society that did not disgust me. To this day my sentimental regard for Ireland does not include the capital. I am not enamored of failure, of poverty, of obscurity, and of the ostracism and contempt which these imply; and these were all that Dublin offered to the enormity of my unconscious ambition. The cities a man likes are the cities he has conquered. Napoleon did not turn from Paris to sentimentalize over Ajaccio, nor Catherine from St Petersburg to Stettin as the centre of her universe.

On this question of ambition let me say a word. In the ordinary connotation of the word I am the least ambitious of men. I have said, and I confirm it here, that I am so poor a hand at pushing and struggling, and so little interested in their rewards, that I have risen by sheer gravitation, too industrious by acquired habit to stop working (I work as my father drank), and too lazy and timid by nature to lay hold of half the opportunities or a tenth of the money that a conventionally ambitious man would have grasped strenuously. I never thought of myself as destined to become what is called a great man: indeed I was diffident to the most distressing degree; and I was ridiculously credulous as to the claims of others to superior knowledge and authority. But one day in the office I had a shock. One of the apprentices, by name C. J. Smyth, older than I and more a man of the world, remarked that every young chap thought he was going to be a great man. On a really modest youth this commonplace would have had no effect. It gave me so perceptible a jar that I suddenly became aware that I had never thought I was to be a great man simply because I had always taken it as a matter of course. The incident passed without leaving any preoccupation with it to hamper me; and I remained as diffident as ever because I was still as incompetent as ever. But I doubt whether I ever recovered my former complete innocence of subconscious intention to devote myself to the class of work that only a few men excel in, and to accept the responsibilities that attach to its dignity.

Now this bore directly on my abandonment of Dublin, for which many young Irishmen of today find it impossible to forgive me. My business in life could not be transacted in Dublin out of an experience confined to Ireland. I had to go to London just as my father had to go to the Corn Exchange. London was the literary centre for the English language, and for such artistic culture as the realm of the English language (in which I proposed to be king) could afford. There was no Gaelic League in those days, nor any sense that Ireland had in herself the seed of culture. Every Irishman who felt that his business in life was on the higher planes of the cultural professions felt that he must have a metropolitan domicile and an international culture: that is, he felt that his first business was to get out of Ireland. I had the same feeling. For London as London, or England as England, I cared nothing. If my subject had been science or music I should have made for

Berlin or Leipsic. If painting, I should have made for Paris: indeed many of the Irish writers who have made a name in literature escaped to Paris with the intention of becoming painters. For theology I should have gone to Rome, and for Protestant philosophy to Weimar. But as the English language was my weapon, there was nothing for it but London. In 1914 the Germans, resenting my description of their Imperial political situation as Potsdamnation, denounced me as a fatherlandless fellow. They were quite right. I was no more offended than if they had called me unparochial. They had never reproached me for making pilgrimages to Bayreuth when I could as easily have made them to the Hill of Tara. If you want to make me homesick, remind me of the Thuringian Fichtelgebirge, of the broad fields and delicate airs of France, of the Gorges of the Tarn, of the Passes of the Tyrol, of the North African desert, of the Golden Horn, of the Swedish lakes, or even of the Norwegian fiords where I have never been except in imagination, and you may stir that craving in me as easily—probably more easily—as in any exiled native of these places. It was not until I went back to Ireland as a tourist that I perceived that the charm of my country was quite independent of the accident of my having been born in it, and that it could fascinate a Spaniard or an Englishman more powerfully than an Irishman, in whose feeling for it there must always be a strange anguish, because it is the country where he has been unhappy and where vulgarity is vulgar to him. And so I am a tolerably good European in the Nietzschean sense, but a very bad Irishman in the Sinn Fein or Chosen People sense.

For the first couple of years of my life in London I did nothing decisive. I acted as ghost for a musician who had accepted a berth as musical critic; and as such ghosts must not appear, and I was therefore cut off from the paper and could not correct proofs, my criticisms, mostly very ruthless ones, appeared with such misprints, such mutilations and venal interpolations by other hands, so inextricably mixed up with other criticisms most offensive to my artistic sense, that I have ever since hidden this activity of mine as a guilty secret, lest someone should dig out these old notices and imagine that I was responsible for everything in them and with them. Even now I can hardly bring myself to reveal that the name of the paper was The Hornet, and that it had passed then into the hands of a certain Captain Donald Shaw, who was not related to me, and whom I never met. It died on his hands, and partly, perhaps, at mine.

Then my cousin, Mrs Cashel Hoey, a woman of letters, daughter of the aunt who played the tambourine with her beautiful hands, gave me an introduction to Arnold White, then secretary to the Edison Telephone Company. He found a berth for me in the Way Leave Department of that shortlived company; and I presently found myself studying the topography of the east end of London, and trying to persuade all sorts of people to allow the Company to put insulators and poles and derricks and the like on their roofs to carry the telephone lines. I liked the exploration involved; but my shyness made the business of calling on strangers frightfully uncongenial; and my sensitiveness, which was extreme, in spite of the brazen fortitude which I simulated, made the impatient rebuffs I had to endure occasionally, especially from much worried women who mistook me for an advertisement canvasser, ridiculously painful to me. But I escaped these trials presently; for I soon had to take charge of the department, and organize the work of more thick-skinned adventurers instead of doing it myself. Further particulars will be found in the preface to my second novel, The Irrational Knot. The Edison Telephone Company was presently swallowed up by the Bell Telephone Company; and I seized the opportunity to recover my destitute freedom by refusing to apply for the employment promised by the amalgamation to the disbanded staff. This was the end of my career as a commercial employee. I soon dropped even the pretence of seeking any renewal of it. Except for a day or two in 1881, when I earned a few pounds by counting the votes at an election in Leyton, I was an Unemployable, an ablebodied pauper in fact if not in law, until the year 1885, when for the first time I earned enough money directly by my pen to pay my way. My income for that year amounted to £112; and from that time until the war of

1914–18 momentarily threatened us all with bankruptcy, I had no pecuniary anxieties except those produced by the possession of money, not by the lack of it. My penury phase was over.

The telephone episode occurred in 1879; and in that year I had done what every literary adventurer did in those days, and many do still. I had written a novel. My office training had left me with a habit of doing something regularly every day as a fundamental condition of industry as distinguished from idleness. I knew I was making no headway unless I was doing this, and that I should never produce a book in any other fashion. I bought supplies of white paper, demy size, by sixpennorths at a time; folded it in quarto; and condemned myself to fill five pages of it a day, rain or shine, dull or inspired. I had so much of the schoolboy and the clerk still in me that if my five pages ended in the middle of a sentence I did not finish it until next day. On the other hand, if I missed a day, I made up for it by doing a double task on the morrow. On this plan I produced five novels in five years. It was my professional apprenticeship, doggedly suffered with all the diffidence and dissatisfaction of a learner with a very critical master, myself to wit, whom there was no pleasing and no evading, and persevered in to save my self-respect in a condition of impecuniosity which, for two acute moments (I still recall them with a wry face), added broken boots and carefully hidden raggedness to cuffs whose edges were trimmed by the scissors, and a tall hat so limp with age that I had to wear it back-to-front to enable me to take it off without doubling up the brim.

I had no success as a novelist. I sent the five novels to all the publishers in London and some in America. None would venture on them. Fifty or sixty refusals without a single acceptance forced me into a fierce self-sufficiency. I became undiscourageable, acquiring a superhuman insensitiveness to praise or blame which has been useful to me at times since, though at other times it has retarded my business affairs by making me indifferent to the publication and performances of my works, and even impatient of them as an unwelcome interruption to the labor of writing their successors. Instead of seizing every opportunity of bringing them before the public, I have often, on plausible but really trivial pretexts, put off proposals which I should have embraced with all the normal author's keenness for publicity.

Thus, after five years of novel writing, I was a complete professional failure. The more I wrote and the better I wrote the less I pleased the publishers. This first novel of mine, though rejected, at least elicited some expressions of willingness to read any future attempts. Blackwood actually accepted and then revoked. Sir George Macmillan, then a junior, not only sent me a longish and evidently considered report by the firm's reader, John (afterwards Lord) Morley, but suggested to him that I might be of some use to him in his capacity as editor of the Pall Mall Gazette.

All such responses ceased with my second novel; and I had no means of knowing, and was too young and inexperienced to guess, that what was the matter was not any lack of literary competence on my part, but the antagonism raised by my hostility to respectable Victorian thought and society. I was left without a ray of hope; yet I did not stop writing novels until, having planned my fifth effort on a colossal scale, I found at the end of what were to me only the first two sections of it, that I had no more to say and had better wait until I had educated myself much farther. And when, after an interval of critical journalism, I resumed the writing of fiction, I did so as a playwright and not as a novelist.

Four of the five novels of my nonage, as I call them, at last got into print as described in the preface already cited. But the first of them never got published at all. Opening the old parcel, as I do now (it is like opening a grave that has been closed for forty-two years), I find a pile of cahiers of twenty pages each, and realize with some dismay that I am face-to-face with a novel containing nearly 200,000 words. The title is Immaturity. The handwriting, which slopes slightly backwards, has all the regularity and legibility of my old cash book. Unfortunately, the mice have eaten so much of two of the cahiers that the ends of the lines are missing. This is awkward; for I have just told myself that I must make no attempt to correct the work of the apprentice with the hand of the master; that such as it is it must remain; that I am too old now to touch it without producing new incongruities more disagreeable than any that are possible between the style of 1879 and the taste of 1921. Yet, if the mice have eaten much, I must play the sedulous ape, like Stevenson, and imitate my own youthful manner like any literary forger.

It may be asked why I should print the thing at all: why not let ill alone? I am quite disposed to do so; but somehow one must not do such things. If Beethoven had destroyed his septet for wind instruments when he had advanced to the ninth symphony and the Mass in D, many people who delight in the septet and cannot make head or tail of symphony or Mass would suffer a wanton deprivation; and though my early style now makes me laugh at its pedantry, yet I have a great respect for the priggish conscientiousness of my first efforts. They prove too that, like Goethe, I knew all along, and have added more to my power of handling, illustrating, and addressing my material than to the material itself.

Anyhow, I have little doubt that Immaturity will be at least readable by the easygoing bookbuyers who will devour anything in the shape of a novel, however ridiculously out of fashion it may be. I know that some readers will like it much better than my later works. There must be a certain quality of youth in it which I could not now recapture, and which may even have charm as well as weakness and absurdity. Having re-read the other four novels for publication and republication at one time or another, I can guarantee the propriety of my early style. It was the last thing in correctness. I have never aimed at style in my life: style is a sort of melody that comes into my sentences by itself. If a writer says what he has to say as accurately and effectively as he can, his style will take care of itself, if he has a style. But I did set up one condition in my early days. I resolved that I would write nothing that should not be intelligible to a foreigner with a dictionary, like the French of Voltaire; and I therefore avoided idiom. (Later on I came to seek idiom as being the most highly vitalized form of language). Consequently I do not expect to find the English of Immaturity idiomatic. Also, there will be nothing of the voice of the public speaker in it: the voice that rings through so much of my later work. Not until Immaturity was finished, late in 1879, did I for the first time rise to my feet in a little debating club called The Zetetical Society, to make, in a condition of heartbreaking nervousness, my first assault on an audience.

Perhaps I had better add a word as to the characters in the book. I do so with some reluctance, because it is misleading to mention even the smallest circumstance connecting a fictitious person with a living one. If Shakespear had happened to mention that he made the Prince of Denmark carry a set of tablets and make notes in them because he had seen Sir Walter Raleigh doing so, it would by this time be an invincible tradition in English literature that Raleigh was the original of Hamlet. We should have writers following up the clue, as they would call it, to the conclusion that Raleigh was the real author of the play. One day, as I was sitting in the reading room of the British Museum, beginning my fifth and last novel, An Unsocial Socialist, I saw a young lady with an attractive and arresting expression, bold, vivid, and very clever, working at one of the desks. On that glimpse of a face I instantly conceived the character and wrote the description of Agatha Wylie. I have never exchanged a word with that lady; never made her acquaintance; saw her again under the same circumstances but very few times; yet if I mention her name, which became well known in literature (she too was writing a novel then, probably, and perhaps had the hero suggested to her by my profile), she will be set down as Agatha Wylie to her dying day, with heaven knows how much more scandalous invention added to account for my supposed intimate knowledge of her character. Before and since, I have used living models as freely as a painter does, and in much the same way: that is, I have sometimes made a fairly faithful portrait founded on intimate personal intercourse, and sometimes, as in Agatha's case, developed what a passing glance suggested to my imagination. In the latter case it has happened sometimes that the incidents I have invented on the spur of such a glance have hit the facts so nearly that I have found myself accused of unpardonable violations of personal privacy. I hardly expect to be believed when I say that I once invented a servant for one of my models and found afterwards that he actually had just such a servant. Between the two extremes of actual portraiture and pure fancy work suggested by a glance or an anecdote, I have copied nature with many degrees of fidelity, combining studies from life in the same book or play with those types and composites and traditional figures of the novel and the stage which are called pure fictions. Many of the characters in this first novel of mine owed something to persons I had met, including members of my family (not to mention myself); but none of them are portraits; and with one exception the models are unknown to the public. That exception was Cecil Lawson, whose early death lost us the only landscape painter who ever reminded me of the spacious and fascinating experiments of Rubens in that branch of painting. When I lived at Victoria Grove the Lawsons: father, mother, Malcolm, and two sisters, lived in one of the handsome old houses in Cheyne Walk, Chelsea. Cecil and another brother, being married, boarded out. Malcolm was a musician; and the sisters sang. One, a soprano, dark, quick, plump and bright, sang joyously. The other, a contralto, sang with heartbreaking intensity of expression, which she deepened by dressing esthetically, as it was called then, meaning in the Rossettian taste. Miss Lawson produced this effect, not by the ugly extravagances which made the fashionable milliners' version of the esthetic mode ridiculous, but by very simple grey and brown gowns which somehow harmonized with her habitual expression of sadness and even suffering; so that when she sang "Oh, dont deceive me: oh, never leave me," she produced a picture as well as a tone poem. Cecil, who had just acquired a position by the few masterpieces which remain to us, was very much "in the movement" at the old Grosvenor Gallery (now the Aeolian Hall), then new, and passing through the sensational vogue achieved by its revelations of Burne Jones and Whistler.

Malcolm was conducting a Gluck Society, at which I had discovered Gluck through a recital of Alceste, in which Theo Marzials, who had a charming baritone voice, sang the part of Hercules. My mother had met Marzials in the course of her musical activities: he introduced her to Malcolm Lawson: she lent him a hand in the chorus of the Gluck Society; and the result was that I found myself invited to visit the Lawsons, who were at home in Cheyne Walk every Sunday evening. I suffered such agonies of shyness that I sometimes walked up and down the Embankment for twenty minutes or more before venturing to knock at the door: indeed I should have funked it altogether, and hurried home asking myself what was the use of torturing myself when it was so easy to run away, if I had not been instinctively aware that I must never let myself off in this manner if I meant ever to do anything in the world. Few men can have suffered more than I did in my youth from simple cowardice or been more horribly ashamed of it. I shirked and hid when the peril, real or imaginary, was of the sort that I had no vital interest in facing; but when such an interest was at stake, I went ahead and suffered accordingly. The worst of it was that when I appeared in the Lawsons' drawingroom I did not appeal to the goodnature of the company as a pardonably and even becomingly bashful novice. I had not then tuned the Shavian note to any sort of harmony; and I have no doubt the Lawsons found me discordant, crudely self-assertive, and insufferable. I hope they, and all the others on whom I jarred at this time, forgave me in later years, when it turned out that I really had something to assert after all. The house and its artistic atmosphere were most congenial to me; and I liked all the Lawsons; but I had not mastered the art of society at that time, and could not bear making an inartistic exhibition of myself; so I soon ceased to plague them, and, except for an occasional chance meeting with Malcolm, passed out of their lives after touching them very lightly in passing.

Cecil Lawson was the spoilt child of that household. He pontificated on art in a wayward grumbling incoherent musing fashion of his own. When, following my youthful and very irritating system of contradicting everyone from whom I thought I could learn anything, I suggested that Whistler was something short of the greatest artist of all time, he could not form a sentence to crush me with, but groaned inarticulately for a moment, like a

clock about to strike, and then uttered the words Titian Turner
Rembrandt Velasquez Whistler. He was goodlooking, not a big
man, but trimly built, with just enough crisply curled hair to
proclaim the artist without compromising the man. I had seen his
work in the public exhibitions (never in private); and, thanks to
my boyish prowlings in the Dublin National Gallery (as a boy
I wanted to be a painter, never a writer), I knew its value. His
untimely death, which occurred soon after my visits, must have
broken up the Sunday evenings at Cheyne Walk very badly. I did
not venture to intrude after it.

I used him in Immaturity as a model for the artist Cyril Scott,
an invented name which has since been made famous by a British
composer. I chose it because Cyril resembled Cecil metrically,
and because I thought Lawson was a Scot (he was, I learn, born in
Shropshire). But I must again warn the reader against taking the
man in the book as an authentic portrait of the great painter, or
inferring that his courtship and marriage or any of the circumstances I have invented for him, represent facts in Lawson's life.
I knew nothing whatever about him except what I saw of him
during my few visits to Cheyne Walk; and I have learnt nothing
since. He set my imagination to work: that was all.

I have now told as much as seems to me necessary of the circumstances and relevant antecedents of my first book. It is the
book of a raw youth, still quite out of touch with the country to
which he had transported himself; and if I am to be entirely com-
municative on this subject, I must add that the mere rawness which
so soon rubs off was complicated by a deeper strangeness which
has made me all my life a sojourner on this planet rather than a
native of it. Whether it be that I was born mad or a little too sane,
my kingdom was not of this world: I was at home only in the
realm of my imagination, and at my ease only with the mighty
dead. Therefore I had to become an actor, and create for myself a
fantastic personality fit and apt for dealing with men, and adapt-
able to the various parts I had to play as author, journalist, orator,
politician, committee man, man of the world, and so forth. In this
I succeeded later on only too well. In my boyhood I saw Charles

Mathews act in a farce called Cool as a Cucumber. The hero was a young man just returned from a tour of the world, upon which he had been sent to cure him of an apparently hopeless bashfulness; and the fun lay in the cure having overshot the mark and transformed him into a monster of outrageous impudence. I am not sure that something of the kind did not happen to me; for when my imposture was at last accomplished, and I daily pulled the threads of the puppet who represented me in the public press, the applause that greeted it was not unlike that which Mathews drew in Cool as a Cucumber. Certainly the growls of resentful disgust with which my advances were resisted closely resembled those of the unfortunate old gentleman in the farce whose pictures and furniture the young man so coolly rearranged to his own taste. At the time of which I am writing, however, I had not yet learnt to act, nor come to understand that my natural character was impossible on the great stage of London. When I had to come out of the realm of imagination into that of actuality I was still uncomfortable. I was outside society, outside politics, outside sport, outside the Church. If the term had been invented then I should have been called The Complete Outsider. But the epithet would have been appropriate only within the limits of British barbarism. The moment music, painting, literature, or science came into question the positions were reversed: it was I who was the Insider. I had the intellectual habit; and my natural combination of critical faculty with literary resource needed only a clear comprehension of life in the light of an intelligible theory: in short, a religion, to set it in triumphant operation. It was the lack of this last qualification that lamed me in those early days in Victoria Grove, and that set limits to this ungainly first novel of mine, which you will not lose very much by skipping.

AYOT ST LAWRENCE
   *Summer*, 1921

# BOOK THE FIRST
## ISLINGTON

# CHAPTER I

AT four o'clock in the evening of the shortest day in the year 1878 a young man passed from a main street in Islington into a quadrangle through an arch, over which was an iron plate inscribed *Dodd's Buildings.*

Dodd's Buildings enclosed a flagged square of which each side was only sixty feet long; yet the square contained eleven severely respectable houses. It was a quiet spot in a noisy neighborhood, and conveyed an impression that Dodd, though unimaginative as an architect, was a strictly pious man.

The young man, when he had despondently surveyed the court for some time, turned to the left, and knocked at the door marked No. 3. After an interval, a voice within screamed "Rose!" It was the voice of a woman losing her temper; and from this most unpleasant of all sounds the visitor shrank. Presently he knocked again, causing another and more hysterical invocation of Rose.

For the next few minutes he idly wondered whether Rose would prove as pretty as her name. When he had expressed by a third knock rather a remonstrance than a demand for admission, a buxom girl of nineteen, dressed in a black gown, scantily cut, and partly covered by an old Paisley shawl, hurried into the court; opened the door of No. 3 with as little noise as the latch would permit; entered the house; hastily deposited her bonnet and shawl beneath a movable flap which served as a hall table; and addressed herself to the patient occupant of the threshold as though she had just come up from the kitchen.

"I have taken some rooms here" said the young man.

"Mrs Froster" interposed a male voice from the second floor: "I think there is a knock at the door."

"And do you expect me to take my servant's place, Mr Fenwick?" retorted, from the first floor, the same person who had called Rose. Mr Fenwick must then have stolen back to his apartment; for he was heard no more; whilst the landlady ran down to the hall, and, overlooking in the dim light the slender figure of the

3

stranger, began, through her shut teeth, "*I'll* let you know, Miss."

"The gentleman has come" interrupted Rose, as loudly as she dared.

Mrs Froster checked herself; bade Rose, in an unsteady voice, to take herself downstairs; and lighted a candle with trembling hands.

"Will you come up with me, please, Mr Smith" she said subduedly. He ascended; and she followed him. At the third step, she broke out again. "You dont know what that girl's temper is, Mr Smith. There is a wicked devil in her. I have spoken to the minister about her. My tenants encourage her. There is no speaking to Mr Fenwick. But pride will have a fall." Here the landlady gave a painful laugh, which was checked by the stumbling of her companion on the unfamiliar steps at the second floor landing.

"This is your room" said Mrs Froster, opening a door, and ushering the new lodger into a small apartment, which contained two cane chairs, a mahogany bed, some common bedroom furniture made of deal stained yellow, and two wooden boxes sent in that morning by Mr Smith. The walls were covered with white paper ornamented with little blue flowers; and the narrow shelf above the fireplace supported a mirror framed in black wood with a gilt beading. The room was clean; and the fire blazed cheerfully; but the reflection that this was to be his home struck cold to the heart of the tenant as he waited for the landlady to withdraw, which, when he had told her how soon he desired his tea, she presently did.

Robert Smith, sitting alone before the fire and ruefully stroking his shins, was a youth of eighteen, with closely cropped pale yellow hair, small grey eyes, and a slender lathy figure. His delicately cut features and nervous manner indicated some refinement; but his shyness, though fairly well covered up, shewed that his experience of society was limited, and his disposition sensitive. When he had warmed himself so much that he was unwilling to leave the fire, he rose; inspected the chest of drawers; and began to unpack his trunk and boxes. From the trunk, which contained his wardrobe, he transferred to one of the larger drawers a suit of

4

black evening dress, which he handled carefully. With these he placed a single white tie, two linen-breasted shirts, a faded stud case, and a pair of kid gloves of that pale primrose hue which passes for white by gaslight. Turning then to one of the wooden boxes, he produced an illustrated family Bible, a Shakespeare, and an album for photographs, all three handsomely bound. The album was the gift of a schoolfellow. The others had been accumulated in monthly parts during a period of two and a half years of his boyhood, and were the proceeds of such morsels of pocket money as he had extracted by occasional importunity from his parents, who had been too poor and too careless to make him any fixed allowance. When the books had been carefully laid with his evening clothes, he locked the drawer, which henceforth constituted his cabinet of treasures, to be opened only at such rare intervals as the danger of moths rendered advisable.

He now proceeded to the disposition of his everyday apparel. Besides the decent walking suit which he carried, he had one, much worn, for use in the house; a respectable black cut-away coat to be donned when visiting, an overcoat and travelling cap which he hung on a peg in the door, the bowler hat he had just taken off, sometimes called a billy-cock, and a tall silk one, not of the latest fashion, which was swathed in tissue paper and sheltered by a bandbox. His shirts for ordinary wear, four in number, were of stout blue cotton, striped; and his socks had been knitted by hand. Other underclothing he had none. He had a box of the best German paper collars; but as they cost three halfpence apiece and were unwashable, whereas linen collars, though less resplendent, could be washed for a halfpenny, he had a supply of the latter for ordinary occasions. They shared his two boxes with his half-dozen cotton handkerchiefs, his Sunday cravat, and a number of chattels such as cheap paint boxes, a glass retort with its stand and spirit lamp, a few carpenter's tools, prints cut from illustrated papers, a scrap book containing pyrotechnic receipts and some foreign stamps, two toy brass cannons, and a common iron-monger's pistol. The proprietor of these articles, as he gazed at the old tool chest which contained most of them, seemed dejected by the prospect. They were relics of his boyhood, and proofs of his homelessness; for who ever removes such things from his father's house whilst any of his kin are to be found there? Smith shook his head, and placed the box in a corner with as much care as if he were still interested in miniature artillery and experimental chemistry. He then set forth his library on the chest of drawers. It comprised schoolbooks, dictionaries, and a number of standard works in the cheapest editions, some of which were ragged, and bore marks of boyish handling, especially the works of Byron, the engravings in which were embellished with swords and moustachios sketched with pen and ink. It presently appeared that he had a taste for music; for he produced a couple of pieces entitled respectively Raffaelle: a Nocturne, and The Bivouac, with a pianoforte tutor on the cover of which it was stated that any person might become a perfect executant by playing the contents carefully some sixteen times each day during a year. Evidence of a culture unusual in Dodd's Buildings was completed by a framed photographic reproduction of a drawing representing a knight accompanied by Death and followed by a demon, both of them grotesquely goatish, by Albert Durer. When this was suspended to the wall, and the mantelpiece decorated with a tin alarum clock, a letter balance, and a portrait in a velvet case, Smith took a scribbling diary and writing materials; put his boxes and trunk aside; and made the following calculation.

| | | | | |
|---|---|---|---|---|
| Interest on Mamma's £800 invested in land in Cork | . | £40 | 0 | 0 |
| My salary from Figgis & Weaver . . . | . | 52 | 0 | 0 |
| | | £92 | 0 | 0 |

| | | | | | |
|---|---|---|---|---|---|
| Rent, fire, and gas . . . . | . £20 | 0 | 0 | | |
| Laundress . . . . | . 3 | 0 | 0 | | |
| Food . . . . | . 31 | 10 | 0 | | |
| Clothes . . . . | . 10 | 0 | 0 | | |
| Tram fare to City and back . . | . 5 | 4 | 4 | | |
| Subscription to Library . . . | . 1 | 1 | 0 | | |
| | | 70 | 15 | 4 | |
| | | £21 | 4 | 8 | |

Smith put down his ruler. "What with theatres, and Christmas boxes, and the newspaper, and one thing and another" said he, "I know how soon that will go. I must give up the idea of hiring a piano. I ought to be able to live on my salary. I wonder have I made any mistake."

But he had made none. So he put up his diary, and rang for his evening meal, pending the arrival of which he took a book; stirred the fire into a blaze; and gave himself up to that contented laziness which usually follows the achievement of an irksome piece of business.

He was not long suffered to remain at ease. The demeanor of Rose as she arranged the tea tray confirmed the doubts which he already entertained of his landlady's amiability. The girl handled her mistress's china as if it was her mistress's head; and her movements were so abrupt, and her breathing so loud, that Smith felt relieved when the door at last banged behind her. She was not long gone when a din of voices, occasionally rising to shrillness, and anon falling into a plaintive murmur, rose from below. An odor of tobacco which presently reached Smith's nostrils seemed to stop it. After an interval of silence and smoke he heard Mrs Froster hastily ascend to the room beneath, and there enter into a loud altercation with the occupant. Smith had just resolved not to pass a second week in Dodd's Buildings, when he was startled by a sound of footsteps without, followed by a rap at the door.

"Come in" said Smith.

Immediately there entered a young man of dissipated appearance, whose dirty-fine dress and manner displayed the combination of shabbiness and pretence characteristic of the sort of poor dandies who are naturally slovens. Had his boots been whole, his linen clean, his eye bright, and his step firm, he would have been considered a well-looking youth. But the boots were of patent leather somewhat bursten, and partially covered by a pair of dirty grey extinguishers. His cuffs and collar were limp and soiled. His eyes were watery; his blotched complexion was an unwholesome yellow; and he bore himself with the feeble swagger of one who made it a habit to be as insolent as he dared, and who durst but little.

7

"Sir" said he: "do you object to my smoking in my own room?"

"No" said Smith, repelled by the aspect of his visitor: "certainly not."

"I felt sure you were too much of a gentleman to do so, sir" said the other. Then, in a lower tone, and looking inquisitively about the room, he added "I think she has gone down." Smith said nothing. "I hope you will excuse my intrusion" he continued, with an accent, meant to be aristocratic, which he had forgotten in his excitement to affect at first. "My name is Fraser Fenwick. I live in the drawing room, and will be happy[1] to render you any little service you may require."

Smith bowed.

"It is so unpleasant for a gentleman to be exposed to the tongue of a woman of her class" said Mr Fenwick, relapsing into irritation.

"Yes" replied Smith.

Fraser Fenwick scrutinized the lady's watch chain of thin gold which Smith wore, and secretly estimated the price of his attire. He looked at the portmanteau for a label, and would willingly have lingered in the hope of discovering something concerning the new lodger. But Smith did not offer his visitor any encouragement to stay; and after a further apology for his intrusion, Mr Fenwick retired, satisfied that the new lodger was an upstart, by which he meant a person who did not look on his acquaintance as an honor.

Smith finished his tea in very low spirits, and, had he been ten years younger, would have crept into bed and cried himself to sleep. As it was, he gazed wistfully at the fire, and vainly strove to escape from holding imaginary conversations with his landlady the shrew, and his roof-fellow the blackguard. At half-past seven he heard the latter go out. Shortly after this Mrs Froster was heard calling to Rose from the hall to discharge certain

---

[1] People had not at that time begun to say that they were "very pleased." They would have thought it vulgar. "Very pleased" and "thanks very much" were later fashions.

domestic offices forthwith. Then the house door was slammed. A minute later, Rose appeared.

"Ev you done with the tea things?" she said coaxingly.

"Yes, thank you."

Rose collected the china on a tray; fidgeted a little; and resumed.

"Will you be wanting me again, sir?"

Smith told her that a jug of drinking water and a tumbler would supply his requirements for that evening. Rose brought them at once. Five minutes after she had left the room, the house door was again closed, this time with the penetrating noise which is usually produced by an effort to make any operation inaudible. The clock then seemed to tick more loudly than before; and Smith, rightly conjecturing that he was alone in the house, became more tranquil. But he was still determined not to stay more than a week in Dodd's Buildings; and a declaration to this effect shaped itself in so many speeches, which he delivered to himself over and over again, that he took a newspaper from his pocket, and tried to fix his attention on a leading article, which opened with a disquisition on the Pagan festivals, and concluded with a eulogium on the Christmas excursions arranged by certain railway companies. But his mind strayed back to his former distressing reflections; and, dropping the paper, he sat staring into the fire until the rattle of a key in the street door roused him. The noise ceased; recommenced; and ceased again. Just as Smith had sulkily resolved that it was no business of his to open the door, the owner of the key knocked. The knock was of an unexpected character. Mrs Froster could not have handled a knocker so delicately, nor Mr Fenwick have struck so firmly. Rose would have given a single knock; and this was what is called a double one: that is, it comprised about eight concussions, disposed rhythmically. Smith, in his eighteenth year, could conceive a romance in a few seconds. Informed by the evidence of a latchkey that he was in no danger of encountering a stranger to the house, he went down; turned up the gas in the hall; and opened the door.

There entered then a young woman who was enveloped in a

waterproof, the hood of which was drawn over her headgear. She only said "Thank you" in a Scotch accent, and went upstairs.

He, pleasantly overpowered, stared after her until the fog, coming in through the open door, chilled him.

"She must be a lodger" said he, as he returned slowly to his room. From that time he thought no more of leaving Mrs Froster's house.

# CHAPTER II

NEXT morning, at half-past eight o'clock, Smith left his apartments, and travelled in a tram car to a counting-house in Aldersgate Street, where he worked daily for Messrs Figgis and Weaver, a respectable firm to whom he attributed most sordid views of existence. From them he gained a salary of one pound per week, and a critical knowledge of carpets and oilcloths, in which they carried on a wholesale trade. In return, he spent nearly two-thirds of his waking existence recording their transactions in large canvas-covered ledgers. Smith had some ability, and he liked work; but he hated the duties of his clerkship as barren drudgery, which numbed his faculties and wasted his time. Nevertheless, his unjustifiable contempt for Figgis and Weaver, who were, within their scope, useful if prosaic men, induced him to do his work conscientiously, lest he should become their debtor for any part of his salary which, through slackness, he should leave unearned. In this point of view the smallness of his emolument, as compared with what he could have earned by condescending to the vulgarity of retail trade, was a consolation to him. His employers thought highly of him, concluding that he liked his functions because he so scrupulously fulfilled them, and not suspecting that he ascribed the readiness to oblige which propitiated them to his own cowardice. When he addressed Figgis as "sir," despising him in his heart, he loathed his own servility. When he laughed with the other clerks at Weaver's jokes, he felt himself the most degraded toady in the office. Nevertheless he did not change his behavior, because churlishness, of which he was incapable, seemed the only alternative.

At six o'clock each evening began that part of the day which belonged to Smith. During it, he effaced business from his mind so carefully that he resented even a dream of the office as a trespass on the part of Figgis and Weaver. On the Monday following his arrival at Dodd's Buildings, he got back to his fireside at half-past six, and had just begun to read, when he was startled by a

11

continuous clacking in the adjoining room, very distracting to a student. It irritated him; and when Rose entered with the tea, he asked her about it.

"What is that awful noise?" said he.

"It's Miss Russell's sewing machine, sir" said Rose.

"Miss Russell?"

"She has the back room, sir. She's a dressmaker."

"Is there any one else—I mean besides the gentleman downstairs?"

"Yourself, sir" said Rose.

Smith was disappointed. In his fancy a dressmaker was either a woman clad in unwomanly rags, singing the song of the shirt, or a flippant young milliner without culture or dignity. Neither of these characters harmonized with his impression of the person for whom he had opened the hall door on the previous evening. He had remarked her accent; and dressmaking seemed to him an unnatural occupation for a Scotchwoman.[1] Fully three minutes elapsed after Rose's departure before it became impossible for him to imagine Miss Russell in any other capacity than that to which the rattling of the machine bore witness.

On Christmas Eve Smith returned to his lodging, rich, but dissatisfied with himself: Figgis and Weaver had presented him with five pounds, which he had not had the courage to refuse, although his pride revolted against accepting a gratuity. In vain did he assure himself that nothing was more natural than that his employers should hold a certain portion of his salary under their control. His fellow-clerks, who had been unanimous in considering the sum too large, and that awarded to themselves too small, had appeared mean to him; and he believed that he shared their degradation. From these reflections he was diverted by a knock at the door.

"Come in" cried he.

The door opened, and discovered a fair woman with soft grey eyes, who entered and addressed Smith with extraordinary grace

[1] Smith always called Scotswomen and Scotsmen Scotch. He would know better now.

of movement and self-possession of manner. Recognizing her as the person he had seen on the night of his arrival, he rose, fascinated by the sweetness of her smile, and awed by the impression of power which he received from her fine strong hands and firm jaw. She had a letter in her hand.

"I hope you will excuse me" she began.

"Not at all" said Smith.

"I have just got a letter from a French lady for whom I work; and I cannot tell what may be in it. I thought perhaps you could translate it for me, if you would be so kind, as Mrs Froster told me you were a good scholar."

Smith expressed his doubts of his competence, and his delight in being of any service to her, hastily and not very coherently. He also offered her a chair; and she, believing that Smith, as a gentleman, knew what was proper for a young woman to do under the circumstances, seated herself. He then, taking the letter, read aloud a few words, from which she rapidly constructed the entire letter. When he had finished, he offered to write it out for her, lest she should forget it; and she, not liking to refuse, produced a card and asked him to write it on the back of that. He stole a glance at the printed side, and distinguished the name Miss Russell in large letters, and Ladies' Own Materials more minutely set down beneath. He wrote the translation in his commercial style, which he had perfected by practice in the ledgers of Figgis and Weaver. Then she, thinking that she had been quite long enough in Mr Smith's apartment, thanked him, and went out with the grace of a lioness. Smith, accustomed to see women walk like parrots, felt his breast glow with admiration, and went into the streets, where, with his five pounds in his pocket, he looked at the Christmas display in the shop windows until his elastic step and spirits began to flag.

He turned homeward by way of the Euston Road. This thoroughfare was a favorite of his, because of the bookstalls which it contained; and he seldom passed along it without stopping to examine the calf-bound volumes of theology, statistics, and travel, which were offered there at a few pence apiece. On this evening, however, he found nothing which he cared to purchase until he arrived within a short distance of Dodd's Buildings, where he saw on a stall a cheap copy of Tasso's Gerusalemme. Determined not to return without some new acquisition, he resolved to learn Italian, and entered the shop. The first person he saw there was Miss Russell, who, busy bargaining, did not perceive him until the shopman had agreed to accept two-thirds of the price originally demanded by him for a work which, as Smith had in the meantime observed, purported to be a method by which the French language might be perfectly acquired in one month without a master. Uncertain whether he ought to address her, and extremely anxious to do so, he paid for his book, and then, affecting to notice her presence suddenly, made her a deferent bow.

Miss Russell, an unprotected young woman of good appearance, was not easily approached by men; but the nervousness which Smith deplored in himself, gained him the confidence of women. She not only returned his bow, but allowed him to accompany her home. Judging from what she had seen of him, she liked him as a polite young gentleman; respected him as a good scholar; and pitied him as an innocent boy who had given one-and-sixpence to a bookseller who would gladly have taken sixpence.

"I see you are going to learn French" said Smith, as they went along.

"I see you are very sharp" retorted Miss Russell.

"I do not think you will find that book a good teacher" he continued.

"It will do me very well" said she. Having bought the book, she was determined to defend it.

"But, Miss Russell" said Smith, "you dont know anything at all about it: do you?"

This time she had no answer ready. Smith, seeing her displeased, hastened to soften his triumph.

"I think there is often much time thrown away in learning which I think I could save for you, if you would allow me. But" he added, lest he might have gone too far, "perhaps you think that intrusive."

"Oh no!" she said, more humbly. "I should be very glad of your help."

"Ha! ha!" thought Smith. "You dont feel so old as you did a minute ago." Scarcely had he indulged in this chuckle when he saw an absent expression in the face of his companion. Fraser Fenwick was standing in the archway which led from the street into Dodd's Buildings, in conversation with a young man who might have passed for a damaged and discarded attempt at a copy of himself. They stood aside as the dressmaker entered the passage; and Fenwick saluted her by raising his hat. She passed on without a sign; and Smith's first impression of her strength and grace returned so strongly upon him as she did so that he forgot the two men until a coarse laugh, followed by a discomfited titter, inspired him with a wish to return and assault them. He parted from her at the door of his room, and thought of her continually during the rest of the evening.

Meanwhile Fraser Fenwick was explaining his rebuff to his companion.

"She is a dear girl" he said; "but we had a little breeze the other day; and she has taken up with that puppy by way of revenge."

"Why dont you kick him?" said the other.

"Pooh!" said Fenwick: "it's not the thing for a gentleman to get into a row over a stitcher. She will drop him soon enough. She was annoyed about little Selina, down at Bigley's. Where are you going to, now?"

"Well, Ive nothing particular to do with myself. Do you live here?"

"Just for the present" said Fenwick, conscious of having given his associate reason to expect a more fashionable residence. "She lives upstairs." Here he smiled, and his associate leered appreciatively. "I suppose you wont come in" he added, very inhospitably.

The other responded by going in immediately; and Fenwick, disappointed, ushered him into his room with the best grace he could assume. The visitor, whose name was Samuel Box, professed to be well pleased with the apartment, in the arrangement of which the neatness of Mrs Froster was counteracted by the slovenliness of her tenant.

"These are snug diggings, Fenwick" said Box. "Where abouts does *she* hang out?"

"Will you have some grog?" said his host, almost rudely.

"Thank you" said Box. "I dont mind if I do."

Fenwick produced some whisky and water, and mixed them silently. His recent discomfiture rankled with increasing bitterness within him, as he surveyed by gaslight the disreputable aspect of his guest. Miss Russell, he thought, could not be expected to let her new acquaintance imagine that she knew a person who so far forgot his position as to converse openly with a man so ill dressed as Box. The knowledge that the latter had enjoyed the scene was an additional grievance; and Fenwick grew malicious as he drank.

"A nice thing for a gentleman to be cut by a common shirt-maker with a few shillings a week between her and the streets" he cried. "It's an honor, I'm sure, to live in the same house with her. What a pity it is she dont take a drawing room instead of living in the garret. I suppose she thinks I care whether she knows me or not."

"I thought it was on account of little Selina," said Box, with a grin.

"What the devil is it to you?" retorted Fenwick.

"Oh, nothing at all" said Box, with an uneasy affectation of coolness.

"That upstart thinks he can do what he likes, because I took some notice of him the night he came. Ha! Ha! Perhaps he's proud of his name. The Fraser Fenwicks are pretty nearly as uncommon as the Smiths."

"Well, whats the odds, anyhow?" said Box cheerfully.

"Odds!" cried Fenwick. "I suppose it makes no odds to you what people think of me, with you hanging after me round the streets."

"Who are you?" said Box, becoming suddenly pale, and springing to his feet.

Fenwick rose also and looked scornfully at his guest; but he was so frightened that he could not speak. Box, equally terrified, kept repeating "Who are you?" more with his white lips than with his voice.

"I am master of this house" panted Fenwick at last. "Theres the door!"

"Oh, I'm going, fast enough" said Box, gaining confidence as he escaped from the room, "but not at your bidding, Mr Master of the House. It's a pity" he continued, railing on Fenwick as he went downstairs, and raising his voice as he receded, "that you dont get on better with your lodgers, since youre a gentleman. I'm sorry I aint good enough to be seen with you. I hope you pay for your back drawing room as well as you paid old Bigley for them liquors. How about that"—Here an angry step seemed to indicate that Mr Fenwick was giving chase; and Box fled, shutting the house door with a slam that made the floors vibrate.

Fenwick had had but a brief interval of peace, when Mrs Froster tapped at the door. He became pale as he bade her come in. She was tall and angular, with black eyes set close to either side of an aquiline nose.

"Well, Mr Fenwick" she said in a strained voice. "This is nice conduct."

"I dont want to have any row, if you please" said he, in sulky desperation.

"I dont want to have any pot-house swaggerers shouting through my house" she retorted. "I wont have a curse brought on my house. I wont have it."

He shrugged himself, and said nothing.

"Do you hear me, Mr Fenwick? Are you going to answer me?"

"How can I help a man being a cad?" he expostulated. "If a man cant behave himself in a gentleman's house, is it my fault?"

"And since when has this house been yours?"

"I mean the room."

"And since when" she repeated, "has the room been yours?" Mr Fenwick avoided her glance and did not reply. Then, with sudden ferocity, she cried, "Are you going to pay your rent and leave?"

"I have promised—"

"Can I live on your promises?"

"I cant possibly—I wish to God youd let me alone" he exclaimed in great agitation.

"Do not dare to blaspheme under this roof," she cried. "He will punish you. He will punish you with fire."

"Stop, stop" sobbed Fenwick, falling into a chair, and bowing his head in his hands. "Ive been very wicked; but I'm very wretched. Nobody will speak to me or know me. I'm going to die. If I'm only spared I'll never touch another drop. I'll go to church tomorrow: indeed I will. I intended to all along."

Mrs Froster, checked by the sudden prostration of her victim, and exhausted by her passion, began to be infected by his terror. "I hope you will, Mr Fenwick" she said solemnly.

"You dont think I'll die in the night?" said Fenwick, trembling.

"Heaven forbid I should think such an awful thing" she replied, moving towards the door.

"Wait a minute, Mrs Froster" he pleaded, stretching his shaky hand across the table as though to clutch her dress: "only another second. I'm afraid to be alone. You wont leave me here to die, will you?"

Mrs Froster tried to speak; but her tongue clove to the roof of her mouth; and her limbs seemed about to fail. She hastily left the room, and made her way to her bed, on which she shivered and sobbed alternately until midnight.

Mr Fenwick, left alone, moaned for some minutes. He then looked fearfully round, and, reassured by the bright glare from the gas and the fire, rose and procured some whisky, of which he drank a glassful. Having thus purchased a few minutes' self-command, he undressed himself and went to bed, not daring to extinguish the light, and was presently rescued by a heavy sleep from the horrors with which his imagination peopled the corners of the room.

# CHAPTER III

"I CANNOT help thinking that today is Sunday" said the entire population of the United Kingdom and several foreigners, on the 25th December of the year in which Robert Smith took lodgings in Islington. He, strolling towards Hyde Park, said it in a tone which implied that he did not approve of the resemblance. Feeling in the humor for exploring new localities, and being little acquainted with the maze of streets called Mayfair, he turned from Piccadilly into Shepherd's Market, and presently found himself in a court where several persons were hurrying towards the door of a schoolhouse. Smith was curious and observant. He had also a love of adventure; and to enter a strange place uninvited seemed to him audacious. Accordingly, he went in at the schoolhouse door, and was no sooner past the threshold than a girl handed him a tract. He thanked her, and walked along a passage, where he encountered in succession an earnest boy who begged him to accept a little book, a man who thrust one on him austerely, and a smiling person who slipped a leaflet into his hand as if it were a doctor's fee, and gently pushed him into the schoolroom. The front seats were occupied by females, principally young girls accompanied by sour-looking old women. The rest of the audience were respectable tradespeople, half-a-dozen soldiers, and some youths who seemed to be scoffers. Nearly all the women were solemn; but many of the men smiled constantly and wrung the hands of the newcomers. Smith sat down, and read his tracts, which he found neither credible, Christian, nor interesting.

The meeting was opened by some hymns, which were fairly sung: many of the singers reading from books printed in nearly every variety of musical symbolism except the ordinary staff notation. Thus, though the bulk of the congregation either followed the tune or improvised a drone bass which only moved at the cadences, there was a tolerable attempt at part singing; and Smith found no fault in the performance. Four hymns were given in succession, the last having the words "We will all be happy over there" for its burden, in which the phrase "over there" was repeated in all the parts, one answering the other. This antiphonal device was very popular; and the congregation repeated the last verse of their own accord. Smith joined his colorless baritone voice to the harmony, but soon ceased, fancying that a young girl who sat close by was listening to him. Observing this, a man proffered him his hymnbook, which he accepted, and held a corner of until the music came to an end. Then there arose a young man, earnest and proud of his oratory, who offered up a long prayer, in the course of which he suggested such modifications of the laws of nature as would bring the arrangement of the universe into conformity with his own tenets. When he was done, several others delivered addresses; but they lacked variety, as the speakers were all very ignorant. The addresses of one or two men who related the atrocities committed by them before their conversion disgusted Smith; and he watched for an opportunity of retiring quietly. Before any occurred, a man of about thirty, with dark circles about his eyes, a pointed moustache, and long black hair, rose, and was greeted by the women with a hum of expectation. Smith resolved to wait and hear him speak. Unlike the orators who had preceded him, he wore a shooting jacket of grey tweed, and a bright-colored scarf. A large felt hat lay on the bench from which he had risen. Although frequently interrupted by a cough, he spoke with remarkable fluency and fervor, and illustrated his discourse by many anecdotes. He concluded by declaring that he was about to die; that his physician had offered him life on condition of complete repose from evangelistic duties; but that he was resolved to persevere to the end, trusting to a still greater physician for his reward. With this peroration, he sank on the bench, coughing violently; and a perceptible emotion among the congregation testified to the justness with which he had calculated his effect. Smith, to whose more cultivated sense the climax seemed exaggerated, was grinning at it, when he suddenly met the glance of a modest-looking girl close at hand, whose eyes, filled with tears, gazed on him with reproachful surprise. Proud of his cynicism, he looked as scornful as he could; and she, taking his expression to be a display

20

of contempt for herself, inspired by his superior social position, turned away. Smith, who had the sense to appreciate his own follies, without the presence of mind to check himself when tempted to commit them, repented immediately, and watched the girl until the meeting broke up, which it did after a long prayer and three or four hymns. Whilst the congregation dispersed, those who had spoken stood receiving the compliments of their admirers. The man with the black hair, who was the most popular, was so mobbed that he had at last to break away and hurriedly approach the door. He passed Smith in the entrance, and was escaping into the street, when the girl who had been moved to tears by his address stopped him and said earnestly:

"Oh, Mr Davis, I want to speak to you about something very particular."

The preacher then entered into a conversation, in which they were still engaged when Smith, after curiously loitering about the room and passage, left. As he passed them he heard the preacher say:

"I will go to him this very night, this very instant."

"Oh, not today, Mr Davis" said the girl. "I did not mean to spoil your Christmas."

"I am ready for the call of my Master at all seasons, Miss Watkins. I know well that I have no time to lose" he added, with a cough.

When Smith re-entered Piccadilly, he mounted to the roof of an Islington omnibus. At Oxford Circus, he was surprised to see Mr Davis clamber up the vehicle, and sit down beside him. For some time the preacher sat resting his hollow cheek on his hand, which was adorned by a gaudy ring. He glanced occasionally at Smith, and seemed disposed to enter into conversation with him. They were nearly at the end of Portland Street when he ventured to ask him the following unexpected question.

"Perhaps you could tell me, sir, if we will pass near a place called Dodd's Buildings?"

Smith replied that the Angel at Islington, where the omnibus stopped, was within ten minutes' walk of the place referred to, and added that he lived there.

At this Mr Davis stared, having supposed from Smith's appearance that he was a gentleman, a conclusion which he thought incompatible with residence in Dodd's Buildings. Feeling more at ease, he said:

"Did I not see you at our meeting this evening?"

"Yes. I was passing; and I went in without knowing what was going forward."

"Youll come again?"

"It is rather out of my way, I fear."

"Dont say that. I'm sure you take ten times the trouble every day for less reward."

Smith thought of Figgis and Weaver, and sighed involuntarily.

"Come!" resumed Davis, perceiving this: "I see you feel that I'm right; and so I am, though not in my own wisdom. I'll tell you where I live. I live at Emmersmith. Dodd's Buildings is further out of my way than Shepherd's Market is out of yours; but that dont matter to me. Ive come up ere this day to snatch a young man from the devil, whose slave he has become. And with the elp of God, I will so snatch him. If you knew ow appy the work makes me, youd join me."

"No doubt every man is happy who has work to do which he likes and believes in."

"Theres plenty of the same work for every one; and youll find youll like it."

Smith shook his head, and said nothing. He could not believe that a man who dropped his aitches could have anything to teach him. He was only eighteen.

"Ow do you think this work was provided for me?" said Davis. "This young man that I'm going to see today—Christmas Day— was engaged to a cousin of his. The cousin saw him falling step by step into evil courses, and didnt know how to save him. One day she came to our meeting, and er art was touched. The Lord shewed her the way then; and this very day she spoke to me as I was going out into the public street as it were. 'Oh Mr Davis' she says to me, 'speak to him. He'll listen to you. You know how to talk straight into a human soul; and you can save it better than any clergyman. So I came straight away to find him; and if the power is vouchsafed to me, I will bring him back to her a newborn man."

Smith politely wished him success.

"I thank you, sir" returned the other; "but I had rather have prayers than wishes."

"The majority of prayers are very little else than wishes."

Davis looked at him doubtfully. Smith broached the subject of the weather, the tendency of every Christmas to be less like Christmas than the one before, and so on. At the Angel, they descended; and Smith proposed to conduct Davis to Dodd's Buildings, adding that it was close at hand.

"It would be rather an awkward thing" said the preacher, uneasily, "to call on a stranger, if it were not on a holy errand."

Smith thought it an impertinent thing, but did not say so.

"I have been misunderstood and reviled sometimes" continued Davis; "but I have thought to myself how a better and greater than I suffered worse. That is a good cure for thinking too much of yourself."

"I dont know" said Smith dubiously. "A man might contend on the same ground that it is no disgrace to be hanged. Besides, a habit of comparing your circumstances with those of great men would rather aggravate egotism than destroy it."

"I think you have some peculiar ideas" said Davis, smiling.

Smith replied quickly that he never could understand why a piece of common sense, when it clashed with a popular prejudice, should be contemptuously set aside as a peculiar idea.

"I ask your pardon, sir" said Davis, humbly. "Heaven forbid that I should speak contemptuously to one whose soul is as precious—nay, more precious—than my own."

"I didnt mean that at all, I assure you" said Smith, taken aback. "This is Dodd's Buildings" he added, as they turned into the archway.

"Oh, indeed" said Davis. "I am greatly obliged to you. Perhaps you will add to your kindness by directing me to No. 3."

"Here it is" said Smith, opening the door with his latchkey.

"Well, how oddly things come about!" exclaimed the preacher. "Depend upon it, this is not a mere chance. Do you know a Mr Fenwick, who lives here?"

"Mr Fenwick aint in at present, sir" said Rose, who had just appeared in the hall.

Davis looked so blank at this intelligence, that Smith saw nothing for it but to ask him into his own room, although he felt ashamed of the poor entertainment he had to offer him. From this embarrassment he was relieved by the appearance of Mrs Froster, who, to his surprise, begged him to bring his friend into the drawing room. Davis bowed in acknowledgment; and the three entered the front drawing room, Mrs Froster's room of state, which she never let. The table was walnut, and was covered with a crimson cloth, in the centre of which a case of stuffed birds stood on a Berlin wool mat. On the mantelpiece were an ornamental clock, a velvet watch-stand, and two plaster of Paris vases under glass shades. A convex mirror, encircled by a gilt frame of earnestly ugly design, hung on the wall opposite the pier glass. The window was draped with red damask curtains, which contrasted with the green Venetian blind; and the appearance of the whole room was worthy of the gentility to which, through many years of struggling, Mrs Froster had never relinquished her pretension.

"I wish I knew the fellow's name" thought Smith, as he entered. "I suppose I am expected to introduce him." But Mrs. Froster relieved him again.

"I little thought, Mr Davis" said she, with emotion, "to have the honor of welcoming you in my house on Christmas Day. This is Miss Russell, a friend of mine. Harriet: this is the gentleman of whom I have often spoken to you."

Miss Russell, sitting by the fire, betrayed a momentary consciousness of the existence of Davis, who made a too low bow, and then, at the hostess's invitation, sat down. So did Smith. A seed cake and a bottle of marsala were produced, and partaken of by all present, except the dressmaker.

"You very seldom come to us at Finsbury now" said Mrs Froster.

"No," replied Davis: "I work altogether at the west end. There is not a more barren wilderness in London than Yde Park, and there cannot be too many voices to cry there."

"Do you go to prayer meetings?" said Miss Russell apart to Smith, whilst Davis enlarged his comments on London infidelity to the proportions of a gospel address.

"No" whispered Smith. "I went today accidentally, because I had nothing else to do, and felt curious. I met *him* on my way home; and as he wanted to call here, we struck up an acquaintance. I think he intends to revive Mr Fenwick. Have you ever heard him preach?"

"Indeed I have not" said Miss Russell, as though the question aspersed her good sense. She did not lower her voice as she spoke; and Smith began to think that she was not very considerate when her sympathies were not engaged.

"How are you getting on with the French?" said he.

"That is nothing to you, Mr Smith" she replied.

Smith grinned: "You will ask me to help you before you are half-way through the first chapter of that infallible method" said he.

"Did you find the prayer meeting interesting?" she said coldly.

"Not particularly. I dont think you ought to be angry with me for finding out your secret when you told it to me yourself."

"I am not angry" said Miss Russell. "But I think you are varra pairseverin." Then, as she heard the cadence of her own sentence, she hastily added "Very persevering indeed."

Smith, content to have shaken her self-possession, abandoned the topic, and began to talk about himself. He was interrupted by Davis, who had been vainly hoping to secure a larger audience than Mrs Froster, and now addressed himself directly to the dressmaker.

"Have I had the pleasure of seeing you at any of our little meetings, Miss?" said he.

"Harriet" said Mrs Froster sharply, after a pause: "do you hear?"

Miss Russell turned, and with the brightness of a smile provoked by one of Smith's witticisms still on her face, looked inquiringly from Mrs Froster to the preacher, who grew paler.

"Have I?" said he, referring to his question.

"Have you what?" said she, as though she were beginning to suspect Mr Davis of being a greater fool than he had at first appeared.

"Mr Davis was asking whether you had been to the meetings at Finsbury" said Mrs Froster.

"I never go to prayer meetings" said Miss Russell.

"You never go anywhere, Harriet" said Mrs Froster; "and Mr Davis will not think any the better of you for it."

"I suppose not" said Harriet, scarcely concealing her contempt for his opinion.

"May I ask what are your objections to us?" said Davis, who did not feel grateful to Mrs Froster for her remark.

"I was brought up by my father to believe that there is no good in such things" said Harriet simply. Here Mrs Froster, overcome by reminiscences of Mr Russell, uttered a groan.

"I wish I could speak to your father" said Davis, with a confident smile.

"I wish you could" said Harriet. "He is dead."

"Oh!" exclaimed Davis, and added, making his flexible face sad, "Dear me!"

"He has a great deal to answer for. He has a very great deal indeed to answer for" cried Mrs Froster.

"That is enough about my father now, Mrs Froster" said Miss Russell. Mrs Froster for a moment looked rebellious. Then she quailed, and let the subject drop.

"I wonder has Mr Fenwick come in yet?" remarked Smith, anxious to create a diversion.

"Yes indeed: I wonder has he" said Davis. "I came all the way from the other end of London to see him. I have a few words—words in season, I hope—to say to him."

"I am very glad of it" said Mrs Froster. "The young men of the present day are beyond my comprehension."

"After all, I doubt if I will see him today" said Davis, looking at his watch.

"At all events, you will not run away yet, Mr Davis" said the landlady. "I will tell Rose to ask Mr Fenwick to join us the minute he comes in."

Miss Russell rose. "I must go now, Mrs Froster" she said.

"There can be no objection to your meeting Mr Fenwick when I am here, and Mr Davis" remarked Mrs Froster.

"I did not mention Mr Fenwick. I have some work to finish before I go out."

"Harriet! You are not going to work on Christmas Day!"

"Those who make holidays should give people the means to keep them" said Miss Russell, making a slight bow to Davis as she left the room, and taking no notice of Smith.

"A very headstrong ungovernable girl" said Mrs Froster, annoyed. "Her temper is unbearable; and she gives way to it without restraint. She will not listen to reproof; and talking to her is only tempting her to say sinful things."

"A relative of yours, I presume?" inquired Davis.

"Certainly not" replied Mrs Froster. "I should be sorry that any one of my family had such ideas. Her aunt is an old friend of mine, and could have got Harriet a very good place with Mr Grosvenor at Richmond; only she thought herself too good for it."

"Then she doesnt live with her aunt?" said Davis.

"Oh no: she lives with me. At least" added Mrs Froster, "in consideration of my knowledge of her, she pays me for a room. She is very independent, and thinks it better to be a stranger in my house and a lonely girl in London, than to live respectably with her aunt in her own station. The young women of the present day are very different to what they used to be."

"Both her parents are dead, I suppose" said Davis. His inquisitiveness was very agreeable to Smith, who was equally curious, but more delicate.

"Her mother died when Harriet was born" said Mrs Froster. "She was brought up in Scotland by her father. I judge nobody, Mr Davis. I am wicked enough myself. But I am sorry for Harriet's sake that she had no better guidance."

27

"Men often stray from the path, when it is willed that their wives be taken to eternal rest: gentlemen especially—though all are equal before the gates of Heaven" said Davis.

"Gentlemen!" cried Mrs Froster. "He was no gentleman, but a gauger and land surveyor, that got his money in bribes, and spent it in drink. He ran away with her mother, and brought ruin on the family, who were most respectable people; for her grandfather was mayor of Nottingham. Her sister, Harriet's aunt, is the only one left now, and has had to become housekeeper to Mr Grosvenor, as I was saying. He's a kind gentleman, and very rich; but I fear he thinks more of his statues and his French pictures than of better things. There will be little comfort in gaudy ornaments when the day comes for us to give an account of ourselves, Mr Davis."

"Little indeed!" said the preacher. "I am sorry to hear what you tell me about your young friend's father."

"I have wondered that fire was not called down on that man's presumption" resumed Mrs Froster. "I darent repeat to you the things he has said to his young child. He would not send her to school, for fear she would be taught to read the Book of Books, where he said she would find nothing but bad examples. The only time I ever went to his house, I gave little Harriet a book that I brought from London called Drops of the Water of Life. He gave it back to me before her face with these very words. 'Harry' says he, 'when you want to do whats right, youll see your way straight enough without the help of religion. When you dont, youll easily be able to invent as good an excuse as youll find in the Bible.' I told him straight out what I thought of him; but he laughed at me, and said things it would little become me to repeat. Then I asked him to let me introduce her to the parish clergyman. 'No, Rebecca' says he, 'not to a parson. I try hard to keep her amongst honest people; and she knows three smugglers already, let alone myself that am a gauger.' You can imagine what the poor child was, indulged and spoiled like that, with as much liberty as a married woman, and nobody but herself to keep house. And it actually pleased him to hear it remarked on. 'Theres nothing like liberty' he used to say. 'My Harry shall go where she likes, except to church; and say what she likes, except her prayers.' Every night regularly he sat in a tavern until eleven o'clock; and perhaps it was the Lord's mercy that in that way she saw very little of him. Four years ago, the doctor gave him a warning; and he sent Harriet to her aunt at Richmond. While she was there he began to drink like a madman; and after arranging that he should be buried and the place sold before she heard a word of it, he died, almost as if he did it on purpose."

"I hope he repented at the last" said Davis, gravely.

"I hope so" said Mrs Froster. "When he came to his senses after the stroke for a few minutes before his death, they brought the minister to him. 'Russell' said the clergyman: 'I'm sorry that this should be our first meeting.' 'Aye, and our last too' said Joseph; 'and if it's any consolation to you to know my mind, I can tell you that if theres a hell for lazy and self-indulgent black-guards I'm going there, and no mistake.' 'Russell' said the minister, solemnly, 'there are comforts in religion for all states.' 'The greatest comfort about it for me at present' said he, 'is that I dont believe in it.' Those awful words, Mr Davis, were the last he ever spoke on earth."

"I suppose Miss Russell was greatly grieved by her loss, Mrs Froster" said Smith.

"If you knew her, you wouldnt think so" said Mrs Froster. "She has no more feeling than a stone. How could she, when her heart has never been touched? He left a letter for her, to be de-livered when he was dead; but she never shewed it even to her aunt or to me, and always spoke about him as coolly as if he were alive."

"Ah!" said Davis: "we dont know what death is till the sum-mons comes to ourselves." This remark, accompanied by a cough, diverted the conversation to the health and labors of the preacher, of whose lung disease Smith was becoming weary. Shortly after-wards, Mr Fenwick returned, and, having been waylaid by Mrs Froster on the stairs, was brought into the drawing room and introduced to Davis, who shook his hand affectionately.

29

"Have you been enjoying a walk, sir?" said Davis.

Mr Fenwick had been at church, in pursuance of his resolution of the previous night, and was partly ashamed of the act, and partly desirous to conciliate Mrs Froster by letting her know of it. So he replied carelessly that he had been to St Paul's in the morning. "A fellow will do almost anything to kill time on these confounded holidays" he added.

Mrs Froster, feeling that the conversion of her lodger should be effected in private, now rose; pleaded some forgotten instructions to the servant; and with many apologies left the room. Smith was willing to follow her example, but lacked presence of mind to devize a happy excuse. Mr Davis coughed; fixed his dark eyes intently on Fenwick's face; and, carefully pitching his voice as low as possible, began thus.

"I have never met you before this day, Mr Fenwick. But I have heard of you, heard anxiously of you, from a young lady who knows you very well. I mean Miss Watkins."

Fenwick blushed. His cousin was the daughter of an Italian warehouseman in Bishopsgate.

"She has found appiness, great appiness" continued the preacher.

Fenwick, taking this to be a compliment to himself, looked a little foolish, and replied, "She's a very good little girl, and well worthy to be spoken to by any man, no matter what his station may be. But there is nothing settled."

"I do not speak of that transient appiness afforded by the vain delights of the world" said Davis, in a threatening voice. "I speak of a peace that passeth all understanding, the consciousness of being saved. Mr Fenwick: are *you* saved? Have *you* found that peace? Oh Mr Fenwick, how is it with your soul, with your precious, your immortal soul? Are you ready to face the great day of wrath? Oh, dont arden your art, Mr Fenwick. That day may be nearer than you think. The signs of the times shew that that day is at and. Noos is in from Russia yesterday—"

"Just excuse me for two minutes, Mr Davis" said Smith, hastily making his escape.

"All that about Russia is great rot" observed Fenwick. "Why didnt the day come after the Crimean war?"

"It was not the Divine will that it should."

"Well, why should it be the Divine will now any more than it was then?"

"And what are you, Mr Fenwick, that you should judge the times and seasons of the Almighty? Remember that it is for your good, and in the service to which I have unworthily devoted myself, that I say these things to you. Dont think of such a worm as I am. I was once as great a sinner as you are—"

"Hello!" exclaimed Mr Fenwick, in a tone of remonstrance.

"Aye, and a far greater one" continued Davis. "I was the servant of the devil. I spent my time in public-houses. I played skittles with the wicked, and never opened my mouth without calling on the awful doom that would surely have been my lot had I been snatched away in my sin. I did worse again than that."

Mr Fenwick tried to wink, but failed.

"But a call came to me at last, as it came to Saul of Tarsus; and I was saved out of the Valley of the Shadow of Death. My eyes were opened. I saw what a sinner I'd been. And I felt I was saved, yes, saved, Mr Fenwick. Oh" shouted Davis, throwing up his arms, "what a blessed thing it is to be saved! Oh, what a glorious thing it is to be saved! To know that you are one of the elect! To see a place prepared for you before the throne! Oh, what a joyful thought! Oh, what a happy, blessed thought!"

"Draw it mild, old man" said Fenwick. "You aint there yet, you know."

"I have a better assurance of it than all the bonds in the Bank of England" returned Davis. "Think well before you reject that assurance. You may be nearer death than you think. [Mr Fenwick turned pale] I'm as strong-looking a man as you are; and I havnt two years to live. I know it well; but I'm appy in the thought of it. Can you say as much?"

"But theres nothing the matter with me."

"How do you know that?" said Davis. "I was speaking to a young man last week: a gay, strong man, puffed up in the pride of his health. I said to him what I say now to you. 'I'll send for you, Davis' says he, 'when I feel bad. I cant stand religion yet says he, 'my constitution's too good for it.' But the hand of death reached him for all that. Two days ago, on the day before Christmas Eve, his sister says to him, 'William' says she: 'come to meeting with me tonight just this once. It wont do you no arm, and you neednt go again if you dont like it.' 'No' says he: 'I'll be damned before I do.' And he walked out of the house. He was brought home an hour after on a shutter, a common deal shutter, Mr Fenwick, dead from the Aymarket, where he'd ad a stroke. Dont think you can tell yourself how youre good for twenty year more. Dont keep saying 'It's time enough.' You dont know where you may be tomorrow."

"No more I wont in any case" said Fenwick, shaken.

"Yes, you will" said the preacher. "Youll know that you cant come to worse in this world, and that you will come to better in the next. Youll be free from the fear of hell. Think of that, Mr Fenwick. Think of what hell is! Youve read in histories of people being tortured. Youve read of the rack that pulls you asunder, of the vices that squeeze you till the blood busts out from under your thumbnails, of the slow roastings, the steepings in bilin ile, and the red-hot gridirons. What are they to what you must suffer in hell? Fancy them all made a thousand times more fearful, and you suffering them for ever and ever. Think of that! No end to it, not a moment's rest, no chance of ever getting out, nothing but weeping and gnashing of teeth to all eternity. Thats what hell is, Mr Fenwick; and thats what you will come to as sure as you are sitting in that chair if you dont repent. But you will repent. The Lord is all merciful, Mr Fenwick. He wants you to come: he longs for you to come. He loves to see people happy and good. He hates nothing but sin. Oh, will you come? Will you be washed whiter than snow? Will you be born again? Will you come into the fold like a little child, and lay down your burden for ever?"

The preacher stopped, gasping for breath. Fenwick, appalled, and deprived of his presence of mind by collision with a more intense nature, muttered some deprecatory words, and stretched out his hand towards the decanter.

"No" said Davis, interposing: "dont turn to that for strength to harden your heart. Be thankful if you feel your sins and your danger; and keep away from that curse, which has led to more infidelity than anything else in the world. *I* need no stimulant but faith: why should *you?*"

Mr Fenwick was about to reply when he was interrupted by a rustling of silk without, followed by the entrance of Mrs Froster, whose dolman of black silk and beads, ornate bonnet, and moire antique dress, indicated her intention of eating her Christmas dinner abroad. Miss Russell appeared in the doorway, waiting for the landlady.

"I'm afraid youll think my manners very bad" said Mrs Froster; "but I have promised to spend the evening at Richmond. You must not let my going out disturb you."

"I must be going myself" replied the preacher, looking at his watch. "Is Miss Russell going with you?"

"She is" assented Mrs Froster. "We have to catch the half-past five train."

"If you will allow me" said Davis, "I will go with you as far as King's Cross. I am going to Emmersmith; and we will be travelling part of the way together."

This proposition was approved of by Mrs Froster; and the preacher, having received from Fenwick a promise to attend a meeting on the following Friday, and to think over their conversation in the meantime, declared himself ready to start. Miss Russell immediately went downstairs with Mrs Froster; and Davis, after pausing to turn the seal of his ring outside, pull his cuffs into view, and glance at the mirror, followed them.

Mr Fenwick, left by himself, listened breathlessly until the house door was closed. He then seized the decanter; inverted it upon his lips; and poured half a pint of its contents partly into his stomach, and partly over his neck and breast. Checked by the sound of Rose's footsteps ascending the stairs, he took a final gulp, hastily replaced the stopper, and left the room. Rose passed him on the landing; and being informed by a strong smell of marsala of his recent proceedings, rightly calculated that another glass might safely be laid to his account. This glass she accordingly drank in honor of the day.

# CHAPTER IV

ON Saturday morning, Smith was eating his breakfast, and warding off the shadow of Figgis and Weaver which impended over that meal by the contents of a newspaper propped in front of him by the milk jug, when he was disturbed by a tap at the door.

"Come in!" roared Smith; and immediately Mrs Froster appeared smiling, with a slate in her hand. On this slate was recorded the amount due for food and lodging by Mr Smith to his landlady for the week then expired, being the first of his sojourn in Dodd's Buildings. He looked at the total, and paid. Although a practised bookkeeper, he could as easily have seized Mrs Froster and waltzed round the room with her as added her figures whilst she stood beside him. This weekly settling of accounts was, in his estimation, the greatest trial to his feelings entailed by living in lodgings; and with a woman like Mrs Froster, who seemed to be always ill at ease, the transaction was specially awkward.

"You mustnt be surprised if the washing is more than that next week" said she. "You know you brought nearly all your clothes clean when you came."

"Oh yes, I know. Certainly" said Smith.

"Bread has gone up a farthing" continued the landlady; "so you neednt be surprised at my charging a shilling for three loaves."

"Of course not" said Smith. "I know it's perfectly right."

Mrs Froster took up her slate; fidgeted a little; and said, "I was thinking of going down to Richmond for a fortnight, on account of my health."

"I'm very glad to hear it" said Smith. "I mean that I hope it will do you good."

"I will come up occasionally to look after the house; and Miss Russell has offered to help Rose in the housekeeping when I am not here. I am sure you will find yourself properly attended; so perhaps you wont mind my being away."

Smith, whilst admiring a degree of conscientiousness which his experience of London lodging-house keepers had not led him to expect, felt relieved at the prospect of her absence. He expressed his approval of the arrangement, and his anxiety that Mrs Froster's health might be established by it. She then gave him some account of the symptoms from which she suffered, and of the troubles to which she mainly attributed them.

On his return from his office in the afternoon, he found the house deserted; and as Rose appeared some three hours later, to inquire if he had rung the bell, she having been out for a few minutes to the vegetable shop at the corner of the street, he concluded that Mrs Froster was already at Richmond.

At eight o'clock he was sitting before the fire, reading, when a letter, which served him as a bookmarker, slipped from the page to the hearth. He hastily stooped to recover it. The letter lay lower than his feet, which rested on the fender, and he had to dive until his face disappeared between his knees, in order to reach it. Consequently he recovered his letter and lost an indispensable button simultaneously.

"Damn!" said he, ruefully.

Having thus expressed himself, he cautiously picked up the button, tightened the brace which was now his sole dependence, and rang the bell. Apparently Rose had returned to the vegetable shop; for he rang in vain. He thought of Miss Russell, and wondered whether it would be proper to knock at the door of her room, where she was now audibly working with her sewing machine. Recollecting that she had not hesitated to call on him when she required a small service, he thought she would scarcely be offended at his taking a similar liberty. So he crossed the landing, and knocked at the door of the back room. The noise of the machine was stopped, and the door was opened by the dressmaker, who looked at Smith with some surprise.

"I beg your pardon, Miss Russell" said he; "but I could not get Rose to answer the bell, and I want the loan of a needle and thread, if you could oblige me with it."

"White thread?" asked she, thinking of his shirt.

"No" said he, blushing slightly: "strong black thread, if you please."

"Is it anything I can do for you, Mr Smith?" said she, with a woman's natural compassion for a man driven to the needle by loneliness.

"Oh no, thank you" he replied hastily. "I can do it myself."

Whilst she searched for the required articles, Smith, standing in the doorway, surveyed the apartment. It was longer than his own, and was lighted by a window in the wall opposite the door. On the right the corner was enclosed by a screen covered with dark red baize, and a curtain of the same color, forming, in effect, a separate bedroom. The table, which was a large one, was covered with leather, and had shallow drawers beneath. It had evidently been made for the counting house or boardroom. Close to it was a sewing machine fitted with a treadle, and between the two the chair from which the dressmaker had just risen. The remainder of the furniture consisted of a looking-glass tall enough to reflect an entire figure, a mahogany wardrobe, a small writing table, and three chairs of much handsomer appearance than that before the sewing machine. The general appearance of the room surprised Smith; for not only did it contain chattels which he would scarcely have thought within the owner's means, but it was also quite different from the nest of spotless chintz and fresh flowers which had filled its place in his imagination. There was nothing of a purely ornamental character to be seen; and save for the writing table, which had been designed with some view to prettiness, the place might have been the workshop of a man milliner who had survived the illusions of his youth. It was quite orderly and clean, except the table, on which lay a skirt turned inside out, a smoothing iron, a piece of candle, two pairs of scissors, and a confused litter of remnants of calico, linen, and breadths of a material similar to that of which the dress was made, mixed up with pins, pieces of whalebone, skeins, paper patterns, and rolls of fringe.

"I am afraid I disturb you" said Smith apologetically, as he saw the dressmaker pulling out drawer after drawer without finding the black thread.

"Not at all—if I could only find some housewife thread that I put up the other day. I hope the rattle of the machine doesnt annoy you."

"On the contrary, I like it. It is company for me."

This was the greatest lie Smith had been guilty of since his moral sense had developed itself. And yet it subsequently became true enough.

"Had you a pleasant evening at Richmond on Christmas Day?" he said.

"It was dark when we arrived there. We dined and had tea with my aunt, and then came back."

Smith, conscious of an absence of enthusiasm for her aunt's entertainment on the part of the dressmaker, resolved to generalize.

"Richmond is a very pretty place" he remarked.

"It is pretty—for England."

"Why? Dont you like English scenery?"

"Any of it that I have seen is nothing but lawns, trees, and a canal."

"It must look tame after the barrenness of Scotland."

"Have you ever been in Scotland?"

"No."

"Oh!" said Miss Russell, shortly, resuming her search, which the above conversation had interrupted.

"I confess that my ideas of Scotland are mixed up with Rob Roy and the fiery cross, and such things" said Smith. "Londoners have generally very ridiculous notions of other countries."

"Nearly as ridiculous as they have of their own" said Miss Russell. "Will you be wanting a needle?"

"If you please, Miss Russell. Thank you very much."

The clatter of the sewing machine recommenced as he reached his own room. As he sat listening to it, he recollected that she had looked surprised when she opened the door. She evidently thought that his visit was in bad taste. Again, how insipidly he had conversed! He had not made a single remark that might have led to an understanding between them. He had asked her about a family gathering with which he had no concern. He had called her native land "barren." Now that he came to think of it, this was the most comprehensively contemptuous term he could possibly have used. He had disturbed her at her work. He had looked awkward as he stood in the doorway. From these reflections Smith roused himself with a sigh; locked the door carefully; divested himself of his injured garment; and sat down before the fire to repair it.

Shortly afterwards, a violent fire poking, door slamming, saucepan scraping, parsley chopping tumult below proved that Rose was within, and anxious that no one should suspect that she was out of the house. Miss Russell's machine stopped; and her bell sounded. Practice had refined Rose's ear to such an extent, that she could ordinarily distinguish with certainty whether a given summons was the first ring of simple requisition, the second of impatience, the third of remonstrance, or the fourth of indignation, to be followed by an angry shriek over the balusters. But Miss Russell's bell was always rung quietly, and although Rose detected something ominous in its tone, she doubted whether it might not be simply an echo in her own conscience, or rather in that reluctance to be found out which served her for a conscience. She acted at once and with decision. A glance at a small mirror convinced her that her appearance was far too neat for a diligent maid of all work. She snatched up a very dirty apron, which had done two days' duty as a clout; and tied it on. Next, she pulled off her cuffs, rolled her sleeves up to her elbows, and plunged her hands into a mixture of dirty water, grease, and tea leaves, which stood conveniently on the table. Finally, she disturbed her hair, which was sleekly brushed over her forehead, rubbed three of her fingers first on the kettle and then across her face, and ran upstairs.

"Well miss?" said Rose, holding the handle of the door in a corner of her apron to save it from contamination.

"Rose" said Miss Russell, "you have been out for the last hour, and you were out the whole afternoon before."

Rose flushed and released the door handle. "I declare to you, Miss" she said, "that I havnt been outside the door once the entire day cept for the vegetables for Mr Fenwick's dinner."

"Mr Smith, who wanted something particularly, had to come

to me for it" continued Miss Russell; "and I dont choose to have gentlemen coming to my room when I am busy—or at any other time."

"Theyre very slow in that shop" said Rose; "and I have to keep at them all day to get the things in."

"Mrs Froster told the gentlemen before she left, that I would see that the house was kept in order" said Miss Russell. "If the house is not kept in order, and the bells properly answered, Mrs Froster must come back. Thats all."

Rose's tongue failed her when she tried to reply. Crimson with mute rebellion, she left the room, shutting the door with the abrupt clap of sulkiness instead of the trenchant slam of rage with which she was used to finish her differences with Mrs Froster.

"Youre no joke" she muttered, as she went downstairs. "Youre a oner, you are."

On her way it occurred to her that she might relieve herself by ascertaining whether Mr Smith had really wanted anything, and repeating to him the tale of the vegetable shop. So she returned and tapped at his door. A scramble, accompanied by the words "In one moment," suggested to her that Mr Smith was not prepared to receive company.

"It dont matter, sir. I thought you rang the bell" said Rose reassuringly, and retired to the kitchen.

On Sunday evening, Fraser Fenwick dressed himself with special care. After examining a disreputable black frock coat, and a waistcoat made from the skin of some animal which had, when alive, apparently suffered from mange, he slowly hung them up again, and gave his ordinary garments a thorough brushing. A scrap of chamois leather and some jeweller's rouge brightened his rings, breast pin, and watch chain; and a liberal application of soap and hair oil did the same service to as much as was visible of himself. When he had put on a clean shirt front, collar, and cuffs, he looked for a moment almost respectable. At the end of that moment, he was further invested with an overcoat of which the fur collar seemed to have been infected by the sealskin waistcoat, and a pair of dogskin gloves whose condition bespoke the desperate fortunes of the owner. As for his hat, it had so often been his pillow in the open air during his intervals of intoxication, that although he had on the previous afternoon paid a hatter sixpence for ironing it, the rest of his attire seemed decent by contrast with it.

The first object which attracted Fenwick's attention as he left the house, was the face of Davis the preacher, at sight of whom, he retreated into the hall, and resolved to deny himself in case of a visit. Davis, however, did not leave the main street, but passed the archway walking slowly, and looking askance into the court without turning his head. He, also, had attired himself with unusual pretence, and wore a jacket of bronze-colored velveteen, to avoid spoiling the symmetry of which he carried his Bible in his hand instead of in his pocket. The book seemed out of keeping with his dark eyes and locks, his broad felt hat, and his costume, as if an artist were going to church. Mr Fenwick watched the retreating velveteen coat till it disappeared round the corner, and then hurried away in the opposite direction.

After a brisk walk along the City Road, Mr Fenwick arrived at Bishopsgate Street Without, and knocked at the door of a shop which bore above its shuttered windows the inscription:

ITALIAN P WATKINS WAREHOUSE.

"Is Mr Watkins at home?" said Fenwick to the servant.

"No, sir. Miss Fanny is a-settin by herself in the drorn-room."

Mr Fenwick placed his hat and overcoat on a chair; mounted the stairs with alacrity; and tapped at the drawing-room door. He was at once invited to enter, and on doing so, discovered Miss Watkins sitting near the fire, attired in a plain black dress, reading The Leisure Hour.

"Hallo, Fan! How the deuce are you?" cried Mr Fenwick with animation, attempting to steal a kiss. "Whats wrong with you?" he added, more soberly, as Miss Watkins repulsed him, and sat down, evidently struggling with an inclination to cry.

"I wish you wouldnt speak to me in that way, Fraser."

"What way?" said Fraser, taken aback.

"That nasty, flippant, vulgar way you try to put on."

At the vulgar, Mr Fenwick reddened, and seemed to search himself for a retort. Not finding one, he turned towards the door, with a movement expressive of mortification and resentment. Miss Watkins choked; bit her lip; and looked straight before her at her tears.

"I am going" said Fenwick. "I think it would have been just as easy to tell me flat out that I wasnt wanted."

"You know very well that I never thought of such a thing."

"No, of course not. However, since youre not accustomed to the manners of gentlemen, perhaps it's natural for you to prefer fellows from Whitechapel, or that swell canal boatman from Stratford, whom you were probably expecting when I was fool enough to come in."

"I think thats the meanest thing you could say" said Miss Watkins, jumping up and confronting him. "If Mr Hickson isnt a gentleman, he always talks to me as if I were a lady."

"Indeed? I wonder where he learnt how to talk to ladies."

"I wonder where you learnt how to talk to women."

Mr Fenwick, thus vigorously attacked, changed his ground. "You seem to be in a precious temper" said he. "I thought we made it all up at the meeting on Friday."

"Yes" said Miss Watkins bitterly, again giving way to her tears. "And after I left, you denied to the Peterses that I was your cousin, and then walked home with one of Miss Mancini's shop-girls."

"She asked me to see her home; and what could I do?" said Fenwick, confounded by these accusations.

"You told her you were a Captain."

"I did not. If she said so, she's a liar."

"How can you say such things? You know you said it. You are always pretending to be an officer."

"I only said it in joke. Besides, if people are such snobs as to think an army man better than anybody else, is it my fault?"

Miss Watkins did not condescend to answer. She turned her back to him, and sat down in silence.

"I suppose I had better go" said he, shortly. "I had no idea that you were that sort of girl."

"Youre very unkind. I dont care whether you go or not. If you go, you neednt come here again" said she, but immediately bowed her head on her hands, and sobbed.

Mr Fenwick hesitated, uncertain whether to obey his pride, which clamored for a dignified withdrawal, or his prudence, which suggested that it would be well to try and soften the bad effect of his indiscretions on the previous Friday. Whilst he stood irresolute, the sound of a latch-key was heard below, and was followed by the appearance of Mr and Mrs Watkins, who greeted Mr Fenwick with sarcastic politeness.

"This is a honor, Cap'n Fenwick" said the host. "It is indeed."

"It's so good of you to remember your poor relations on a Sunday" said Mrs Watkins; "though of course you cant be expected to know everybody on weekdays, Fridays especially."

"You dont look a bit proud over it, neither" said Mr Watkins. "Thats what *I* like about you."

"Let him alone, father" said Miss Fanny, touched by the annoyance and humiliation of her lover. "He'll think youre in earnest if you dont stop." Here she whispered to her mother.

"What!" cried Mrs Watkins. "Invite an officer to tea! I darent do it."

"I dont want any tea" said Fenwick.

"It's champagne you generally ave at the Orse Guards, aint it now?" inquired Mr Watkins.

Mr Fenwick uttered an inarticulate imprecation, and walked out of the room, making the windows rattle as he swung the door behind him and descended the stairs. Mrs Watkins laughed as loudly as she could; her husband, dissatisfied with himself for pushing his jest so far, and irritated by Fenwick's violence, stood irresolute, affecting indifference; and Fanny, disregarding her mother's contemptuous request that she should not be a fool, ran downstairs, where she found Fenwick wrenching his overcoat over his shoulders.

"Come, Fraser" said she, "father didnt mean anything. You

know he was only joking." Fenwick did not reply. "Youre not going away like that" she continued, catching his arm.

Mr Fenwick released himself with a jerk, and went out into Bishopsgate Street. Miss Watkins watched his retreating figure for a moment with a long face, made a convulsive effort as though to swallow her chin, and retired to her room to cry.

"A damned pack of cads" repeated Fenwick to himself again and again, as he hurried back to Islington. When he came opposite Dodd's Buildings, he checked himself in the act of crossing the street as he saw the light from the lamp which stood by the archway reflected by the bronze velveteen coat of Davis.

The preacher, whose ordinary pallor was increased by fatigue, was again passing slowly by the archway, into which, as before, he glanced furtively. He then walked quickly away, and after looking behind once or twice in the direction of the lamp, turned down a by-street and disappeared from Fenwick, whose curiosity was excited by a suspicion that the preacher had been wandering about the neighborhood during the past hour. A policeman, who had been standing opposite this by-street, now slowly resumed his beat. He stopped close to Mr Fenwick, and without requesting him to move on, made him so uncomfortable that he was glad to do so of his own accord. He then made a tour of Dodd's Buildings with his lantern, and returned as far as the arch, inside which he posted himself, invisible to passengers until they came abreast of him. This manœuvre was remarked by Fenwick, whose curiosity was reinforced by a sense of apprehension; he having a dread of burglars, like many people who possess nothing worth stealing. Presently he saw the velveteen coat emerge from a side street parallel to that already mentioned, and connected with it by a road which ran past the rear of Dodd's Buildings. Davis had evidently made a circuit, with the object of again passing the archway. He approached it rapidly, but when within a few yards slackened his pace, and at length stopped close to it, unconscious of the stolid gaze of the policeman. Davis then went cautiously into the court, and gazed at the windows of Mrs Froster's house. The policeman watched him in doubt; for his expression, though fatigued and even wild, was sentimental rather than burglarious; and it is unusual for housebreakers to go to work with bibles in their hands, and bronze-colored velveteen coats on their backs. After standing in the court for more than a minute, the preacher, disturbed by the opening of a window, hastily retreated, and, as he did so, was much disconcerted by the sudden flashing in his eyes of a bull's-eye lantern. However, he passed on and walked away rapidly. The policeman, in whom the self-consciousness produced by many years of public prominence in a uniform had engendered a taste for such theatrical effects, closed his lantern, and paced off slowly in the same direction.

At about this time Miss Russell, who had been spending her Sunday at Richmond, left the train at King's Cross, and proceeded home on foot. For she possessed neither carriage, manservant, maidservant, nor even a dog to escort her; and, therefore, in common with some hundred thousand other young working women similarly situated, was accustomed to make her way alone through London at all hours and seasons.

On the present occasion she had traversed the Pentonville Road for some distance, when she perceived a man, who had been approaching her at a great pace, hesitate suddenly, and apparently consider whether he should advance or return. As she attempted to pass him, he started, and addressed her by name. She bowed in acknowledgment.

"You must let me see you safe home. You must indeed, Miss Russell" said he, accompanying her. He gasped, and added, "You came so close upon me, that you startled me. Just as I was thinking about you, too."

"You need not come out of your way on my account" replied Miss Russell, "I would just as soon go by myself."

"Oh, it's not out of my way" said the preacher. "I called on Mrs Froster this evening; but I found she had gone to the country on a visit. I hope she will be the better for it." Miss Russell nodded, and walked with unabated speed.

"I like the country myself" continued Davis; "but I have little opportunity of seeing it. Not that I have reason to complain. No, thank God, I am well off, being foreman to one of the largest furniture manufacturers in England. Indeed, I earn more than I know what to do with. My sisters are well settled; and I have no one to support except myself."

"You are very fortunate" said the dressmaker, who took no interest in Mr Davis's affairs, but could sympathize always with worldly prosperity.

"And after all what use is it to me?" said Davis. "I am a lonely man."

Miss Russell glanced at his face, and began to walk faster.

"I suppose you find occupation in your preaching" she remarked.

"Only for that, I dont know what I should do" said he. "I am thought a good deal of as a preacher. I have made myself respected more than many clergymen in surplices. I have brought more strong men to the Lord, perhaps, than the great archbishop of Canterbury himself in his pride. But I feel, I know, that man was not intended to be a solitary. In the hithe of my popularity, I feel that I am alone. There are men that think to laugh at me because I'm not ashamed of the gospel. But I can tell you, Miss Russell, Ive been in the homes of them and such as them; and I know how they treat their wives, and deny their children what they spend in the public-house and on the race-course. I think I could make a woman I loved—"

"Goodnight, and thank you, Mr Davis" said Miss Russell, unceremoniously interrupting him as they reached the archway.

"Goodnight" echoed Davis, made irresolute by this sudden check. Then, as she turned away, he made a hasty step forward, and said, with great earnestness,

"Miss Russell. Stop one moment. Only a moment. I want to speak to you on a very serious subject."

"You know, Mr Davis" said the dressmaker, confronting him with her singular grace and self-possession, "that our opinions on serious subjects are not the same. Goodnight."

The preacher, abashed and bereft of breath, stood helpless as she moved away into the court, as though he had presumed, and

46

been rebuked. Then, feeling weak, he leaned against the lamp-post, struggled with a fit of coughing, and for the first time in his life was seized with terror at the prospect of that which the coughing foreboded.

Next morning, Mr Fenwick received the following letter.

*Sunday night*

My dear Fraser—I was greatly grieved when you went away tonight so angry and I hope you are not offended with us. You did not lose much by going, for Mr Davis, who was to have spent the evening with us, sent word that he was ill and could not leave his house. All the people at the meeting were greatly disappointed, for Mr Davis never misses a day and we are afraid something serious is the matter. We are to have some people to tea on Saturday next and mother will be glad if you will come. I have no more to say at present except that I hope you will not be so unreasonable as to take what passed yesterday in earnest. I remain, dear Fraser, your affectionate cousin          FANNY

# CHAPTER V

On the following evening, shortly before six o'clock, Mr Weaver had occasion to refer to his account in one of the ledgers which it was Smith's duty to post up, to check, to tot, and to balance. Having found what he sought, he closed the ledger with evident pleasure in the exertion required to do so, struck it with his fist, and said,

"A handy volume that, eh, Smith? A pocket edition."

This was one of Mr Weaver's jokes, which he repeated whenever he came to the bookkeeper's desk in good humor.

"Wretched sycophant that I am" thought Smith, "I must laugh." And he did.

"I once knew a man worth a million of money" said Mr Weaver reflectively, "who began life with twenty-five pound ten. He was standing in the Corn Exchange one day, when he heard two fellows chaffering over a load of madder. One offered the other twenty-four guineas, but twenty-five pound ten was asked. This man that I speak of didnt know what madder was no more than the man in the moon. Never heard of it. But he calculated that if it was worth twenty-five four it couldnt be very dear at six shillings more. He went up to the fellow and bought the madder, which turned out to be a sort of vegetable for making red paint, like cochineal, and he sold it next day for thirty. He often bought and sold things that he never saw or knew the meaning of; but the madder started him. As I said, he made a million, and never kept a book in his life. He kept his bills in one pocket and his receipts in the other. That sort of thing wouldnt suit you. Eh, Smith?"

"After all" said Smith, struck by the simplicity of the arrangement, "he would not have had a penny more at the end of the year if he had kept the strictest accounts."

"No, but his bookkeeper would" said Weaver. And he left the office with a gay sense of having been too many for his young clerk, at whom his fellows laughed loudly until the door closed behind Mr Weaver, when they became grave.

48

"Well" said one of his seniors to Smith, "you have a nerve to talk up that way to old Weaver."

"Oh bother!" said Smith, putting his ledgers into the safe. "One would suppose the man was a golden calf. I wish he had half as much sense as his madder man."

"I wonder" said Smith to himself, as he walked home, "is there any profession in the world so contemptible as that of a clerk! It offers no work to the cleverest man that the stupidest could not do as well, or perhaps better. So long as there are hosts of creatures who can do nothing but read and write, there will be hosts of competent clerks. Here am I spending my life in making entries of which a thousand will never be referred to again, for every one that will; and if that one were not forthcoming, the world wouldnt stop turning. Here is Weaver, with the example of the madder man to shew him what a fool he is, deliberately spending nearly a thousand a year on a staff of clerks. He could replace us by picking fellows at random out of the street if we annoyed him by shewing the faintest self-respect; and naturally we are a mean and servile pack of dogs. I believe he could get better men if he tried the streets. But being a hammerheaded conventional old nail, that can do nothing except in the usual way, he demands testimonials and experience. The idea of a man with three weeks' knowledge of the world caring about a testimonial! Why, the very first cashier he ever had, held a thirteen years' character for honesty, and had had about three millions pass through his hands during that time. He absconded with twelve pounds two and sixpence, his quarter's rent. Old Simms, the new head bookkeeper, kept books in an insurance office for thirty-six years; and Figgis jumped at him as a treasure of a head bookkeeper. He generally has to ask me what side he should make his entry on, and tells me the way Mr Beauchamp, the secretary of the insurance company, used to have his books kept. There is not a clerk in the office who could be trusted to write a letter; and if there was, old Figgis would snub him and alter his letters, on principle. Being clerks, we're all gentlemen. A railway pointsman, who must have some capacity for acting on his own responsibility, is not a gentleman. Neither is a cabman, who must be a skilled pilot. Plumbers and carpenters, who make things, and whose work gives scope to whatever ability they possess, are common fellows. I dont believe artists would be let into society if they could be done without. I would rather be the meanest handicraftsman than a clerk, except that I would be under the thumb of a trades-union. If that abominable office and every book, carpet, clerk, and partner were consumed to ashes tonight, I would contemplate the ruins tomorrow morning with the liveliest satisfaction."

Smith smiled at his own folly, and then relapsed into that painful yearning which men cherish gloomily at eighteen, and systematically stave off as a nuisance by excitement or occupation in maturer years.

When he got home, he perceived, as he passed through the hall, that the door of Mrs Froster's ordinary sitting room stood open. Thence came Miss Russell, and said,

"Good evening, Mr Smith."

"Good evening" said Smith, dashing himself against the movable shelf that hung on the wall.

"Mr Smith" said the dressmaker, "were you in earnest when you offered to help me to learn French?"

"Perfectly" replied Smith.

"When would it be convenient for you to begin?" said she, a little embarrassed.

"Whenever you like. Now, if you wish" said Smith, putting his hat on the shelf.

"I was thinking" said Miss Russell, "that if you could spare the time after tea, you could come down here and learn me the rudiments."

Smith consented, and forgot his clerkship and his discontent as he went upstairs. In his room he danced and made grimaces at the glass, this being his usual method of expressing delight. When he became calm, he improved his appearance as far as he could without making the attempt obvious; rang for his tea; and, pending its arrival, selected Voltaire's Charles XII from his library as an appropriate volume from which to learn Miss Russell the rudiments. When he had finished his evening meal, he thought it best not to go down immediately, lest his reappearance should seem precipitate. He therefore allowed an interval to elapse, during which he became more and more nervous, so that he trembled as he went downstairs, and knocked at the door of the sitting room with an unsteady knuckle.

"Come in" said Miss Russell.

Mrs Froster's sitting room had originally been furnished in the same fashion as the state apartment upstairs. It resembled a cast-off drawing room with the ornaments removed. Miss Russell was sitting at a table on which were her workbasket and the recently purchased method of acquiring the French language in a month without a master. Smith took up this book with confidence; for, though his knowledge of French was only ordinarily accurate, some opportunities of speaking it which he had enjoyed in his boyhood had given him a facility in dealing with it unattainable by literary study. The dressmaker looked at him with awe as he turned the leaves.

"Have you looked over this at all?" said Smith, unconsciously assuming a magisterial air.

"I have learned the first two lessons" replied Miss Russell, resolutely preventing herself from blushing; "but I dont think I have them properly off, they seem so easy."

Smith immediately propounded "The tailor's hat, and that of the neighbor." Her response made him start. She translated it correctly; but, with the exception of the word "chapeau," with which she was professionally familiar, she rendered the words as if they were written phonetically in English. Smith repeated the sentence himself, as a guide to her.

"That sounds very affected" said she, doubtfully.

"Well, of course it is an affectation to speak with a foreign accent; and I suppose it's the consciousness of this that makes most people so awkward about it" said Smith. "Try again."

Miss Russell tried again, and this time delivered the sentence in broad Scotch. And although, having a quick ear, she soon improved, he remarked that when she spoke English, which she had accustomed herself to pronounce carefully, there was little to distinguish her from a native, but when she spoke French she became unmistakeably a Scotchwoman. Her memory seemed at first so contradictory that Smith was confounded by its caprices. He understood her the less as he had educated himself almost entirely from reading, whereas she was so little accustomed to books that the process of deciphering was still one of which she was conscious. When he at length saw this difference clearly, he found that the apparent inconsistency of her acquisitive faculty was due to it, insomuch that she remembered perfectly all that he told her, and forgot all that she read. He found her quick to seize isolated explanations, and impenetrably stupid when he endeavored to make her see analogies in the construction of the language, which he had a pedantic taste for drawing.

The first lesson was necessarily a brief one. When she had recited her two exercises, she said,

"Will I ever speak French as well as a Frenchwoman?"

"Not unless you live long enough in France to forget your own language" said Smith; "and then you will probably speak better French than the natives. At least, if you dont, the French must speak their own language much better than the English do."

"But when I know all those rules and verbs that you speak of, what more have I to do?"

"Only to learn the language. The rules only give you an idea of how to use the language when you know it. I know a good deal more of the language than I do of the rules."

"And what do you call the language then?"

"Well, knowing the French for dog, cat, yes, and no, is knowing the language. That's the real difficulty after all."

Miss Russell began to have doubts of the advisability of troubling herself with foreign tongues; but she said nothing. She thought she would like to denounce French as useless after she had learnt it; but to do so at present would be retreat, and therefore ignominious.

"French" said she, "is of great advantage to a dressmaker."

"Are you fond of dressmaking?" asked Smith, wishing to discover how far she had the feeling of an artist about her work.

"I *am* a dressmaker" she replied. "I thought you knew that."

"So I did" said he; "but—" Feeling that explanation was hopeless, he added, "For the matter of that, I am a merchant's clerk; and I dont like it."

"Then why dont you do something else?"

"I dont know. I suppose because I am fit for nothing better."

"Couldnt you teach in a school?"

"It is the rarest gift in the world nearly, to be able to do that" said he. This was so astonishing to the dressmaker, that she began to doubt the soundness of her preceptor's mind.

"It is waste of time to quarrel with your bread and butter" said she, gravely. "The happiest thing in life is that we can never be so comfortable as to have no hope of bettering ourselves."

"That is a very philosophical reflection for a young lady to make" said Smith.

"It is what my father always said when anyone was discontented."

The conversation now threatened to halt; and Smith felt that it would be advisable to retire.

"How will we arrange for our lessons in future, Miss Russell?" said he. "I am at liberty after seven every evening."

"Mrs Froster is generally out on Mondays and Thursdays" said she; "so we could have this room in the evenings."

"I wonder whether she will mind us" said Smith, who was doubtful as to the propriety of these interviews from a conventional point of view.

"I have spoken to her about it" said Miss Russell; "and she is rather glad that I am going to educate myself, particularly as you are a friend of Mr Davis, whom she thinks one of the best men in the world."

"So he may be" said Smith; "but I met him accidentally on Christmas Eve for the first time in my life, and have never seen him since."

"Mrs Froster is satisfied with the arrangement, at all events. Perhaps you had rather not have it so?"

"By no means" said Smith hastily. "It will be a great pleasure to me."

"Then, if you will be so kind, we will have another lesson on Thursday."

"On Thursday?" assented Smith, and returned to his own room.

"Well, certainly" said he, as he stirred the fire, "that is the most insensible woman I ever saw. I believe she has no soul. If she were only conscious of her unaccountable grace, she would be poetry personified."

From that time forth Smith's intercourse with the dressmaker became intimate and regular; and it soon began to take effect on him in many ways. It made his isolation more complete by depriving him of his reasons for desiring society. She was the only person in London whom he knew; for he played before his office associates a part which he did not believe to be a true representation of himself; and he was satisfied with his one friend, even to the point of guarding himself from contracting any new interests. The necessity of reconsidering his knowledge from the point of view of a teacher put life into the fragments of learning which had been mechanically thrust upon him at school; and the explanations which he felt bound to offer his pupil (who seldom demanded them) led him to arrange the odds and ends of knowledge which he had picked up in the course of much desultory reading, and to supply the missing links by fresh research. Furthermore, he began to acquire an insight into human nature, subtle, if not impartial; for he constantly had it before him in its extreme aspects: in Woman, whom he regarded as the visible step between savage and intellectual humanity, and Man as he appears disembodied in the produce of his loftiest powers. Smith taught the dressmaker, and read Ruskin, Mill, and the poets. Soon he became intolerant of everything that fell short of his highest ideal of beauty and power. He contracted prejudices against all works that had not survived from some former time; threw aside Byron, of whose poetry he had been fond, and substituted Shelley; refused to appreciate what was merely entertaining and prettily conceived; and only read the newspaper when he found himself in a restaurant with no alternative between doing so and doing nothing. He planned an austere religion for the worship of Truth; and made an attempt to become a vegetarian, which was frustrated in three days by the inability of Rose to vary a regimen of boiled cabbage. He was credulous when a reformer pointed out abuses, and sceptical when a conservative defended institutions. He adopted strong views as to the natural inferiority of the female sex, and maintained that women were destitute of scientific curiosity, capable of learning that A was equal to B and that C was also equal to B, but incapable of inferring therefrom that A was equal to C, incorrigibly personal in their application of the broadest principles, certain to give wrong reasons for right conclusions, and eager to learn conventions, in order to save themselves the trouble of ascertaining principles. In short, he entered upon that unpractical phase of development in which acute perception, hatred of falsehood, love of liberty, pregnant truths, and scrupulous purity, are complicated with mental color blindness, unconscious sophistry, intolerance, platitudes, and subtle epicureanism. Being through the defective induction of inexperience unable to discriminate accurately the natural from the accidental, he acquired that fine instinct for the prettiest half of the truth which makes young men thorough in partisanship only.

Meanwhile Miss Russell seemed to remain stationary. The evening lessons soon expanded beyond their intended scope; and the dressmaker became acquainted with many facts of which she had previously been ignorant. But she did not assimilate them; and her new accomplishments, instead of changing her position in relation to the world, seemed to attach themselves externally to her, as barnacles do to a ship. Of French, she soon had sufficient to make such remarks as ordinary conversations require, and beyond this she never progressed. For translation she had no facility; and she took so little interest in Charles XII, that Smith substituted Racine, whom she liked less. He then tried Molière; and this succeeded. The dressmaker, it is true, cared nothing about the writer or the skill displayed by him in delineating character. But she entered heart and soul into the amours of the Valères and Leandres, and never felt reassured as to their ultimate success until the last scene, so much had the catastrophe of Le Misanthrope (which, by chance, was the first play she read) shaken her confidence in the course of true love on the stage. Speculative works she would have nothing to do with; and the only literature she cared for besides romantic fiction, was that department of descriptive travel which approaches it most clearly. Smith had at first some difficulty in choosing books for her to read. Modern novels discouraged her: she mastered hardly half a chapter in a week. In one of his enthusiastic moments he proffered her the works of Shelley, which to his great astonishment she returned as "a good book, only fit for children." In revenge, he gave her Robinson Crusoe; and she, quite unconscious of the sarcasm, not only read it diligently, but contended for the truth of the narrative afterwards in an animated discussion with him. Struck by this, he followed it up with The Pilgrim's Progress, which she accepted with a bad grace as having "good" characteristics, but finished nevertheless. The Vicar of Wakefield finally convinced her that reading was a pleasure, she having before considered it an irksome educational process; and she even displayed a relish for information which Smith would have rather expected to have wearied her. Thus, though she knew nothing of pictures, she read an old volume of Vasari, which Smith had brought into the room to supply the place of a castor which had come off the table. She remembered all the stories she read, but never the name of the author, and did not make the slightest distinction between John Bunyan and Walter Scott; although she quite appreciated the gap between Christian fighting Apollyon, and Ivanhoe charging the Templar. Smith was constantly puzzled by the contrast between her shrewdness and her simplicity. She looked on him as a very great scholar; but her admiration of his learning was tempered by doubts whether he did not know more than was good for him. She appreciated his intellectuality and freedom from vulgarity. Still, she could not believe in the real worth of attainments which left their possessor with an income and position no better than that of many ignorant persons. She saw that he did not push his own interests, and that he was weak and backward in practical matters. Although she listened in silence to his occasional denunciations of laws and habits which she had always looked on as part of the nature of Man, she felt sure that he was wrong and the world right in most of their differences. She respected what he had made of himself without having the least faith in his future success; and, being an ambitious utilitarian of strong purpose, and little sentiment, she held him in a regard which partook, more than she knew, of that pity which is akin to contempt.

The element of romance that entered into their relations, though always present to Smith, was indefinite. The only person who contemplated practical results from it was Mrs Froster. She felt as though Harriet were a member of her own family, and therefore considered that dressmaking was an avocation below her social position. Smith, on the other hand, was a clerk, well behaved and respectable. Knowing that he had inherited a very small income, she was accustomed to describe him as a young gentleman of private means who was learning business. Mrs Froster had been trained to believe that marriages in which the wife was the elder, were irreligious; but having only saved herself from celibacy at the age of thirty-two by wedding a man of twenty-five, she had modified that opinion so far that she now held that it was a woman's first duty to get married; and as she knew that this was not always easy of fulfilment, she urged Harriet to take the first reasonable chance without raising objections which were only expedient for ladies whose opportunities were secured by their fortunes. Accordingly, she did not obstruct the lessons in any way, having so high an opinion of Smith that she believed him free from the prevailing wickedness of an aversion to matrimony, and felt confident that he would not permit his wife to work except in Berlin wool and at household matters. Smith himself never suspected that an elderly woman would look on him as fit for marriage. He soon lost the sensation of delight which his first meetings with Harriet had produced; yet he never seemed to get nearer to her as their lessons progressed; for from the outset she treated him with such frankness, and made it so much a matter of course that there should be no ceremonious reserve between them, that she left no barriers to be broken down. And yet she was so independent of him that he felt that there was a distance between them which he could not diminish. He often longed to elicit from her some token of mutual understanding more sentimental than a fellowship for the purpose of promoting culture; and this desire sometimes tempted him to say something tender—he did not exactly know what—to her. But when he sat beside her, he felt the impossibility of so befooling himself; and next day, when he had recovered his tone, he felt terrified at the indiscretion he had been about to commit.

# CHAPTER VI

ONE evening the Watkins family sat in their house in Bishopsgate Street, drinking tea. Mrs Watkins was a tall woman with black eyes, thick black eyebrows, thick lips, hard seamy complexion, and a carriage which, in spite of her forty-eight years, was spirited. She wore stays without inconvenience, and produced a general impression that she valued the smallness of her waist, and was not a woman to be trifled with. Her husband was a small, neatly made man, with thin brown hair, small straightly cut features, and an appearance of physical weakness and mental craft which came from his moist dun skin, and mistrustful eyes, which continually moved as if avoiding some object.

"I met Mr Davis coming out of Broad Street station" said Fanny, who had just come in from walking; "and he says he's going to call on you tonight, mother, about your not letting me go to his meetings."

Mrs Watkins looked sternly at her daughter.

"Mind, mother" continued Fanny, "I didnt tell him about it; but Mrs Robson did, and he taxed me directly with it. I hadnt a word to say to him, I felt so foolish."

"Well, I suppose he had better come" said Mrs Watkins, grimly. "I wish Mrs Robson would mind her own business."

"Ah" said Mr Watkins, glancing furtively at the wall, "them preachers is all very well for a while; but they dont wear."

"No need for you to go out of your way to put notions of that sort into the child because this Davis has had his head turned" said Mrs Watkins.

Mr Watkins, unmoved by this retort, stole a look at his wife, and said, "D'ye mean to see him, Flossy?" Mrs Watkins's christian name was Florence.

"I will. And I'll tell him what I think of him too."

"Hark!" said Fanny, as a knock at the door was heard.

"That aint him" said Mr Watkins. "I know his hand. Thats young Larkins the treasurer. You may talk to him about it

59

Flossy: he's come about it. Davis thinks it best to sound us afore coming himself."

Larkins, who presently appeared, was nicely dressed, spoke in a soprano voice, and was cheerful in his manner. He was an active member of the congregation at which Mr Davis preached, and was popular as a speaker. His powers lay chiefly in a mild vein of humor, and it was his habit to rally the sinner rather than to threaten him.

"I come" said he, "fearing that something was the matter in the household. Wherever have you been for the last fortnight, Mrs. Watkins?"

"I dont like going where I cant bring my daughter" said Mrs Watkins.

"But surely" said the treasurer, "your daughter has often been with us, and often will again, please God."

"Ah" said Mrs Watkins, "I dont know whats come to Mr Davis. I wouldnt have believed it. I tell you plump, Mr Larkins, that I wont go to meeting or let Fanny go while he goes on as he does."

"Mr Davis! Oh! Oh! Oh!" cried Larkins. Having thrown all the amazement and remonstrance he was capable of expressing into these ejaculations, he gazed at Mrs Watkins with sorrow. Curiosity then set in; struggled with sorrow; and displaced it. "You dont mean" he said, "that Mr Davis—Mr Davis! has done anything wrong."

"I dont impute anything to him" said Mrs Watkins. "But I never saw a man so changed for the worse."

"But how, Mrs Watkins? In what way?"

"I have noticed it ever since last Christmas; and more than me has noticed it too."

"It aint struck you at all, eh?" said Mr Watkins drily.

"Not at all" said Larkins emphatically. "Hoy ave always considered him as one of the most special called, as one may say, of our brethren. He has a great gift to move the heart."

"Humph" muttered Mrs Watkins.

"You just tell him what you want to, Flossy; and have done with it" said her husband.

"Do you remember about last Christmas, the discourse he made at Finsbury?" said Mrs Watkins.

"I do well" said Mr Larkins with enthusiasm. "He spoke on the text 'The heart knoweth its own bitterness.' There was not a dry eye in the room."

"You spoke yourself afterwards, and said you thought that was the way the apostles used to speak" said Fanny.

"Ah" remarked Mr Watkins, "he was all for fever, and death, and going out on the mission to the Kaffirs."

"It's a pity he didnt go out" said Mrs Watkins.

"Oh, mamma!"

"You hold your tongue" said Mrs Watkins; "it's for your good I speak about it. Well, Mr Larkins, ever since that time, Mr Davis has not been the same man; and I think he has strayed far from the path, though it's not for me to judge him. It's not religion that is on his lips now, nor in his heart either, I'm afraid. Do you ever see him talking and reproving and exhorting now among the young men? Or among their mothers? No: it's the innocent young girls, and the women that are fonder of their chains and brooches than of their souls, that he's so confidential with now."

Mr Larkins, evidently outraged in his most cherished impressions, gazed dumb at Mrs Watkins.

"And what do you think he has to say to them?" continued Mrs Watkins. "Is it faith and prayer? No, but sympathy of souls, his loneliness, the want of somebody to love him, and such wicked nonsense."

"Oh no" said Larkins. "You must be mistaken."

"I am not mistaken" said Mrs Watkins. "I havnt opened my lips without being sure. The whole meeting sees how that little Mrs Meares twists him round her finger, and makes believe to feel for him, as if she cared a scrap for any man, with her husband always away travelling—"

"Flossy" interrupted Mr Watkins, "do you go on with what you have to say; and dont mention other people's names."

Mrs Watkins repressed an impulse of sulkiness, and resumed. "Theres no need to mention names. It's only too well known to everybody. A fortnight ago he began to talk to Fanny about a young man that paid her attention; and he very soon came round to the same thing, his sympathy, and desolation, and all the rest of it. He says he longs to die, too, as if the Lord's time wasnt good enough for him. Fanny, like a fool, came home nearly crying about him, and told me what he had been saying. I know what that sort of thing means of old."

"She dont mean, mind you" said Mr Watkins, "that he wants to do anything wrong."

"No. Far from it" said Mrs Watkins. "But he's got to think about nothing but himself; and he isnt healthy company for any girl, much less fit to be a minister of the gospel. And once for all, he may go to the Kaffirs, or he may stay at home; but Tom and me will find some other meeting house to go to while he's let go on as he does at Finsbury."

Overwhelmed by the charge thus suddenly brought against one whom he had ardently imitated as a model above reproach; and, as treasurer, alarmed at the defection of Mr Watkins, who subscribed five pounds a year to the Finsbury chapel sustentation fund, Larkins lacked presence of mind to form a sentence of comment or protest. Mrs Watkins closed her lips, and busied herself with the tea tray. Fanny sat with her eyes cast down towards a handkerchief which she was hemming. Her father sat silent and furtively vigilant. The silence was broken by a loud knock at the street door. Mr Larkins reddened; but no one moved except Fanny, who dropped her work, and looked at her mother in consternation. Then the servant announced "Mr Dayvidge"; and the preacher entered. He was altered in appearance. His earnest expression and springy gait were modified. He had gained some flabby flesh; he carried himself less uprightly; his manners were more insinuating; and his step softer. None of these changes were very marked; but they perceptibly affected the impression conveyed by his personality.

Mrs Watkins looked at him with rigid features as he gave her daughter's hand a prolonged shake. She determined to refuse her hand and inform him by a distant bow how he had fallen in her estimation. Mr Davis advanced, with his brilliant black eyes fixed on her. For the moment her powers of resistance were dissipated. Indignant but helpless, she submitted to a similar shake, concluded by a confidential squeeze which increased her anger. The remaining ceremonies accomplished, Mr Davis accepted Fanny's timid invitation to sit down, and, happening to look at Larkins, perceived that the treasurer avoided his eye in confusion. After a moment, during which no one broke silence, he began to suspect some misunderstanding. He coughed.

"Fine arternoon, Mr Davis" said Mr Watkins.

"Glorious, glorious!" said Larkins, in his soprano voice. Then, feeling that by this exaggerated display of gaiety he had betrayed his uneasiness, he hung his head guiltily.

"I didnt notice you at our two last meetings, Mrs Watkins" said Davis.

"I wasnt there" replied Mrs Watkins curtly.

"The business of the world will interfere with the best of us" said Davis. "But for the sake of example, it is well to be regular. Youll excuse my saying so."

"Mrs Watkins is going to leave us" said Larkins, letting his voice break from its ordinary pitch into the partial tones thereof in his perturbation.

"To leave us!" echoed Davis. "And why?"

"I have explained myself to Mr Larkins" said Mrs Watkins.

Davis rose, shocked, and said austerely, "I wouldnt have believed this, Mrs Watkins. I didnt believe it when Mrs Robson told me of it. Well I know, after two years of fighting again it, how hard our meetings is beset with scoffers, that try to make us a laughing stock. I said to myself, their laughter is the crackling of thorns under a pot. I dont mind such as them: I can leave them to their own consciences. But when my friends, and those I know for godly people, lend an ear; when, after all my labor to place myself above suspicion, my words are took up, and myself made out to be a wild libertine of the town, it cuts me. It's hard. It's very hard." Here Davis sat down, and bowed his face upon his palms.

Mrs Watkins, quailing, took refuge in offence, and said, "Thats the first time I ever was called a scoffer."

Davis lifted his head, and mastered his emotion. Then, with a forced smile upon his lips, and a tear in each eye, he rose and took his hat.

"I ask pardon for being so weak" he said; "but my ealth is not what it might be. I oughtnt to give way. Mrs Watkins: I wont ask you to shake hands with me now. I know from within that youll understand me better some day. Until then, may you have peace and prosperity, and every blessing that a good woman can have. If ever you feel like to reproach yourself about me, dont do it; for I am a sinner and deserve it in many ways; and for past kindnesses I will not forget you when I remember my friends in my prayers. Miss Watkins: I know youve took my part; and that is a greater comfort to me than riches. But let nothing ever tempt you to go again your mother. Mr Watkins, if I may take the liberty, sir, I'll speak to a friend of mine belonging to the Aldgate Society Chapel, where I never go now, and where youll hear far better speakers nor me. Theyll receive a member such as youve proved yourself to be, with joy. Larkins, youll give me your hand?"

Mr Larkins sobbed, and grasped his colleague's hand fervently. Mr Watkins also advanced and went through the same friendly ceremony with an unusually steady gaze, in which criticism and admiration were blended.

"I thank you, sir" said Davis with emotion. "God bless you all." He hurriedly went out.

Mr Watkins resumed his seat in silence. Mr Larkins pressed his handkerchief to his eyes, and sniffed in distress. Fanny bent her head over her work, vainly trying to restrain the tears which dropped on it in fast succession. Mrs Watkins could not speak. She had never before realized what it is to encounter forgiveness in the place of resentment; and pride was useless as a defence against it. All listened to the preacher's footsteps as he descended the stairs. At the street door a murmur of voices arose as if he were speaking to the servant. Then came the noise of the door closing. Then, a scuffle and a stifled scream from a female voice.

"Who is that larking with Selina?" said Mr Watkins. Larkins turned pale.

"Dont you dare to do it, sir" said the voice of Selina. "I wont take it from you." Immediately after this, the door was flung open sharply by the servant, who announced "Mr Fenwick" with indignant abruptness.

Fenwick, who was abashed by the consciousness that Selina's loud protest must have made his recent gambols known to the occupants of the drawing room, was coldly received. So he hastened to divert his relatives with lively conversation.

"I met old Davis at the hall door" said he, "looking as virtuous as the busy bee." This sally was received in silence.

"Thats a downy bird, that Davis" he continued. "I dont think he'd be so easy in his mind if he knew how many of his games I happen to be up to."

Larkins rose excitedly. "After Mr Davis's noble behavior here tonight" said he, "I wont hear anything said against him behind his back."

"Oh, very well" said Fenwick, disconcerted. "Theres no use in making a row about it. Since he belongs to the chapel he cant do wrong. If he was anybody else, it might just be remarked that when a fellow goes hanging about all night after a girl—"

"Fraser!" said Mrs Watkins fiercely. "Remember where you are."

Fenwick left his innuendo unfinished, and became sulkily silent. Larkins, disgusted by the inopportune visitor, took his leave. Then Mrs Watkins rose; took the tea tray; and left the room without noticing her nephew. Fanny, obeying her glance, followed her.

"Fraser" said Mr Watkins, "youve been at the liquor again."

"I havnt indeed" protested his nephew. "I havnt touched it this two months until today, when I met an old chum who has just dropped into a good thing, and we took a drop together."

"Why cant you hold your tongue before the women?" said Mr Watkins. "Flossy has found out Davis, and sent him to the right-about; but she gets mad when you go chatting about him. He hasnt been up after the girl lately, has he?"

"Not he" said Fenwick. "She soon let him know she didnt want him. She's a regular vixen; and besides, she's taken up with that milk-and-water puppy, Smith. I see Davis passing occasionally; but he hasnt been on the beat for a long time; so I dont think he comes specially. It's a rum thing Aunt Flossy turning against him after all."

"Ah" said Mr Watkins; "and she'd give her eyes out of her head to be in with him again. He gammoned em all here just before you come in, till they were ready to cry for losing him. But Flossy wouldnt have it said that she gave in to a mistake; so off he went. Leery. Thats what he is, Fraser: he's leery. And itll bring him through anything."

A pause ensued, during which Mr Watkins brought his chair closer to his nephew.

"Fraser" he said, in a low voice, "is there anything in about that mare of Gilhooly's?"

"Nothing fresh" said Fenwick. "Look here, uncle: have you anything on her?"

"Me bet!" said Mr Watkins sternly. "Ive given that up; and if youll take my advice, youll give it up too. Look ye, Fraser, I havnt swallowed a glass of spirits, smoked an ounce of tobacco, or put a penny on a horse since I married Flossy. When I was on the turf, as I was for nigh fifteen year, I learnt to be pretty sharp; and if I could only have stopped when I was in luck, I might a made a nice thing of it. When Flossy took me, I put some of my sharpness into the shop, and the rest into my pocket; and Ive got on. You aint sharp: youre silly; but take to the steady tack and itll pay you. Those meeting house chaps dont take me in; but they get on; and it's the right thing for young girls; and it pays; and I back it accordingly. Do you take to the meetings, and learn when to hold your tongue, and youll get on. All the same, it dont prevent me from knowing whats moving in the world, on the quiet. To tell the truth, I cant break myself away from it altogether; and though I never lay a halfpenny, there aint a horse in the kingdom I dont know the odds on. Thats why I ask you about Gilhooly's mare."

"It's well to be able to give a friend the straight tip, if you dont use it yourself" observed Fenwick.

"Do you take me for a fool?" said his uncle, with disdainful emphasis.

"Why?"

"When I am" said Mr Watkins, "I will take to putting money into other men's pockets, but not before."

"But it wouldnt cost you anything."

"Youve become very virtuous and disinterested all of a sudden" said Mr Watkins, with a sneer. "Here: youd better come down to the back parlor, and square matters with your aunt."

# CHAPTER VII

SMITH was not an habitual patron of the theatre. He was still one of those who go to the play as a special festivity, who wait for the farce,[1] and to whom stage illusion is independent of a voluntary surrender of the imagination. He retained the boyish preference for remoteness in scene, action, and costume. He had great patience with grave exposition and sentiment in a drama; and though sensible to fine acting when he saw it, he was readily imposed on by any effective mannerism which did not jar on his taste. The latter condition he seldom found fulfilled by the velvet clad swordsmen in romantic plays and operas (Maritana, The Bohemian Girl, and Il Trovatore were his favorites); and to modern comedies, wherein a more natural style of acting prevails, it never occurred to him to go. Consequently he was ignorant concerning theatrical matters; and when that intolerance already mentioned developed itself out of the solitary intercourse which he held with himself, both directly, and reflectively through the dressmaker, he ceased to concern himself about them at all. From the commencement of his tenancy at Dodd's Buildings until the last week of August, when he achieved the adventure which follows, he had been inside a theatre but once. On that occasion he had induced Miss Russell to go with him to Covent Garden Theatre, to witness a representation of Les Huguenots, of which they had lately translated a tempting description from a French newspaper. He felt that it would be a reproach to him to live within reach of a performance of so fine a work by the greatest artists in the world, placed on the stage with a completeness unknown in any other country (for such, he assured Miss Russell, was guaranteed by the reputation of the great London opera house), without going to see it. Accordingly, one evening in June, they mounted to a

[1] In Smith's boyhood theatrical performances still began and ended with farces; and his father had doubtless often sat out programs containing five items: say a tragedy, a melodrama or Christmas pantomime, and three farces.

stifling gallery, for the privilege of admission to which they paid half a crown apiece, and obtained a misty view of the greatest artists in the world, very much fore-shortened, shouting and gesticulating in the abyss beneath. None of the special beauties enumerated by the French newspaper were made apparent to Smith; but he attributed this to his own ignorance, and to national jealousy the conduct of a German who sat next him, and who spoke of singers, players, and conductor indiscriminately as hogs. Miss Russell was disappointed, and declared not only that she did not consider that what they were listening to was music or proper singing, but that nothing would induce her to go to the Opera again. She added that she thought it a very strange thing for a woman to come out dressed as a man before a crowd of people, apparently not in the least ashamed of herself. She approved of some of the dresses, but was surprised that the Queen of Navarre's riding habit was made of silk velvet when cotton-backed was available and would do well enough for the stage. Smith felt that the operatic experiment was a failure, although he maintained that the performance was a splendid one, and, in proof, read to her next day the criticism in the daily paper, which fully confirmed his view. Miss Russell remarked that he had often shewn her that the papers made ignorant mistakes about books and pictures, and that they were just as likely to be in the wrong about music.

In the autumn, she told him that she intended to take some holidays, as her aunt had invited her to Richmond for a fortnight. The house there would be empty during that time owing to the owner's absence on the continent; and as it contained many art treasures, and was surrounded by a park which extended to the river's edge, she anticipated a pleasanter time than her means would allow her to spend elsewhere. Of this project Smith cordially approved, the more so as he considered that the change would be beneficial to her health; for, although the dressmaker seemed to be proof against even those transient derangements which the variable climate of London produces, her paleness and the deliberate regularity with which she worked, made him long

H           69

to see her free in the open country. Smith himself, being too poor to enjoy idleness, hated holidays, and only accepted an annual week because to have refused it would have rendered him odious to his fellow clerks. However, he always put it off as long as he could; and his turn seldom came until October was far advanced.

It was on a fine autumn evening that he carried his portmanteau, which he had lent to Harriet for the occasion, to King's Cross Underground, thereby saving her the expense of a cab. She walked beside him with more animation than usual. Her matter-of-fact tranquillity, though always graceful, was sometimes oppressive, particularly during those revolts against his circumstances and loneliness which sometimes occurred to Smith. Now setting out in quest of pleasure, and about to change for a while the habits of nearly eight months, she recalled to him by her look and bearing some of that hesitancy and faint flush which had so captivated him on the evening when she had first appealed to him. But for the bumping of the portmanteau against his leg, he would have succumbed to the influence of the sunset and become sentimental. They were close to the station before he spoke.

"I shall feel quite strange when I have passed a week without seeing you."

"I was just thinking" said Harriet, unconsciously relapsing into her native accent, "how I seem to know ye so much longer than six months."

"I can scarcely realize it" said he. "I feel as if I had always known you."

"You had better give me the portmanteau now" said she, as they entered the station. "The man wont let you pass."

"If he doesnt, I'll take a third single to Farringdon Street, and have him that way" said Smith. "I will certainly see you into the train." So saying, he took her proffered purse, and purchased her ticket, knowing of old that any attempt to pay for it himself would be futile. Then the ticket collector letting him pass, and rather resenting his explanation than otherwise, he accompanied her to the platform. In taking leave, she gave him her hand for the first time.

When he reached the street again, he felt that to spend the evening at home after such a parting would be impossible. He therefore started briskly towards the west end, and soon hailed an omnibus, which carried him to Hyde Park Corner. Here he alighted, and finding himself in a congenial frame of mind, passed the remaining hour of daylight pleasantly wandering by the Serpentine. Shortly before nine o'clock, having been expelled from Kensington Gardens by a policeman, he set his face to the east, and at half-past nine arrived in the half foreign, half theatrical region which surrounds Leicester Square. Infected by the prevailing atmosphere, he was seized with a desire to see some entertainment in harmony with the aspect of the place. He heard a young man who had just been stopped by an acquaintance, say "I am off to the Alhambra." [1] Smith had heard the Alhambra spoken of as a wicked place, but had never visited it. Determining now to see it for himself, he made his way thither quickly, and paid a shilling for the privilege of admission. On entering, he found himself in a huge circular theatre, lighted by small lamps arranged in continuous lines around the auditorium. The centre of the floor was occupied by seats of various denominations, according to their degree of proximity to the stage, and surrounding these and separated from them by a barricade was a narrow strip forming the extreme circumference, which was unprovided with seats, and to which Smith discovered that he was limited by the modest sum he had disbursed for his ticket. As the curtain was down when he entered, and the crowd who shared this promenade with him either moving to and fro or drinking in the various holes containing bars which were placed around, he walked about, observing the throng, feeling uncomfortable, and

[1] The old Alhambra, on the site of the later Alhambra. It is proper to state here that the establishment of the London County Council, about ten years after Smith's visit, led to a municipal control which made the moral atmosphere of the new Alhambra quite different from that of the old, as truthfully described in the text. The controlled variety theatres of London are immeasurably more refined and artistic, even in their immoralities, than the old music halls and *opéra bouffe* theatres. The old Alhambra caught fire one night. I saw it burn gloriously.

hoping that he might not be discovered by any of his acquaintances in such a place. There were many old men present and many young ones, who looked on their seniors with that intolerance of dissipation which depraved youth exhibits when it perceives its own weaknesses reflected in old age. There were a few soldiers, a number of women, and some officials in uniform, whose chief duty seemed to be the protection of the edifice from conflagration by smokers. The atmosphere was hot, and flavored with gas, cigar smoke, and effervescing liquors. Just as Smith had concluded that a wicked theatre without a performance was quite as dull as a virtuous one would be under the same circumstances, the band assembled. He enjoyed their playing, which, though coarse and slovenly, was spirited, and reminded him of the orchestra at Covent Garden, although it was more enjoyable to him. He was obliged to confess that he liked Offenbach. Meyerbeer, on the authority of the French newspaper, he respected. But he could not deceive himself into supposing that he liked him: he could but feel ashamed of himself for not liking him. When the curtain rose, the last act of Le Voyage dans la Lune was performed by many robust young ladies with large voices, which they were endeavoring by all the means in their power to destroy. As the voices Smith had heard at Covent Garden had, for the most part, been destroyed already for the benefit of continental audiences, he could not help preferring the Alhambra artists; and he felt that this preference was an additional proof of his ignorance. He was moderately pleased by the gorgeous dresses and scenery; yawned at the long processions; and laughed at the horseplay; for he loved the humor of harlequinade.

When the curtain descended, it was late; but the audience was increasing; and Smith, on addressing an inquiry to one of the men in uniform, learned that the next entertainment would consist of a ballet entitled The Golden Harvest. The Alhambra was famous for its ballets; and Smith resolved to wait. At length a reedy prelude announced the pastoral atmosphere of the forthcoming spectacle. The curtain rose, and discovered a village, decorated as for a festival. Three young ladies with servants' caps and aprons, but otherwise prepared, as to costume, for the rite of confirmation, appeared and conversed by stamping, motioning with both hands towards the earth, combing their faces with their fingers, and slapping their persons in various places. They then danced. Interrupted by a sound of bells, they bent one knee at a right angle; rested an elbow on it and a cheek on the elbow, stretched the other leg as far as possible behind; and in this attitude, listened anxiously to the now deafening clamor. Satisfied that their ears had not deceived them, they ran away. A company of reapers with sickles entered, each reaper conducting a binder bearing a sheaf. They danced, the reapers sawing the air as though they were cutting the sheaves presented by the binders. Then a canopy appeared, beneath which were borne a bride and bridegroom. The bridegroom was attired in purple knee breeches, a white shirt, and a crimson sash in which was a tiny gold sickle. The bride was covered with a veil adorned with orange blossoms. As the orchestra paused on the chord of the dominant, she threw off the veil, and revealed a light nuptial costume consisting of a waistband and shoulder straps of white satin, to which was appended a skirt of about fifteen inches in length. In addition to the ordinary methods of locomotion, she had acquired the power of walking on the points of her great toes, and of poising herself on either one, and spinning herself about without becoming giddy. These feats admitted of but few combinations; and Smith thought the dancing resulting from them deficient in variety, destitute of charm, and no better than a painful and unmeaning species of gymnastics. Some unintelligible dialogue in gesture ensued; and after a tarentella concluding with more ringing of bells and the withdrawal of the procession, the scene shifted and disclosed a cornfield glowing in an autumn sunset. Here reappeared the reapers and binders, who celebrated the occasion by dancing around a maypole resembling a barber's sign decked with ribbons, which they carried in with them. In these rejoicings the bridegroom took an energetic part, and, long before they were ended, succumbed to weariness, and lay down at the base of a stack of sheaves, where he fell asleep. The bride presently missed him, and, having searched for him on her toes in every place but that in which he was, expressed distraction and ran off. The rest, after kneeling in obedience to the sound of the vesper bell, followed her; and night fell on the scene with tropical suddenness. The music became hushed and full of mystery. A powerful moon cast a halo on the sleeping figure of the bridegroom, and on the stack which sheltered him. Then the sheaves fell asunder, and a transcendent being, the spirit of the harvest field, appeared, enveloped in the hues of autumn, blood-red poppy lightening into gorgeous orange. Cornflowers and golden ears of wheat were twisted fantastically in her black hair. Her dark bright eyes flashed in the limelight. Smith forgot his surroundings. The audience, the lights, the cigar ends, the unpleasant bursts of laughter from the drinking bars, ceased to color his impression of the scene. The stage became an actual cornfield to him, and the dancer a veritable fairy. Her impetuosity was supernatural fire; her limbs were instinct with music to the very wrists; that walking on the points of the toes, which had given him a pain in the ankle to look at before, now seemed a natural outcome of elfin fancy and ethereality. He became infatuated as he watched her dancing in wanton overflow of spirits about the field, with the halo of the moon following her wherever she bounded. When she reminded him of her real circumstances by making a courtesy, he was irritated at the tameness of the applause which followed, cursing the indifference of the herd to refined art, and hammering with his walking-stick on the wooden barricade against which he stood. At one moment he fancied he had caught her eye, and that she was conscious of his presence. At another, he strove to establish a magnetic influence over her by fixing his gaze sternly on her face and holding his breath. He grudged all applause which was not addressed to her. He almost lost his temper when a woman stood up, and obstructed his view of the stage for a few seconds.

Meanwhile the story of the Golden Harvest unfolded itself as rapidly as the discursiveness of the saltatory illustration permitted. The fairy soon discovered the bridegroom; roused him; fascinated him; danced with him; languished in his arms; tantalizingly eluded him; and fell into graceful poses which he contemplated with as much astonishment as he could affect whilst supporting by her belt the hundred and twenty pounds avoirdupois which had no existence for Smith. Throughout a night of fifteen minutes' duration the bridegroom resisted the spells of the enchantress; but at the critical moment when he, overcome at last, was about to place a ring upon her finger, and thus deliver himself into her power for the ensuing century, the cock crew; the fairy vanished; the sun rose; the oboe on a drone bass discoursed in the spirit of the pastoral morning; and the reapers, returning to their work, found the now sleeping bridegroom, and restored him to his bride, whom he received (being, as Smith thought, a tasteless person) without making any disparaging comparisons. Then the curtain fell; and the audience dispersed slowly. Among them was a courtly old man, whose black silk stockings and studied gait proclaimed him a relic of a past generation. He was discussing the performance with a young officer, who had achieved the perfect gentility of the indescribable, having no individuality beyond the general characteristics of the class to which he belonged.

"Good, very good" said the elder. "Dancing is a lost art nowadays; but she has something of the old school about her. She is indeed the only one now who has. I have seen Cerito, Carlotta Grisi, Fanny Ellsler, and the great Taglioni. Taglioni was my *vis-à-vis* in a quadrille once, when I was sixteen years of age." The old gentleman gave his shoulders a slight shrug, which Smith, who had overheard him with the deepest respect and pleasure, interpreted as the expression of tolerance opposed to that pang of mingled tenderness and despair which recollections call up, when they concern an order of things passed away for ever.

"She is a fine straight woman, all game, and no crumb" replied the officer with energy. Smith cast a look of contempt at him, and passed out into the street. Here was a confusion of swift hansoms, clamorous vendors of obscene literature, violet sellers, and crowds of men and brilliantly attired women aimlessly wandering about with just sufficient motion to satisfy the urgent policemen, with a background of the gas-lighted windows of *cafés*, gin palaces, tobacconists, and eating-houses where lobsters predominated redly over the other edibles. Through this tumult Smith rapidly made his way, and reached Dodd's Buildings, as it seemed to him, almost immediately.

For half an hour after midnight he walked up and down his small room, thinking of the dancer, and inventing extravagant expedients by which he might make her acquaintance. He regretted that he had no skill in the art of picking pockets. How easy it would be, he thought, to wait at the stage door of the theatre in order to get near her, to steal her purse, and then to call on her and earn her gratitude by restoring it! This idea was followed by visions of runaway broughams, the Alhambra in flames, shipwrecks, and every disaster in which he could conceive himself united to her by a common danger. He repeatedly checked himself, and laughed at his indulgence in the very follies which he had often found trite in novels; but after each check of this kind, he relapsed again, and was only reminded of the advancing night by a knocking, which Mr Fenwick, umbrella in hand, clad in his nightshirt, and mounted on a chair, was indignantly making on the ceiling of his apartment, as a reminder to his fellow lodger that he could not sleep with a procession apparently passing overhead.

In the morning, Smith, reading the late Mr Mill's essay on religious liberty as an accompaniment to his breakfast, felt ashamed of himself. His pride in thinking comprehensively as a man, was wounded. He put on his boots, and then, finding he had still some minutes to spare before going to the office, he leaned back in his chair, and made this speech, telling off each section on his fingers.

"What are the facts of the case about this woman? (Forefinger.) In order to preserve her gymnastic skill she must pass hours every day in practice which has not one element of mental improvement in it. Therefore she must be utterly ignorant and narrow-minded. (Middle finger.) She is disguised with masses of rouge and bismuth, and, deprived of them, would probably appear coarse looking. (Third finger.) As she certainly dances well, and as excellence in any art is only attainable by much experience, she must be pretty old. (Little finger.) Her profession is a guarantee of her low origin and indifferent character. Were I to observe her closely, I should be completely disillusioned. Consequently I will go again tonight and take up a position close to the stage—Psha!" he added, jumping up and putting on his hat. "What gross sophistry! I shall never enter the Alhambra again."

# CHAPTER VIII

SMITH was at this time in easy circumstances. His material necessities were few, and as he did not frequent any society, he could always calculate his expenditure. Having a strong aversion to debts of all descriptions, he paid for everything as he got it, and so was free from the demoralizing influence of pecuniary embarrassment. But a new expense was imported into his economy on the night when Miss Russell went to Richmond. Hitherto, as has been seen, his patronage of the theatre had been desultory; and the habit, peculiar to dwellers in large towns, of following the progress of art on the stage, and of exchanging the supposititious enjoyment of thrilling adventures for the curiosity which incites the critic to observe how certain authors will treat certain subjects, or what certain actors will make of certain characters, formed as yet no part of his culture. He had taken the first step to its acquirement when he had seen the ballet of The Golden Harvest three times in one week, which was his case on the Saturday following that on which he made his first visit to the Alhambra. In the meantime he had ransacked the lending library for books bearing on the history of the ballet, and had become learned in the traditions of opera. In imagination he revived every celebrated dancer whose literary investment was sufficiently poetic, in the guise of the Signorina Pertoldi, *prima ballerina*, as his enchantress was entitled in the program. A fair and fat rival of hers insisted on being *prima ballerina assoluta*; and Smith hated her with a jealousy cruel as the grave.

His musical tastes received such a stimulus from the Alhambra orchestra that he not only tried to play the airs of the ballet by ear on the German concertina, but purchased and read the treatise of Hector Berlioz on instrumentation, and began to entertain notions of becoming a composer. The dancer, instead of occupying his imagination to the exclusion of everything else, became a centre of mental activity, and caused one of those ruptures of intellectual routine which, when they do not occur too often, and are not consciously sought after, are valuable as occasions of fresh departures in thought. Smith, without considering this, deplored his own infatuation, and held long discussions with himself on the character of his fascinatress. He argued that unless there were at least some good and generous element in her, she would not have attracted him. Then he reproached himself with self-flattery. To his former severe inferences against her he replied that her daily practice was no more demoralizing than the daily occupations of ordinary persons, not even more so than the mechanical reduction of poetry to ink, paper, and grammar. Its athletic virtues did not occur to him: Smith's sole exercise was walking. As to her rouge, women were ugly and pretty on the stage just as they were off it; therefore there was evidently no magic in pigments to improve nature. Painting, he argued, is a mere device to neutralize the glare of the footlights. She is not necessarily old because she is a finished dancer: she may have begun when an infant. It merely implies hard and constant work, conscientiously directed to an artistic end. What could be more ennobling? As to her low origin, he felt himself ashamed of having ever thought of such a thing; and to assert that her profession precluded the idea of a spotless character, was, as he had read in a theatrical paper, to cast an unmanly slur on a body of artists who numbered amongst them women who, whether as breadwinners, benefactors of the poor, or examples of the brightest virtues of their sex, were second to none in the land.

Before long, however, he was compelled to reflect that an expenditure of fifteen pounds and thirteen shillings per annum on The Golden Harvest might result in a famine for himself. Besides, not only was he ashamed of being under the domination of a sensuous attraction: the dissipated loungers among whom he had to move in the shilling promenade at the Alhambra were repugnant to him. He avoided the officials, lest they should learn to recognize him as a frequenter of the place. He ceased to applaud the object of his admiration, lest he should be observed, and the motive of his visits detected. He was repeatedly disappointed by her performance, which was often gone through mechanically as a professional task, rendered possible by training and habit. The variable temperament of the artist was perceptible in despite of rouge, limelight, and gymnastic skill; and it was only on rare occasions that she displayed the jubilant grace which had dazzled him at first. Even then, the audience seemed brutally insensible to it, and reserved an equal, and sometimes a greater share of their applause, for others in whose feats Smith could see nothing but antics and grimaces. Again, what trivial music, and what a lack of sentiment in the tales illustrated! Smith, deriving his ideas of music from books, idealized it to an impossible sublimity; and on learning, to his great astonishment, that Mozart had composed many ballets, reviled the ignorance and little faith of the managers of the Alhambra for leaving these doubtless immortal works in oblivion. Before a fortnight had elapsed, he was so dissatisfied with himself, and disgusted at the theatre, that he wondered why, when the hour came, he felt a restless craving to return to it.

On the first Monday in September, Miss Russell returned to Islington. She travelled by the earliest train, and Smith was still sleeping when she arrived; but he saw her for a moment on the stairs as he went out; and her appearance in the morning sunlight made him feel as though he had just stepped from that vile-smelling midnight vision of gilt sheaves, painted skies, and electric radiance, into a real harvest field, full of fresh air, noisy birds, and sunshine.

That evening the books were left untouched, and the hour devoted to a description of the treasures of Mr Grosvenor's house at Richmond, and of the manner in which Miss Russell had spent her holidays. Mrs Froster was present, listening with interest to particulars as to the titled guests expected by her friend later in the season. Harriet did not entirely approve of Mr. Grosvenor's tastes. She admitted that his house was pretty and comfortable, as well as grand; but she could not understand why he hung dinner plates about the walls instead of keeping them on the kitchen dresser; or why he hid all his nicest pictures in her aunt's room, or in the corridors. Neither did she admire his taste for making his servants wear outlandish dresses, and decorating his rooms with gaudy peacocks, flamingoes, black swans in gold lakes, and other grotesque images. Mrs Froster joined her in reprobating these extravagances, on the ground that arranging a house was no part of a man's business, and that there were other things which it would become him better to think of. She asserted that all the gold he had plastered over his walls would be sufficient to keep ten poor families from hunger for a whole year; but that the rich little knew what poverty was when they scattered their money about on sinful luxuries.

On a subsequent evening, when Mrs Froster was absent, the dressmaker asked Smith how he had been employed during her holiday. He replied, with carefully acted innocence, that he had done nothing except jog along in his accustomed fashion. He then led the conversation back to the house at Richmond. Harriet described to him the great hall wherein Mr Grosvenor gave his renowned fancy balls; and upon this Smith spoke of dancing, and cast his late reading into a dissertation on music, the poetry of motion, and kindred subjects. As an instance of the fact that the art in question still had its representatives, he described The Golden Harvest, and repeated the remark which he had overheard the old gentleman make as he left the theatre. She asked him how often he had been to see this spectacle, thinking as she did so of what Mrs. Froster had mentioned to her about his staying out at night. He answered carelessly that the affair had taken his fancy so much that he had gone to see it again. The conversation then strayed to other topics; amongst them to the dressmaker's affairs, of which she seldom spoke.

"My aunt Angel—"

"Your what?" said Smith.

"My aunt, with whom I was staying—her name is Angel Summers—is very anxious that I should settle at Richmond."

"What on earth would you do there?"

"I mean to set up in business in the town. My aunt says she could help me in many ways to establish a connection."

"Then you are going to follow her advice, are you?"

She shook her head doubtfully. "I have as long as I like to think about it; and I am getting on very fairly here. I doubt if I would be so independent at Richmond. I would rather have to do with everyday ladies, than with great ladies' maids."

"But you have to work for Madame somebody or another here, several hours a day."

"Well, I know my hours. I know my terms; and I can do my work; so there is no compliment between us. Better have one mistress than many."

"You know best. I dont know enough about the business to advise you. How irksome the arrangement of such things is!"

"It is not so to me" said the dressmaker with decision, "and I dont know why it should be to you either. Have you made any verses since?" For Smith had a facility for rhyming which frequently led him to manufacture sonnets, which he felt ashamed of, and yet had got into the habit of shewing to his companion when they were humorously conceived. Certain serious ones he had kept to himself. Unfortunately, he had just composed an unusually florid apostrophe in heroic couplets, which seemed to him to have more warmth and power than anything he had previously written. It was entitled Lines to a Southern Passion Flower; and in it he had vividly depicted his infatuation for the dancer. Instinct warned him not to shew it to the dressmaker. Vanity rebelled against allowing a creditable offspring of his imagination to fall stillborn. He shewed it to her, feeling that he could not bring himself to read it aloud.

"I wonder at you who are a gentleman and a scholar" she said, when she had read it, "to let yourself be taken so with a woman who dances on the stage."

"What have the verses got to do with a woman who dances on the stage?" said Smith, dismayed.

"Have they, or have they not?" asked Miss Russell quietly.

"Why should they not have, then?" replied Smith. "Dancing is a fine art."

"Nonsense!" said the dressmaker. "It is a pretty thing for a girl to know, but not to get her living by, or to do before a crowd of people without being decently dressed. I'm sure no woman who respected herself would do such a thing."

"At any rate" said Smith boldly, "this woman danced so poetic-
ally that she put—or at least the character she acted put—those
verses into my head."

The dressmaker made no reply; and after a silence of nearly a
minute, Smith resumed the French.

From this time forth, the close intimacy between them, which
had been gathering strength for so many months, began to relax.
Her holiday seemed to be the summit of a hill, the sunny side of
which they had climbed together alone, and which they were now
descending in the evening shadow by diverging paths, with fellow
travellers to divide their interests. The attraction of the dancer
made Smith feel that philosophy grew monotonous if not relieved
by what he called a little flesh and blood, a phrase which means,
according to the nature of the individual using it, a great deal of
gross sensuality, or a snatch of innocent folly. But his intolerance
recognized no degrees in debasement; and he resisted the new influence as strongly as he could. Still, philosophy failed both to
argue and to bully the dancer into an object of indifference; and
Smith began to crave for a female friend who would encourage
him to persevere in the struggle for truth and human perfection,
during those moments when its exhilaration gave place to despair.
Happily, he found none such. The power to stand alone is worth
acquiring at the expense of much sorrowful solitude; and Smith,
who now felt for the first time how hard, cold, and narrow his
pupil was, received no encouragement to indulge in that clamor
for sympathy, the whining expression of which is sometimes regarded, not only as consistent with common stability of temper,
but as a sort of trade mark of genius.

The dressmaker, on her part, was disgusted because Smith,
who had risen to a high place in her esteem, and even in her affec-
tion, admired the painted charms of a creature her right to despise
whom she never dreamed of questioning. In all matters depend-
ing upon taste, education, and the exclusiveness which springs
from both, she had deemed him irreproachable. Nothing is less
easy to recover than the faith of a worshipper who has once detected clay feet in an idol. There is a reflected degradation in the

discovery that gives it a sharp sting. This, added to the inevitable woman's comparison between his regard for her and for her rival, intensified all her previous disparaging thoughts of him. So that his visit to the Alhambra produced, on his part, disappointment, and, on hers, jealousy without love, disguising itself as contempt for male weakness.

# CHAPTER IX

WHEN another Christmas had passed away, there came a fine Saturday afternoon in February, on which a man entered the court surrounded by Dodd's Buildings, and looked at the houses with a critical air, which made Smith, who happened to be looking out of the window, think he must be mad. Presently the man was joined by a carpenter, who looked patiently at him, and by a boy with a straw tool bag, who looked at the carpenter. These were soon followed by six little girls with a skipping rope, a male infant with bandy legs, and a street Arab. By this audience of eleven persons, Fraser Fenwick, returning from a walk, was contemplated with attention, so that he retired within doors in confusion. Then the first comer produced a note-book, and having, with the assistance of the carpenter, measured the court, went away. The children, after hooting this disappointing conclusion of the scene, and causing Smith to leave the window hastily by addressing a similar demonstration to him, withdrew also, and left Dodd's Buildings in its accustomed solitude.

On Monday morning when Smith was at breakfast, a tap came to the door; and Mrs Froster entered. Smith, who congratulated himself every Saturday on being rid of his landlady for another week, looked at her with such presentiments as are usually excited by a letter directed in a strange hand, or a sudden warmth in the manner of a distant acquaintance.

"I wished to speak to you, if you had time, Mr. Smith" said Mrs Froster.

"Certainly" said Smith.

"I dont know what you will think, Mr Smith" said the landlady; "but I have come to give you notice."

"Notice!" echoed Smith. "Do you mean notice to leave?"

"I am very sorry for it" said Mrs Froster, a little frightened by the involuntary sternness in her lodger's tone; for she stood in some awe of him, he was so invariably quiet; "but I have sold my lease; and the house is going to be pulled down."

"And how soon must I turn out?" said Smith.

"I have just had warning that the house must be empty by Saturday week" replied the landlady.

"Well" said Smith, resigning himself, "I suppose I must look out for a lodging. Have you taken another house, Mrs Froster?"

"Not in London, Mr Smith. I think I will settle in the country. I have been in this house nearly twenty years; and I dont feel as if I would care to set up a new one."

"But dont you think you will find the country very dull after being so long in town?"

"I always lived in the country as a girl, Mr Smith, and was brought up there. I may say I have been waiting my time to go back there. The thought of going to live near Angel—thats Mrs Summers, Harriet's aunt—much as I used to long ago, has often kept me up. That is" added Mrs Froster, "it has led me to prayer; and praying gave me strength."

"And Miss Russell? Is she going with you?"

"She thinks of setting up for herself in Richmond" said Mrs Froster, smiling in a manner that was very distasteful to Smith; "and of course, if nothing should happen to change her prospects, it's the best thing she could do."

Smith began to desire the departure of his landlady. "I suppose you will leave this house with some regret: you have been so long in it?" said he.

"It has been a very troublesome house to me" said Mrs Froster; "and I scarcely know whether I'm sorry to leave it, or glad that it's to be pulled down. Before there was any talk of selling, I thought every year that I could bear to live here no longer; but now it seems strange to be turned out of it whether I like it or not. I have more reason to regret the lodgers than the lodgings, as one may say, Mr Smith. You have always been most satisfactory; and I'm sure Harriet is much indebted to you for all you have taught her."

When Smith returned home that evening, he thought his room already looked strange. The day before, his residence at Dodd's Buildings had seemed part of the order of nature. Now it was fading into an incidental experience whose very reality seemed doubtful.

"Well, Rose" said Smith, as his tea was brought in, "have you heard the news?"

"Yes, sir" said Rose, grinning; "theyre agoin to turn the ouse into the street."

"Are you sorry for it?" said he.

"Oh, *I* dont care, sir" replied Rose. "I can better myself easy."

"Thats all right" said Smith. "Is Miss Russell downstairs now?"

"Miss Russell, sir! Oh no. She's gone to Richmond for good today. She wont live here no more until Mrs Froster goes out, and the ouse is give over to the builders. She'll be in and out to elp us with the things; but she's took away all her own things already."

"Oh, indeed!"

"Very unsettling thing is moving, sir."

Smith assented; and Rose withdrew after delaying long enough to give him an opportunity of asking her to share his future fortunes, should he be so disposed; for, although a proposal from Smith would have surprised her more than one from any other person she knew, yet the habit of following the simultaneous progress of five different romances in a weekly journal, had prepared her for all possible matrimonial contingencies.

"Well" said Smith, as soon as he was alone, "there is absolutely no reason why she should tell me of her arrangements. Every one to their own affairs; and hurray for being practical!"

During the rest of the evening, he was a little troubled in his mind by the dressmaker's reticence, and a great deal by the question of lodgings, and of the proper amount to offer as a present to Rose on his departure.

When he left Figgis and Weaver's on the following Saturday, he went by train to South Kensington; turning whence riverwards, he scanned the windows of the houses in search of the small card which signifies apartments for hire. The Fulham Road once crossed, card after card invited him to inquire within; but he walked on, unable to make up his mind; and it seemed to him that the farther he went, the worse he fared. The line of houses degenerated into a row of shops, from which he turned away to gaze on the flying buttresses of St Luke's Church, within whose shadow he resolved not to dwell. Soon after he had left it behind he reached the river, where, looking up at a labelled corner, he discovered that he was in Cheyne Walk. The name was suggestive to Smith of poets, artists, philosophers, picturesque old houses, blue and white china, wooden bridges, floating piers, and penny steamers. He determined to seek for a room in some of the less pretentious streets which led away from the river. Rejecting Oakley and Beaufort Streets as having an expensive air, and others as being little better than alleys, he finally entered a narrow thoroughfare labelled Danvers Street, Paulton Square. At No. 90 he made inquiry, and was shewn a couple of rooms, each, as it seemed to him, of about the dimensions of an oven, provided with cheap and flimsy necessaries, which contrasted unfavorably with the solidity of Mrs Froster's furniture.

The landlady was a young woman, who in happier circumstances might have appeared pretty and amiable, but whose expression was careworn and meek. Her timid manner was agreeable to Smith after the constrained kindness of Mrs Froster, in whose presence he had never been free from apprehension. Her name, she told him, was Amelia Tilly; and her husband an engineer, which subsequently proved to mean a worker in metals. They had one child; but as it was the quietest little thing in the world, and had already suffered from whooping cough, no annoyance was to be feared from it. The drawing rooms were occupied by a most respectable photographer, whose wife was well connected, and sometimes played the piano and sang in the evenings, but not so much as to be troublesome. The rent would be seven and sixpence a week. This was a worse bargain than Mrs Froster's; but the proximity of Cheyne Walk was to Smith a sufficient compensation; so he hired the rooms without further ado, paying a week's rent on the spot so that he might be free to remove his goods thither on any day of the following week that should prove convenient. Mrs Tilly thought Smith a nicely mannered and well-spoken young gentleman, which consoled her for having been afraid to ask him for a reference.

Although Smith's room at Islington was held by him from Saturday to Saturday, Mrs Froster would not hear of receiving rent for the portion of the week which he intended to spend there before moving to his new lodgings. Therefore he felt bound to place himself at her disposal in fixing the date of his exodus. The arrangement entered into was as follows. On Wednesday Mrs Froster was to remove her goods to Richmond, with the exception of some furniture which she had elected to send to the auctioneer, and which included that of Smith's room, and of the parlor in which so many French lessons had taken place. In the evening he was to get his tea from Miss Russell: a provision for which there was no necessity, but which was, on sentimental grounds, congenial to all concerned. He was then to escort her to the half-past-eight o'clock train. On his return Rose was to be dismissed to her father's house; and Smith was to sleep alone for the last time at Islington. Next morning, he was to admit a charwoman; make breakfast of a collation of milk and bread spread on the previous evening; consign his boxes to the carrier; and proceed in the evening from his office direct to Chelsea.

All considerations as to Fenwick's movements had been rendered superfluous by his accomplishing on Sunday evening the feat popularly known as shooting the moon. Taking advantage of the absence of the landlady, with its usual result of a visit of Rose's to her favorite vegetable shop, he put on all the shirts, both for day and night, which he possessed, one over the other, and pocketed three socks, two handkerchiefs, a pair of carpet slippers, a brush and comb, and a wet sponge, all of which gave an eccentric outline to his figure. Taking a brown paper parcel under his arm, which contained, amongst other odds and ends, the duplicate tickets for his spare outer garments, which he had pawned the day before, he deposited his latchkey on the shelf in the hall, and ran away. When Mrs Froster returned to her house, the only visible relics of her lodger were the latchkey, an empty bottle, and a miniature, forgotten in his flight, representing a pretty child with golden curls, blue eyes, and a bright expression, sitting, clad in a smart velvet suit, with a toy drum beside him. This was a portrait of Fraser Fenwick at the age of six years.

Monday and Tuesday were passed by Smith in a state of restlessness which would have been intolerable but for the distractions of business. Then the eventful day came; and he found himself at breakfast, uncomfortably awaiting the appearance of the landlady. He had not long to wait. Mrs Froster, with her accustomed good housewifery, had made everything ready for the carrier the day before; and now she was attired in her state costume of black silk, to superintend the removal and enter her new house with dignity.

"Well, Mr. Smith" she began, in gracious confusion: "Ive come to say goodbye."

"I am very glad, for your sake, and extremely sorry for my own" said Smith. This little speech went off well.

"Indeed, no" said Mrs Froster. "I wish I could always have such as you in my house. I suppose you heard how Mr Fenwick treated me?"

Smith had. Rose had demanded of him bitterly whether it was her fault that the lodgers ran away: no small share of Mrs Froster's indignation having been vented on her for absenting herself so inopportunely.

"I believe he went away without telling you" said he.

"He went away without paying me" said Mrs Froster. "A nice thing for a gentleman to do!"

"I don't think Mr Fenwick was a gentleman" said Smith gravely, anxious to sympathize with her.

"Oh, I dont know that" said Mrs Froster. "I know he was befriended by very high people. When he was a boy he was quite a pet with Lady Geraldine Porter. I have been told by a gentleman who is incapable of an untruth, and who knows some relatives of his, that she used to let him play about her country house like one of her own children."

"He does not seem to have benefited much by his intercourse with the aristocracy" said Smith.

"If he had only been awakened to his own good" replied Mrs

Froster, "he had fine prospects. But it was willed otherwise, and he forgot himself. He thought he could drink, and gamble, and go into debt for fine clothes, as if he was a real gentleman. However, he's gone now; and I suppose I must put up with my loss. To tell the truth, I was not sorry to be rid of him. He was very different to you, Mr Smith. Your mother—if you wont mind my saying so—must have been a happy woman, and proud of you."

Smith blushed; but not being conscious of having been enthusiastically appreciated by the late Mrs Smith, he said nothing. A pause ensued, during which he vainly sought for a natural remark, and Mrs Froster fidgeted with her watch chain.

"Well" said she at length, with an effort. "Goodbye."

"Goodbye, Mrs Froster" said Smith. They shook hands warmly; and whilst he was debating with himself whether any further compliments were necessary, she left the room.

"After all" said Smith, much relieved, "she's as good natured as she knows how to be. Thank Heaven, that ordeal is over!"

No. 3 Dodd's Buildings looked more desolate than ever that evening. The curtains and blinds were gone; the single step before the door was muddy; and wisps of straw and scraps of twine lay about. Inside, the stairs were uncarpeted, and the hall deprived of its oilcloth. The staircase windows were dismantled; and on each landing the open doors revealed cheerless glimpses of bare floors and undraped shutters. The novelty of this spectacle exhilarated Smith. He felt that the closeness of the place was gone; and the romance of the bare boards, on which his boots stamped and creaked, tempted him to sing at the top of his voice. Postponing the gratification of this impulse until he should be alone on the premises, he went to his room, which he found much deteriorated in appearance by the absence of the table and pier glass. When he descended to the parlor, he found Miss Russell in the act of placing a wadded cover, resembling in shape a beehive on which a heavy person had been sitting, over the teapot. Feeling that the occasion was one of those on which intervals of silence are awkward, he began conversation at once.

"The house looks very queer, doesnt it?" said he.

"It is because the furniture has been taken away."

"Most probably" assented Smith, repressing a sudden inclination to throw the milk jug at her head. "Has that surveying genius been here since—I mean the man who is going to knock down the house?"

"No" said she, with interest. "I rather liked him. He seemed a quiet, sensible man, used to practical work."

"Which means" said Smith, "that he is exactly as narrow as his profession."

"Or perhaps that he has had the energy to learn a profession that suits him."

"It may be so. He was fortunate to have had the chance of doing so."

"I do not see anything to prevent anybody from doing the same."

"Nobody ever does except those who are in the dilemma" said Smith; "but take my case for an example. In the first place, I dont know what profession would suit me; and in the next, if I did, I couldnt afford to take it up."

"Can you not go into the government?" said Harriet.

"No, I cant" said Smith.

"Why?" said she, in her quietly persistent manner.

"Because" replied he, "I should have to pass a competitive examination."

"Well, surely you could pass any examination."

Smith grinned complacently. "So you think" said he; "but men who have had a long professional training in tripping people up with idiotic questions, are not to be encountered without special preparation under the direction of an expert. It would cost me a year's time and a year's income at the lowest calculation for the chance of a post even in the excise. If they will make me a clerk on my shewing them that I can do a clerk's work, well and good: I am ready. But they will only make me one on condition that I prove my ability to do something else. Consequently, I have no chance, and, like other poor and rationally educated men, must stay out in the cold. Besides, I object on moral grounds to submit my merits to a false test. In fact, I am bound hand and foot by circumstances. I can do nothing."

"You are clever enough to argue for all you do; and I fear that is all the good your cleverness will ever be to you" said Harriet.

"Well" said Smith, "what do you want me to do? I keep the accounts of a carpet shop. I earn the means of supporting myself. What would you have?"

"Push yourself; and get into business on your own account."

"That notion of 'pushing' yourself" said Smith dogmatically, "is a popular delusion—"

"Now, what is the use of your talking like that?" said Harriet, interrupting him deprecatingly, and almost impatiently. "Perhaps you dont like my speaking so freely to you about your affairs."

"Bosh!" said Smith. "I will prove to you in the clearest manner—"

"There is no use in your proving anything in the face of common sense. I know that people who set themselves out to do it can push themselves on and make their way in the world."

"True; but suppose it is not worth your while to set yourself out to do it. Suppose you enjoy yourself more in keeping out of the rush than scrambling in it, spending your life pushing and being pushed."

"You will be left behind, and laughed at, and be sorry afterwards. Thats all."

Smith shrugged his shoulders and made no reply. He felt at that moment in a humor to defy and despise all the practical self-pushers in the world. He was familiar with her view of life both from his own reflections and the admonitions of others; and had long ago decided that it was a view which did not fit his temperament. Besides, the imputation of being unpractical was one which he thought he did not deserve. From a city acquaintance he had learned that Figgis had pronounced him a steady fellow, with a great talent for business, and certain to get on; and, though he laughed at the simplicity of Figgis, yet it helped him to persuade himself that it was elevation of taste, and not want of capacity, that had led him to contemn his daily occupation.

"I suppose you will give up your reading and your French and so on now" said he after a pause, "and devote yourself altogether to business."

"Why should I do that, after giving you the trouble of teaching me? At first, I will have less regular work than usual until I get a connection at Richmond."

"Have you taken a place for yourself, or will you live with Mrs Froster?"

"Mrs Froster is going to live in a cottage on Mr Grosvenor's property. I have taken the upper part of a house in the town, where I intend for the future to live by myself, and carry on business for myself. The rooms are over a confectioner's shop; and the drawing room has plate glass windows, and will make a very good showroom. I will be near my aunt Angel and Mrs Froster, but quite independent. That is, if I succeed."

"It is a bold venture" said Smith doubtfully; "but you should succeed, if you can hold out at first."

"Between what I have saved, and the small sum my father left me, I shall be able to hold out for more than a year; and I hope to be making my expenses before that time. I have got work from three ladies there already."

"You will succeed, never fear" said Smith, with enthusiasm. "Independence, enterprise, and industry never fail. I cannot tell you how I admire you for making your way so resolutely out of this wretched place, and becoming your own mistress. I am sick of seeing fools and irresolute creatures grovelling along in the same old track, never finding the energy to grasp their fate by the throat and lift themselves into a sphere of free activity."

"Why dont you look at your own affairs in that way, Mr Smith?"

"Oh, bother my own affairs" said Smith. "Yours are much more interesting to me. I shall no doubt form plans some day, when I can see my way to do it. You see, you have an advantage over me. You can make a dress. Very few people can make a dress. I can only keep books. Any fool can keep books. Consequently our affairs are not the same; and to look on them in the same way would only lead to confusion."

"Well, I was not born able to make dresses."

"Pardon me" said Smith, who hated his worldly circumstances to be brought thus persistently before him; "but you were. You had the requisite taste and genius, and only required to learn the technics of needle and thread in order to find a material channel for them. However, let it be admitted that I am a weak creature—'

"I do not say so at all" said the dressmaker hastily, coloring at this concise expression of her thought.

"Then we are arguing about nothing" said Smith. "I think I will have another cup of tea."

One of those awkward silences which both feared ensued. Smith thought that the conversation, for a last interview, had hitherto been unsentimental; and he longed to express in some way the emotion with which their parting inspired him. Yet he could not satisfy himself as to the prudence of doing so, in the face of her hard disposition and five years seniority.

"I wonder" said he at last, "whether we will ever see each other again?"

"Why not? Richmond is not Australia—unless you never go there."

"I never do go there" said Smith.

"Then" retorted the dressmaker, "I suppose we never will see one another again."

"Therefore" continued Smith, "if I go there in future, it will be for the purpose of seeing you. Which, perhaps, although you may not like to say so, would not be unmixedly agreeable to you."

"If you think so" said she shortly, "you can very easily stay at home." She rang the bell then, and occupied the interval which elapsed before Rose's appearance in putting on her jacket and bonnet,[1] whilst Smith rued the ill success of his approach to the

---

[1] Women wore things called bonnets on their heads in those days. At the summit of its Victorian development about twenty years earlier the bonnet was an amazing headgear. The woman in Ford Madox Brown's picture of The Emigrants shews the bonnet and shawl authentically.

pathetic aspect of their position, and wondered whether his remarks had been kind and apposite, or brutal and in the worst taste.

Rose, who appeared to remove the tea things, which she had privately determined to leave to the charwoman to wash, had succeeded in inflaming her dry eyes sufficiently to carry a decent appearance of grief at leaving her mistress. This tribute she considered due to Miss Russell's generosity in making over to her a liberal gleaning from her wardrobe; and it cost her some very laborious dissimulation. For, being a buxom young woman with a cheerful expression and good complexion, it was not easy for her to look sad on the verge of liberty, change of scene, and a public appearance in her newly acquired garments.

"You may take down the tray, Rose" said Miss Russell. "Are my boots ready?"

"Yes, Miss" replied Rose in a forlorn voice. "Shall I bring them up, Miss?"

"No" said Miss Russell. "I will go down. I have some things to tell you before I go." She accordingly left the room. Rose followed, sniffing. Smith went upstairs for his hat, thinking meanwhile that if he did not come to a happier understanding with his late pupil before they arrived at King's Cross, they were likely to separate on very doubtful terms. She was waiting for him in the hall when he came down, and they went out together.

"Do you find the house more interesting now that you are looking at it for the last time?" said he.

"It is just the same as ever. It is only fit to be pulled down. We found the woodwork in a shocking state when we moved the furniture. It cannot have been very well built."

"No. I suppose not. It is quite warm tonight for February."

"Yes."

Not another word passed until they arrived on the platform at King's Cross, which they had hardly done when a train rushed in.

"Sec'nd be'ind, third forrerd. Baker Street, Bayswater, Victorier train!" vociferated the porters.

"E-cho, Globe, Evenin Ste-ndawd" sang the newsboy.

The underground railway admits of no leisurely partings. He hastily selected a carriage for her. They shook hands; and Smith, without feeling any preliminary access of emotion, was surprised to find tears in his eyes. As the train went off amidst a salvo of banging doors, he saw in her last nod all that occult charm which had first attracted him to her, and which he had since, in his familiarity with her, regarded as a romantic delusion. Then he strolled away, noticing the grime of the station, and wondering how long it would take a single man to clean it. He endeavored to dismiss this impertinent idea, partly because he wanted to think about the dressmaker, and partly lest it should recur to him in a nightmare. But it would not be dismissed; for he thought of nothing else than of giddily swinging on a ladder among the sooty girders, trying to clean them with a towel and a small basin of water, until he reached Dodd's Buildings.

He went into the parlor, and sat down before the fire to think upon the change in his circumstances. Finding, after two minutes, that his attention was wandering, and that a certain aimless facetiousness was predominating over the feelings which seemed proper to the occasion, he procured a book, and began to read. Rose appeared about an hour afterwards to beg that he would help her to carry up her box from the back kitchen (which served her as a dressing room); and he was soon on the steep flight of stairs, pulling at the higher end of her heavy trunk, and seeking a medium between breaking his shins and precipitating himself upon her head foremost over the trunk. When her property was deposited in the hall, she informed him that she was to send for it the next day, and that she was now going. Smith thereupon, with many misgivings as to the meanness of the donation, presented her with three half-crowns, which she, greatly pleased, acknowledged by permitting her limbs to collapse, and recovering herself when she had sunk about twelve inches.

"Goodbye, Rose" said Smith, opening the door for her.

"Goodbye, sir" said Rose, blushing and departing.

Smith returned to his book and read until past eleven o'clock. Then he took a candle and examined the house. Although he had lived there for more than a year, there were many rooms in which he had never been. First, he descended to the kitchen, where he looked into the drawers of the dresser, and slammed the door of the oven. Passing thence into the washhouse, he lifted the lid of the copper and peered within. Returning to the kitchen, he went to the tea-things which had been left by Rose on the table, and drank the remaining contents of the milk jug. This accomplished, he laughed boisterously, and went upstairs, where he found the state drawing room dismantled, and the neighboring apartment still redolent of Mr Fenwick's cheap tobacco. Then he visited the room lately tenanted by Harriet Russell, which he had seen only once before. It was quite empty, and, there being nothing now to restrain him from taking advantage of its resonance, he lifted up his voice, and sang The Heart Bowed Down with much expression. When he was tired of singing, he resumed his investigation of the premises, and eventually retired to rest with a pleasant sense of having made a merry night of it.

At seven o'clock in the morning, he was roused by the knocks of the charwoman. Unwillingly he rose and admitted her. The following hour was devoted to completing his toilet and cording his boxes. At half-past eight the carrier came, and took them away. Smith then looked for the last time at the blue flowers on the wall paper; handed his latchkey to the charwoman; and passed out through the archway. He had lived in Dodd's Buildings for a year and two months.

# BOOK THE SECOND
## AESTHETICS

*108620*

# CHAPTER I

MR HALKET GROSVENOR, of Perspective, Richmond, was a munificent patron and hospitable entertainer of artists of all denominations. He was a man of easy temper. What agreed best with his mental constitution was trifling. He felt that it befitted him to admire earnestness and strength; but, finding that these qualities collided too roughly and reproachfully with his luxurious indolence, he at once avoided and countenanced them by attributing them to works in which they were only affected. At intervals he grew tired of trifling. Then he organized classes for needlework, cooking kitchens, and institutions for the protection of young English girls studying music in Italy. But as these employed his head for about three days, and his hand as many minutes in signing cheques, he soon fell back into his routine of country, city, continent, gallery, and opera house, with their attendant art cliques and art fashions.

Physically, Halket Grosvenor was a tall man, with a long glossy beard, curly hair, and a modern adaptation of the Roman nose. At thirty-five years of age, his moist eye and spongy flesh had lost their original fire and hardness; but the stage of flabbiness on which he was entering was not as yet unpleasantly pronounced. He was called a finished *gourmet*: in English, a fastidious glutton. As a preliminary to each meal, he swallowed a glass of curaçoa; consequently he was further past his prime than his gamekeeper, who was fifteen years his senior. He had paid almost every distinguished artist in Europe for lessons in all branches of art. At twenty, he had painted a picture of Jacob's ladder; and this work, much faded because of the liberal use he had made of brilliant but unstable pigments, still hung in a drawing room at Perspective, where it created mirth enough to confer on it a celebrity as wide as the personal reputation of the painter. He had begun many works subsequently; but they remained unfinished; and of late years Mr Grosvenor had ceased to speak even of his intentions with respect to them. He felt all sarcasms on his powers as a musician and painter very keenly; and this was so well understood that he seldom suffered from them. On the other hand, he received all aspersions on his excellent hospitality with good humor, replying to the most impertinent suggestions as to the arrangements of his house with jests at his own expense, and ludicrous tales of the inconveniences suffered by former guests from his stinginess or negligence. This feature of his disposition was peculiarly useful to him, although it would seem that a man entertaining polite society could hardly have any occasion to display it; for in the first place, any species of talent, not necessarily associated with good breeding, gained admission to his house; and in the next, he found that his favorite artists were no less remarkable for sudden breaches of good taste, than for instinctive delicacy. His wealth was great; and to him the saving effected by a resolute "No" was not worth the unpleasantness of saying it to a well-mannered beggar.

The first great festival of the year at Perspective took place in Easter week. Easter Sunday afternoon was devoted to an artistic congress from which none of Mr Grosvenor's wide circle of acquaintances cared to be absent. It was anticipated with mingled pride and care by the housekeeper, who had to prepare the house; to ensure the comfort of the guests; and to preside at a table where tea was consumed by successive parties of ladies.

Mr Grosvenor's plan of entertaining was simple. When he expected a large gathering, he threw open the body of his house, consisting of a handsome hall, the dome of which was decorated with fantastic combinations of gold and bright colors, apparently laid on at random. At the end of this hall a broad flight of steps led to a gallery, from which there was access to many handsome apartments. Some of these were saloons draped with crimson velvet, in which large pictures in massive gold frames hung at sufficient distances apart for the isolation of each. Others had walls of pale blue flowered damask, and dadoes painted with processions of pale maidens picking flowers to pieces, reading books, looking ecstatically up, looking contemplatively down, playing aborted guitars with an expressive curve of the neck and fingers, dancing, smiling at themselves reflected from hand mirrors, stooping forward, bending back, or glancing over their shoulders at the ends of their skirts, all on a ground of dead gold. These rooms were for the reception of pictures of moderate dimensions, such as atmospheric landscapes, studies, representations of spirits, seasons, and other abstractions in diaphanous draperies, besides Phrynes and Faustines in no draperies at all, and Marguerites with blue dresses, cartouche boxes, and straps. In one saloon, devoted to spirited cabinet pictures of the French school, the walls were covered with bright yellow satin. The most notable of the galleries was draped with curtains of a dusty green hue, the monotony of which was relieved only by its own festoons and folds, and by the color and surface of the brown polished floor. A few settees, of the simplest form, and covered with very old velvet of the dullest crimson, were the only objects that interfered with the empty sadness of the place, except the pictures, which were Mr Grosvenor's most cherished possessions. They represented remote incidents, derived from mythology, classic history, early Christianity, or personification of influences. A few of them, by their purity of intention, and evidence of a laborious effort to reach a region where even an honest glorying in technical craft would be too earthy an element, made themselves welcome to the capable spectator by the double appeal of their baffled weakness to his sympathy, and their masterly and hard-earned beauty to his admiration. The rest, bad imitations of these, depicted vacant persons with that vague aspect and indistinct eye, which is in nature the symptom of a bad cold in the head. They were foolishly conceived, and ill executed. At the end of the gallery, opposite to the entrance, the visitor might lift the green curtain and pass into a small apartment formed of dark purple velvet. Here hung a picture of enormous size, painted by Tintoretto, the insolent power of which contrasted as strongly with the works in the adjacent gallery as its luxurious purple surroundings with their faded drapery of green. All these apartments were roofed with glass, and fitted with blinds and screens whereby the light could be regulated as the hours progressed.

On the floor beneath, adjoining the body of the great hall, was the music room, which was furnished and fitted in deep-hued oak. The chairs were in the newest style of old-fashionedness; the panes of glass in the bay window were not more than a foot square; the fireplace was a capacious alcove, framed in carved woodwork which reached to the ceiling; the panelled walls were decorated with specimens of old china; and the case of the monster pianoforte, of American manufacture, had been specially designed by an eminent artist, and was covered with arabesques and small figure subjects, painted in oils on a ground of subdued gold and white. In a corner, which could at will be excluded from the rest of the room by hangings of arras, was a small organ of a design as antique as a modern organ builder could be bribed to conform to. Close by, the wall was pierced by a narrow Gothic window, stained to represent St Cecilia listening in ecstasy to a cherub who, springing buoyantly through the celestial ultramarine, sang to an accompaniment of two harps and the Pandean pipes; the performers being angels seated on clouds.

Besides these, there were many other rooms surrounding the hall: painted, panelled, padded, tapestried, blue, green, and gold rooms; with peacocks, flamingoes, jays, and other gorgeous birds depicted on the walls. Bowls, plates, candlesticks, statuettes, and etchings were everywhere. Artistic effect, consciously striven for, was apparent at every step.

Bodily wants were provided for in a few rooms occupied by buffets, where the guests at the large meetings refreshed themselves without ceremony as they felt inclined. Indeed, so extensive were the afternoon assemblages which crowded the great hall and the lawn, that any other method of entertainment would have been extremely inconvenient, if not impossible. Each person could lose himself in the crowd; wander through the galleries; gorge himself at the buffets; be social, solitary, obscure or conspicuous, exactly as he pleased. Those to whom ceremony is as necessary as the gyves to an old prisoner, were not to be found amongst the frequenters of Perspective; or, if by chance such a one appeared, he did not repeat his visit. People who disapproved of felt hats, tweed and velveteen clothes, long hair, music on Sundays, pictures of the nude figure, literary women, and avowals of agnosticism, either dissembled or stayed away; and thus all elements antagonistic to the idealized Bohemianism of the place weeded themselves out. Unpleasant incidents sometimes occurred; but they were of that kind from which no society is exempt. For instance, the conservatories were unlocked only when a sufficient force of gardeners could be spared to prevent wholesale appropriation of the flowers; and indoor objects specially tempting to infatuated collectors were under glass and also under lock and key. A little negligible stealing was indulged in at times by some of the ladies; and occasionally one of those socially agreeable guests who are gentlemen by the accident of birth, but criminals by nature, took toll from an unguarded basket of his entertainer's plate. Sometimes two champions of rival schools carried the warmth of discussion too far, and proceeded from personalities to abuse and threats. It was said that on one occasion a young poet, infuriated by the aspersion of a critic who had in the midst of a circle of young and beautiful women attributed his inspiration to delirium tremens, not only knocked his traducer prostrate on the sward, but was about to roll the lawn-mower over his body, when he was seized by a courageous countess who boxed his ears, and at once became famous in anecdote. But on the whole, the gatherings, considering their extent, their promiscuous composition, and the free expression of opinion which prevailed, were harmonious enough to be of use in promoting good feeling amongst partisans accustomed to wage war elsewhere with all the virulence permitted by the absence of their opponents.

## CHAPTER II

BEFORE half-past two in the afternoon of Easter Sunday, Perspective was already crowded with visitors. At about that time, there approached by the highroad a young man whose costume was sufficiently unconventional to suggest that he might be one of Mr Grosvenor's artist guests. He was dressed in a short loose coat of light grey, which he wore unbuttoned. His hat was shaped in the Swiss fashion, and made of felt of the same color as his clothes. In his right hand he gripped an umbrella almost as if it were a sword: his left was concealed in his pocket. His hair was rich dark chestnut, clustering closely about his head, the occipital development of which was remarkable. His features were salient and inquisitive, and his nervous mouth and distended nostril, with the self-assertive deliberation of his gait, expressed the individuality which distinguishes the craftsman from the mere gentleman. He was small, sinewy, and, on acquaintance, handsome.

The gates of Perspective, tall examples of florid hammered work, were closed; but in the wall beside them was a studded oaken door, furnished with a bell, which the man in the Swiss hat rang. A girl, clad in Lincoln green, with puffed slashed sleeves, and a white cap modelled on one of the types worn by French peasant women, opened the door. The young man, not at all surprised by an apparition which would have led a less accustomed visitor to believe that he had interrupted a fancy ball, looked at her critically, and uttered an inarticulate sound, which seemed to be interrogatory.

"Mr Grosvenor is on the lawn, sir" said the girl. "Shall I send your name, Mr Scott?"

"No, thank you" said Mr Scott, and passed beneath a verandah attached to the gate lodge into the avenue, from which he approached the lawn by a short cut through the trees. Here he joined a large concourse of people. There were, among them, dandies, ostentatious slovens, and men whose costume troubled neither themselves nor—consequently—any one else. There were ecclesiastics, some as unprofessionally clad as possible, and others wearing Roman collars fastened by jewelled brooches. There were artists with long hair, haggard cheeks, and silky moustaches, eagerly talking to women; and artists with stumpy beards and neglected appearance talking to one another. There were young ladies, funny, but pleasant to look upon, dressed in sacks, blankets, or dresses apparently let fall from the sky upon them, slipping off their shoulders, and decorated with large bows stuck on all to one side. There were fashionable girls tottering on high heels, and squeezed out of human shape to shew off the skill of their dressmakers. There were the mothers of these young ladies sitting in garden chairs, conversing with young men who had in vain tried to extract conversation from their daughters. There was, in particular, Lady Geraldine Porter, nearly forty, with light brown hair, pleasant face, and full, but still shapely figure. She, comfortably seated close to where Mr Grosvenor was welcoming his guests, espied Mr Scott slowly approaching through the crowd, umbrella in hand, haughtily regarding those whom he passed, and occasionally jerking his head abruptly in recognition of an acquaintance.

"Do look at Mr Cyril Scott" she said to an old gentleman who sat beside her. "I wish some athlete would give that young man a hearty shaking."

"Eh?" said the old gentleman, with a start.

"I repeat deliberately and advisedly" said she, "that I wish somebody would shake him. He is too old to be whipped."

"But why?"

"Because his conceit is intolerable" said Lady Geraldine. "Look at his cuffs. What business has he to come here with his linen steeped in turpentine?"

"Ah!" said the old gentleman: "these young artists are careless fellows. He has been painting all the morning, and stained himself with his oils, I suppose."

"Nonsense!" said Lady Geraldine. "Who ever heard of a man working with his cuffs down about his wrists. Depend on it, he puts the turpentine on purposely with his brush, because he thinks it looks artistic."

"Haw! haw!" cried a youth who had come behind the seat, and had overheard this conversation. "You are regularly down on Cyril, Lady Geraldine. He's a splendidly clever fellow, a glorious fellow. I was down at his studio yesterday; and he has done a magnificent sky, finer than anything of Turner's, *I* think."

"How long do you usually stay when you visit Mr Scott in his studio?" said Lady Geraldine.

"The whole evening sometimes" replied the youth. "Really, he's a very nice fellow, though he works like a black. Old Bond offered him four thousand—"

"Ernest" said the lady, interrupting him, "will you kindly give us credit for a little common sense, and time to adjust your invention to our credulity?"

"But I assure you—on my honor—ask Woolly."

"I think you had better go and play, dear" said Lady Geraldine, looking sweetly at him. He accordingly retired, casting a rebellious glance at her as he went. When he was gone, she continued, "I have the honor to be that young gentleman's aunt. Amongst ourselves he usually calls me so; but here he conceives that the term would detract from his years and wisdom. I wish young Mr Scott would put down that umbrella. What is he brandishing it for?"

"I am told that he is a rising man" said the old gentleman. "You know I am not versed in pictures; but he has been well spoken of in my hearing."

"I believe he empties several cans of paint on a canvas, and then looks for a landscape in the result, as we look for pictures in the fire. At least that is what it looks like to me. Atmospheric art is rubbish."

"I have been shewn some of those new harmony paintings" said the old gentleman; "and they seemed not unlike certain places which I have seen."

"But they are not like pictures" said Lady Geraldine.

"No" said the other, catching with some relief at this: "that is quite true. Theyre not."

"Well" said she, "people go to galleries to see pictures, and not fogs and lobster salads."

Meanwhile, Mr Scott, having paid his respects to his host, went into the house. In the hall he was warmly received by a few leaders of the latest reaction in art, and scowled at by many professors of the older fashions. He glanced into the tea room, where a Napoleonic caterer, in command of a platoon of waiters, confronted an attacking force of women, all clamoring for a supply of their favorite insidious stimulant. He next tried one of the smaller rooms; and here he found a number of men standing by the walls, behind a row of chairs occupied by plainly dressed women, most of them past thirty-five, and intelligent looking, but not pretty. In the middle of the room, seated in a large chair, was a man to whom a broad brow, square jaw, glossy hair, ample figure, and studied negligence of pose, gave an imposing aspect. He was speaking in a sonorous voice, with studied phrasing and accent, as Scott entered. The latter, not knowing him, appealed by a movement of his brows to Lady Geraldine's nephew, who stood by.

"Macartney" whispered Ernest. "Extraordinary clever fellow. He's the Analysis of Genius man."

"This is a literary lot, of course?" said Scott, looking on the company with suspicion.

"It not unfrequently happens" said the man in the chair, "that from a misapprehension of the true nature of that function of the mind which we have agreed to call the imagination, misty and imperfect conceptions are often considered the result of an uncontrollably vivid fancy. What has been called Far Removedness in art is an example of this, and obtains principally amongst painters, who are, as a rule, so deficient in imaginative power that they are capable of no scenes save those which are mere assemblages of theatrical costumes and bright colors. This inability to perceive what is romantic in contemporary life, and tendency to substitute the contents of old curiosity shops, is the lowest abyss of vulgar sensationalism, and is omnipresent in pictorial art."

Mr Scott uttered a contemptuous snort, and left the room. A young lady who had formed one of a little group near the door, followed him quickly. She was pretty, and wore a costume of primrose sateen and grey towelling, which fitted like a glove on her tightly laced corset.

"Is he not a dreadful blasphemer, Mr Scott?" she said, addressing the artist, who greeted her with a sulky nod. "But he knows nothing about art, I am sure. Or else he was thinking of some vulgar painter like—like Rembrandt, for instance. [Scott started and glared at her.] Rembrandt is marvellous, of course, but a little vulgar, isnt he? Quite a painter of common people."

The artist looked at her with scorn, not at first deigning to answer. Then he said emphatically, "There was only one artist of all who ever lived who was never once vulgar. That artist was Rembrandt." Having delivered himself thus, he turned away contemptuously, and went to the music room.

"Well" said her sister to the young lady in primrose: "what do you think of your dear Cyril now? Is his freedom from conventionality as admirable as you thought it last Thursday, when he tried to snub me?"

"He is a rude little beast" said the young lady abruptly, and returned to the room she had recently quitted.

The music room was crowded. A long-haired young man sat at the piano flapping his hands as he played the last few bars of what he presently informed his audience was a Scandinavian Rhapsody in the form of a study for the loose wrist, composed by himself.

"Look here, Grosvenor" said Ernest to his host, who was his senior by about seventeen years. "I'll put you up to a good thing. Do you see Scott over there near the door?"

"Well?" said Mr Grosvenor.

"Just introduce him to Lady Geraldine, will you? She wants to know him, awfully. If she takes a fancy to him, she'd make old Porter buy up his whole studio in a minute."

"But are you sure she would like it?" said Grosvenor. "Had I not better wait until she asks me herself?"

"She wont do that" said Ernest. "She always abuses Scott's set on principle; and she will not condescend to ask for an introduction to such a small fish as she considers him to be. But if it could be done accidentally, she would be all the better pleased; and it might be a good thing for Scott."

Mr Grosvenor looked at Ernest in doubt. The more professional success and social standing any artist owed to him, the more complacent did he feel; for he liked to play the patron. But he wished that Lady Geraldine's nephew were a little more trustworthy.

And now began a plague of amateur singing. Young ladies with worn-out voices testified to the skill of the most approved native and foreign masters of the declining nineteenth century. With perfect satisfaction to themselves and their parents, they sang sharp; they sang flat; and some of them sang consistently against the pianoforte in a different key. Some glared at the accompanist for being loud and calculated to occupy a share of the attention of the audience: others could get through a song only on condition of the air being hammered on the instrument in unison with them. The men were scarcely less offensive; and the sole relief to the entertainment was afforded by a Celtic lady, possessing some inborn faculty for music, who sang an old English song with a little expression. Finally, a young German played a Turkish rondo by Mozart, which was much appreciated by the jaded listeners.

"What is that piece?" asked an old lady, when the pianist ceased.

"Do you mean that thing of Mozart's?" said the gentleman addressed.

"Mozart?" said the old lady. "Oh no! I dont mean anything classical. That pretty thing!"

"That is Mozart's" said the gentleman. "Mozart in one of his playful moods. Mozart with his German depth temporarily held in abeyance by his Gothic humor and his Latin melodiousness— his infantile vivacity getting the mastery of his profound learning and of that stupendous fatalism which, in the G minor symphony, seems to foreshadow the giant Beethoven."

"Yes, of course" said the old lady. "It's beautiful, most beautiful. But I think the young gentleman played it in a very flippant style, almost as if it was a piece of ordinary dance music."

"Hush" said the gentleman. "Bolingbroke is going to play."

"Oh, how interesting!" said the old lady. "Is Mr Bolingbroke a professional?"

"What!" exclaimed the gentleman. "Dont you know Boling- broke the poet? Eremacausis of Lucifer, Epos of Demogorgon, and so on."

"Theyre irreligious books, arent they?" said the old lady, doubtfully.

Before the gentleman could reply, the poet, a fair young man with large glassy eyes, in which intelligence was overpowered by languor, placed his right foot hard on the loud pedal, and began a formless improvisation, dwelling with evident relish on the most luscious chords he could find. Normally, he played very gently: occasionally and explosively, very loudly. At the end of ten minutes, he struck a discord in a soft passage; stopped abruptly; thought for a moment; shook his head sadly; and left the piano.

"Oh, pray go on" said a young lady who had been listening. The poet looked at her with a regretful smile.

"No" he said. "It is broken now. I could not play another strain though the bribe were immortality."

"What a grand thing it is to be a musician! How I envy you!" said another young lady.

"I am no musician" said the poet deprecatingly. "I do not know the name of one of those ivory tongues that speak to me when I caress them with my fingers. I seek for harmonies; and they come. Mr Burton, who is a student of those diagrams which are sealed books to me, called fugues, symphonies, and double basses, will tell you that I am wholly ignorant of the art. [Burton, who was standing by, nodded emphatically.] Yet I love it, and feel it, though I suppose the learned have no name for what I have just been doing."

"Oh yes, they have" said Burton. "As far as you can be said to have been doing anything, you were experimenting with Italian sixths, and resolving them, for the most part, improperly."

"You speak to me in an unknown tongue, my dear Burton"

said the poet, with a smile of pity. "I know nothing of your ratios."

"Dont you think science is quite antagonistic to true music, Mr Burton?" asked one of the ladies.

"No, I dont" said the musician. "Stringing pretty chords together is no more making music than stringing alliterative words together is making poetry."

Close by, a knot of persons surrounded a lady novelist, who was speaking on the same subject.

"Music" said she, "is the only art which lends a passion to our own dreams, instead of presenting to us the faded glow of another's. When I hear it, I close my eyes, and feel as though I were sitting in a forest with the autumn leaves dropping about me, or wandering on a stony beach under the shadow of some lowering cliff. The music of Weber, when played, as it always ought to be, by soft viols and flutes, without any harsh brass instruments, is a delicious narcotic, whose reveries bring no enervating reaction. For Beethoven I do not care. He disturbs; and his music thrusts itself upon the intellectual perception, which should be left to slumber. He appeals to the understanding: nay, he clamors to be interpreted; whereas the dreamy rhapsodies of Schubert and Chopin die away in cloying cadences that sink straight into the soul, and leave the weary mind at rest. I have known girls to sit for hours whilst their maids passed the comb through their long hair. Oriental potentates sink to sleep before the moving fans of their slaves. What the comb and the fan are to the body, music is to the mind: a soothing minister."

"Yes" said Ernest, "Meyerbeer has worked out that idea in his Africaine. Theres an awfully good fanning song in the last act." Finding his remark ill received, and determined that he would not be put down on a point which he felt confident of having illustrated accurately, he added, "Isnt there, Mr Burton?"

"There is" said the musician; "but of course you would miss the point of it if you didnt keep your wits about you."

"Ah!" said the novelist, divining his thought instantly. "You dont approve of my way of listening to music, I see."

"On the contrary" said Burton, "I think it is a very agreeable plan. I am rather fond of being read to sleep, for instance, which is much the same sort of process. But I dont think that books were written for that purpose; and when I want to enjoy and to understand a book, I generally find it necessary to keep wide awake."

"But surely there is no analogy between a book and a piece of music" said the novelist.

"At any rate" said the musician, alarmed at the prospect of becoming the unpopular champion in a controversy of which he doubted his ability to make his side intelligible, "all great works of art are much the same; and it takes as much brains and sensibility to appreciate the ninth symphony, or the Zauberflöte, as to appreciate Laon and Cythna, or Hamlet, or even a nineteenth century novel."

"Whose ninth symphony?" said the novelist, evidently inclined to dispute this.

"*Whose* ninth symphony?" echoed Burton irritably. "Why, *the* ninth symphony. Beethoven's of course. The last one he ever wrote."

"Oh yes" said Ernest. "I heard Hallé play it at St James's Hall the other day. He played the last five of em, one down and tother come on. Ha! Ha!"

Burton breathed a heavy sigh, and felt that explanation would be useless. "I hope the day will come" said he, "when persons of culture will deem a knowledge of the great classics of music at least as essential to their education as a proficiency in recognizing the bad paintings of a barbarous pack of fools and monks about whom nobody cares a straw." A dozen mouths instantly opened to denounce the prejudices of the speaker; but they were interrupted by a powerful voice brawling forth the coarse dissyllable—

"Gammon!"

"Whats the matter?" asked Mr Grosvenor, re-entering the room at the moment.

"It's a religious row. Theres a thundering Radical going for George Lind" said Ernest, gleefully.

In the organ corner, with one hand resting on the instrument, and the other hanging by his side, stood a young, clean-shaven, pale clergyman, whose attenuated figure stood out from the background of stained window with an effect which, to judge by his bearing, he was not unconscious of. Opposite to him was a large man with short red whiskers and fat cheeks, who was speaking to the clergyman in a stentorian voice, with a frank enjoyment of his own arguments, and the most entire recklessness as to the feelings of the company.

"I say, Gammon!" he shouted. "You dont like Michael Angelo because he was a big man; and the minute you come into collision with a big man, you cant help seeing that the small men whom you are perpetually sticking up as little gods are only pigmies. I dont like old pictures for exactly the same reason as you dont like them if you only had the courage to say so; because theyre dirty, and full of bad drawing and perspective and ugly women. But I admire Michael Angelo. Why? Because I go to Rome, and I see a chapel there, which is the centre of the Christian religion. [The clergyman lifted his hand in protest.] I say, the centre of the Christian religion. On the wall of that chapel is a picture conceived in the true spirit of that religion, and epitomizing it on two thousand odd square feet of plaster. Rain em down; tear em with hooks; batter em with oars; and jam em into hell," continued the Radical, guarding his breast with one arm and rearing the other menacingly aloft, whilst he looked with a frown, not at the clergyman, but down at the floor on his left. "Thats the religion of love, depicted, and depicted truly, by Michael Angelo. Ay, you may all 'hish-sh' as much as you please; but you wont alter that almighty fact."

"How on earth am I to stop him?" said Grosvenor, appealing to Lady Geraldine.

"Send for his wife" replied she promptly.

"I will" said Grosvenor, and left the room.

"Yes sir" continued the stout man: "faith *is* proof against clamor. Youre right there. In the same way, fools are proof against common sense. You have inferred also that it would be better taste on my part if I held my tongue. Very likely it would; but what is good taste? Only an excuse for the cowardice of shouting

with the largest mob. I have no doubt that the founder of your religion, or rather the person on whom you saddle the responsibility of your religion, hurt the feelings of the Pharisees; and that
the elders of the synagogue considered him as bad form."

"Sir" said the clergyman: "I respect your convictions; but I
cannot permit you to make me a party to an argument conducted
in such a strain in a house where I am but a guest."

"The conventions of society should be nothing to a man who
has had the Holy Ghost—"

"Tom!" said a lady, who had made her way through the crowd,
which was now composed almost exclusively of men, and who
stationed herself close to the speaker.

"Yes, my dear" said the man: "I'll join you presently in the tea
room."

"How do you do, Mr Lind?" said the lady, addressing the
clergyman. "I hope Tom has not been going on." The clergyman
smiled vaguely.

"I was only saying what I always will say, whenever—"

"Now *do* stop" interrupted the lady. "Why do you mind him
or answer him, Mr Lind? It only makes him worse; and he says
things he doesnt mean at all."

"I hope not" said the clergyman.

"Why dont you come over to see us oftener?" said the lady,
speaking quickly to prevent a fresh explosion.

"Ay" said the stout man, "why dont you? Come and dine with
us on Friday—or stay: Friday is a fast day. Come on Thursday,
and I'll introduce you to a confidential secretary of the Pope. He's
the best judge of wine in Europe; and he says he is over here only
for his health, which is most likely a lie."

"Tom!" remonstrated the lady.

"I am very sorry" said the clergyman; "but I have a service
every evening at seven."

"Never mind, Sallucci will absolve you."

"Come" said the lady: "we shall lose the train." So saying, she
bade Mr Lind a hurried farewell, and drew away her husband,
who took his leave of the host with the air of a man who had

enjoyed himself.

The exodus of guests, which had begun in a desultory manner about half an hour before, now became more active; and Mr Grosvenor, standing on the stone terrace which led by a flight of steps at each end from the great hall to the lawn, was busy receiving the compliments of his departing guests. When the greater number were gone, he remained more at leisure among the loiterers who, having no engagements, were more disposed to lounge about the terrace and galleries, chatting, or watching the sunset, than to enter upon a dull Sunday evening in town.

"Ernest" said Lady Geraldine, as she stepped, fur clad, from the hall to the terrace: "*are* you coming?"

"Here I am, Aunt Joldie" replied her nephew. As she approached Grosvenor, he was standing beside Cyril Scott, who was looking at the setting sun with a workmanlike attention which contrasted with the gloomy absorption affected by some others present. It was a good opportunity for an introduction. Lady Geraldine looked at the painter with a slight smile. Grosvenor took it for an expression of interest; and performed the ceremony before either party suspected his intention. Lady Geraldine turned with just enough curiosity to imply that her attention was now for the first time called to the doubtless clever young man before her, and bowed gracefully and deliberately. He, on the contrary, made a hurried bow, and fidgeted in silence. Ernest stood grinning in the background.

"I hope I have not interrupted a lesson from nature, Mr Scott?" said Lady Geraldine, with a glance at the sky. The artist smiled vaguely, and allowed his gaze to turn momentarily in the same direction.

"I am always anxious to claim your favor for my poor artist friend" said Grosvenor, "you are so renowned a critic." Scott's nostril dilated at the word poor, and contracted at the word critic.

"Dear me!" said Lady Geraldine, with an affectation of concern. "I believe I am renowned for not understanding pictures, particularly modern ones. But I have come to take my leave; and my train will not wait for me. I suppose any compliments on the success of the day would sound trite, Mr Grosvenor." And her ladyship, having bidden her host farewell, and received from the artist an uneasy bow in return for a composed one, left the terrace, followed by her nephew, who, now that his jest had succeeded, was beginning to feel apprehensive of losing the countenance of Grosvenor, who had dismissed him with marked coldness.

"What a jolly funk Scott got into when old Grosvenor trotted him out, eh?" said he.

"And what a pleasant thing it must be for you, Ernest" said Lady Geraldine, "to be able to go through such a ceremony with perfect confidence and self-possession?"

"Well" said Ernest modestly, "you know I am used to it."

"Besides" continued she, "you are in a good position; and you never forget that at least half the favor of an introduction is conferred by you. And you know so well that you can converse entertainingly; and are so pleasantly free from any of that absurd *mauvaise honte* which attacks proud and sensitive people, who are afraid of being misunderstood."

"But I assure you Scott is not a bad fellow when you come to know him" said Ernest; "and you neednt be down on him because he is not a perfect gentleman like—well, like, for instance—"

"Like you?" suggested Lady Geraldine.

"No, hang it, you know what I mean. Besides, I'm a Republican, and dont care a straw for such distinctions. Scott is an immensely clever fellow; and in spite of all our old pedigree bosh, I would think it an honor to change places with him today."

"No! Would you really? How very disinterested of you!"

"Chaffing again, as usual" said Ernest. "You are getting a bad habit of being sarcastic. This morning, Scott was the greatest puppy in England; and now, because it suits you to compare him with me, he is set up as a sensitive nature and all that, on the strength of your putting him out of countenance. But it is only a habit, which you cultivate because you can do it well; and I can tell you it will make fellows dislike you. Ive heard it remarked, in fact."

"Yes" said Lady Geraldine, amused: "there is just sufficient acuteness in the observation to convince me that you did not originate it. At my age, it would be painful to fall beneath the displeasure of fellows. I wish you would stop ploughing that grass border with your heels, and walk on the gravel."

# CHAPTER III

FOR two months Smith had lived alone at Danvers Street. Each morning he rose early, and went to the city in a steamboat. In the evenings, when he was tired of reading, he walked along the embankment, watching the barges proceeding sideways like unskilfully ridden horses, and listening to that distant rattle and shriek of trains, which had sounded to his father as the death knell of sylvan sentiment, but which was to him as characteristic of the country as the song of a blackbird. To his eye, a landscape was barren without the familiar row of white poles supporting an endless stave of music on which the insulators were the only crotchets, and which, by placing the ear against the pole, might be heard humming thunderously. Even across the Thames, and surrounded by gas works and factories decorated with tubes like colossal bassoons, they were the visible link between the maze of brick and stucco on the Middlesex side and the broad commons of Surrey and the downs of the South Coast.

One moonlit night, Smith had extended his walk as far as the prison of Millbank,[1] and was considering whether the mere aspect of this structure was not enough to repress any feeling of good will towards the community which a criminally disposed passer-by might still retain, when he suddenly thought of the Alhambra, at which he had not been for some months. After the fortnight which succeeded his first visit, during which he had gone there almost nightly, he had vowed to restrict himself to one visit in each week; and the violations of this resolve which occurred at first were more than compensated by his subsequent abstention for periods of three weeks and a month at a time. At last his visits ceased altogether; and now the idea of going had an air of novelty to recommend it. He accordingly went on to Westminster; passed along Whitehall; crossed Trafalgar Square; and shortly afterwards reached his destination, where, to his disgust, he met one

[1] This hellish thing has since been happily replaced by the Tate Gallery.

of his fellow clerks, a young Irishman named Kennedy, who was proud of his intimate knowledge of the private life of every public person in London.

The performance was that with which Smith was familiar. One small item in the entertainment was, however, new. This was the appearance in the chorus of a man with flaming black eyes who behaved and impressed himself on Smith's attention as if he were a principal performer. As nothing came of it the effect was ludicrous; but Smith did not laugh; for something in the man's personality vaguely stirred his memory. Kennedy, who had many particulars to impart concerning all the principal performers, repudiated all interest in or knowledge of a chorister, and accepted Smith's questions as a proof of his inexperience and mental weakness, an estimate in which he was confirmed by his companion's refusal to occupy the intervals between the acts in drinking. However, as Smith listened with complete credulity to Kennedy's tales of behind the scenes, and Kennedy enjoyed telling lies even more than drinking, to say nothing of its being cheaper, he abstained for the first occasion of the kind in his life. When the ballet of The Golden Harvest was well on its way, one of the accidents of the stage gave his imagination a cue. The beautiful dancer was waiting to be revealed to the audience by the opening of a harvest stack. It was the business of the manipulator of the limelight to keep his rays away from this stack until the moment arrived for the appearance of the dancer. Smith had often admired the dexterity with which these illuminating devices were carried out; but on this occasion the radiance wandered prematurely to the spot, and betrayed to the attentive spectator not only that the stack was constructed to fall asunder, but that somebody in short skirts of a bright hue was concealed behind it. Immediately Smith heard, in spite of the music, the voice of the dancer for the first time; and it was the voice of a very angry woman. Its tone was not lost on the Phœbus of the cornfield; for the gilded stack was immediately more obscured. Smith shuddered. Kennedy, who had also observed the incident, laughed, and said,

"Old Biddy Muggins is riling up over the lights."

"Old Biddy Muggins!" repeated Smith, with a pang of disillusionment.

"Aye: Mrs Muggins: there she goes" said Kennedy, as the sylph sprang from her hiding place and acknowledged the applause which greeted her by a droop of her head and a dainty upturning of her palms. "What age would you take her to be?"

"I should say well past thirty" said Smith, with a critical air.

"And the rest of it" said Kennedy. "She confesses to thirty-five; but I know for certain that she's forty-three. She's a whale to dance though, if she was eighty. If she put a little more spice into it, she'd be as good as any of the rest."

"Is she married?" said Smith.

"Dont I tell you?" replied Kennedy. "Her name is Muggins; and she's been married longer than she likes to say, and has four grown-up kids, two boys and two girls. The youngest fellow is her pet; and he's in Düsseldorf, studying to be a painter. That was a queer start too."

"What was that? her son's going to Düsseldorf, do you mean?"

"Well, I may as well tell you, Smith" said Kennedy patronizingly. "Old Biddy is as deep as a draw-well, and has queer notions. She gave her children a first-rate education, and kept them at school as long as she could; and she never let one of them inside a theatre or know what her profession was; though she took care to let them have plenty of amusement when they were home for the holidays. One night she got a ticket for Exeter Hall,[1] and gave it to Horatio, the eldest fellow, for him to go and hear The Messiah, a sort of religious singsong that some of the opera singers were in. So off goes the young buck by himself, and passes by here on his way. He had heard some of the chaps in the school talking about the Alhambra and what a roaring place it was for a jollification. So he thought to himself how he'd go on the sly; say nothing about it; and let them think at home that he'd been to the Exeter Hall. In he goes, sir, and gets shocked at the women in tights and all the rest of it; but, of course, takes to it like anything.

[1] A concert hall once famous for oratorio performances, now replaced by the Strand Palace Hotel.

Then he gets talking to a girl, and stands treat to her pals, thinking that he is cutting no end of a swell, and getting pretty well screwed by the time the ballet comes on. Next thing he sees, sir, is his own mother kicking up her legs about the stage in short petticoats; and what with the fright and the drink and always thinking her a regular angel, he goes wild; catches an old gentleman's opera glass and smashes it on the floor; and pitches into a fellow that he overheard making a remark about her. At last three bobbies[1] carried him out screaming, crying, and ran him in. He wouldnt give his name or address; and next morning he up and asked the beak to send him to penal servitude for life. Instead of that his worship gave him a lecture; hoped it would be a warning to him; and let him off, as he had had a night in the cells. He went home, and found them in the devil's own state about him; but he wouldnt tell where he'd been; and he went into such fits of hysterics when they bothered him about it that they were afraid not to let him alone. One day he let the murder out to Sebastian, the brother, who was a year younger than himself. Sebastian was by way of studying to be a painter. He was a regular laddo, and used to gammon his mother and get heaps of money out of her by way of buying paints and things at South Kensington, where she believed he was studying when he used to be jollifying amongst all the artists and their models in St John's Wood. He wanted to go to Düsseldorf, because he said the teaching at South Kensington was all rot, and he could lick the head master into fits at painting, any day in the week. But she wouldnt trust him alone on the continent, and couldnt bear to part with him. So things went on until the brother told him what he'd seen. Sebastian didnt care a dam, and laughed till he was ready to split at the way old Biddy had kept them in the dark about her games. Then he went right off to her, and asked her for ten shillings to get a study from the life of a dancing girl. She told him she wouldnt have him studying dancing girls from the life; and he told her that this was as nice a woman as herself, and would as soon think of sitting for the nude figure as she would. Old Biddy felt rather queer, as you may imagine;

[1] Middle-class slang for policemen at this period.

but when he kissed her, and said that he'd make a great name, and owe it all to her, she gave him a pound, which was how most of their squabbles ended. That night, away went the lad to the Alhambra in full dress, and plants himself right in the front row of stalls. Just before the ballet she came to take a look at the house; and the first person she set eyes on was the brave Sebastian. She refused to dance that night; and there was a fearful row behind the curtain. It ended in her taking old Crow, the manager, by the collar and pitching him out of her dressing room. She had to pay fifty pounds for breaking her engagement. But that was nothing to the blow-up at home. The affair about Horatio came out, of course. The father took the boys' part, and said that it was all for the best, as they must have found it out soon, and he had always been against keeping it from them. Sebastian said the only thing he was sorry for was that he hadnt seen her dance; and she sent him off to Düsseldorf the same week, after crying for a whole morning like mad. What do you think of that, eh?"

"I think it is rather frightful" said Smith, looking at the figure on the stage with a new interest. "Why should she be ashamed of her profession; I should have supposed, from the way she dances, that she had all the feeling of an artist about it."

"I dont know as to that" said Kennedy. "She says it's the greatest profession in the world, and looks down on actors and opera singers as if they were dirt; but she dont think most people come to look at it in the proper spirit; and thats the reason she couldnt bear to have her children sitting amongst them. Old Biddy knows how to preach as well as a parson, when it suits her."

"Is she a well conducted woman?" said Smith.

"Well, *we* know what women are" said Kennedy. "But she's never been found out, anyhow; so she can afford to give herself airs."

"What countrywoman is she?" asked Smith. "She looks like a Spaniard; but her name is an Italian name, I suppose her maiden one."

"Italian be blowed!" said Kennedy. "She was a Wexford girl of the name of Delahunty, and ran away with a circus or something when she was a child. After the Lord knows how many years, she turned up at Prague as a star dancer, and appeared afterwards at Milan and Paris. Then she was engaged for the opera in London; but she was so prudish and ready with her hands—she has a devil of a temper—that the swells soon turned against her. While she was here she married a builder named Muggins, and gave up the stage. But she soon went back to it; for he was always away on business; and she couldnt stand idling and giving up all the excitement and fun. She's been waltzing away all over the world since, coming back to Muggins and the kids when she can. She likes continental engagements because she thinks the people there appreciate her better; but she comes here pretty often on account of being at home."

"And now, Kennedy" said Smith, "one more question. How do you know all this about her?"

Kennedy winked and shook his head. Then, relenting, he said, "Well, the fact is, my Uncle Tim is in the theatrical line, and has dressed nearly every star that has come out here for the last fifteen years, at one time or another. If you only set him going about the Opera, he'll never stop. He saw her the first time she appeared in London, in Masaniello. It is from him that I know how she started; and I picked up the rest here and there. The whole story's well known."

Smith believed it all because it made him feel completely disillusioned. Men easily mistake the shock of disillusion for the impact of brute truth. As a matter of fact the whole tale, from the first anti-climax of Biddy Muggins to the final improvisation of an imaginary Uncle Tim, was a shameless fiction. Kennedy could no more help fabling in this manner than he could help breathing. Had he known the truth, which was that the dancer, Erminia Pertoldi, born in Trieste in 1850, was twenty-eight; that she was desperately struggling to uphold the tradition of the grand school of Italian dancing against the British ignorance of it which expects nothing from a stage dancer but loose morals and the power to kick off a man's hat in a cancan; that her extraordinary grace and impetuosity of movement was very suitably accompanied by a beautiful singing voice which she never could be prevailed on to use on the stage, Smith would have fallen in love with her more hopelessly than ever, and perhaps learnt the lesson that the chief objection to fictitious romance is that it is seldom so romantic as the truth, and, as manufactured by a twopenny-halfpenny Cervantes like Kennedy, is as often as not a cynical iconoclasm. As it was, the story did its work of making Smith realize that the dancer was a human being, and his dreams about her something that could never be realized even if he rescued her every night from a runaway hansom,[1] much less if he obtained an ordinary introduction to her. Perhaps it was the best thing that could have happened to him then. Since she could not, off the stage, be the fairy visitor from the stars whom he adored, she might just as well have been Biddy Muggins, *née* Biddy Delahunty of Wexford, as been Erminia Pertoldi of Trieste. He never went to the Alhambra again until one night when he saw a great glare in the sky, and, hastening Leicester Square way in pursuit of it, found the theatre in flames, and wondered that it did not set all London on fire with the amazing volcano of sparks that shot up from it.

He parted from Kennedy after the performance, not without difficulty; for the fabulist clung hard to his gull; but Smith escaped by taking the Islington bus, quite forgetting for the moment that he no longer lived there. When he remembered, a desire took possession of him to indulge in the pleasures of reminiscence, on the spot where he had met Harriet Russell. The strange looking chorister at the same moment recurred to his memory, and confirmed his half formed resolution to proceed; although he could not see any connection between the two. His thoughts were occupied by the dancer, the chorister, and the dressmaker until he arrived at his old residence.

Here he found the archway closed by a temporary wooden gate, secured by a padlocked bar, and surmounted by a board in-

---

[1] Hansoms were the vehicles that plied for hire in the London streets before taxis were invented. They were very dangerous, and so improbable in build and aspect that nobody who has never seen one will ever believe that it could have existed.

scribed *No admittance except on business*. There was a wicket in the gate, against which Smith tentatively pushed. The only result was a clank of the bar and a deep toned bark from within which relieved him of all desire to intrude. As he turned away with the intention of proceeding homeward without further delay, he was surprised to see the chorister leaning against the lamp-post and looking at him intently.

"You have come, like me, to view scenes of the past" said the man, in a hollow voice, folding his arms.

Smith paused in embarrassment, and muttered a few words.

"Perhaps you dont remember me" continued the man. "I am changed, Mr Smith, no doubt."

"I ought to know you" said Smith; "for your appearance is familiar to me. But I really cannot recall your name at this moment."

"My name is Cartouche" said the man solemnly.

Smith began to feel uneasy. The name suggested ideas which were not reassuring at midnight in a lonely street. "I certainly dont know you by that name" he said.

"No" replied the man, with a melancholy smile. "I was in another line when you knew me, Mr Smith. There is little in my wasted features now to recall the once prosperous and respected preacher, St John Davis."

"Oh, to be sure: of course: I beg your pardon" said Smith, laughing at his own forgetfulness. "What a fool I am!"

The chorister for a moment looked as though he considered this flippant; but seeing that Smith was proffering his hand, he relaxed the theatrical severity of his manner, and accepted the greeting.

"I thank you, sir" said he. "I bear you no malice, although I have good reason to curse the hour in which you led me to this fatal spot."

"How is that?"

"It is a long story, sir. And yet it might be told in one word."

"Well" said Smith, "I am going west, towards Brompton, if you are coming that way."

"I will accompany you for some distance, if I may be so bold" said Davis bitterly.

Smith expressed his pleasure with a sincerity which was due more to curiosity than to any prepossession in favor of his companion.

"Mr. Smith" began the chorister: "have you ever been in love?"

Smith thought of the dancer, and of Harriet Russell. But after a moment's deliberation, he answered, "No."

"Ah!" said Davis, "so much the better for you! You dont know what it is to be consumed, scorched up, drove to madness by the thought of one woman. I do, Mr Smith. You dont know what it is to spend sleepless nights longing and desiring like Dives for a drop of water to moisten his tongue. I do, Mr Smith. You dont know what it is to be trampled upon, despised, rejected, and laughed to scorn. I do, Mr Smith. God grant you never may know it! I dont talk about myself; for the heart knoweth its own business. But I know what I know, how I suffered, and what I bore. And why not, Mr Smith? Why not? I was in a very good position. I was looked up to by respectable people. I made three pound a week from my business, and had all my expenses from the brethren. It wasnt because I was against fighting as a Christian that I couldnt take my own part if I'd wanted to. Worse looking men than me find girls to run after them every day in the week."

"Of course" replied Smith encouragingly. "Did the lady—?"

"I'm coming to that presently" said the other. "When I come here that day to see that young man, I seen *her.* That was the beginning of my downfall. I went mad over her. No man ever loved like what I did, Mr Smith. Them as you read of in novel books and such couldnt love like earnest men, as I could. I was practised to throw my whole heart and soul into a thing when I once felt it. Other men had their souls to think of; but I hadnt. Mine was saved; and I well knew it. I knew I was doing God's will when I fell in love. It's ordained in the Bible that we should. I didnt obey the Bible by halves, Mr Smith. I flung myself into it; and I well nigh worshipped her. I came about the place at night to look at the house that held her. Often have I walked that court when you were sleeping, only to think that I was near her. You wouldnt have patience with me if I told you the way I devoted myself to her. One night I met her not far from where we stand now. She was coming back from the train; and she had a little bag over her arm. I spoke to her then; but she put me from her with scorn, as if she was a lady in silks and satins. I wrote to her; and she sent me back the letter with a note to say that it was all a mistake. That was what she thought of my sufferings. A mistake! But pride will have a fall; and maybe some day she'll be glad to take up with a worse than me, and be sorry when she thinks on what she threw away. She wont easy find a man with such a heart to give her."

"And was that the reason you gave up the preaching?"

"Indirectly it was, Mr Smith. I suppose you heard reports about me. They were in everybody's mouth."

"No" said Smith. "I lead a very retired life; and matters of current interest often escape me."

"It's not easy to let your heart bleed drop by drop, and not complain" said Davis. "What is life without sympathy, Mr Smith? When I sought for it amongst my congregation, I was misunderstood. Some of the women had been coming to hear me, and thinking of other things besides religion; and what with their being jealous, and never having gone through what I suffered, they kept away their daughters, and spread evil rumors of me. I forgive them heartily, and hope they may be forgiven above. But I thought it best to leave the chapel. They gave me a handsome presentation when I went, Mr Smith: a gold watch and chain with my name cut in the lid, in a Morocco leather case lined with blue; and a bead purse with twenty-five guineas in it. It was not so much the money I valued, as the feeling it shewed. They asked me to stay, too; but I was loth in my unworthiness to give cause for scandal; and I went."

"That was very nice, very nice indeed" murmured Smith. "Have you entirely given up your public career?"

"Well" said Davis, "I am thinking of going on the stage. I always had a taste that way. I have been told that I have a fine singing voice; and I have been cultivating it of late. In fact, I am fulfilling an engagement at one of the principal theatres, though I do not wish it to be known. Perhaps you may see me in the Opera yet, Mr Smith; for I'm told they pay anything there for a good voice. I can read music well, having studied in a tonic sol-fa class that was got up in connection with the chapel. However, it dont matter now what becomes of me. There was a time when I cared; but it's all over. There are things that a man gets over; but a broken heart is one of the things that gets over him. Well, well! It wont be for long. It wont be for long."

"I'm afraid this is the last bus" said Smith; "and I live a long way off; so I think I'll take it. I hope to find you in better spirits when we meet again."

The ex-preacher smiled sorrowfully; shook Smith's hand; and turned back. Smith climbed to the roof of the passing vehicle, and, as he looked at the retreating figure of Davis, thought that the manner in which Harriet Russell had kept her counsel concerning his proposal was another proof of her utter want of his coveted delusion, a sympathy leading to complete confidence and un-jealous community of thought.

# CHAPTER IV

CYRIL SCOTT spent the second week after Easter at Perspective. He elected this period for his visit because there were then but few members of his own profession to be found beneath Mr Grosvenor's roof. There were scarcely four artists in England whom Scott liked, and not more than two who liked him. The majority of the picture makers denounced him as a puppy, a charlatan, and such commonplaces of envious mediocrity. The most liberally disposed of them, too well established to fear his rivalry, admitted that he was a clever fellow who might do good work if he only knew how to draw. In return, Scott allowed the merits of his enemies with a bitter magnanimity which, in effect, depreciated them. On their shortcomings he said little except to his intimate friends; and to them he said a great deal. He withered beneath sarcasm, a sort of attack to which his school was peculiarly exposed; and he was unable to retort in kind because he was so in earnest that his own irony, labored and sometimes coarse, seemed less a weapon than a wound. His manner towards strangers was not cordial. In spite of his youth and growing reputation he was disposed to revenge himself on the world for its neglect of him before he had obtained a reluctant recognition which had come only after many disappointments, and for which, considering that it was not frankly tendered, he felt no gratitude. He had both diffidence and self-confidence, produced by the contemplation of great predecessors and petty contemporaries. Thanks to being handsome and self-willed he was a little spoiled superficially, and had certain affectations in his dress and manner which tempted many persons at first sight to ridicule him as Lady Geraldine had done.

The morning after his arrival at Perspective, he rose early, and descended to the great hall. He found nobody there; and knowing from experience the usages of the house, he determined to search the adjacent rooms for some breakfast.

"Good morning, Mrs Angel" said he, discovering the housekeeper in the tea room.

"Good morning, Mr Scott. You are the first down."

"How soon will the rest make their appearance, Mrs Angel?"

"Not many, I'm afraid, Mr. Scott, before three-quarters of an hour. Will you have breakfast now, or—?"

"I'll wait till I get it, Mrs Angel, and no longer. That is, if it wont inconvenience you. I hate making a business of grubbing."

"To be sure" said Mrs Summers, ringing the bell. "Many of the gentlemen come down early on purpose to escape the crowding and talking that begins after half-past nine. What would you like for breakfast, Mr Scott?"

Scott, at home, was in the habit of eating porridge in the morning, but seeing none, he had not the courage to suggest it to the housekeeper, and so was compelled to satisfy his appetite with ham and eggs. Whilst he made his repast, Mrs. Summers presided at the head of the table as though she were entertaining fifty guests, a proceeding which would have embarrassed a younger man. But Cyril was twenty-eight; had worked enthusiastically for twelve years, and steadily for five. He was therefore not easily dashed where his appetite was concerned.

When he had finished, he went for a stroll through the galleries, to see what new art treasures his host had acquired since his last inspection. The blue gallery was his favorite one; for there hung Fretted with Golden Fires, the picture which had raised him from obscurity. It had brought him forty pounds, and cost Mr Grosvenor four hundred and fifty. He rarely visited Perspective without taking some such opportunity as the present to gaze on it unobserved, and note how the colors were standing. When he entered the gallery, he was surprised to see a woman there. She wore a plain drab dress, admirably fitted to her figure, with a skirt which was neither festooned, tied back, covered with bows, horizontally crumpled, nor in any way robbed of the simple dignity of a flowing robe. As Scott entered, she was moving down the room; and as she did so, he remarked a strange grace in her action and in the carriage of her finely shaped head, which reminded him at once of a panther and of the Venus of Milo. He wondered who she could be. She did not look at the pictures like an artist; she was out of

bed too early to be a musician; and yet she looked something more
than a lady. She was not a servant, because Mr Grosvenor dressed
his servants in ruffs and fancy headdresses; and she had not even a
brooch or a cuff adorning her, although, following an artistic habit
of studying hands, he presently perceived that her right middle
finger was decorated with a silver thimble. Scott looked at her
figure again, and coughed. She looked up; and he bowed. She
acknowledged it slightly, and approached the door. Scott became
nervous as he saw her face. Hitherto he had divided her sex into
four sections: conventional women, to whom he was indifferent;
clever young women, whom he disliked; clever old women, of
whom he was afraid; and female artists, whom he despised. The
woman in drab would not fit into any of these categories; and reminiscences of a certain pleasure he had found in the society of
comely girls before he had devoted himself wholly to his art
began to stir within him.

"Pray dont let me disturb you" said he.

"Not at all."

"But I am afraid I have" said he, "since you are going. *I* will
go, if you find me intrusive."

"Excuse me, sir" said she, after hesitating a moment; "but I am
only the housekeeper's niece; and I have no business here."

Scott made her another bow, as if her speech were an introduction, and said, "Mrs Summers is an old friend of mine. I am greatly
indebted to her for the kindness with which she has always entertained me here. I hope you wont run away from the pictures; for
I shall feel as if it were my fault."

Harriet looked at him with some suspicion, and then, saying
simply "Thank you," returned to the other end of the room, and
resumed her study of the pictures. Scott, wishing to avoid any appearance of forcing on a conversation, pretended to occupy himself similarly; and for about a minute the two listened to each
other's footsteps, and were only restrained from gratifying their
desire to look at one another by the fear that both might choose
the same moment for doing so.

"You are fond of pictures?" he observed, at last.

"I like some pictures" she replied.

"You dont draw, yourself, do you?"

"I have often drawn maps, but not pictures."

"Maps!" said Scott, confounded by this reply. "Well: they are useful, at all events."

"Of course they are more useful in a certain way than pictures; but I would rather have the pictures."

"Indeed? What sort of pictures do you prefer?"

"I like large figure scenes of some story best" said Harriet, yielding to a prepossession which Cyril's face in the first place, and his adroit consideration of her aunt as his hostess and equal in the second, had inspired her with. "The ones that please me most are by the old masters. They were painters that lived a long time ago; and some of their pictures are still to be seen at the South Kensington Museum, and in the National Gallery. Did you ever hear of a painter named Raphael?"

"I believe I have."

"I like his pictures, although they have blackened very much. Still, when you get to know them—they are not very pleasant at first—they are really very fine."

"Yes" said Scott, with a grin, "I am quite an admirer of Raphael myself, you must know."

Miss Russell suddenly became diffident, and said no more.

"So you like landscapes" said the artist. "For instance, do you care for any of these pictures?"

"Only a few of them" said she. "They are all very affected looking. I prefer the drawings and engravings."

"Affected looking" said Scott, warmly. "What do you mean by that? What is the word affected supposed to convey?"

"I mean affected looking" replied Harriet, a little abashed, but resolved not to shew it. "As if the painter was thinking a good deal about himself."

"Humph!" said Cyril. "Let me see one of those works which you dismiss in one word so readily. Just one example."

Her face assumed an expression of quiet determination. "There!" she said, pointing to his own picture.

Scott winced. "How do you know" said he, turning to her, "how much study and work that picture may have cost the man that made it? What do you object to in it? 'Affected' means nothing. Is it like nature? If it differs from the blue and white skies you are accustomed to in pictures, is it because it is more truthful or less so?"

"The more study it cost, the more ridiculous it is" said Harriet resolutely. "It is not pleasing. Besides, what is the use of talking about nature? A painter cannot copy nature with a box full of gaudy clays made into mud with oil." This remark, of which Scott had often felt the truth, she borrowed from her former preceptor Smith, who had declaimed it one evening in a fit of unusually intolerant transcendentalism.

"That is a very sage and incontrovertible remark" he retorted. "But it does not destroy the relative truth which pictures have, and which can be compared easily enough. There is the evidence of a man's mind in pictures too, which makes them more interesting than nature. How often have you seen that sky?"

"I only noticed it for the first time a few minutes ago."

"Yes; and you dont find it pleasing on a few minutes' acquaintance. You said a minute ago that even Raphael did not satisfy your critical eye all at once. Perhaps if you spent a little more than a few minutes in judging of the result of years of labor and thought, you might learn to mistrust the value of thoughtless conclusions."

Harriet felt that the argument from her experience of Raphael was a forcible one, and also that her companion was rather short tempered. So she yielded the point, and said, "I wonder how much it cost."

"What has that got to do with it?" said Scott roughly.

"Nothing" said Harriet sweetly; "only I wanted to know."

"I believe Mr Grosvenor gave four hundred and fifty pounds for it" said he, thrusting his hands into his pockets and looking with a frown at the window.

"Four hundred and fifty pounds!" repeated Harriet, astonished. "But then Mr Grosvenor is so rich and generous. I suppose the painter was a poor young man, whom he wanted to encourage."

Scott could not trust himself to reply, but still looked at the window, through which the morning sun shone upon his face. Harriet looked at him; saw that he was in a rage; and admired him ardently. He seemed to her thoroughly a man, susceptible, intense, and altogether different from the pale scholar of Islington, whose thoughts were like bloodless shadows of conscience and logic. She wondered at his being so disturbed by her criticism, and resolved to discuss a subject whose merit was, she thought, unquestionable.

"There is an engraving of a splendid picture in my aunt's room" she said. "I have often wondered why it was not placed in the galleries."

"Humph!" said Scott, trying to recover his good humor. "Whose is it?"

"I cannot remember" said she. "It is a picture of a railway station. The dresses are quite old-fashioned—crinolines and large bonnets; but the picture is most lifelike and interesting. There is a bride—"

"Yes" interrupted Scott. "I know the picture. It is Mr Frith's."

"Don't you like it?" said she.

"I have nothing to say against it" replied the artist, resolved to be just. "Mr Frith is undoubtedly a very clever man." He could not refrain from adding, "And he found in a railway station a very suitable field for the exercise of his genius."

Harriet paused in doubt. She saw that he did not share her admiration of The Railway Station. Her glance wandered to the Golden Fires opposite; and he saw comparison in it, which he shrank from. He was spared by the appearance at the door of Mrs Summers, whose dismay at finding her niece, whose good sense she had always respected and even feared, conversing with one of her master's guests in the picture gallery with her thimble on, was visible in her face.

"Harriet" said she: "it's just nine o'clock."

Harriet started and said, "I had no idea it was so late." Then she bowed to the artist, and left the room with her aunt.

"Who is that gentleman, Aunt Angel?" she said, as she descended the staircase.

"That is Mr Cyril Scott" replied Mrs Summers: "a young gentleman of whom Mr Grosvenor thinks a great deal. He is a painter; and Mr Grosvenor gave four hundred and fifty pounds for that picture of his that he was shewing you upstairs."

Harriet now understood what had passed. She said nothing of it to her aunt, but hurried on, lest she should meet him again.

"Harriet" said Mrs Summers timidly: "I hope you didnt offer to speak to Mr Scott of your own accord."

"Nonsense, Aunt Angel! I offered to go out when he came in. I even told him who I was; but he spoke of you as a friend, and put it in such a way, that I could not very well have walked off."

"He is a truly nice gentleman" said Mrs Summers; "and I know your good sense, Harriet. Heres Miss Woodward coming down to look for him, I'll be bound." As she spoke, the same young lady who had appeared on Easter Sunday in primrose sateen, and had then been snubbed by Scott, came into the hall, looking as fresh as the early morning, an enormous straw hat, and a pretty costume of holland could make her. Harriet looked disparagingly at her, and went downstairs, preparatory to departing to business at Richmond.

Miss Woodward, after a glance into the tea room, and a brief stroll on the terrace, went to the blue gallery, where she found Mr Scott before his picture, divided between pride in its merits and a desire to destroy it for the sake of the imperfections which his more recent experience would have enabled him to avoid.

# CHAPTER V

EARLY in the afternoon, as Lady Geraldine Porter, who was also a guest at Perspective for the second Easter week, was sitting in the lawn reading the newspaper, she was interrupted by one of the young ladies in Lincoln green.

"If you please, my lady, there is a person at the lodge wishing to see you. The person's name is Fenwick."

"You were quite right not to let him in. Thank you."

"Your ladyship will not see him?"

"Certainly not."

The young lady in green, evidently gratified, returned to the lodge, where Mr. Fenwick stood, leaning against one of the pillars of the verandah, and furtively glancing through the latticed window at a well spread table which stood within the pretty residence of the gatekeeper. His clothes were threadbare, stained, frayed at the edges, and clustered in wrinkles about his knees and elbows. His dirty collar, too limp to stand up, draggled over an old printed handkerchief which served him for a neckcloth. His boots were broken; and his bare feet, covered with dust and mud, were visible through them. A pair of soiled paper cuffs, and the remnant of a dogskin glove on his left hand, shewed that he was anxious to appear well dressed when visiting Lady Geraldine. An eager expression came into his face as he saw the girl returning. She, with a hard look at him, first opened the oaken door, and then said shortly,

"Lady Geraldine Porter cant see you."

Fenwick looked at her in consternation, and seemed about to make some appeal. But her expression as she held the door open was inexorable. He hesitated; glanced again at the luncheon table; gulped; and walked out with a painful swagger. But, unable to endure the idea of yielding without a struggle, he asked, as he crossed the threshold,

"What time would it be most convenient for me to call again?"

By way of reply, she shut the door in his face; and he cursed her frantically as he turned away. He walked quickly, until weakness, and a reluctance to give up all chance of obtaining his object by quitting the neighborhood of Perspective, checked him. The road was enclosed by the brick wall of Mr Grosvenor's park on one side, and by a damp ditch, on the further bank of which grew a hedge, on the other. He crossed the ditch; lay down in the sunlight on the long grass on the bank; and began to brood sullenly over his position. He felt languid and rather sick. Suddenly a conviction seized him that he was about to die; and in his terror he feared to rise, lest he should rob himself of the hope that he was still strong enough to walk. He felt his pulse; and when he found it rapid and unsteady, did not know whether that sign was favorable or the reverse. As he listened to it he became conscious of the beating of his heart, and the possibilities of disease there filled him with fresh apprehension. He wished he had never endangered it by smoking. Then he longed for a scrap of tobacco to soothe him. The prospect of begging occurred to him; but he had still pride enough left to resist the hunger that he nevertheless felt must soon drive him to it. He had nothing left that he could pawn; and so, without food, and almost without hope, he fell asleep, the sun warming his ragged form, and extracting a golden gleam from his yellow hair, which straggled about his neck in dusty mats.

Later on, Lady Geraldine borrowed one of her host's landaus, and paid a few visits in the neighborhood. As she returned to Perspective by another road, her attention was attracted by the recumbent figure asleep in the hedge. Lady Geraldine was proprietress of a dairy farm, and wife of a magistrate. She had an eye for tramps, though but seldom an ear. So she prepared to scan this vagabond as she passed. As he lay, with a pinched, wistful expression of hunger on his brow and mouth, the disordered handkerchief at his throat betraying the absence of any shirt beneath his wretched garments, he was far beneath any sentiment but pity. Lady Geraldine's first impulse, on recognizing him, was to drive on as fast as possible. Her next, to stop and address him. Before she could act, the rumbling of the wheels roused him: he cast a languid glance at the carriage; and immediately staggered to his feet, with an imploring look at Lady Geraldine.

"Come to the gate, and wait outside until I send for you" she said sternly.

A minute later she had disappeared; and Fenwick was standing at the oaken door, hastily endeavoring to arrange his clothes neatly.

When the carriage entered the grounds, Lady Geraldine alighted, and went into the lodge.

"Gwendoline" said she to the young lady in Lincoln green: "is your mother in?"

"She is up at the house, my lady."

"Well, can you lend me your parlor, or any room, for a few minutes?"

"Certainly, my lady."

"I want to see the same person who called this morning; and I do not wish to bring him to the house."

To obtain the good will of Miss Gwendoline, it was only necessary for her social superiors to call her by her name, which she loved. She led the way to a pretty drawing room, with a tiled fireplace, oak furniture, latticed panes, and trophies of the chase. Here Lady Geraldine placed herself, and requested the girl to admit Fenwick. She accordingly opened the oaken door and said,

"Step this way, if you please."

Mr Fenwick entered haughtily, and trifled with his remnant of a glove. Gwendoline led the way into the hall of the lodge, and, pointing to the drawing room door, informed the visitor that Lady Geraldine was prepared to see him. He thanked her with an affected politeness which from a more dignified figure would have been insulting, and tapped unsteadily at the door. An imperious "Come in" frightened away his affectation in a moment; and he obeyed, shrinking from the stern regard of Lady Geraldine with an air of mingled shame, fear, and entreaty.

"Well! What do you want?" said she, with a severity which cloaked an impulse to laugh.

Fenwick fidgeted with his hat, and mumbled inarticulately.

"Put that thing out of your hand, and speak properly" said Lady Geraldine impatiently.

Mr Fenwick hastily dropped his hat. Then, encouraged by her tone, which, if alarming, was more familiar than before, he began,

"I am very sorry to take the liberty of troubling you, Lady— of troubling your ladyship. I have been very unfortunate lately. I have been out of employment."

"Why did you leave the employment you were in?"

"Which one do you mean?" said Fenwick.

"Your place at Mr Linton's."

"There was a misunderstanding about a trifle; and I had to resign; but—"

"You stole; and you were dismissed" said Lady Geraldine. "Is that what you mean?"

"No, upon my honor" said Fenwick, sincerely horrified. "I wouldnt do such a thing. Indeed I wouldnt. I only borrowed it. It was on the twenty-eighth of the month; and the money was really due to me. I would have replaced it in two days, and nothing would ever have been known about it. I had to pay a debt of honor."

"Whats that? A tradesman's bill, I suppose?"

"No: I wouldnt have done it for fifty tradesmen. I lost it on the turf. It was not my fault; ask Mr Porter if it isnt well known that Topsy was pulled—"

"So you are a gambler as well as a drunkard, sir. And what do you expect me to do for you on the strength of these recommendations? You have had chances that very few men get. You were offered good nominations; and you would not work to pass your examinations. You have been put into one office after another, and have lost them all by drink, idleness, and insolence. Finally, when Mr Linton employs you as a favor to my solicitor, who asks him to do so as a favor to me, you rob him in order to supply yourself with funds for gambling. I am sure I cannot understand why he did not send you to prison. That would at least have kept you at work and away from drink."

"I know I havnt been steady. But I have always tried to do

what you told me. I have never forgotten that I should always act as a gentleman."

"How dare you say such a thing to me!" said Lady Geraldine. "Have you ever acted as a gentleman in your life? Are drunkenness and theft the virtues of gentlemen?"

"It was not a theft" pleaded Fenwick. "I had earned the money: I had indeed."

"And the woman with whom you lodged at Islington, and from whom you ran away, leaving me to pay your rent: had you earned her money too? Or the many people you have cheated by using my name and parading my letters to you: had you earned their money? Fraser" said Lady Geraldine gravely: "you are a bad boy; and I am afraid I may have had some hand in spoiling you. I do not think you can tell me one unselfish action done by you in all your life."

"But I mean to turn over a new leaf" said Fenwick. "I havnt drunk anything for a long time; and I will take the pledge tomorrow. I'll be steady. Ive had my fling; and I see what it's brought me to. It's not so much my fault; for everybody is down on me except you. Youve always been my friend. Give me one chance more; and see if I will not be a credit to you. I intend to go to church regularly—"

"How often have you broken the same string of promises?" said Lady Geraldine, sharply interrupting him. "No: I will have nothing further to do with you. In encouraging you I have only given you the means to prey upon others. I am done with you." And she made a movement towards the door.

"But, Lady Joldie" cried Fenwick, in the voice of a child about to cry, stretching out his hand as though to clutch her dress, "I am hungry!"

"Have you brought yourself to that at last?"

"I havnt eaten anything today?" said he, with a convulsive sniff; "and I had only a penny loaf yesterday. I've pawned everything I possess, except some things at my lodgings; and the people there wont give them to me nor let me in. Ive lived the life of a dog for the last two months. I'm going to die. I often thought so before; but I know it now; and I'm not fit for it. I dont know why I was ever born, if I am to be always miserable." Here, overcome by weakness, he sat down in a chair, and howled suddenly, his tears making white channels in the dust which powdered his face.

"If I trust you with some money to get food and clothes, I suppose you will spend it on a single night's carousing" said Lady Geraldine.

"Upon my solemn oath—"

"Fraser!"

"I will spend it properly, and work hard, if I have to sweep a crossing" said Fenwick more calmly. "You will find me all right, if you will only try me this time."

"Where is your uncle to whose daughter you are engaged? You may remember that the last two chances you got were to enable you to marry her."

"I dont go there now" said Fenwick. "We had a misunderstanding. At least, he would have nothing to say to me after that affair at Linton's."

"So the match is broken off?"

"I suppose so. I havnt seen Fanny since. I'm not good enough for her now."

"If you would think a little less about being good enough for other people, and set up a standard of self-respect, there might be some hope for you. You are not good enough for any young girl to trust her happiness to, you most unfortunate fool. Now, listen to me. I am about to give you ten pounds. [Mr Fenwick's eyes glistened.] Go back to town and get yourself proper clothes; pay your rent; and release any of your property that may be worth it, from the pawnbrokers. Call on me at Wilton Place next Tuesday at half-past eleven; and bring the receipt for your rent with you. If you come drunk, or look as if you had been drinking, you will know what to expect. I want to hear no thanks, no protestations. I am content to risk this money; and if you like to spend it all in play or gin, you can; only in that case do not call on me again. And mind, you must be prepared to take what employment I can get for you, whether it suits your dignity or not. Now you may go."

"Oh Lady Joldie—"

"Thats enough" interrupted Lady Geraldine. "Go to Richmond, and get something to eat. Here: you had better have a few shillings in change. Now, go!"

Fenwick repressed the expression of his gratitude, and left the room humbly. As he shut the door, he chuckled with delight. The next moment, with ten pounds four shillings and sixpence clutched in his hand, he swaggered through the verandah; looked disdainfully at Gwendoline, who sat reading a novel; and let himself out with a bang into the highroad, which he traversed rapidly, buoyant as a trodden daisy, and luxuriating in the hunger which he now possessed the means of stifling in luxury.

# CHAPTER VI

Miss Isabella Woodward was at this time twenty-four years old. Her eyes and hair were of that hue which passes as black when not contrasted with the true color; and her expression, animated and pretty when she conversed with men, was peevish and wearied when she was idle amongst her own sex. Originally of good capacity and impatient disposition, she had received the customary education for a life of fashion, and had left school discontented, violent of temper, capricious, insincere, and competent to converse after a fashion in the French language; to sing four songs; and to play M. Prudent's fantasia for the pianoforte on airs from Lucia di Lammermoor. She had one taste and one accomplishment: the first, for exciting literature, the second, flirtation. The latter was more an instinct in her than an art. To charm a man by a glance, or a flattery, and at the next encounter to treat him with indifference or pretend to forget him, was so natural to her, that she believed flirting to be a vulgar habit of which she was incapable.

In her twentieth year, finding herself restless and unhappy at home, she quarrelled with her family, and refused to live with them. Soon after this, a religious acquaintance pointed out to her that perfect happiness was only attainable in the bosom of the Roman Catholic church. Without reflecting that the acquaintance seemed to be as far from perfect happiness as herself, and being vaguely desirous of some change in her inner life, she, in despite of the representations, threats, and entreaties of her family, transferred her faith to Rome at the church of the Oratorians in Brompton. Discovering presently, however, that Isabella the Catholic was precisely the same as Isabella the Protestant, and that the attractions of mass at six o'clock every morning were modified by the approach of winter: becoming, moreover, tired of the old women of her present faith, who ostentatiously kissed and petted her, and of those of her former one, who treated her as a silly child; and above all, disgusted with her confessor, who, though an ex-officer of the Guards, had retained none of the gallantry of his former profession, she relaxed the rigor of her observances, and was prevented by superstitious fear only from reclaiming her spiritual independence. Her mother dying at this time, she returned to her home on the terms of a domestic treaty, one of the items in which was, that although she was to attend any place of worship she preferred, her father, an Irish Protestant member of parliament, was to be at liberty to kick downstairs, break the neck of, or otherwise maim any emissary of the Pope who should presume to cross his threshold. She thus made her duty as a daughter a refuge from importunity as to her duties as a neophyte; and thenceforth she sought for solace in enthusiasm for art, in simulating which she for the first time found an easy and pleasant occupation.

She had had six offers of marriage. The first was from an artillery officer, who proposed to her when she had just left school. She refused him at once because he was thirty-four, matter of fact, nervous lest she could catch cold, and in the habit of walking without gloves. The second arrived during the triumph of refusing the first, and shared his fate. The third suitor she loved up to the date of his declaration, and even after it; but he married some one else whilst she was putting him off with evasive coquetry. Hereupon she declared that her career was over; offered her services (which were declined) as hospital nurse; and eventually changed her religion as before described. So long an interval elapsed after this, that she began to think the rule of society which enjoins that persons shall always accept invitations whether they mean to take advantage of them or not, equally applicable to offers of marriage; and from that time forth she invariably replied to such proposals in the affirmative. She had in this way become engaged to three gentlemen without securing a husband. For, of these three, the first objected to her accepting the second pending his engagement; the second repudiated her for having concealed from him her contract with the first; and the third retired for some months to Scotland, whence, having induced her by his silence to reproach him, he wrote to the effect that no woman who had doubted his honor could ever be anything to him, and that he wished her every happiness with the man upon whom she should confer her hand. Upon which, being by this time able to endure such reverses with fortitude, she told her friends that she had broken off the match, and awaited the advances of a seventh suitor. Happening then to become acquainted with Scott, and inducing him, by some ignorant comments on his art, to treat her with open contempt, she determined that he should be this seventh, if possible, and swore to herself in the watches of the night that if Cyril would only give her the chance, she would cast all her former wretched life behind her, and be to him the truest, fondest, and most unselfish wife that ever took upon herself half the burden of an artist's existence. Such vows were not infrequent on Miss Woodward's part.

At about five o'clock in the afternoon of the day on which Fenwick paid his visit to Lady Geraldine, Miss Woodward, with a roan cased sketching block under her arm, entered a portion of Mr Grosvenor's demesne which sloped to the river edge, and was wooded with elm and chestnut. Here she saw through the trees Scott standing by the margin of the water, and looking on the scene before him with an air of dissatisfaction which the young lady attributed to the absence from the landscape of fog, in the delineation of which he excelled. Whilst she was yet at some distance, he turned and saw her; and, although she was unusually attractive with the patches of sunlight shining through the branches upon her large straw hat and light summer dress, he hastily turned his face again riverwards. In this position he heard her steps approach through the grass, and stop close behind him. He did not look round. She did not address him, knowing that he was aware of her presence, and not loth to punish him for ignoring her. The artist held out obstinately until he felt the back of his neck becoming crimson. Then he turned, with an unsuccessful attempt to simulate surprise.

"Well, Mr Scott?" said she, with satirical politeness.

"Well?" said he bluntly. Finding it difficult to focus her at a distance of only two feet, he took a step backward as he spoke.

Recollecting just in time, that this movement must deposit him in the Thames, he recovered himself with a stagger, in executing which he inadvertently dealt her sketch book a blow which scattered its loose leaves on the sward. Miss Woodward, who had an Irish perception of the ridiculous, began to laugh.

"I beg your pardon" said Scott, sincerely but petulantly; for he disliked being laughed at.

"I have been sketching all the afternoon" said she, becoming sad as she helped him to re-collect her papers; "but the more I strive, the further off appears the goal I aim at." The artist continued to huddle the sketches into the book without looking at them. "I suppose" she added with a faint laugh, "my efforts appear very silly and presumptuous to you."

"I have never seen any of them."

"I have often thought of asking you to look at them, and to advise me; but knowing how deeply you think of your own work, I never dared to trouble you with such impertinent daubs as I produce."

"I should be very glad—of course—but I dont see exactly how I could advise you" said he slowly.

"Oh, I know you could!" she said with enthusiasm. "If you would only tell me your real opinion of one of my sketches— only *one*—I would learn more from that than from years of groping in the dark by myself. Other artists, like old Mr Vesey, pay me empty compliments which only humiliate me. You will tell me the truth, will you not?"

Mr Vesey was a follower of the old school. Cyril scratched his forehead; shrugged himself; and said,

"Very well, Miss Woodward. I will give you my opinion if you like. You can take it for what it is worth."

"I'm half afraid" said she, glancing up at him with a smile, as she hesitated with a sketch half drawn out from her budget. Her coyness had no effect on Scott, who unceremoniously seized the sheet of paper, and studied it with a gloomy countenance.

"Is it *very* bad?"

"Oh no: it's not *very*—at least—. The truth is, Miss Woodward, that this sort of thing cannot be done by an amateur as a pastime. I assure you it takes a man all his life, working as hard as he can, to get any sort of power to paint. You go at it for once in a way to amuse yourself; and you select a subject that *I* dont know enough to attempt. It's pretty, no doubt; but, of course, it's worthless."

"I suppose I must give it up" she said forlornly.

"Oh no" said he tolerantly. "If you try simpler effects, and have nothing better to do, you might as well waste your time at that as at anything else."

"Thank you" said she, beginning to feel, on reflection, a little annoyed. Scott had spoken so much less vehemently than he felt, that he was quite unconscious of the severity of his remarks, and believed that he had expressed himself with forbearance. Fearing that he might be tempted to speak out if the subject went any further, he put up the sketch, and said,

"We must not forget the hour, by the bye. It will soon be time to dress for dinner."

"Ah!" said Miss Woodward, "I am sure you hate having to dress."

"I dont like it" said he. "But there is no use in grumbling. Come on."

"Do you get up early every morning to look at your own pictures, Mr Scott?" she said, as they walked together toward the house.

"Why?"

"Because you ran away from the blue gallery this morning in such a hurry when you saw me, that I felt quite sure you had been indulging in a look at Cleansing Fires."

"I am not aware that I have ever given such a name to a picture" said he, with his nostril writhing.

"Most likely you know what I mean. It is the picture old Mrs Summers thinks so much of. I saw you having quite a long conversation with her afterwards in the hall; and I supposed you were talking about it."

"I am glad you follow my movements with so much interest,

Miss Woodward."

"That is as much as to say it was like my impudence to watch you."

Scott did not deny.

"I am very sorry, Mr Scott" she said with affected earnestness. "I cannot tell you how sorry I am."

"I dont know, Miss Woodward," he retorted with deliberate emphasis, "why you should have done me the honor to select me as the victim of your wit. Perhaps my profession has given me a habit of taking things too seriously, and so unfitted me for that refined and very intellectual sphere in which you shine; but I fail to see that you have any right to make my private actions the subject of your humorous misconstruction."

After this speech, one of those on which Scott based a high opinion of his power as a satirist, the two walked together for some time in silence. As they emerged from the wood into the open park, Miss Woodward tossed her hat from her forehead, and gaily sang a snatch of a ballad. The artist looked indignantly at her, and increased his speed to a degree which compelled her to devote her lungs solely to respiration.

"Speaking from your experience now, Mr Scott" she observed, "do you think artists are as a rule pleasant in society?"

"When you consider the sort of beings who constitute society, Miss Woodward, and the amount of thought and work which artists have to go through, you may perhaps understand how they feel in drawing rooms. If an artist is, as he must be, sensitive, one fool is enough to put him out of temper for a whole evening."

"Dear me! I thought artists were always so sweet tempered."

"Of course then, I suppose they are. No doubt you understand them better than I can pretend to."

"Confess now, that you are in a dreadful rage with me." They entered the hall as she spoke.

"I see there is no one here; so I conclude that the bell has been rung" said Scott coldly. He then flung down the sketches on a table, and walked away to his room. Miss Woodward picked up her portfolio, and followed his example merrily, but not quite sure that she was not angrier than he. On this point her maid, who arrayed her for dinner, did not share her uncertainty.

Mr Grosvenor was in the habit of finding in his drawing room so many diverse castes, that he had long ago, as the only means of withholding offence, adopted the plan of systematically violating all rules of precedence. It was believed that on the only occasion on which a bishop had crossed the threshold of Perspective, he had brought down an opera singer; whilst his wife, four couples ahead, descended the stairs on the arm of an engraver. On the present occasion, Mrs Mainwaring, a married sister of Mr Grosvenor, acted as hostess. In her neighborhood the conversation was subdued; no opinions were delivered; and polite acquiescence was accorded to harmless remark. At the opposite end of the table the host and Miss Woodward, Lady Geraldine and Cyril Scott, Ernest and Miss Woodward's younger sister Clytie, with some journalists and critics, formed a loquacious group. Mr Lind the clergyman was there also, apprehensively watching his radical antagonist, who sat opposite to him eating largely.

For some time Cyril Scott was silent. He was trying to overhear Miss Woodward, who was relating to Mr Grosvenor, in a low voice, an amusing anecdote about somebody falling into a river.

Lady Geraldine, who expected to be talked to, became impatient. "What will we have from you in the Academy this year, Mr Scott?" she said.

"I! Oh, nothing, nothing particular."

"Nothing is very different from nothing particular. Perhaps I should not have asked."

"Not at all" said Scott, blushing and laughing. "I have two pictures; but one of them was painted three years ago, and the other wont be popular."

"Another step" said Miss Woodward to her host, "and he would have been in. And then he got into a rage with me, and absolutely bullied me all the way home. I am in his black book with three big crosses against me in consequence."

Grosvenor laughed, and changed the subject by addressing

one of the critics.

"Have you seen those sonnets of Hawkshaw's?"

"He sent them to me yesterday" replied the critic. "Admirable, oh, admirable! Quite the finest things of the kind since Suckling."

"Yes" said Ernest. "I saw the proofs. The name of the fifth sonnet, The New Endymion, was a tip of mine. Theyre wonderful, splendid! By George, theyre magnificent."

"There is no doubt" said Grosvenor, "that Hawkshaw is a consummate master of the French forms. But I hear he is going to edit the Elizabethan dramatists."

"Not that exactly" said the critic. "I happen to know what he is really doing; but it is to be kept secret. The fact is, he is making a complete reading of Hamlet for Simonton, who will open the Gymnasium Theatre with it next month. He has given Simonton a study of every scene; and it will be simply a revelation."

"That is extremely interesting, sir" said Mr Lind. "I greatly admire Mr Simonton's elocution. What a wonderful work Hamlet is!"

"Wonderful!" echoed another critic. "I object to that term, or to any other, applied to Hamlet. If you qualify a work, you profess to understand it. And who understands Hamlet? In the sixteenth century there appeared a grand monument which every one can admire, but the mighty inscription on which none can decipher. There it stands in the nineteenth, inscrutable as ever. Dare any man say he has deciphered it?"

"Thats very true, of course" said the first critic; "but I think many of Hawkshaw's ideas are extraordinarily near the inner motive of the play."

"Despite the celebrity of this Mr Hawkshaw, I do not remember his name" replied the other. "I presume he is a young man; and I take leave to doubt his capacity to grapple satisfactorily with a subject which has baffled the maturest intellects."

"Oh, I say" remonstrated Ernest: "look at his Wheat Sheaves!"

"Is Hamlet mad?" continued the critic, ignoring this interruption. "There is a simple question. Answer it who can. Is Hamlet mad?" As he spoke, he looked slowly round; but no one met his gaze except Lady Geraldine, who smiled blandly at him. Finally, he looked at the burly gentleman beyond him, who was busy eating, but who, becoming conscious of the critic's inquiring look, threw down his knife and fork, and was about to reply, when a servant took away his plate.

"Hallo" said the gentleman, whose voice overpowered every other sound: "you just hand me back my dinner, will you?" Then, having recaptured his food from the startled domestic, and glanced joyfully at the reproachful face of his wife, he said to the critic, with boisterous courtesy, "I beg your pardon. You asked me a question?"

"I was merely putting the futile, ever-recurring question, Is Hamlet mad?"

"Deuce a mad, sir. But theres too much of him. The play's too long. Neither actors nor audiences are able for it nowadays." And he recommenced eating.

"That man is the most refreshing barbarian" said Lady Geraldine to Scott.

"Who is he?" said the artist.

"His name is Tomline Musgrave" replied Lady Geraldine. "He is a barrister, and a great authority on the subject of international law. As all the people who know him either like him or detest him, I suppose he must be clever. His chief social accomplishment, besides eating, is a remarkable aptitude for violating decorum, particularly by abusing religion in the presence of clergymen. He likes doing so, partly because it amuses him, and partly because it annoys his wife, who never knows what fresh outrage he will perpetrate, and consequently lives on thorns. He does it of malice prepense too; for he can behave himself perfectly when he chooses."

"Is there anything new about the Covent Garden tenor?" said Grosvenor, addressing a journalist of musical reputation.

"It is settled that he is to appear. Gye has got him; and he will have to defend six actions for breach of engagement, three in Italy, one in Marseilles, and two in Madrid. He is a wonderful artist. Poor Mario's place will be filled at last."

"Indeed" said Grosvenor. "I just missed hearing him at the San Carlo. Where does he come from? Whose pupil is he?"

"He has been studying for ten years with Lamperti; and he certainly shews it. He is master of all the secrets of the true old Italian *bel canto*—phrasing—command of the *mezza voce*—blending of the registers: all perfect. Magnificent actor!"

"In fact he is just the same as all the successors of Mario who have appeared and failed for the last ten years" remarked Lady Geraldine. Then, in a lower tone to Scott, "How I hate music!"

"Eh?" said Cyril, surprised.

"I hate it" she repeated. "It is bad enough to have to listen whilst otherwise sensible young men and women make themselves ridiculous at the piano, without being pursued at one's meals by this cant which proves to the satisfaction of no one, that detestable lazzaroni converted into howling dervishes, whom even the English public can scarcely be induced to tolerate, are profound artists and accomplished gentlemen."

"I know all about the new tenor" said Ernest. "He was boots at a hotel in Naples; and old Lamperti heard him sing three operas straight through while he was polishing his balmorals. So he snapped him up."

"I have been made acquainted with a singular anecdote respecting him" observed Mr Lind, at the sound of whose voice Musgrave became attentive. "He studied for ten years, during which his master only permitted him to sing some exercises which were contained on a single sheet of music paper. At the end of that time, he requested to be allowed to learn a song. His master in reply, turned round and said: 'Young man: go. You are the greatest singer in the world.'"

"The revising body ought to incorporate that story with the new edition of the Bible" said Musgrave. "Its extreme antiquity, extravagant improbability, and the universal acceptance it has obtained, savor strongly of inspired revelation."

Mrs Musgrave sighed as she saw her husband look lazily round with his appetite satisfied, and his face beaming with post-prandial good humor.

"I have often thought" said he, "what a capital instance of the survival of blind faith—which some fools suppose to be dead— the authority of musical criticism is. Except when they prophesy after the event, musical critics are invariably wrong. I know that by comparing their verdicts with subsequent experiences. Yet the more they are found out, the more they are believed in. Thats because they have such a lot of technical jargon at hand. If a man uses a single term which I dont understand, I of course cannot measure his superiority to me, and naturally give him credit for stupendous erudition. He knows more than I do: thats enough for me, whether he has the advantage of me in one word or fifty sciences. Consequently, when a fellow tells me that there are consecutive fifths, or false relations, or what not, in Wagner's music, I feel ignorant; and, seeing that he knows such a lot more than Wagner as to be able to pick a hole in his work offhand, I think it a great pity that he doesnt go and write something perfect himself. Eh, Weekes?"

Mr Weekes, the musical critic, said blandly, "My dear Musgrave: you know you are talking nonsense. Suppose I reply that it is a pity you dont produce perfect musical criticism, since you can pick a hole in the ordinary article offhand?"

"So I do" said Musgrave; "so I do. I form my own opinion about music, and reason from what a performer is, instead of dragging a notion of what he ought to be out of a fog of tradition and reputation, and then being afraid to say he is anything else. That is what perfect criticism is, as far as such a rotten conceit as criticism can be perfect in this world. I know what I like; and I wont be dictated to about my tastes by a parcel of camp followers. Yes, sir: I am the public: I lead; and the critics follow; catch at my opinions; apologize or apostatize if they pick em up wrongly; and state them so verbosely that I feel ashamed of them when I read them."

"But then, on your own shewing, you must agree with the critics."

"Up to a certain point, which we will fix at one generation ago, they agree with me, because they have followed me so far. But that generation is the distance which I, representing the world, am ahead of them; and consequently we do not agree, except on points which have been settled for half a century to the satisfaction of every reasonable man. We have settled that Beethoven could write music. Weve even got as far as Schumann; and after some thirty years of knocking their heads against a stone wall, the critics are ratting as fast as they can to Wagner, to avoid being left too far behind. Considering how fast the world moves nowadays I have no doubt that if I went to sleep for twenty-five years, I should wake up pretty level with contemporary criticism."

"I will positively leave the table if they dont stop talking about music" said Lady Geraldine to Scott. "Pray say something to create a diversion."

The artist, thus suddenly appealed to, was contemplating the blank which he found within himself, when, to his relief, Lady Geraldine exchanged glances with Mrs Mainwaring, and in a few minutes the men were left alone with the wine. At Perspective the hall was the place of assemblage at all hours. Thither the ladies now went, certain of being joined immediately by most of the young men. Mr Grosvenor was fond of wine; but he drank on many occasions during the day; and as he considered the custom of the men remaining at table to drink after the withdrawal of the women a survival from Saxon barbarism, out of harmony with the culture which he desired to make his house noted for, he abridged it as much as possible. Hence the dining room was soon deserted. Mr Lind, apprehensive of the humor of Musgrave, left first; and the rest followed his example, with the exception of the host, Musgrave, a few art critics, and Scott, who began to discuss the prices recently given for pictures, and to tell stories of offers he was daily receiving from men who, two years before, had affected ignorance of his existence. As his tone was bitter, the critics soon tired of their wine. Musgrave was fast asleep. The host accordingly rose, and led the way to the hall, where the company were chatting and drinking coffee. Miss Woodward was sitting on the steps of the grand staircase, listening to Mr Lind, who quoted poetry as he looked admiringly up at her from the step below; a state of

things which she had brought about in the hope of making Scott
jealous. He, unmoved by the spectacle, went upstairs, and returned presently with a hat. On his way to the terrace he was
stopped by Ernest, who said, with a careless air,

"Jolly evening, isnt it?"

"Jolly!" said Scott. "Do you think this infernal talking jolly?
I have been almost driven out of my wits at dinner, listening to
stuff that Grosvenor's footmen must be ready to hang themselves
for having to listen to."

"I was rather enjoying myself, I confess" said Ernest, taken
aback by the ill humor of the artist. "It's really a jolly house, you
know."

"Pah!" said Cyril. "It stinks of money. The idea of a man like
that pretending to hang pictures! with his Tintoretto stuck in a
Bluebeard's closet to shew that he knows the difference between
a Venetian master and a Fulham one." Here, recollecting that he
had often despised other men for flattering Grosvenor before his
face, and abusing him behind his back, Scott checked himself, and
made his way to the deserted terrace, where he looked disparagingly at the moon, which was not such a one as he loved to paint.
The rustling of a woman's dress disturbed him. He immediately
put on his hat; descended the steps; and disappeared in the gloom
of the lawn, whilst Miss Woodward, disappointed, returned to
the hall.

# CHAPTER VII

SINCE his first meeting with Mrs Tilly, the landlady of 90 Danvers Street, Smith had perceived an amelioration in her appearance. She had begun of late to smile often, and to pay attention to the adornment of her person. Smith had often watched her with interest as she went out on Sunday afternoon, smartly dressed, and accompanied by her husband, a young man whose slouching gait contrasted with the self-assertiveness by which he expressed his resentment of the social disadvantages of his position. His aspect improved with his wife's; he gradually lost a sodden condition which had rendered his habitual sulkiness repulsive; he carried the child on the Sunday afternoons; and when the infant rubbed its cheek against his, he no longer strove to conceal his parental delight by a swaggering deportment. A further improvement was apparent in his language. Hitherto, when at a loss for an idea in the course of his remarks, he had interpolated the word "bloody" without any regard to its relevance, just as more polite conversationalists use "hm," "er," and such sounds. This habit he had almost rid himself of. On the whole, he seemed to be advancing both in happiness and respectability; and Smith, who had a strong aversion to his landlord at first, was able to congratulate himself at Easter on having been in no wise inconvenienced by him. He was therefore disagreeably surprised, on his return late at night to Chelsea after his visit to the Alhambra and to Islington, to hear a confused din of voices from the kitchen. He was too tired and sleepy to trouble himself about the matter then; but next day, when Mrs Tilly, who waited on the lodgers in person, brought him his breakfast, the old careworn expression was on her face, and all her recent cheerfulness quenched. He referred this change to the disturbance of the previous night, and judged, by the timid deprecation of the landlady's manner, that she dreaded complaint on his part.

As he was returning from the city that evening, he saw Mr Tilly at the corner of the street reeling out of a public house. Evidently his landlord's recent improvement, and the increased happiness of his wife, had been caused by an interval of temperance, from which he had taken advantage of the Easter holidays to relapse. Smith avoided him, and went into the house, where he had to ring the bell thrice before Mrs Tilly arrived with his tea. She was almost in tears, and apologized for the delay with the remark that William had worked very hard of late, and that he was a little overtook. Smith did not enjoy his tea. A murmur from below, in which Tilly's menacing voice alternated with the remonstrances and coaxings of his wife, made him nervous. At last a crash of breaking crockery determined him to endure the noise no longer; and he went out: a rumbling shock informing him as he did so, that an effort of Tilly's to ascend the kitchen stairs had failed.

Smith did not walk far. It seemed cowardly to leave Mrs Tilly without any person to appeal to in the event of her requiring protection from her husband's violence. The possibility of an encounter with Tilly filled Smith with dread; but this made him the more uneasy about his own conduct. After some hesitation he went back to the house. He found the kitchen maid waiting bareheaded in the street, and listening eagerly at the railing.

"Is there anything the matter?" said Smith.

"Marster's a murderin of Missis downstairs" replied the girl, with a grin.

Smith stared at her for a moment, and then hurried into the house, and approached the stair which led to the basement. He paused before descending; for the fragment of conversation which reached him through the open door of the kitchen seemed to indicate a less extreme state of affairs than that described by the maid.

"Willie: dont go out again. Now dont. Youve had enough to drink tonight."

"Le' go."

"Youre not fit to go out. Youll be taken, and lose your place. Cant you stop with me?"

"Who isnt fit to go out? I'm as fit to go out as any man; an' I'like to see who'll stop me. Le' go, will you, damn you?"

"I wont let you go. I wont have the bread taken out of the

159

child's mouth for you to go and destroy yourself." There was a short pause after this.

"Loo' here, Ameliar. I wish to go out to see a fren. Merely to see a person. I'll bring in su'think for the child."

"Wait till the morning. Come and get into bed, Willie. Youll be all right in the morning."

"Will you lemme go?" This was a drunken roar. Smith hesitated no longer. As he rushed down the stairs, he heard a scream; and he reached the kitchen door just in time to see Mr Tilly bring down a saucepan on his wife's head with a bang which felled her to the ground. Her face became suddenly white as she dropped on the flags; and Smith felt sick as he ran to her assistance, and tried to lift her. She moaned, and raised her hand to her head. Embarrassed by the weight of her shoulders, which he was supporting in an inconvenient position, and unwilling to leave her lying on the hard floor, Smith looked helplessly at Tilly, who, sobered by a misgiving that he had committed murder, had dropped the saucepan, and was now contemplating Smith's proceedings with remorse and consternation. They were disturbed by a heavy footstep on the stair. Immediately afterwards, a policeman, attended by the kitchen maid, entered the kitchen. He paused just inside the door, looked cautiously around, and said,

"Whats this?"

Tilly looked doggedly at the policeman, and replied dramatically, "I done it. I'll swing for her. I done it."

"Dont you be in such a hurry with your tongue" said the constable sternly. "You may be sorry when it's brought up again you, as it will be if I have to charge you." At this moment Mrs Tilly, with the assistance of Smith, rose; sat down on a chair; and began to cry.

"I hope you are not hurt" said Smith.

"Come, Melia" said the culprit, approaching her awkwardly: "you know I wornt in earnest. I wouldnt urt you for all the world." Mrs Tilly turned her face away, and wept the more.

"I suppose youre her husband" said the constable.

"I am" retorted Tilly.

"There's nothing serious the matter with the woman, is there?" said the policeman, turning to Smith, whom he took to be a medical student, or apothecary's assistant.

"Oh no, I hope not. I think she's all right now" said Smith, unconscious that his words carried the weight of a professional opinion.

"Now" said the policeman, addressing Mrs Tilly, "do you intend to charge your husband? And if you do, do you intend to stick to it?"

"I dont intend anything" said Mrs Tilly sobbing. "It's no business of yours. I never sent for you."

"Very good" said the policeman. "You take care of yourself, my man, or youll overdo this some day or another; and then I'll have some'at more to say to you." Having so delivered himself, he went out with the indifference of one familiar with domestic violence.

"Can I get you anything, Mrs Tilly?" said Smith, anxious to withdraw.

"No, you cant" she replied. "And I hope you wont get a policeman into another person's house again until you are asked. I always thought you too much the gentleman to mix yourself up in what isnt your affairs." Here she began sobbing afresh.

"Aye" said Tilly: "youre so damned busy: arnt you now?"

Smith, surprised and hurt by this attack, looked at Tilly with mechanical imperturbability, and walked out of the room. Had there been another roof in London beneath which he could have claimed shelter, he would have walked out of the house. As it was, he went upstairs and to bed, where he lay greatly disturbed in mind. The more he strove to think on indifferent or agreeable matters, the more did the insult he had received compel his attention. If he forgot it for a moment, it was only to think of Mrs Tilly falling with her white face upturned, and to feel again the sickness which the reality had caused him. After two hours, which seemed to him half a night, he fell asleep, and escaped from himself until morning, when he arose in a calmer, though still irritable condition. He had no appetite for solid food; and the dread of seeing

Mrs Tilly prevented him from ringing his bell. He left the house without having breakfasted, and went into a confectioner's on his way to the city. Here he drank three cups of tea, and lingered to read the newspaper; so that he arrived at the office five minutes late. On the stairs he met old Mr Simms, the chief bookkeeper.

"Hurry up, hurry up, Mr Smith. Mr Figgis is in the office, and has been calling for you. He's in a terrible temper. Up with you."

"Oh, hang Mr Figgis!" said Smith. "What does he want with me?"

"Tut tut! Mr Smith" said Simms, who took an interest in his junior, and entertained a high opinion of his good sense: "that was not spoken like yourself. Pray shew yourself. Youre late."

Smith leaned against the wall to indicate that he did not intend to hurry himself. Then, assuming with an effort the burlesque strain in which he often amused himself at the expense of Mr Simms, he said gravely,

"I understand you to say, Mr Simms, that Mr Figgis has so far forgotten himself as to mention my name before ten o'clock. What does he want?"

"Now, dont be incorrigible, Mr Robert. There is a time for everything. Mr Figgis had occasion to refer to Kennedy's accounts, and he found that they had not been posted up for nearly a fortnight. Then he asked for your ledger, and grumbled because you were not there."

"I am surprised at his audacity" said Smith. Then, feeling indisposed for further banter, he went up to the office, feeling angry that his unpunctuality, which was quite exceptional, should have been commented on by his employer.

In the middle of the room stood Mr Figgis, surrounded by a ring of awestruck clerks, and confronted by Kennedy, who retorted his magisterial frown with an insolent grin.

"Have you anything to say?" said Figgis sharply.

"Oh no!" said Kennedy familiarly: "Ive nothing to say."

"Mr Forsythe" said Figgis, becoming purple with rage.

"Yes, sir" said the cashier, starting.

"Give this fellow his month's salary, and let him go."

"Fellow yourself" said Kennedy, reddening. "Fellow yourself!"

"Thatll do" said Figgis, turning to a desk to avoid further altercation. Here, turning the pages of the ledger with a shaking hand, he stood whilst Kennedy was being paid, remonstrated with, coaxed, and bustled out of the office by his fellow clerks, who had at first stood aloof from him, but subsequently thought it best to try to soothe his loud assertions that he was as good a man as any in the room, and had stood up to better than any upstart that had made too much money to remember his place. These remarks fulfilled their purpose by making Mr Figgis very angry. He was feared by his clerks, to whom he seldom spoke: his partner usually keeping the office in order, and doing the requisite bullying in all except flagrant cases of wrongdoing.

"Smith" shouted Figgis, turning to his junior bookkeeper.

"Sir?" replied Smith in a stifled voice, pausing in the act of putting on his office coat.

"Oh! Youre there at last, are you?"

"I am" said Smith, surrendering himself to a sudden impulse of intense rage. Silence fell on the office.

"You are, are you?" said Figgis. "Perhaps you will remember that the hour here is half-past nine. If that doesnt suit you, you can leave."

Smith made no reply, but deliberately began to divest himself of the office coat. A thrill passed through the staff as they watched him. Figgis, though a burly and self-confident man, could not help feeling relieved when, to the disappointment of the clerks, it became apparent that Smith had only removed the coat to make room for that which he wore in the street. Having made the exchange, he said politely, in reply to Figgis's last remark,

"Your terms do *not* suit me, sir. I will leave."

"Please yourself" said Figgis contemptuously, as, after a pause of incredulous astonishment, he turned to the ledger again. Smith placed the key of his desk on a table, and walked out, addressing a parting "Good morning, gentlemen," to the staff as he did so. Outside, he laughed to himself in a transport of joy, feeling that he had made his exit with dignity. As he descended the stairs he met old Mr Simms, who was returning to the upper storey without having witnessed what had passed.

"Goodbye, Mr Simms" said Smith jubilantly.

"What d'ye mean?"

"It means" said Smith with a flourish of his arm, "that I have trodden on that arch scoundrel, that personification of all that is sordid, that incarnate offence against the loveliness of high art, Figgis, the carpet fiend, to whose depravity I have too long pandered."

"Stop, stop!" said Simms. "You really musnt talk like that. You havnt done anything wrong in earnest, have you?"

"Wrong! Certainly not" said Smith. "To express myself vulgarly, Mr Simms, I have given Figgis and Weaver the sack. I want you to make up my office coat and the few things that are in my desk into a parcel, which I will call or send for whenever I can. The hair-brush with the mirror on the back I bequeath to you as a token of my esteem. You will excuse its being cracked."

"But what has happened?"

"Figgis had the audacity to speak disrespectfully to me; so of course I had no alternative but to walk out and leave his business to the ruin which my assistance has hitherto staved off."

"Dont be so ridiculous. I hope it wasnt on account of your being late."

"The very thing."

"But then youve been very foolish. You were in the wrong altogether. But I cant believe a word you say."

"On my word" said Smith seriously, "Mr Figgis spoke to me without the least provocation, in such a way that I took him at his word, and went off. You will hear all about it from the fellows upstairs. I dont like to wait in the place any longer now; so will you make up the parcel for me?"

"I will indeed" said Simms. "But for a young man of your talents to throw away your livelihood like that! Think a bit. What good have you done yourself? What have you got by your foolish ideas?"

"Liberty!" said Smith, shaking the hand of his senior. "No longer your fellow clerk, I bid you farewell in the proud capacity of your fellow man. My foot, Mr Simms, is on my native heath: my name, McGregor." With this rhodomontade, he ran downstairs, leaving Simms shaking his head.

At the street entrance, he was stopped by Mr Weaver, who seldom reached the office before ten.

"Hullo!" said Weaver: "going out already, Smith?"

"Yes, sir" replied Smith, who felt that to be respectful was now a luxury.

"How soon will you be back? Ive something for you to do."

"Never. I am leaving the office, Mr Weaver."

"Eh! What! Why?"

"I was unfortunately five minutes late this morning; and Mr Figgis spoke to me about it in such a manner that—at his suggestion—I left."

"Nonsense! Mr Figgis never meant anything of the sort. Pooh! Come back with me; and I will settle the whole affair."

"I am much obliged to you; but it is out of the question."

"Come, come! youre annoyed about it. We wouldnt wish to lose you that way. Mr Figgis was hasty; and he doesnt know as much about the office as I do. Five minutes late! Bosh!"

Smith felt almost in the toils again. "I have made up my mind" said he. "I assure you that nothing would induce me to return."

"Dont be in a hurry, young man" said Weaver with an air of wisdom. "You are hot on it at present. Just take a while to think; and then we'll see. Mr Figgis thinks a great deal of you; and so do I. I want you to run over to Mason's, and ask when Mr Brown will be in. They will tell you sooner than they would Kennedy. You can take your time. It will do if you let me know in an hour or so; and then we can talk matters over."

"Thank you, sir" said Smith. "I shall call at Mason's."

Twenty minutes later a clerk from Mason's waited on Mr Weaver to say that Mr Brown would be in during the afternoon. He added that Mr Smith had requested that the message might be sent, as he was not returning to the office himself.

Meanwhile Smith was striding past Temple Bar, free. He pitied the lawyers' clerks who hurried past as they might have pitied him had they known his plight. The streets seemed gay to him; and the sunlight and bustle of the Strand harmonized with the hopefulness and energy with which he faced the future.

In this exultation he, walking by the riverside route to his lodging, arrived at Westminster. It was long since he had been in the Abbey. As a clerk, bound to return next day to his ledger, he had never cared to visit it. Now, being free and happy, he entered, and trod the aisles with the old religious sense of their peace, but without the old constraint in which the restful calm of prostration before eternal goodness was marred by the consciousness of discharging an incomprehensible duty in a suit of clothes reserved for the occasion. As a man far removed from past ages finds a romance in history of which the persons in that history had in their time no sense, Smith could breathe the atmosphere of the cloister with an appreciation impossible to those whom it still overawed. A discerning observer might have marked him by his hushed step, impressed bearing, and reflective calm, as a confirmed freethinker very happy.

He wandered thus for about an hour, avoiding the portions of the building set apart for commercial purposes. At length his revery lightened; his seclusion from the bustle of the world without became less complete; and he yawned. Then, feeling that he might add the past hour to his small stock of happy memories, he left the Abbey, and returned to Westminster Bridge, where he went on board a penny steamboat.

As he sailed down the river, he, for the first time since his defiance of Figgis, felt a shadow creeping over his spirits. The boat had scarcely passed Lambeth Palace when he sat down and set himself to the task of thinking out his future. He began by carefully stating his case as it stood. He was out of employment. He had saved no money. He could not live on his inheritance of forty pounds a year. He was a competent clerk. He had a good character; but Figgis might refuse to bear witness to it. This, however, troubled him but little; for he was resolved that only in the most desperate extremity would he again work at a ledger. As he had no experience of any other lucrative occupation, no alternative presented itself to his mind save to live on pease pudding and lentil soup at the rate of sixpence a day until some suitable chance should offer itself. He thought once or twice of the stage, and beguiled some moments with a vision of himself attired in a fur-edged coat and hessian boots singing The Heart Bowed Down to an enraptured audience. He thought of teaching, but was diffident of his knowledge and of his power of commanding respect. He thought of going to sea, and even of sweeping a crossing. At last, disgusted with his common sense, which condemned these fancies, but did not prevent their occurring to him, he determined to think no more of the matter until the morrow, when he could read the advertisement sheet of The Times. He knew that he could as easily look at the paper at once; but a spirit of procrastination induced him to put it off in order to be free from business for at least one day.

As he approached his lodging, he recollected his interference in the quarrel of the Tillys, which had been temporarily effaced by the excitement of the morning. As he thought of his reluctance to meet Mrs Tilly that morning, he resolved to give no further quarter to such squeamishness. Accordingly, his first proceeding on entering his apartment was to ring the bell. He was at no loss for an excuse to do so; for the room was in disorder, it being the landlady's custom not to clean it until the day was well advanced. Mrs Tilly presently appeared, in garments suited to the occupation of scrubbing, and having her head tied up with a handkerchief. She looked ill, and evidently viewed her lodger's unexpectedly early return with uneasiness.

"I merely wished to let you know that I was home for the day, Mrs Tilly" said Smith. "I would like you to finish my room as soon as convenient."

"Yes, sir" said Mrs Tilly weakly. "I would have had it ready; only I never thought you would be in. Your bedroom is quite ready, sir."

To his bedroom Smith retired until Mrs Tilly had finished her task. He waited for her to go before he came out, but hearing her linger and cough once or twice, he concluded that she desired to speak further with him. So he rejoined her.

"Is there anything else, sir?" said Mrs Tilly, fidgeting with her duster.

"I suppose there is" thought Smith, "or you would not stand there disturbing my soul." But he only said, "Nothing, thank you, Mrs Tilly."

"I hope" began Mrs Tilly with much hesitation, "you wont mind what passed last night, Mr Smith."

"Oh, it's of no consequence at all. Pray dont trouble yourself about it." He had no sooner said this than he began to doubt whether it was not rather a flippant dismissal of the breaking of a woman's head.

"It's not so much what William said" said Mrs Tilly; "for I'm sure you wouldnt hold him to account and he not knowing what he was doing or saying; but I'm afraid that in my worry I may have spoke unbecoming-like to you, that should have been only too thankful for your kindness to me and your forbearance to him."

Smith protested that he quite understood her. Her mention of his forbearance to her husband made him blush; for he now remembered for the first time that, according to convention, he should have revenged by a knockdown blow the ruffianism which had led Mr Tilly to lay a saucepan on a woman save in the way of kindness.

"I dont know what came over him last night" she said. "He has been as steady as a man could be ever since Christmas. You musnt think from what passed that William's a bad man. Very far from it, sir. When he's himself, he wouldnt hurt a fly; and he never raised his hand to me before last night. It was my fault to come in his way, and he in such a state, poor fellow. If it wasnt for the drink, no one could say a word against him on any score."

"I hope, for your sake, that he will keep from it in future."

"I hope so, indeed. I wouldnt mind so much" said Mrs Tilly

with a stifled sob, "only for the child. I wish the government would shut up them wicked public houses, and keep honest men, that would never unhappify their homes without them, from temptation. I never had a policeman in my house before."

"I should perhaps tell you, Mrs Tilly, that I did not send for him."

"I know it well, sir; and I'm sure I beg your pardon again for what I said. The girl told me how it was. To think that I should have spoke to you—"

"Pray say no more about it. I hope your hurt is not painful."

"Oh no, sir" replied Mrs Tilly hastily. "It's nothing at all. Indeed it was more an accident, as one may say, than anything else. I was took aback at first; but it was nothing to signify, I assure you. I'm detaining you from your books, Mr Smith, I see. Thank you, sir." With these words, Mrs Tilly, who evidently desired to avoid discussing the injury to her head, left the room.

Smith spent the ensuing hours in looking through his boxes; burning a few useless letters; reading old scraps of poetry, some of which suggested to him the idea of obtaining employment with Madame Pertoldi as a footman; and calculating whether the thirty-seven shillings and sixpence he had left would last him until he received his next quarter's interest. At last this idleness made him hungry; and, as his usual dinner hour was past, he went out to a neighboring restaurant, where he dined. This done, he was at a loss for some occupation, and for a moment felt that he could willingly amuse himself at posting up a column of Figgis's ledger if the firm would consent to treat him as an independent amateur. At last he went for a walk. As he passed from Beaufort Street into the Fulham Road, his attention was attracted by a vehicle without windows, with large plumes of black feathers stuck into the roof. It was drawn by four long-tailed black horses draped in black, each horse having a plume of black feathers fixed between its ears. The color of the animals, and the beady glitter of their eyes, heightened the grotesque effect of their accoutrement. The driver, a hard-featured, tall man, was attired in Wellington boots and a long-skirted black coat, which seemed to have been exposed to many showers. From his hat flowed a long scarf of crape which imparted a degree of eccentricity to his otherwise grave aspect. On each side of the vehicle, which contained a corpse rolled up in lead, there walked six men dressed in black, with white ties, and append-ages to their hats similar to that worn by the driver. Each man carried a black staff tipped with brass. Behind these came a coach with a black hammercloth, driven by a coachman resembling the driver of the first vehicle. It was occupied by four persons whose sad countenances had a strange appearance in the fantastic pageant of which they formed a part. Smith had seen many such funerals before; but custom had rendered him as indifferent to them as to the contents of a butcher's shop. Judging that the destination of this one was Brompton cemetery, and never having visited that place, he resolved to proceed thither. He soon outstripped the slow march of the hearse, and had left it at some distance behind when he reached the cemetery.

Here, strolling through a multitude of tombs, he amused him-self by reading the inscriptions, which seldom went beyond mere statement of fact into verse or quotation without becoming either trite or funny; and the latter quality was not lost on Smith, who found his sense of the ludicrous unusually stimulated. He marked, with melancholy irony, the grandeur of the monuments which were the most emphatic in their graven declarations that the thing beneath was only a cast skin whose assimilation by a host of worms was of no consequence. He also observed that many of the tombs were those of persons whose eternal welfare was spoken of in their epitaphs as an ascertained fact; and that all the graves which were decorated with fresh flowers bore recent dates. When he had passed the chapel, he arrived in the midst of an open space sur-rounded by catacombs, to the gates of which flights of stone steps descended at intervals. Smith went down to one of these gates, and peered through the bars. He found nothing except a strange smell, a whitewashed shelf on which were laid some dirty coffins, and a few rotten wreaths of so-called *immortelles*. After gazing at these coffins with the curiosity which no other description of rubbish receptacle can inspire, he returned, somewhat disgusted, to the surface of the cemetery, and pursued his walk. Occasionally a clergyman with surplice, book, and umbrella, hurried across his path. Turning into a side path to avoid a funeral, he came upon a woman clad in mourning, who knelt by a grave, tending some flowers which had been planted on it. Smith recoiled. Not only did his delicacy warn him not to intrude on the scene, but a perverse inclination to laugh came upon him as he conceived the idea of the transmutation of the corpse through hideous stages of decomposition into the very flowers she was handling with such solicitude. At some distance he saw a workman digging, watched by an old gentleman with long white hair. The two seemed to be exchanging some remarks; and Smith, thinking of Hamlet and the gravedigger, strolled towards them, hoping to overhear some of their conversation.

"People are always buried in leaden coffins here, my friend: are they not?" said the old gentlemen.

"Them as can afford to buy em is" replied the workman. "Them as cant is run into shells."

"What becomes of the shells?"

"They rots and busts up."

"Dear me!" said the gentleman. "I believe a body never decays in a leaden coffin."

"Dont they?" said the digger sulkily. "It's there they *does* decay. They blows the coffins hout like barrels."

"How very interesting! What do you do with them then?"

"Drills a hole into em, and lets the gas fiz out."

"The gas! God bless us!"

"Aye, the gas" said the gravedigger. "Ive knowed a man take to his bed an' die from gettin a breath of it. I should 'a thought the old rip wot owned the coffin had done arm enough to workin men in his lifetime, without blastin em wen e was dead."

The old gentleman looked at his informant with an air of discomfiture, and walked away. Smith hastened towards the nearest gate of the cemetery. He fancied that the air was heavy and tainted, and that the rain on the grass was a dank sweat. Oppressed and nauseated, he walked as quickly as he could until he escaped into

the old Brompton Road, where, as soon as he had left the cemetery at a distance behind, he ventured at last to breathe freely.[1]

[1] In 1878 this scene was something more than a description of the
macabre side of a young man's fancy. It was a plea for cremation,
which was then a much more controversial subject than it is now. And
it was a repleading of Dickens's protest against the grotesque mum-
meries of the old-fashioned funerals.

# CHAPTER VIII

Next morning Smith rose at his usual hour, and, having dressed himself carefully so as to be ready to reply in person to any advertisement, went out and purchased a copy of The Times. The morning was fine; and instead of returning home with the paper, he carried it to Kensington Gardens, and seated himself in an iron chair which he found pleasantly situated in one of the vistas which stretch from the round pond to the Long Water. For this accommodation he was presently compelled to disburse a penny by a morose man with a money-bag. On the retirement of the official, Smith opened his paper, and glanced over it in search of advertisements. In doing this, his attention was arrested by a paragraph with an interesting heading. He read the paragraph, and then glanced at a couple of articles. Eventually he read all the news without having looked at a single advertisement; and when he had finished, he felt inclined to take a walk round the park and postpone business for another day. But he roused himself with a shake, and set to work. The first advertisement that met his eye was:

"Wanted, a secretary. Call for two days at 300 Queen's Gate, South Kensington, before 12 noon."

This announcement gave Smith a new idea. Why not be a secretary? Then he began to doubt. Was a secretary not at the same disadvantage with a footman, as a governess with a housemaid? Was not the servant of a public firm more independent than the servant of a private family? But Smith argued against himself in vain; for he had, though he did not know it, decided in favor of the secretaryship at the first thought. It promised a scope for the display of individuality which was forbidden by bookkeeping. Queen's Gate was a more refined sphere than the City. This last consideration was decisive. Smith looked at his watch. It was half-past eleven. He trembled as he found himself close to the ordeal of a personal application for employment. But his spirits rose adventurously at the same time. He sprang to his feet; thumped himself on the chest with his fist; and started towards Queen's Gate at a great pace.

His ring at the door of No. 300 was answered after a long interval by a very un-English manservant in a red livery coat, but otherwise clad in grey tweed.

"I have called in answer to an advertisement in this morning's Times," said Smith.

The footman became grave, and thought for a moment. "Yes" he whispered confidentially. "Step inside; an' I'll tell the masther. You havnt a card about you now: have you?"

"I have" said Smith, producing one, and handing it to the manservant, thereby leaving himself in possession of ninety-nine out of the first hundred he had ever purchased.

"Thats all right" said the man, encouragingly. "Now do you sit down; and dont say a word til I come back." So saying, he went away with the card. In a few minutes he returned on tiptoe.

"Well?" said Smith, after a pause.

"Whisht!" said the man in a low voice. "His dawther's up wid him. Make yourself aisy: I'll bring you to him when he rings the bell. Youre in luck."

"How so?" said Smith.

"Theres been hundhreds an' 'thousan's here already afther the place before he was out o' bed. He isnt five minutes up from his breckhusht; an' youll have the furst chahnce. I wish you may git it; for it's been the divvle's own work openin the hall doore."

"Thank you" said Smith, who had some difficulty in understanding the man's accent, "I hope I will."

"It's a high fammley to get into" said the man impressively. "An' where may you come from, sir? Whisht, theres the bell! Come along; an' dont be afeerd."

Smith, who had turned pale at the sound of the bell, followed his conductor through a door covered with green baize, into a long corridor, at the end of which was a conservatory. As they entered the corridor, a young lady with black eyes and hair, pretty, but discontented looking, approached them from the other end. Her expression brightened as she perceived that the servant was followed by a man; and as they passed, Smith felt a slight thrill as the dark eyes furtively observed his person. This was succeeded by a feeling of indignation when, on the green doors closing behind the young lady, his conductor looked round at him and winked. Then they stopped; and the man knocked softly with his knuckles at a door near the conservatory.

"Come in" roared a voice.

"In wud you; and spake up to him" whispered the man, throwing the door wide open. Smith entered, and found himself in a large, untidy room, fitted as a library. Letters, newspapers, directories, blue-books, stationery, pens, paper clips, and spectacle cases, were littered together around a bespattered desk which stood on that end of the table which was nearest the window. The chairs were much the worse for wear; the corners of the room were occupied by portmanteaus, heaps of coats, and dusty boxes; a couple of plaster busts stood upon the book-cases; and behind the door was an assortment of sticks, umbrellas, fishing rods, and broken blind rollers. A large fire burnt in a carelessly polished grate. The floor had been imperfectly swept; and the globes on the gasalier were covered with dust. The disorder of the room, and the dull red color of the wall paper, gave it a dingy appearance, which detracted from the effect of its spaciousness.

Before the desk sat a grey-headed gentleman of about sixty years, with a puzzled impatient expression which, with the state of the apartment, led Smith to judge that he was unpunctual and untidy. He was a handsome, and when not stooping over his desk, an uprightly borne man of majestic stature and powerful frame. He was unshaven; and all of his dress that was visible was an old greatcoat, the unbuttoned collar of his nightshirt, and a pair of carpet slippers.

"Will you sit down; youll find a chair there" said he, as Smith entered. "Just one moment til I finish this."

Smith sat down, and watched him whilst he signed a letter, and looked about for a clear spot on which to leave his pen. Not finding one, he stuck it in the inkbottle. He next searched for a piece of blotting paper, and, after tossing about a great many letters, muttering all the while, found a torn and much used scrap. Then he took his pen again, and, having placed it in his mouth, began another search. At last he lost patience and exclaimed, with his teeth gripping the pen handle:

"Where the mischief have they put the envelopes?"

Smith, seeing a packet lying under a corner of the newspaper, ventured to hand it to him.

"Oh—ah! thank you, thank you" said he. "It's the most infernal thing to live in the house with untidy people. Not one o' them cares a dam where they pitch anything. Now," he resumed, after folding his letter and closing it: "the coast is clear. You came to see about the berth here, eh? How old are you?"

"A little more than nineteen" said Smith.

"That's very young" said the gentleman. "What school have you been at? Are you a university man?"

"I have been at business since I was sixteen."

"Oh!" said the gentleman. "Then perhaps it wouldnt be worth your while to come here. And what business were you at?"

Smith, a little ashamed of Figgis and Weaver's trade, explained his circumstances briefly.

"The fact is" said the gentleman, "Ive got a great deal of correspondence to get through; and what with one thing and another, and the infernal slovenliness and procrastination of everybody and everything in this house, it's more than I can manage by myself. I tried one young fellow here that used to write paragraphs for the sixpenny papers; but he was no use to me at all. Divil o' such a fool I ever saw in my life. Theres enough work to take up your whole day—your whole morning, anyhow."

"I can place the whole day at your disposal, sir" said Smith, "if necessary."

"Oh well then" said the gentleman, "I suppose it's all right."

"And what salary would I receive, sir?"

"Youre an Englishman, arnt you?" said the gentleman, laughing.

Smith admitted his nationality with a misgiving lest the gentleman, who was evidently an Irishman, should regard a Saxon secretary with envy and hatred.

"I thought so from the way you said that" said the gentleman.

"I'm Irish." Smith tried to look surprised. "Well: a hundred a year is what I usually give, eh?"

Smith, who had toiled in the city for little more than half this amount, felt a thrill of joy, which his business training warned him to conceal. But he scorned the admonition as a taint of the carpet warehouse, and said, "That will content me very well, sir."

"Suppose you just try how you like it for a week, or a month" said the gentleman. "How soon can you begin?"

"I can set to work now, sir, if you wish" said Smith, rather taken aback by this prompt way of concluding a transaction which had cost him three interviews, and many references, at Figgis and Weaver's.

"Well, is it a bargain?" said the gentleman.

"If you please, sir" said Smith. "But would you not wish to make some inquiries?"

The gentleman seemed worried. "Yes, I suppose so" said he. "You can just give me an address; and I'll see about it. I'm afraid I havnt time today exactly. Are you anything to the Smiths of Hackettstown?"

"No" said Smith. "I dont belong to any particular family. Smith is a very common name in England."

The gentleman grinned at this attempt to enlighten his Irish ignorance, and said, "Well, suppose we get to work. God bless my soul, the mornings run away before you know where you are. While I think of it, let me tell you theres one thing I will expect from you always; and that is tidiness. When youre as old as I am, youll know the value of it. Believe me, Smith: if a man were to live as long as Methusalem, he wouldnt have time enough to afford to be untidy. Now let us have no more talking, but fire away at once."

"What shall I begin with, sir?" said Smith, putting aside his hat.

"Gad" said the gentleman, scratching his head, "I dont know exactly yet. Just hold on a minute; and we'll get to rights presently."

"If you will allow me" said Smith, "I think I could occupy myself arranging some of these papers."

"Aye, indeed: so you might" said the gentleman. "But be very careful about them. I like to have them all ready to hand; and if you think there is any chance of your putting them astray, youd better not touch them."

Smith promised to be careful, and began to collect the letters which bore that day's postmark. They were addressed to Foley Woodward, Esquire, M.P. He then set aside from the litter a supply of stationery and stamps; so that when he saw the old gentleman looking about him, he was enabled to hand him what he required the moment he learned what it was, thereby soon convincing him that he had found a treasure in his new secretary. He also collected, endorsed, and arranged many old letters in alphabetical order. In less than an hour the table was in order.

"I think" he ventured to say, looking at a pile of prospectuses, old envelopes, and other useless papers, "that a waste-paper basket would be a great convenience here."

"So there is one, under the table. Here—eh?" The old gentleman paused as he looked down and saw that there was no basket. He uttered an imprecation, and began shouting "Hamlet" furiously. Smith, who had never met with this name off the stage, was surprised to see the man who had opened the door for him enter the room.

"Yes, sir?"

"Wheres the basket that was here under the table?"

"I don' know, sir."

"And why the dickens dont you know?" cried Mr Woodward, enraged at this reply. "Go and get it at once: do you hear?"

"That I maytnt sin" began Hamlet whiningly, coming a step nearer, "but I never seen—"

"Be off and get it" interrupted Mr Woodward. "Smith: hit him an infernal dig with the shovel, and send him flying out into the passage." The man, to the relief of Smith, fled without waiting for this order to be executed, and, after some delay, returned with a clothes basket, which seemed to have been just emptied of some clayey vegetable and hastily scrubbed with soap and water. This he deposited beneath the table, watching his master's movements meanwhile, as though he apprehended a sudden assault from him. When he was gone, Smith asked whether Hamlet was really his name.

"Quite a common name in some parts of Ireland, like your own here" said Woodward. "He's a Carlow man, though he comes of county Louth people, and a great blackguard. I'll astonish him some of these fine days."

"Then Hamlet is his surname?" said Smith.

"Yes, Cornelius Hamlet. [Here Hamlet reappeared.] Talk of a certain person! Well, what do you want now?"

"If you plaze, sir, Miss Izzabella sez youre goin out to dhrive in the phaytn wid her afther lunch; and she wants to know wont you come up and ate a pick furst."

"Tell her I'm too busy" said Woodward.

"But she bid me not come back widhout your honor" persisted the footman coaxingly. "Arra do, sir: come up an' have a bit. Whats the good o' killin yourself over thim ould letthers?"

"Very well, very well: tell her I'll be up in a minute" said Woodward resignedly.

"God bless yer honor!" replied Cornelius briskly, and retired.

"Well, certainly" thought Smith, who had expected to see the man discharged on the spot for his familiarity, "these Irish are most extraordinary people."

"I'm afraid I can do no more today" said Woodward. "I have to go and dress myself; and indeed I suppose youre in a hurry to get away yourself. So off with you."

"At what time shall I be with you tomorrow, sir?" said Smith.

"Come as soon after eleven as you can. I'm generally down here before twelve."

Smith began to feel some qualms about accepting a hundred a year on such easy terms. He suggested deferentially that he should come earlier; receive the day's letters; and answer some of them from such instructions as his patron might scribble on them in bed or at breakfast. He could also proceed with his task of endorsing the arrears of letters. Mr Woodward was astonished at the foresight and method shewn in these plans, and approved of them, warning the secretary at the same time not to attempt too much, as it was better to start with a little and keep it up than to be like a new broom, which only sweeps clean at first. He told him further not to mind putting up the papers, as the servants were instructed to leave everything exactly as they found it. Then, bidding him good day, he left the room.

Smith had taken up his hat, and was about to go, when Hamlet entered.

"Has he tuk you?" he said in an eager whisper.

Smith, desiring to maintain a distance between them, but not knowing how to do so, replied in the affirmative.

"Good luck t'ye" said Hamlet. "Shure he's no betther nor an owl' fool, God forgi' me. You can do what you like wid him if y'only kape your finger in his eye. The whole lot that was lookin for the place come back since; and aich o' them went off like an ass in a shower o' tundher when I tould them we was suited. Whisht! There he is tearin away at the owl' bell, bad luck to it." Here Hamlet hastily departed; and Smith left the house. In the hall he passed a tall man in evening dress. This was the servant who answered the house door after three o'clock in the afternoon, Cornelius Hamlet being too prone to the commission of social solecisms to be trusted with such a post in South Kensington at that hour.

Smith looked at his watch as he came out. It wanted a quarter of three.

"Well" he said to himself as he walked along, "for more than three mortal years have I toiled nine hours a day in a cheerless den amidst sordid money grubbers for a pound a week. Now for nearly twice that money, an unfortunate Irish gentleman is glad to get me to help him to do in an hour what usually takes him a day, and would take me, single-handed, about five minutes. My worthy Figgis, my excellent Weaver: I have not been a day out of employment; and I got my job precisely by that virtue of being late which you so signally failed to appreciate." He snapped his fingers gaily at his former employers, and proceeded eastward to get his dinner.

On his way back he felt so accustomed to the west end, that he almost bought a pair of gloves. He checked himself, however, and took a walk through Rotten Row instead, where he was gratified by seeing Mr Woodward drive past with his unsatisfied-looking daughter by his side. Smith was surprised to see how handsome a gentleman his employer was when his nightshirt, greatcoat, and carpet slippers were replaced by decent garments. He also wondered whether Miss Isabella had been at all struck by his own appearance that morning.

# CHAPTER IX

Miss Woodward had been a day absent from Perspective. She had gone up to London on Thursday afternoon; and now, at noon on Saturday, she was in her room at Mr Grosvenor's, putting aside the dress in which she had just travelled to Richmond. She was joined by her younger sister Clytie, who, after wandering about the room for some moments, said listlessly:

"Well?"

"Well?" said Isabella crossly, mimicking her sister.

"Oh" said Clytie, "I see we're amiable this morning." Isabella did not retort. At length Miss Clytie spoke again.

"Has the governor been making a fool of himself in any way since we left?"

"He has got a new secretary, a boy who was an acrobat or something."

"What do you mean by an acrobat?"

"He was either that or in a carpet shop, I dont exactly know which. I know he had something to do with carpets. Papa is delighted with him because he is tidy. I suppose he used to have to roll up everything when the shop was shut. Dear me! I wish it was time to dress for dinner."

"But did you see him? Is he nice?"

Isabella pouted and shrugged her shoulders. "I scarcely saw him. He's just the sort of creature you would expect to be very tidy. He is more like two yards of tape than anything else. However, he will do very well for papa to swear at when his letters are lost."

"What's his name?"

"What should his name be? Smith, of course. He looks such a prig! Cornelius says he's a boyoh, and puts his comether on the masther finely. The servants are all gone to the very devil. I never saw the house in such a state."

"And how old is the carpet man?"

"Oh, I dont know. For goodness' sake dont bother me about

him. He looks twenty. Now dont sit down on my sealskin, you little fool, you."

"You neednt be afraid, Bella: I'm not going to. By the bye, what have you done to set Cyril Scott's tongue against you of late?"

"Clytie!"

"Dont get into a passion, my dear. You would have needed all your temper if you had heard what he said last evening in the porch. What a spiteful little wretch he is!"

"I dont care what he said about me; but your brutal vulgarity is past bearing. I wonder why it is that you think the fact of our being sisters a sufficient excuse for perpetual squabbling. I wish you would either speak civilly or hold your tongue."

"Indeed" said Clytie. "You are so very charming always yourself, I suppose. Who began snapping, I should like to know?"

"You may as well tell me what Cyril Scott said about me" said Isabella after a pause. "I am dying to hear it because it is something nasty; and you are dying to tell it to me for the same reason."

"We are becoming philosophical" said Clytie, with affected gravity. "Yesterday evening I was sitting on the terrace. My chair was against the house, and quite close to the door. Scott and the great Mogul came into the porch; and after looking to see whether they were alone everywhere except under their noses—just like fools of men—they began to chat. Scott wanted to talk about his pictures; and I think Grosvenor was sick of them; for he kept dodging back to the subject of Scott himself, and at last asked him whether he ever thought of settling. Men always talk of settling instead of marrying, by way of muffling the clank of the chain."

"Pray go on, and dont waste your clever little sayings on me" said Isabella impatiently. "Of course you listened."

"Of course; and so would you if you had been in my place. Then Grosvenor said in his jolly-good-fellow, patronizing way, 'Come, my dear boy: theres poor Belle Woodward throwing herself at your head. She would make your house the fashion in a week; and her father will come down handsomely if you shew him you can do without his money. Besides, he is an Irishman; and he will think more of you for coming of a Protestant family than for being the cleverest man of the day in your own line.' There was a pause; and I could *hear* Scott's nose twisting up. 'I tell you, Scott, that you might do worse' said Grosvenor. 'Is she not pretty?' Scott gave a snort. 'Clever?' He gave a louder snort. 'A good girl?' He snorted so dreadfully then that he had to use his handkerchief. 'No doubt her husband will be a very fortunate man' said he. You know the way he says things that he means to be cutting. 'You dont mind her being a Catholic, surely?' said the great Mogul. 'For the matter of that' says Cyril—conceited little beast!—'I have no doubt she would turn fire-worshipper if I made a point of it.' Then he thought that sounded too complacent; and he tacked on a saving clause, 'that is, if she really honors me as much as you say, which I am loth to believe.' I think Grosvenor suspected that Scott was only putting him off, for he went on to say, 'But on your honor, Cyril, if an old friend may ask'—old friend, indeed!—'dont you care a little for her?' Scott swelled like a turkey at this. 'What! I!' said he, 'care for Isabella Woodward, a made-up creature of stays and heels, a flirt, who wants me to save her from a sixth unsuccessful season, an *amateur*!' You should have heard him spit out that word *amateur*. It was so bad that I was afraid to listen any more, for fear they would say something so outrageous that I could not very comfortably confuse them by letting them know that they were overheard. So I got up at once, and walked straight in like a clap of thunder. You should have seen their faces! When they recovered themselves Grosvenor coughed and tried to look amiable. Scott scowled at me as if he would have liked to dash my head on the terrace flags. Then he looked pointedly at my chair, and went off with himself. The great Mogul came in with me like a lamb, hoping I was not chilled, and that I had not wet my feet in the grass. That was to make believe that he thought I had come in from the lawn. But they know that I overheard them as well as I know it myself; and I hope they feel happy."

"I suppose" said Isabella in a hard voice, "this is not a pack of lies. Or is it?"

"You can believe it or not, exactly as you please. There is that fool Ernest dawdling about the lawn. I will make him bribe the gardener to steal me a camellia. I love making a mean man's purse bleed."

For some time after Clytie's departure, Isabella was conscious of nothing but pain; and the first thought that defined itself was a wish that she had heard the conversation herself. There would have been some poetry in her despair, she thought, had she heard the words pronounced by his voice; some drama in appearing before him and passing on with a silent reproach in her white face. (In moments of excitement she was apt to forget that the bloom of her complexion was due to appliances which were not affected by her emotions.) But to receive the insult through a younger sister, who did not disguise her enjoyment of it, and whose mean espial had probably seemed to the artist a natural outcome of her domestic associations, was not only painful, but humiliating; and at that moment Isabella hated her sister with such intensity that only her superstitious fears withheld her from praying that some unspeakable calamity might overtake her. Even in her listless moods, she was accustomed to regard Clytie as her natural enemy. As to Grosvenor and Scott, she resolved never to meet them again, but rather to quit the house at once without taking leave of her host. Then, abandoning this project as certain to expose herself alone to ridicule, she thought of cutting Cyril Scott pointedly, so as to inform all the world (Queen's Gate, Brighton, Perspective, and a few other places) that the artist had deceived himself in supposing that she was willing to turn fire-worshipper for love of him. This plan she also rejected, lest he should revenge himself by publishing her provocation, which he would understand too well. As she brooded over his personal remarks, she began to suspect that some rival had been traducing her to him. How, she argued, could Cyril Scott, whom no one had ever seen in society four years ago, know that this was to be her sixth season? But she could not stifle the conviction that the artist had found her out by his common sense and her common reputation; and at last, wearied by her tormenting reflections, she looked at the mirror as a preliminary to joining the guests at luncheon. She saw her state of mind so faithfully reflected in her face, that she attempted to improve her appearance with rouge. On this occasion, as she possessed little skill and less patience, the artifice was too apparent; and after washing the color off, she contemplated her white face and wistful black eyes in despair. Then, perceiving suddenly how she might turn these to account, she put on a lace-trimmed white muslin dress with hanging sleeves, and caused her maid to procure a lily, which she placed in her bosom. In this attire she descended to the hall with slow steps, and a tristful expression. The first person she encountered was Cyril Scott, whose complexion deepened to brick red as he turned hastily aside into the music room, pretending not to have seen her.

Since the night before, when Scott had discovered, by the position of Clytie's chair on the terrace, that his words had been overheard, and were likely to be repeated to Isabella, his mind had misgiven him that she was not so bad as he had represented her to be. If that were so, then he had slandered her, and, by running away from her as he had just done, had acknowledged his guilt. This he could not bear; for he had no magnanimity, although his impulsive generosity often made him perform actions of which the more rational virtue would have stopped short. Nevertheless he was ashamed of having retailed vulgar gossip concerning her to Grosvenor, a man whom he did not respect; and he determined to return and seek her out, in order to soften by some small attentions the harshness which had called that sorrowful expression into her eyes, if he could do so without appearing to be sneaking back into her favor. Accordingly, he went to the terrace, where he saw her among a group of young people, for whose amusement a painter was making caricatures. As Scott approached, she, without seeming to see him, left the group, walked slowly to a lonely part of the terrace, where she leaned on the balustrade and looked sadly at the landscape. He followed her; but when she looked round at him, wincing slightly as she did so, he felt so uncomfortable that he wished himself back again in the hall, and wondered that he had not had the sense to see that the case was of a nature to make softening impossible, and explanation an insult.

"Lovely afternoon, is it not?" said he at last.

Miss Woodward bit her nether lip, and did not answer. Scott was alarmed. If she were going to cut him, his position was very awkward.

"Perhaps you dont want me to talk to you" he said bluntly.

"Not at all" said she, looking languidly at him.

"Making studies for future sketches, perhaps" said he, indicating the landscape with a nod.

"No" said she. "I have done with painting."

"I hope you have not been discouraged by me."

"Not discouraged, but convinced. I believe your opinion was a candid one, although I exposed myself to an intruder's welcome in asking for it."

"That is the worst of criticizing a lady" said Scott. "You believe, of course, that what I said to you as a fellow student [he forced this word out with some difficulty] was the expression of my personal feeling towards you."

"Oh dear, no!" replied Miss Woodward. "Your personal feeling is always expressed too freely and forcibly for its objects to have any excuse for confounding it with your artistic sympathies."

"Humph!" thought Scott. He added, aloud, with affected gaiety, "I am afraid I often say more in a day than I will stand to in a year. I hope you dont keep account of all my outbursts."

"I do not keep account of what you say at all, Mr Scott, when I can help it. If some of your remarks stick, it is not my fault."

"I must guard my tongue, in that case."

"It matters little. When a thing is thought, it is better—or at least more honestly—said as well."

"Sometimes people say what they dont think. At least I often do, when I am out of sorts."

"Yes, Mr Scott, but that is in the presence of those of whom we speak. When they are absent we are more sincere."

"Not unless we are time-serving hypocrites" said he severely.

Miss Woodward, startled from her sorrowful composure by this impudent evasion, cast an indignant look at him, and resumed her contemplation of the landscape in silence.

"Is Mr Woodward coming down tomorrow?" said the artist, after a pause.

"He is coming tonight."

"He is quite well, I hope."

"Thank you. Quite well."

"Grosvenor was saying yesterday that he expected to break up tomorrow with a larger gathering than that of Easter Sunday."

"Yes. I was not here yesterday; but Clytie told me what passed in my absence!"

"It will be a pleasant change for Mr Woodward: he so seldom leaves town."

"Very."

"I say, Scott" interrupted Ernest, appearing suddenly behind them with Clytie: "youre losing all the fun."

"Yes, indeed" said Clytie. "We have been caricaturing both of you for the last half hour as Romeo and Juliet on the balcony."

"Porson has made no end of a sketch of you, Cyril" said Ernest. "And he has hit off Miss Woodward's back in two strokes."

"The one of Mr Scott is the best" said Clytie. "The nose is so like. And the costume is the same as the Troubadour's in the Pampeluna picture."

"Indeed" said Cyril. "It is an honor to be selected as lay figure by Porson. I am glad his wardrobe and property room are getting exhausted. It may suggest to him the advisability of studying nature at last." So saying, he left the terrace, and crossed the lawn in the direction of the gate. Isabella remained, and refused to look at the sketch until it was placed in her hands by the artist, who presented it to her with mock solemnity as a memento of the occasion. She received it with a show of good humor, in deference to Mr Porson's age and celebrity. At that moment she secretly concurred in the opinion which had often been expressed in her hearing with reference to him, that a man who disliked talking about art; romped with children when any were present; and refused to read modern poetry, could not be a truly great painter.

# CHAPTER X

CYRIL SCOTT, after quitting the terrace, went out upon the high-road, and walked to the town of Richmond to make some purchases. Within a short distance of the bridge, he passed by a confectioner's window, at which, from a habit which had survived his taste for sweetmeats, he looked idly. His attention was thus led to a new brass plate on a door next the shop, with the inscription, MISS RUSSELL, MILLINER AND DRESSMAKER. The artist stopped, and crossed the street in order to obtain a view of the first-floor windows. Nothing was to be seen there but white curtains and a figure which stirred Scott's pulses until, on scrutiny, he saw that it terminated headlessly in a brass collar. He recrossed the street, half resolving to ring the bell and pay the dressmaker a visit under pretext of buying a bonnet. Whilst he hesitated, the door opened; and Miss Russell, in a black costume of more ornate design than the drab dress she had worn at their first meeting, appeared on the threshold. For some seconds they stood motionless, startled at coming upon one another unexpectedly.

"How do you do, Miss Russell?" said he, recovering himself. "I stopped here, seeing your name on the door; and in an instant you popped out and took my breath away."

"I beg your pardon, I am sure, Mr Scott" replied Harriet a little humorously, but quietly. "Good evening." She shut the door; bowed to him; and walked quickly away. As he stood gaping after her, it occurred to him that she might be going to visit her aunt; and he calculated that by taking another way, and making good speed, he could easily rejoin her outside the town, and walk with her thence to Perspective. But his tactics were baffled by his ignorance of the terrain; and at the end of three minutes he found himself back in the same street. There was now nothing for it but either to relinquish his intention or frankly run after Harriet. He decided to run; and his race attracted much attention. But neither jeers and cheers, nor the indignity of scampering in chase of a dressmaker, delayed him; and when he reached the road which led to Perspective, Harriet, although a fast walker, was only a little distance ahead.

"It seems" said he, as he overtook her, panting, "that we are both going in the same direction."

"I am going to my aunt, Mr Scott" said she, her grave manner rebuking him. "You seem to have run all the way from Richmond."

Scott pretended to consider this a joke. "I had to walk very fast to overtake you when I caught sight of you" he gasped; "and it has put me a little out of breath."

Harriet knew that he had chased her in the public eye. Had she been displeased, he would have had cause to repent it. As it was, she walked demurely on, accepting his company with perfect self-possession.

"I have been looking for you in the galleries every morning on the chance of getting some more ideas on art from you" said he.

"It was very foolish of me to talk as I did without knowing who you were."

"Oh!" said he, noting for the first time that she had used his name at their encounter outside the confectioner's. "So you did not know that I was the affected dauber you were so hard on. I thought you knew very well all the time, and were giving me a sort of left-handed lecture on my sins."

"Then you had no right to think my manners were so bad. I would not do such a thing; and I think you should have told me who you were" said Harriet seriously, with her Scotch accent perceptible.

"Ha, ha!" cried Scott, "so that you might have told me what you didnt think of me! That would have been very sensible."

"I did not speak of you, but of your picture. And I would not have said what I did not think. I would have held my tongue."

"So much the worse for me by one honest opinion. And as I have not arrived at the stage of buying my own pictures, I am the only person you could disparage them to without injuring me."

"That is true" said Harriet, who could appreciate a commercial argument. "Still, I am very sorry."

"Listeners never hear any good of themselves, Miss Russell."

"That is the reason why they are so much disliked: they make those whom they overhear so uncomfortable."

"Then you dislike me?"

"Not at all" said Harriet, with a faint blush.

A suspicion that he was about to fall in love with the dressmaker silenced Scott for a time. Her last remark made the pause rather embarrassing to Harriet; but she shewed no sign of this, and walked steadily on. The artist looked stealthily at her, and involuntarily compared her with Miss Woodward.

"I think if we go round by the river, we will save a few minutes" he said presently. "Have you ever been that way?"

"Yes" replied Miss Russell. "It is a full quarter mile longer."

"The shortest way round is the longest way home, in that case" said Scott, discomfited, and wishing that she would not walk so fast.

"You seem to be in a desperate hurry" he said, at last.

"I am walking too fast for you" said Harriet, moderating her pace. "I am a good walker; and I forgot that I was not alone."

"I can walk as fast as you like. As I have inflicted my company on you, it is my business to keep up with you. I suppose it is because I dont forget that I am not alone that I fail to see the necessity for so much haste."

"Was it for the same reason that you wanted to take the long way round by the river?" said Harriet.

In spite of her quiet manner, the artist mistook this for coquetry, and replied, looking boldly into her eyes, "Of course it was."

"If I had known that, I would not have walked with you at all, Mr Scott" she said resolutely, but not coldly. "It is a difficulty to me, in my position, to have gentlemen like you speaking to me at all; but I cannot forbid them on pretence that they must be seeking me for the pleasure of my company."

"Humph!" said Scott, offended. "Indeed? It never occurred to me that there was any harm in speaking to you as I would to any other lady of my acquaintance."

"It ought to have" replied Harriet calmly.

"I am greatly indebted to you for your good opinion. You have an admirably delicate way of calling a man an intruder." To this she did not reply; and after walking for some distance, he had to renew the conversation.

"I understand then that you do not intend to speak to me any more."

"I cannot make you understand if you choose to be so quarrelsome" said Harriet, with some impatience.

"You completely misunderstand me: completely" said Scott, in a rage. "Quarrelling is a thing quite foreign to my character; although doubtless I have my defects. You are the first person who ever called me quarrelsome, or thought me so. You quarrelled with me without the slightest provocation."

"I did not quarrel with you at all" said Harriet, endeavoring to turn away his wrath with a soft answer.

"Of course I have nothing more to say. A lady can always silence a gentleman by contradicting him flatly."

"What do you expect me to do when you say such things?" said Harriet, roused by his aspersion of her politeness, to which her station made her sensitive. "You have lost your temper, Mr Scott; and you are trying to lay the blame on me."

"When you know me better, you will scarcely accuse me of losing my temper. I admit that I have naturally a dangerous temper; but I have also the will to control it. I made up my mind long ago to master it; and I have done so."

"Certainly, if this is one of your quiet moods, you must be very dangerous when you are angry."

Scott scowled at her; saw that an impulse to laugh had disturbed her former calm; was infected by it at the moment when he most desired to look severe; and in the ensuing struggle with his features, grinned so constrainedly that the dressmaker could hardly prevent herself from laughing outright. Thus they reached the gate of Perspective, at which stood a cab, from which the driver was sulkily allowing Cornelius Hamlet to pull down a portmanteau.

"Good evening" said Harriet, with a bow, and a blush at the smile which she could no longer restrain. She then passed quickly through the gate; and Scott, though still chafing, thought what a graceful bow and blush it was, and how different from the glances which had gained Miss Woodward so many admirers and so few suitors. Meanwhile the cabman grumbled from his box.

"Good enough for you to take it down yourself. You want the worth o your shillin, and somethink over."

"Musha, youd be kilt wud the weight of it, wouldnt you now, poor man?" retorted Hamlet. "It's a pity you didnt ax the masther to dhrive you on the box, and let you have your sleep inside."

"Calls himself a genleman, I spose" said the cabman indignantly, "an' gives a man his bare fare to a place where theres not a chance of a job back. Comes from the same shop as you do, dont he?"

"Very well for you to get it" shouted Cornelius. "Your betthers has been dhrove the lenth an' breath of Dublin for sixpence; an' the divil another ha'penny would I ha' given you to save your soul. G'alang" he added contemptuously as the driver flourished his whip at him and drove off.

"Hallo, Hamlet" said Scott: "is that you? Is Mr Woodward here?"

"Wh'then is that yourself, Misther Scott?" replied Hamlet. "The masther is gone up to the hall doore wud Miss Bella."

"How is he?" said Scott, lingering at the gate to avoid overtaking Miss Bella.

"Finely, sir, I thank you" said Hamlet, hoisting the portmanteau to his shoulder. "Long life t'yer honor" he continued, as Cyril helped him to lift it. "Sure it's a wary owl' thing to bring out for a clane shurt and a suit of black close."

"Why did you not make him drive you up to the house with it?" said Scott, walking along beside Cornelius.

"The Lord knows! Whin the masther seen Miss Bella waitin for him at the gate he got out an' ped the dhriver, lavin me wud the thrunk. He's only seen her wanst since Good Frida'; an' he was glad to walk up wud her acrass the grouns. He idolizes her, God bless her."

"Have you any daughters of your own, Hamlet?"

"What a fool I am! Not but what Miss Bella is a fine young slip, axin your pardn, sir. On'y she spens a power o money on dhress, an' thinks nothin o payin two poun tin for a pair o boots that she has to walk like a hin on a hot girdle in. Women is the divil, anyhow. Wan o them ud ruin a poor lad like me quick enough. I wondher is it round here I'll get to the back doore."

"Yes, to the right" said Scott, turning towards the terrace. "Goodnight."

"Goodnight; an' thank your honor."

There was at Perspective at this time one James or Jim Vesey, a landscape painter, who had cultivated a knack of painting ruins and moonlight until he had become celebrated for his views of Melrose and Muckross, of which he painted as many each year as the dealers would buy. His works were all alike, and were recognized without reference to a catalogue by frequenters of the galleries, to their self-satisfaction, and the advancement of his reputation. He was approaching his sixtieth year; and, being easy tempered, reconciled to the world, and able to make a sufficiency of money easily, he was a pleasant companion in an idle hour. He had been separated from his wife for many years, and was childless.

On Saturday night, the guests of Mr Grosvenor retired early. At midnight the hall was dimly lighted by a few lamps; the great central light having been extinguished. Now and then a group of men came from the smoking room[1] and ascended the staircase. The servants were yawning, and hinting in various little ways that they would be glad to go to bed.

Cyril Scott had been reading in the library. Finding the hall

[1] Neither Queen Victoria nor any other lady would in those days have tolerated men smoking all over the place. Even smoking rooms and smoking carriages were innovations; and the older ladies still expected their guests to smoke out-of-doors or up the kitchen chimney if they must indulge in so abominable a habit.

deserted, he went into the smoking room in search of society. He found Mr Vesey alone, seated in an armchair, with his legs on a stool, a tumbler full of grog on the table beside him, and a cigar in his mouth.

"Hallo" he said lazily, as Cyril entered. "Come and sit down. I want somebody to keep me company while I finish my cigar. They all seem to be in a deuce of a hurry to get to roost tonight."

Cyril sat down on a corner of the table.

"Well, my young friend" said Vesey: "whats the news with you? You should take to smoking. Have some whisky?"

"No, thank you" said Scott. "I want to find out your opinion about something. As it concerns matrimony, I have no experience to help me to an opinion of my own, I'm happy to say."

"Quite right" said Vesey. "But you dont mean it. You will buckle-to one of these days. I know the sort of fellow you are."

"Well, I have the more need of your opinion. Suppose an artist makes up his mind to marry! Has he any chance of getting on well with a woman who knows nothing about art, and takes no interest in it?"

"My dear boy: theres no such thing as a woman who knows anything about art, except one or two in the profession, from whom may the Lord deliver you, because two of a trade never agree, much less two of a fine art. So that narrows the question to whether you ought to marry a woman who will take an interest in your painting."

"Well, not myself in particular. Whether any fellow ought."

"Very well. We'll consider you only for the sake of argument. Now, I am a man of experience. I'll tell you my experience presently. But first, my advice to you is, never let your wife interfere with your business. Look at your city men, who are perhaps the best family men in England. Is there one of them who can stand his wife going to his office? Not one. Some of the young women try it: in fact, most of them do; but you wont find many civic matrons that have done it three times. It's the same in art. Keep your wife out of your studio, except when you want her to sit to you. And unless she's a very fine model, you will find a professional more comfortable to deal with, if your wife is not too much given to making unpleasantness about such things."

"Well, thank heaven I have nothing to do with models. I dont see the analogy between a city tradesman and an artist. Surely if a man had a proper wife—one who understood him—he would paint the better when she was beside him."

Vesey looked at Scott; shook his head; and took a drink. "I told you a minute ago" said he, "that I would tell you my experience; and I will. You know that I dont live with my wife. Did you ever meet her anywhere?"

"Yes. Somebody brought her to a private view of mine once."

"Come now: tell me honestly what you thought of her."

"I only spoke to her for a short time. I really dont know."

"Come! Out with it! You thought something or other."

"I thought her a very nice good sort of woman. She seemed to take a great interest in art; but she didnt know much about it."

"There!" said Vesey, slapping the table: "thats what she is. She's the best of women, excellently brought up, virtuous, resolved to do her duty, and versed in Shakespear and the musical glasses. She ought to have married a parson, or a sheriff. I wish she hadnt married me."

"Why did *you* marry *her*?" said Scott, laughing.

"I dont know. My case was a common one. I remember two nice girls who would have taken me; but like most young men, I was cautious; went further; and fared worse. At last I got tired of having no home; and so I resolved to settle down before it was too late. Emily happened to be there to my hand: a good girl, and not bad looking; so I thought I couldnt do better. So much for a prudent marriage! By Jove, Cyril, that woman was a wife, and no mistake! I wanted to have a run in Paris for the honeymoon; but she said she would prefer going to a quiet seaside place; and I believed her, and gave in. She really wanted to go on the Continent, where she had never been; but she thought the seaside place would be pleasanter for me, because it was cheap and I could sketch there. So *she* gave in. She could tell lies by the dozen in the way of duty and self-sacrifice. We both went down

to this infernal place, pretending that we liked it beyond anything. There was no one to stand between us but a bathing man;
and our living cost us less than a pound a week. In three days
the sound of her voice made me sick. Then she set upon me for
neglecting my work. She thought it was her duty to encourage
me to persevere; and she believed I was only kept from it by the
fancy that she would consider herself neglected. I felt at that time
as if I could never handle a brush again; but anything was better
than sitting staring at her or tramping about the place with her
beside me. So I arranged sketching excursions; and she came
with me. She did indeed, my boy; for I couldnt very well refuse
to let her; and she was determined to take an interest in my work.
I sketched the whole place up hill and down dale: she sitting by
me all the time. I shall never forget her sticking to her duty,
striving to understand me, and driving me out of my wits with
her little bits of encouragement. When I could bear it no longer,
I said my paints were used up, and gave her all the sketches to
keep, which she does still, I believe, most religiously. She
wouldnt have me drop my work though, and self-denyingly let
me go up to London by myself to buy colors. She said if she
came, I would have to go second class, and that she would rather
stay where she was. I promised to be back next day; and she had
a little surprise of a supper ready for me. My heart bled for the
poor woman; but I couldnt go down and face her again; so, after
making a roaring week of it, and putting her off one way or
another until she wrote to me that I had spent more than her fare
to London in telegrams, I told her to come up; and we went into
lodgings in Torrington Square. By that time her enthusiasm had
cooled; but she had got a high opinion of her eye for a picture.
So she took to lecturing me, sustaining me, keeping me up to
the mark and so forth. We managed to pull along for a few years,
not knowing any better, poor fools that we were. Had I been as
wise as I am now, I wouldnt have held out two days. She *would*
interfere. The more I threw off the mask, the more she stuck to
me, thinking it was all her own fault in not making herself a sympathetic companion. I felt my temper and digestion getting worse

every day. Sometimes, when I lay on the sofa after dinner pretending to take a nap to keep her from talking to me, I used to think of the matches I might have made but for my prudence; and when she moved about as quietly as she could for fear of waking me, I used to wish that I had married a housemaid, or some badly brought up woman that didnt know what duty was. The worst was that she had no suspicion of what I felt, because I was as amiable with her as I could: indeed, she gave me no excuse; for she was determined on principle to believe all my incredible excuses for avoiding her. Consequently I was a long time bringing myself to let her know that I had had enough of her and her solicitude. I was afraid it would kill her, unless she was prepared. That tells you what an ass I was. Well, when I could stand no more of it, I went to a solicitor, and told him the state of affairs. He took it quite coolly, and said that he supposed I did not intend to return home. When I mentioned my fears about the effect a sudden break-up would have on her, I saw a look in his eye that set me thinking. He pointed out to me that if I did not care to face the disclosure, I could go back and live with her; but if it was to be made, it might as well be done then as thereafter; and he strongly advised me to leave the transaction in the hands of a professional man. I took the hint, and I never went back. The solicitor arranged the whole matter. How she took it I dont know; for I never could get anything out of him but a 'hmm,' and a shrug. However, Ive no doubt she soon found out that it was a relief; and whenever I have seen her since, she has always looked uncommonly well!"

"Do you speak to each other, when you meet?"

"I generally dart into a shop or down a side street when I see her coming; but I was once introduced to her at an At Home by a lady who thought I was a widower. On that occasion we talked a little about the weather; and I left her, I suspect, wondering how she had ever cared much about me; for I had grown out of my good looks. We not only talked like strangers, but I really felt as much so as if she had been a casual acquaintance whom I had not seen for ten years. What do you think of that story?"

Scott, puzzled by the question, only smiled.

"It has a moral that applies to your question" said Vesey; "and I tell it to you because you are a young man, and often think about marrying. Come, my young friend! you neednt deny it: every man who is not a fool has to think which state he will elect to live in. I also tell you because I like people to know the true reason of my separation, to prevent them from imagining worse ones. However, that doesnt concern you. What *does* concern you, is the lesson you may learn from my experience on the very point that has posed you. Marry a woman who is just able to give you, when you ask her for it, a rational opinion of any picture which you havnt time to go and see. Marry a woman who has the sense to know that she is the wife of the man, and not of the artist, and who keeps in her place accordingly. But dont marry a devoted helpmeet like Emily; because you may not be able to get rid of her so easily as I was. Remember, my boy, that where there are children, a separation cant be managed off-hand."

"It's very easy to say, 'Marry this,' and 'Dont marry that'; but the most knowing men make mistakes in matrimony."

"Of course they do. And why? Because a man only learns how to select a wife by experience. We are not very fond of talking about art to critics, because, between ourselves, the critics sometimes shut us up; and many of them—give the devil his due, Cyril—know a good deal about pictures. But just set one of them to paint, and what is his knowledge worth? Similarly, philosophers, novelists, and such fellows know a good deal about women: they can talk about them, and explain the matrimonial mistakes of other men very ingeniously. But when they marry, where are they? They may have a better chance than a fool; just as a critic might have a better chance of painting a picture than a fellow who had never thought about what a picture was. But there would be as little probability of Shakespear fitting himself better than an experienced widower who had buried two wives, as of a critic surpassing, at the first attempt, the things that the fellows draw on the flags in Piccadilly in summer. Therefore take my advice, and if you marry—for though we all know that marriage is an unnatural institution and a desperate undertaking, still, we do submit and risk it—marry whomever you fancy best; and dont make a fool of yourself trying to do scientifically what you dont know how to do at all."

"Do you mean to say that a man ought to pair off with the first woman he fancies, without regard to circumstances?"

"I do. I say this. Take a hundred men, sagacious, and accustomed to the study of social science and human nature. Let fifty, with full liberty and time for consideration, select their wives. Marry the other fifty to women of their own social standing, whom they have never seen, and whom they have selected by drawing their names out of a hat. You will find the average of happy marriages as high for the one lot as for the other."

"Perhaps so. That can be neither proved nor disproved."

"Very few things can; but whether a theory is true or not, if you find it recommending itself to the instinctive belief of one intelligent man, you will find that it has some significance or another. Why do you suppose, now, that most people marry?"

"Because it is the custom, I suppose. Some people are fond of saying that the real motive is mere animalism. I'm not a philosopher, and have not troubled myself about the matter. Perhaps theyre right."

"No, theyre not. Marriage is a restraint upon such motives. What is your idea of what a man ought to marry for?"

"Hm! It's hard to say. Loneliness. A desire for somebody to be fond of, who will be fond of you. Sympathy; and spiritual companionship, and so forth."

"All possible without marriage. And none of them are things to be got on lease. Try again."

"I can conceive nothing else that could induce a man to marry."

"Do you like children?"

"No!"

"Well: that is what you marry for. Children of your own, hostages to fortune, and forms in which you see your youth renewed, sound old-fashioned phrases nowadays; but they are as true as ever. There is no gratification of soul or body which a woman can afford you, that will not be sweeter when the woman is not your wife, except the possession of boys and girls to continue the record when you are in your coffin. Therefore marry the woman who will bring you the finest children, and who will be the best mother to them; and you will never find out that you might have done better by choosing elsewhere. And now, are you aware that it is a quarter past one, Sunday morning?"

"Is it so late?" said Scott. "Well, good night." He shook hands with Vesey, who had risen, with many groans and yawns, from his comfortable chair.

"Good night, good night. Oh Lord! I wish I were in bed without the trouble of going there. Oh dear me! Yaw!"

"What an old cynic!" said Scott, as Vesey withdrew. "I wonder is he right about the folly of prudent marriages." Feeling sleepy, he went into the hall, where the reproachful looks of a solitary man-servant apprised him that he was the last guest stirring in the house. When he was gone, the domestic extinguished the remaining lights; and, after flitting round the gallery with a single taper, like a liveried ghost, vanished and left the great hall in darkness.

# BOOK THE THIRD
## COURTSHIP AND MARRIAGE

# CHAPTER I

MISS RUSSELL had been successful as a milliner and dressmaker at Richmond. The wife of a local clergyman, a woman remarkable for exclusiveness and for economy in the disbursement of her husband's stipend, had ascertained from her servant that a neighboring lady's maid had been admirably fitted with a mantle by the new dressmaker on reasonable terms. The mantle was borrowed, and paper patterns constructed from it; but a disparity between the proportions of the maid and those of the clergyman's wife rendered this expedient useless. The lady then went to Miss Russell; explained that she had influence in Richmond society; and offered the patronage of her circle in return for a considerable reduction in terms to herself. The offer was rejected. On the same evening, Harriet told Mrs Froster and her aunt of this incident, expressing some indignation at the nature of the proposition. Mrs Summers declared that her niece's prospects were ruined, and that the offended lady would use her influence to prevent her getting work from the townspeople. She suggested that an acceptance of the offer, accompanied by an apology, should immediately be sent.

Mrs Froster followed more severely, inveighing against too much independence in the young and humble. Harriet said nothing; and her elders, who were secretly afraid of her, thought her silence so ominous that they allowed the subject to drop. But they shook their heads and recommended her to be more careful as they bade her good night; and she returned to her new premises in a worse mood for conciliating customers than ever. In spite of this, she received, before a fortnight had elapsed, so many orders that she had to employ two assistants. This unexpected success was due to the advertisement given her by gossip about her spirited repulse of the clergyman's wife, whose exclusiveness and censoriousness had made her many foes. The story of her proposal had been communicated by Miss Russell's assistant to the owner of the mantle; by her to the parson's servant, who added details as to the cutting out of the pattern; and by all three to acquaintances who soon spread the tale through the parish.

The new dressmaker thus became notorious. Customers were attracted by the professional eminence which her independent conduct seemed to indicate, and in some cases by the prospect of praising her and exhibiting her handiwork in the unpopular lady's presence. Harriet proved her skill in executing the orders of ladies who knew how to dress themselves, and her taste in dictating to those who did not. A long-established rival, who had for ten years been bullied and underpaid by the local aristocracy, was almost ruined by the new comer, to whom, amongst other consequences of prosperity, came offers of insurance agencies, bill discounting agencies, brandy-disguised-as-perfume agencies, and capitation fees on pupils introduced to preparatory schools. From all these byways of moneymaking Harriet turned with disdain, alleging that her business was dressmaking, and not agency. Both Mrs Froster and Mrs Summers urged her to profit by these offers with such persistency, that she at last ceased from mentioning such matters to them. The regular procurers of venal recommendations soon left her in peace; but she remained subject to the solicitation of ladies who gave her orders, and, when they were executed, suddenly declared themselves governesses, and offered a liberal fee for a situation. Her customers unwittingly intensified the temptation by confiding to her so many details of their domestic troubles and wants and ailments, that she often longed for ungenial clients who would treat her with entire reserve.

Meanwhile, the knowledge she was acquiring of the lives of gentlewomen unprovided with the independence which a handicraft confers, with no resource but marriage, made her proud of her own position, and contemptuous of that from which her patronesses looked down upon her. Nevertheless, since she had become acquainted with Cyril Scott, she had once or twice checked herself in the act of wishing that she could be looked upon as his social equal. When she had learned after Easter from her aunt that there would be no visitors at Perspective until September, she had involuntarily felt disheartened at the length of the interim. Then she checked herself again, and resolved to think no more of the artist. She succeeded partially; for she was very busy; but in her leisure moments she thought so much of her resolution that she had to confess that she might as well think directly of Cyril himself.

It was her habit to spend Sunday with her aunt at Perspective, going thither on Saturday evening, and returning early on Monday morning. On the second Saturday after the departure of Mr Grosvenor's guests she had just passed from the streets of Richmond into the country road when she saw Scott coming towards her. Her first emotion was one of pleasure. Then she felt angry, suspecting that the meeting was intentional and disrespectful on his part, and knowing that to countenance it would be to invite its repetition. Accordingly, when he raised his large felt hat with an affectation of having been unconscious of her approach, she bowed to him sternly and passed quickly by. He stood for a moment discouraged, and made an undecided movement in pursuance of his way. Then he turned; followed her; and overtook her. She stopped.

"Good evening, Miss Russell. May I see you safely on your way?"

"Thank you" said Harriet. "You were going towards the town. I will not delay you."

"Oh, it will not delay me, I assure you. I am not going anywhere. In fact, I wished to meet you, to apologize for my rudeness on Saturday week."

"You were not at all rude, Mr Scott. I am much obliged to you; but I think I had better go alone."

The artist looked jealously at her. "I beg your pardon for interrupting you" he said. "I thought you were going to Perspective as you were before, by yourself."

"So I am. I am used to go about alone. Indeed, I can scarcely go otherwise in my position."

"Well" said he, reassured, "unless you would prefer me to go home again, I wish you would let me go with you just this once. I want to speak to you: at least I would like to—" Here his voice changed to a vague murmur. Harriet, half reluctant, and bewildered by a sudden sensation of delight, yielded, and walked

with him for some distance without speaking. Then, with an uneasy laugh, he continued: "I assure you I came out from town on
purpose to meet you."

She was about to warn him against so coming again; but she
could not. Scott, seeing only her calm face and resolute step, was
more and more at a loss for words. The beauty of the spring evening, with its long shadows and distant noises, made all ordinary
conversation seem unworthy of the hour and of his love.

"Are you fond of the country?" said he at last.

"No. I prefer the town."

"Indeed! I suppose you find yourself lonely here?"

"It is not that. I prefer to be alone. I am more independent so."

"That is very cruel."

"Cruel! To whom?" said Harriet, looking at him sharply, as
she detected a sentimental tone in his voice. She drew a line between emotion, which she respected, and sentimentality, which
she despised as sloppy.

"To everybody who might care for your society" said he.
"Such attractions were not meant to blush unseen in out-of-the-
way places."

To this, which was spoken foolishly and awkwardly, Miss
Russell replied by a look of contemptuous surprise. He saw it;
made a gesture as though to fling some encumbrance behind him;
and said impetuously,

"That nonsense is not what I came to say. Ever since I first saw
you—Are you listening to me, Miss Russell?"

Harriet, who was walking fast, and looking at the ground before her, assented with a nod, her color notably deepening.

"Please stop for a moment. I cannot speak to you whilst you
walk at that pace."

Harriet stopped and confronted him, still looking downwards.

"I am in love with you" said Scott. "That is all."

"How dare you tell me such a thing?" said she, as she raised her
eyes, and looked at him with an expression of wrath of which he
had not supposed her features capable.

"How dare I!" said he, with equal sternness. "Why not? Why

not? If you dont care to marry me, can you not tell me so civilly?"

"It is manners to wait to be asked" replied Harriet, startled and softened.

"I did ask you."

"You did not."

"And how dare *you* think that I meant anything else?"

"You should remember the difference in our positions, Mr Scott. I beg your pardon."

"What could make me think of positions at such a moment?" said he, his anger subsiding into anxiety. "Now that you do understand me, will you not give me an answer?"

"Thank you" said she, slowly resuming her walk. "I have seen a great deal of marriage; and I would rather remain as I am."

"Yes, yes: so have I; and I know that it is commonly a miserable business. But it would not be so with us. We should be prepared for the trifles that upset ordinary people. Besides, you cannot always remain as you are. People who do not marry repent it even more than those who do."

Harriet shook her head.

"Of course" he continued, a little bitterly, when he had waited in vain for a more explicit answer, "if you dislike me, that settles the matter. Women very seldom do care for men who are fools enough to fall in love with them."

"There are many other things besides liking or disliking to be considered in marriage" said Harriet quietly.

"I can make a thousand a year easily, if that is what you mean?" said he shortly.

"Thank you. I have no occasion to marry for money."

"I dont want you to marry for money. I want you to marry for love."

Harriet looked at him with a laugh of pleasure which she was for a moment unable to repress. Then, as she saw its reflection in his eyes, she became grave, and said, "It is impossible."

"Do you mean that you refuse?"

"I cannot help it."

"You can help it very easily if you like."

"I think we had better say no more about it for the present" said she, a sudden instinctive anxiety to escape overcoming her courage.

"No" said Scott resolutely: "you may require time to make up your mind as to marriage; but you must know as well as you ever will whether you care for me or not."

"What right have you to expect me to answer such a question, Mr Scott?"

"I have a perfect right. I want to know whether there is any use in my coming down again?"

"There is no use in your coming down again."

"You are a most unreasonable woman. Why is there no use in it?"

"I cannot make you understand an answer if you are determined not to" said Harriet, offended.

"Very well. In plain English, you dislike me. That is quite sufficient."

"I did not say that" said Harriet quickly, momentarily relapsing into broad Scotch.

"Then what objection have you to consider my proposal?"

"Mr Scott" said she seriously, stopping as they came within sight of the gates of Perspective: "I am afraid I have not expressed my thanks properly for your offer; but I assure you I take it as a great compliment. I would not be a suitable wife for you; and I know that after your first fancy had worn off you would not like to have your lady friends coming to see you in dresses that might be of my own making, and looking down on you on my account."

"And if they do" he said, interrupting her, "it will be very easy to bundle them into the street. What do I care about such people? You dont understand my position. I am not a hanger-on to society. I have no occasion to court it. I am an artist; and society cant do without me. It is glad to run after me, and will be glad to know my wife. Besides, the friends whom I value are men of culture, who will never ask what you *were*, as long as you *are* the handsomest and cleverest woman in London."

"You must not think that I am at all ashamed of what I am. But if anybody else was, it might make you so too; and I could not run the risk of being exposed to that."

"But if I were ashamed, or likely to be, would I have proposed to you? Why am I to be made miserable for life for the sake of a few fools who are of no mortal use or interest to me? Respect for the opinion of such people is nothing but moral cowardice, pride, selfishness: anything but love. If you cared for me half as much as I do for you, you would not throw me over for fear of being snubbed by nonentities."

"You may not always care so little for them or so much for me." The last five words came out in spite of her, to her great terror.

"I will never care for them" said he vehemently; "and I will always care for you. I cannot tell you so more plainly than I have already. I will care for you more than anything else in the world except my work; and even that I feel I cannot do without you."

"What would your family say?"

"I should like to see them dare to criticize any course I choose to take. You are only trying to invent objections."

"I think they are very natural objections, Mr Scott. I should be your family if I married you; and I might criticize. We know very little of each other; and our tempers might not go happily together."

"I cannot see why. You seem to have no more temper nor feeling than a block of marble. And I am not aware that my temper is a bad one."

"I think you would soon get tired of an unreasonable woman without any feeling."

Scott, about to make a passionate appeal, was checked by this retort, and could not trust his temper to reply. He fumed silently. So Harriet held out her hand, and bade him good evening.

"Well?" said he: "am I to come again?"

"I have already explained."

"You have not given me an answer" said he fiercely. "You have mentioned plenty of reasons for not marrying me, for all of which I do not care one straw. I want to know would you *like* to marry me if the objections were put out of the way?"

"There is no use in answering ifs. I think we had better drop the subject."

"Then you will not give me any satisfaction. Is that it?"

"I had rather not say anything more. Good night!" And she held out her hand again. He, with an angry look, ground the dust beneath his heel as he turned from her, and walked away in what she thought literally a very pretty rage. When he disappeared at a curve of the road without having turned his head once, she went on her way to the gate.

Mrs Froster had come to Perspective early in the afternoon to have a chat with her old friend for some hours before the arrival of Harriet, in whose presence they seldom conversed without a feeling of restraint, due partly to her impatience of their lamentations over the degeneracy of the age, and partly to the fact that her own prospects in life formed their favorite topic. On that evening they had discussed her four-and-twenty years, her pride, her discouraging manner towards men, and the offers of marriage which she had rejected.

"You seem in wonderful spirits tonight, Harriet" said Mrs Froster, as they sat at tea.

Harriet laughed and blushed slightly.

"I hope you have reason for it" continued Mrs Froster. "We were talking about you before you came in. I have lain awake thinking about you, often and often, and wondering what will become of you."

"Twenty-four is a great age for an unmarried girl" said Mrs Summers; "and young men are often led to think there must be some bad reason for it."

"Marriage was ordained for our first parents" said Mrs Froster; "and I would be sorry to think that any girl I cared about was no better than a Roman Catholic nun."

"I must say I dont think it natural for a young woman to live by herself and make her own living" said Mrs Summers.

"It was never intended, and was never thought of when I was a girl" said Mrs Froster. "It is not as if you were ugly. But dont forget in your thoughtless pride that your good looks will pass away, and leave you sick and sorry, with no one left to care for you."

Then, for the first time in the experience of her aunt and Mrs Froster, Harriet laughed heartily.

"Harriet" said Mrs Summers anxiously: "what is the matter with you this evening?"

"Well, certainly!" ejaculated Mrs Froster. "To think of *you* breaking out like that!"

"Of all the gentlemen you know, aunt, which would you select for my husband?"

"It little becomes you to speak of gentlemen" said Mrs Froster. "You would do well to put such foolish thoughts out of your head, and look for a home to some honest tradesman in your own station in life."

"Harriet" said Mrs Summers, more intuitively: "has any gentleman proposed to you?"

Harriet leaned back in her chair; closed her lips secretively; and smiled.

"Surely Mr Davis has not come round again?" said Mrs Froster, disconcerted. Then, irritated by the scorn which appeared in Harriet's face at this suggestion, she added quarrelsomely, "May you never meet with worse than he! and you will be able to think yourself lucky, as independent as you are."

Mrs Summers trembled as she heard her friend's tone, and saw the softness disappear from her niece's face.

"Never mind about Mr Davis now, Rebecca. Tell us who it really was, Harriet."

"I have just been thinking that as I refused him, I ought not to mention his name. Perhaps I was wrong in mentioning it at all" said Harriet thoughtfully.

"But it cant matter if you only tell it to *us*, dear" said Mrs Summers.

"Not if it were my business only" said Harriet.

There was a pause, during which they waited for her to speak further. But she did not. Then Mrs Froster rose and said, "I will get out of the way, Angel. I know it's no business of mine."

"Now dont get angry, Rebecca" said Mrs Summers, rising to detain her visitor. "You do turn on a person so suddenly for nothing at all. Sit down, wont you?"

"Yes" said Mrs Froster: "my temper is well known; and so is my tongue. I am not fit to be trusted with the affairs of children. I am not good enough for a girl who receives proposals from gentlemen."

"What nonsense!" cried Mrs Summers. "Why will you take up things in that way? Harriet meant nothing of the sort, I'm sure."

"How dare she try to trample on me?" said Mrs Froster, turning angrily towards Mrs Summers, who recoiled from her tall gaunt figure, gleaming eyes, and distorted features. "Does she take me for one of her workwomen?"

"There is no need for you to raise your voice here, Mrs Froster" said Harriet, rising determinedly as though addressing an unruly child. "The servants will hear you."

"What do I care for the servants?" retorted Mrs Froster passionately.

"My aunt cares very much for them. As long as you remain in her room, you will have to consider what she cares for, if you are capable of considering anything in your present temper."

"Harriet" pleaded Mrs Summers: "dont aggravate her."

"How dare you!" said Mrs Froster.

"Nonsense" said Harriet. "Sit down; and quiet yourself. You are not fit to go into the streets or to be seen by the people about the place in your present state."

Mrs Froster's throat became convulsed; and she looked menacingly at Harriet, who returned her gaze resolutely. Then she had a fit of trembling, and fell back into her chair, where, after a brief struggle with her tears, she began to cry piteously.

"There, there, deary: theres nothing the matter" said Mrs Summers soothingly, rocking her friend's head on her bosom. Mrs Froster resisted her at first, but presently submitted and hung on her friend, shaken by an occasional sob.

"Come!" said Mrs Summers: "youre better now, Rebecca, arnt you? Cheer up!"

"I have been told that I'm not fit to be seen" moaned Mrs Froster. "The servants are thought of before me, because I have not a decent reputation."

"No, no" remonstrated Mrs Summers: "think no more of it now. Youre worn out."

"I'm not strong enough even to go when I am turned out of the house."

"Dont dream of such things. You will never be asked to leave my house, Rebecca."

"Such things were never said to me before."

"Take her into your bedroom, aunt" said Harriet quietly but peremptorily. "Make her lie down. If you sit by her and let her alone, she will rest herself quietly."

Mrs Froster trembled again at Harriet's voice; muttered a protest; and left the room leaning on the shoulder of Mrs Summers. When they were gone, Harriet, with a gesture of impatience, turned to the window, and looked out at the twilight, angry with Mrs Froster for intruding on her memory of the artist. Then she suddenly thought of Smith; and as she had enjoyed his intimate acquaintance, and won the admiration of Scott, she felt with pride that her place was in the society of artists, scholars, and gentlemen, instead of the lodging-house keepers, tradesmen, and field preachers amongst whom her social lot had led her. Whilst she was musing, she heard her aunt passing softly without, vainly entreating Mrs Froster to stay. When a few minutes had elapsed, Mrs Summers re-entered the room alone.

"Well?" said Harriet: "has she gone?"

"She has. I could not induce her to stay. I think she was afraid to see you again. You oughtnt to have spoken to her in that way."

"It will spare her in the long run" said Harriet. "You will find that she will never lose her temper with me again."

"She cant help it" pleaded Mrs Summers.

"Everybody can help it if they choose."

"It's a great pity. Only for that one failing, she's the best of women. But even as a child she used to lose herself the same way. I'm sorry you were so short with her. It's not easy for a woman of her age to bear being put down by a girl. It's humiliating to look on at, much less to feel oneself."

"She has herself to thank" said Harriet inflexibly. "It is not true kindness in the end to encourage her in being outrageous. If she will not control herself, she must be made to, like other people."

"Perhaps you are right" said Mrs Summers meekly. "Poor Rebecca! It's a great thing to have a strong mind, Harriet; but I hope it will not ever make you hard."

# CHAPTER II

MR WOODWARD, though he had complained at first when called upon to master some trifling details of the arrangements adopted by his new secretary, was now, for the first time in his life, able to have his papers found for him immediately when he wanted them, and free from arrears of correspondence. He was a member of parliament, but not an active one, seldom contributing more to debate than a facetious remark, which the House, having learned to look on him as one of its Irish jesters, laughed at as a matter of course. His Irish estate was in the hands of an agent, the acknowledgment of whose annual remittance and account constituted the only business its management entailed upon the landlord. These accounts were now handed to Smith, who spent two nights vainly trying to discover the principle on which the tenants were permitted to deduct the poor rate and other imposts from their rents, and what a gale day meant. He thought at first that it was a misprint for gala day.

After a short time, Smith, though anxious to make work for himself, could rarely find a pretext for spending the whole day with his employer. Leisure soon modified his appearance and habits. He purchased a new hat at Lincoln and Bennett's, and wore dogskin gloves. Mrs Tilly's little maid of all work one day said to her mistress that Mr Smith was getting a good deal of style about him. He saw little of his employer's family. Clytie had come to the study once or twice to arrange the hour of a meal or meeting with her father. On some of these occasions, she vouchsafed a Good Morning to the secretary, who conceived a strong dislike to her.

One morning Cornelius announced "Misther Hawkshaw."

"What does *he* want, I wonder" grumbled Mr Woodward.

It appeared presently that the poet wanted an order for admission to the House of Commons for one of his relatives.

"He has come up from the country, my dear Mr Woodward" said Hawkshaw; "and I should feel obliged by your making the order a perennial one. He comes to me every night, and persecutes me to go with him. What an accursed thing it is to have relatives!"

"Humph!" said Mr Woodward. "Why dont you try reading your poems to him?"

"He does not like them" said Hawkshaw, with a smile. "I fancy you think he is right. But I suppose you never read any of my wares."

"Ive read one or two."

"What did you think of them?"

"Well, to tell you the truth, I thought there was a good deal of blatherumskite in them. But I am no judge of such things."

"Youre quite right. There is" said Hawkshaw affably.

Mr Woodward, baffled and silenced, stared helplessly at his unwelcome visitor until he was rescued by the opportune entrance of Isabella. She greeted the poet gushingly whilst Smith pretended to busy himself writing, and listened, conscious of his own deficiencies in polite intercourse, to the poet's gossip with the lady. When this had lasted for some minutes, Mr Woodward, who had looked askance at his guest several times, got up and left the room, promising to return directly.

"Yes" said Hawkshaw, continuing the conversation: "I was there. Bazaars rather amuse me. I leave my money at home, except a single half-crown which I not uncommonly contrive to reserve for my cab fare back."

"How very mean!" said Isabella.

"Shocking, is it not?" said Hawkshaw, smiling, and half closing his eyes. "I admired nothing there but your dress, which was a day dream. Pray who designed it?"

"Oh! that peacock blue thing."

"Stay" said Hawkshaw, opening his eyes. "Peacock blue, with its aesthetic associations, reminds me of my unfortunate friend Cyril Scott. Is it true that he has gone mad?"

"Cyril Scott gone mad! Impossible!"

"Then you have not heard."

"I have heard nothing of him since Easter, when I believe he was staying at Mr Grosvenor's. Let me think. Yes: I remember seeing him there quite distinctly; and he seemed no madder than usual. Of course you are not in earnest?"

"I am always in earnest until three o'clock, when I assume my cap, bells, and cardcase. I assure you, Lizzie Scott told me yesterday that Cyril came home last Saturday evening looking ill and excited. He has been shut up in his studio ever since, and has locked the door against the whole world. He! once the most social of men. When they attempt to question him, he becomes quite a bear."

"I do not know that there is anything very unusual in that."

"Ah! you are too hard on him. I saw him about three weeks ago, immediately after his return from Richmond; and he talked in an extraordinary fashion; disparaged art; sermonized me, and was as unlike Cyril Scott as the most sordid Philistine could possibly be. I concluded that he had fallen in love at Perspective. I was almost disposed to give you credit for his aberration."

"I dont know why you should" said Isabella, very coldly. "Mr Scott distinguished himself at Richmond by some unaccountable adventures with a lady who was kindly identified with me, but who turned out to be the housekeeper's niece." Here Miss Woodward, with a slight shrug, turned towards the secretary, and found him looking at her. He immediately resumed the attitude of diligent work proper to his position.

"Was she a Scotchwoman?" said Hawkshaw, not noticing this episode.

"I dont know, I'm sure" said Miss Woodward listlessly. "Why?"

"Nothing particular. Something that he let drop induced me to rally him on the subject of a Scotchwoman; but I did not then believe that she had any real existence."

"Perhaps Mr Smith can tell you. He knows all sorts of the most extraordinary people."

"I happen to know the niece of Mr Grosvenor's housekeeper" said Smith, in response to Hawkshaw's politely inquisitive regard. "She is a Scotchwoman."

"Indeed! Is she very attractive?"

"She is a person of remarkable character, personally very attractive; and she is not ignorant of artistic matters, although her information is perhaps rather scattered. It is the unconsciously acquired culture which comes from a lonely struggle with the world that really individualizes her."

Hawkshaw and Isabella stared at the ex-carpet salesman.

"Pardon me" said the poet, recovering himself; "but what is her social position?"

"I am not sufficiently versed in such matters to say" said Smith cautiously. Then, changing his mind, he added, "At the time of my acquaintance with her, she was what is called a *modiste* [Miss Woodward's lip curled]; and I believe she has an establishment of her own now at Richmond."

"Oh" said Hawkshaw. "Then there is of course no question of his marrying her."

"Possibly not" said Smith. "But she is an exceptional woman; and I am sure that Mr Scott would not have the slightest chance of making her acquaintance in the character of a trifler."

Miss Woodward, paler than usual, looked at Smith, who resumed his writing. Hawkshaw coughed, and was about to change the subject when he was interrupted by a sound of footsteps in the corridor. Cornelius then appeared.

"Heres—wheres the masther, Miss Bella?"

"Upstairs. He will be down in a moment. What is it?"

"It's Mister Scott. Walk in, sir" said Cornelius.

"Oho!" cried Hawkshaw: "here comes Raphael Rembrandt Titian Turner Scott. What have you been doing this many a day?"

"Something that would do you a great deal of good if you followed my example" replied Scott. "I have had a week's hard work."

"Work!" said Hawkshaw. "You make me shudder."

"What is there to live for but work?" said Scott. "Everything else ends in disappointment. It's the only thing that you never get tired of, and that always comes to good."

"Amen" said Hawkshaw, with a significant look at Miss Woodward. "You have become a bottomless well of edification lately. So everything else ends in disappointment, does it? What else have you been trying? Do you mourn that e'er you knew a girl so fair yet so deceiving?"

Scott looked angrily at the poet. Then, detecting Miss Woodward in the act of observing him narrowly, he said,

"Perhaps it will amuse you to learn that I have been repulsed in an affair of the heart."

"What, jilted?" said Hawkshaw.

"Not even jilted; but refused point blank."

"You came, you saw—"

"And I was conquered. You see I am generous enough to give the world the gratification of laughing at me."

"I believe you are joking" said Isabella. "Or else you must have greatly aspired to have so greatly fallen."

Scott looked at her; and she returned his gaze with one of unconcealed triumph. Smith bent over his letter and grinned.

"I wish you would give me the recipe for getting over a disappointment so quickly as you seem to have done" said Hawkshaw.

"Simply work" said Scott. "A week has sufficed in my case. I spent the first day spoiling a canvas, the next looking at it in despair. Next day I wiped it out and began again. I got hold of something that time; and now I have some good work safe for the winter season."

"Indefatigable man!" said Hawkshaw, with a sigh. "If I had only your power of work, I should be the author of a dozen epics, instead of a poor sonneteer. Well, there is no point in rallying a man who knocks his fellow-creatures down with a cool confession of his fall. But what brought you here at this unfashionable hour, if I may ask the question?"

"I did not expect to find any one here except Mr Woodward" said Scott; "and I want an order for the House from him."

"What! the same errand as mine" cried Hawkshaw. "Have you also a country cousin?"

"No" said Scott; "but I have been offered a commission in my old line. I want to draw a sitting of the House for the wood.[1] I mean to go in for paying business."

"Heaven preserve your wits, my poor fellow" said Hawkshaw. "You have been hard hit."

Mr Woodward, who had been putting on a shirt and collar, now returned. He greeted Scott with more cordiality than he had shewn to the poet. After the two young men had obtained the desired orders, their visit was brought to an end by an obviously embarrassed invitation to lunch, which was tactfully resisted by Hawkshaw on the plea of another engagement, and refused bluntly by Scott without excuse.

"I dont like that Hawkshaw. He's a puppy" said Mr Woodward.

"He is at least polite" said Isabella, "which is more than can be said for Mr Scott."

Mr Woodward pocketed his spectacles, and left the room. His daughter, to the surprise of the secretary, remained, but seemed unconscious of his presence as she looked at the window. Smith took advantage of her inattention to attach a pair of cuffs to his shirt wrists, and to pass a pocket comb through his whiskers. He had risen, and was about to go, when Miss Woodward turned.

"I have just been thinking, Mr Smith" said she, "and I feel quite sure that I have seen the young lady of whom we were speaking when I was at Richmond."

"Very possibly" said Smith, admiring Miss Woodward's eyes.

"Is she not a dark woman, with a pretty, cunning face, and—"

"Oh no!" interrupted Smith, astonished at this description. "Not at all. She is the exact reverse."

"Dear me! Then the person I remember seeing with Mrs Summers is not the same. But you are not very complimentary to her."

"How so?"

"You said she was the reverse of pretty."

[1] In those days black-and-white draughtsmen drew on boxwood blocks, which were then engraved by hand.

"I did not mean that. You spoke of a certain kind of prettiness. It is not easy to describe Miss Russell. You would never dream of referring her to any standard outside herself. She is in every sense of the word a strong-looking woman; and yet there is a softness about her face and a grace about her movements which make her almost fascinating. To a stranger I have no doubt she would appear quite beautiful. I saw her so frequently at one time that I got out of the habit of considering her appearance."

"Nevertheless you describe her very eloquently."

"She is a sort of person to make a striking impression on an observer. I can understand an artist admiring her, her figure is so very natural, and her character so unconventional."

Miss Woodward, who corseted herself like an hour glass, looked at Smith when he spoke of Miss Russell's figure as natural, but seeing no trace of any second meaning in his expression, and being subject to a delusion that no man could detect the presence of stays beneath her own dress, she dismissed her suspicion, and said dispiritedly,

"She seems to be a wonderful person, this *modiste*. Excuse me, Mr Smith; but may I ask whether you are related to her in any way?"

"Oh no!" said Smith, discovering by his feelings at this question that he was not so thorough a republican as he had believed himself to be.

"I should not have asked" said Isabella, perceiving his discomposure; "only all her circumstances seem to be the reverse of what might be expected."

"You must not suppose that I had any other feeling than that of disclaiming an advantage" said Smith, repenting of his worldliness. "However, I only made her acquaintance accidentally. I lodged for a year in the house where she lived."

"And is she a very scornful beauty?"

"I have no doubt she could be, on occasion" said Smith, imagining the repulse of Scott with some satisfaction.

Here the conversation was interrupted by Hamlet, who, having expected to find the room empty, started as a properly trained London footman should have died rather than have done, and gasped at the pair.

"I ax your pard'n, Miss Bella. I come in to put the room to rights."

"Very well" said Miss Woodward. "Put it to rights, unless Mr Smith requires the room." Then, with one of the glances which she shot at men as a matter of habit, she bade Smith good morning, and went out. He, having waited long enough to avoid overtaking her in the hall, followed her example, and left the servant alone in the study.

"A'thin, bad luck to *your* impidence" said Cornelius, unable to bear his fright in silence, and menacing the absent secretary with his fist, "makin up to a gintleman's dawther. An' a bitther young clip is the same lady. She'll be afther me next, I suppose. No matter, I have me eye on the pair o' yous. See that now!"

Meanwhile, Smith found that, in describing Harriet to Isabella, he had for the first time defined to himself the attractions of the woman whose intimacy he had let slip away from him. A desire to see her again came upon him. On the way from his lodgings to Chelsea railway station, which he thought would be a good place in which to consider whether he should go to Richmond or not, he argued with himself thus.

"You are committing an egregious folly" said common sense.

"One must commit follies sometimes" said romance.

"She does not want to see you" said common sense.

"How do you know?" said romance.

"You have no pretext for calling on her" said common sense.

"I may meet her in the street by accident" said romance.

"How do you propose to put yourself in the way of doing so?" said common sense.

"Time enough to think of that when I get there" said romance. "Besides, even if I do not see her, a day in the country will do me good. And, after all, I may decide not to go when I get to the station."

An hour later he was in Richmond, wondering where he would find Harriet. Being too irresolute to ask questions, he walked through the streets in search of her place of business. Then, becoming hungry, he entered a confectioner's shop where he obtained some refreshment, and inquired of the young lady who stood at the counter whether she knew the whereabouts of one Miss Russell, a milliner.

"Upstairs, sir. Ring at the hall door on the right as you go out; push it open; and go up to the first floor."

Taken by surprise, and conscious that his informant was watching him through the window, Smith obeyed her instructions before he had time to consider how he should present himself to the dressmaker. He rang the bell; a wire clicked; and the door moved. He pushed it open; ascended the stairs; and found himself on the first floor landing opposite a glass door, through which he could see a mantle disposed on an effigy of wire. The place seemed unfitted for the reception of his sex; and he entered with trepidation, as he might have entered a ladies' bathing place. From the adjoining room the sound of a sewing machine reached his ears, and reminded him of the lonely evening at Dodd's Buildings when it had first disturbed his meditations. He coughed and immediately Harriet came from the other room, attired, he thought, for some special occasion; for her black habit, though simple, was much more elegant in design and costly in material than the plain drab dresses, soft shawls, and weather-stained waterproof cloaks which she had worn at Islington. She had a like impression after her first surprise at seeing him, as she noted his frock coat, his glossy hat, and gloves. She received him with a cordiality which quickly dispelled all his doubts as to the advisability of his visit. Contrary to what he had expected, the reserve which she had never before, even in their most familiar hours, entirely thrown aside, was now undiscernible; and her manner was further ameliorated by a gaiety which, notwithstanding her shrewd humor, she had never before displayed.

Her favorable reception of him arose partly from pleasure at his visit, and partly from her enlarged experience of men, which had taught her that in those qualities for his deficiency in which she had despised him, he was not so inferior to the rest of the

world as she had supposed. The esteem which accompanies a reaction against an injustice; the fact, undervalued by her before,
that he was her only intimate friend; and her feminine sensibility
to the external change in appearance and manner which had followed his dissociation with the counting house of Figgis and
Weaver, all disposed her to welcome him. She sat with him for
some time in the show room; and as the hour was too late for
business, they were undisturbed save by the monotonous rattle
of the sewing machine worked by Harriet's assistant in the next
room. She recounted to him how she had established herself in
Richmond; and she described the retreat of Mrs Froster, who
was, she said, as hard to get on with as ever. In Dodd's Buildings
she had never discussed the temper of the landlady. Smith, in
return, told her his history, and was pleased to find that she approved of his conduct with regard to his former employers, and
considered that his present avocation was far better suited to his
taste and ability than city bookkeeping. In reply to his inquiries
as to her cultivation of literature and art, she told him that she
had in her leisure moments resumed of late the study of Mr
Ruskin's works, with journalistic quotations from which (the
prices of the books themselves were far beyond their means) he
had occasionally edified her, although she had not then taken
much interest in them. She accounted for this by the picutres she
had seen at Mr Grosvenor's house. Smith thereupon described
his visit to Perspective, and mentioned that the gentleman to
whom he was attached as secretary was a Mr Woodward, a friend
of Mr Grosvenor's.

"Mr Woodward!" said Harriet. "How oddly things come
about! Has he not a daughter?"

"He has two" said Smith: "one a beauty, the other a beast—I
mean in disposition; for she is passably pretty."

"What is the name of the beauty?"

"Isabella." Harriet was disappointed. "By the bye" continued Smith, "she is jealous of you."

"Of me!" said Harriet. "She never saw me, and can know
nothing about me."

Smith then repeated the conversation which had taken place that morning between Hawkshaw and Miss Woodward, and the confession subsequently made by Cyril Scott. "And of course" he concluded, "you got the credit of being the person he had proposed to. My mentioning that seems like asking you whether you were or not; so perhaps I ought to have held my tongue."

"I was the person; but I think Mr Scott might have kept his own counsel. I suppose he thought I would boast of it, and that it was best to be beforehand with me."

"I dont think so. I fancy he said it on the impulse of the moment in defiance of their banter. He seems to have a very good opinion of himself; and I think you must have astonished his self-conceit. Miss Woodward told him so to his face."

"Indeed!"

"And when he was gone, she asked me all sorts of questions about you: that being the first occasion on which she deigned to notice my existence."

"I hope you told her nothing about me."

"I had to. I treated her to a glowing picture of you, at which she did not seem to be particularly pleased. [Harriet could not restrain a smile]. It did not occur to me at the time; but now that I come to think on the matter, I suppose every adjective I used must have added to her disgust. I wonder is she in love with Scott herself!"

"It is certainly strange that even the quietest people cannot escape becoming common talk, the moment they have any affairs which they care to keep private."

"Well, if you choose to destroy the peace of mind of the most notable artists of the day, and scatter the hopes of the loveliest members of society, what can you expect? You were not born to be obscure, and you must pay the penalty of popularity."

"Nonsense!" said Harriet. All the same, she was not displeased by this jest. "I am glad to hear that Mr Scott had the good sense to turn to his work and forget all about me. You must not speak about this, or let it be known that I spoke to you about it, Mr Smith."

"Certainly not" said Smith. Then he laughed.

"What are you laughing at?" said Harriet gravely.

"At the idea of Mr Scott forgetting you in that offhand way. Whenever a man makes up his mind to forget anything, he only succeeds in making his recollection systematic."

Harriet, having had some experience of this in her own thoughts of the artist, made no reply, but changed the subject by asking Smith to take tea with her. He declined, fearing to cause her inconvenience, and protesting that he must return to London by the next train.

"You know you are welcome to stay" said Harriet.

"I would stay, really, if I could" said Smith with the earnestness of a liar. "But I assure you it is impossible." Reflecting on his previous doubts as he descended the stairs, he said to himself,

"Why should she not have been glad to see me? How stupidly I torment myself by supposing that the commonest human feelings are suspended when I am in question!"

# CHAPTER III

ON the evening of a fine Sunday in June, the sward on either side
of the path which crosses Hyde Park from the Marble Arch to the
eastern end of the Serpentine was occupied by circles of idlers
and worshippers, to each of which an orator expounded some
doctrine, chiefly the impending damnation of everybody in the
park excepting the speaker and his supporters. A few proved from
scripture the Christadelphian alternative of annihilation or a
share in the millennium. Others identified the English nation
with the lost tribes of Israel, and derived vaticinations concerning
the Emperor of Russia from the prophets. Here and there a crowd
surrounded a prayer meeting which had been interrupted by the
intrusion of a Secularist, or a Secularist meeting which had been
challenged by a Christian Evidence champion, the point at issue
being whether somebody of the opposite persuasion to the
speaker had or had not been sentenced to three months' hard
labor for some disgraceful offence, religion being totally forgotten in the heat of the dispute. Though most of the unmolested
preachers made the same appeal almost in the same words, they
differed in manner. There were supplicants who flung their arms
aloft, and shrieked with discordant voices which seemed on the
point of breaking. There were robust men who seemed to bully
their hearers into heaven by sarcastically enumerating the delights of the way to hell. There were dispensers of platitude, who
sought for sermons in stones and good in everything. There were
devotees trembling with earnestness, who urged the change that
had been wrought in themselves, and implored the world to
share their ecstasy. There were young men, elated by the discovery that they were not without the power to move assemblies,
arraigning adverse arguments and confuting them with triumph.
There was a retired officer, scorched by the sun of India, who
had brought out his family, a supply of campstools, and a Bible,
from which he was reading in a voice ill adapted to the purpose.
There was a bearded gentleman, calling himself a Comprehen-

sionist, who had discovered metaphysics for himself, and, being persuaded that his discovery was entirely new, called upon the people to enrol themselves as Violet Volunteers for the promulgation of a home-made philosophy of the most abstract kind. There was also Mr Larkins, who harangued a large and orderly congregation under some trees near the Marble Arch, his soprano voice carrying his words to the outermost ranks of the crowd. When he had concluded his address, a hymn was sung, and amongst those who sang most reverently was Fanny Watkins, who was interrupted in the middle of the second verse by a nudge from a person standing close behind her.

"How de do, Fan?" Miss Watkins had not heard that accent for months; and her voice faltered as she recognized it; but she was too devout to neglect her act of worship, and she kept her eyes on her book. At the end of the verse the salutation was repeated; and she turned hastily, whilst Mr Larkins gave out the succeeding lines, to Fraser Fenwick. His appearance surprised her; for he was not only well dressed, but his complexion was so much healthier, and his eyes so much clearer than of yore, that Fanny returned to her old opinion of him as the handsomest and most dashing of gentlemen. She said, "Good evening. You mustnt speak to me until after the hymn," and turned away to begin the third verse.

"Hymn be hanged!" said Fraser. "Come and take a walk somewhere out of the crowd."

"Sh-h-h!" hissed a woman who stood close by.

Fanny shook her head, and sang as loudly as she could. During the long prayer which followed the hymn, Fenwick kept his hat on lest any one should suppose that he was so poor of spirit as to be a worshipper. When the end was at last reached, Fanny was glad to withdraw him from a position equally unacceptable to himself and his neighbors.

"Why, I havnt seen you for months, Fan" said he, when they had walked apart from the crowd. "Take my arm."

"Stop, Fraser. I scarcely know whether I ought to speak to you or not."

"Why not?"

"I dont know; but father would be angry if he knew; and mother has forbidden me ever to see you again."

"Stuff! what do we care? Besides, that was when I was hard up. Theyll change their note quick enough now. Ive got on to a good thing; and I'm as steady as a preacher. Havnt touched a drop for two months, I assure you. 'Pon my soul, Fan, it's absurd when you think of a man like me turning to and taking the pledge."

"I'm sure I hope you will keep it, Fraser."

"That depends" said Fenwick, becoming serious. "I had better go to the devil and have done with it. It's all thats left to me."

"Why? Dont talk so wickedly. On Sunday too!"

"Whats the use of life to a man when he's thrown over? I turned steady for you. Ive worked hard for you. And now you give me up. I suppose youre engaged to Hickson by this time."

"I am not. You have no right to say such things. It was you who gave me up. You said you would not lower yourself by speaking to a tradesman's family any more."

"Yes: that was when your father put me out of the house. No doubt you have plenty more of what I said to throw in my teeth. That wasnt the way I thought of you when I was starving. I said to myself, I could bear to die if I knew that Fanny was true to me."

"Starving! Dy—!" exclaimed Fanny, almost crying, "Oh, Fraser, what do you mean?"

"I *was* starving. I was lying in a ditch on the point of death, because I was too proud to beg, when a lady of title whom I had known in happier days drove up in her carriage, and brought me to a mansion where I was revived. She was too real a lady to think the worse of a gentleman because he was reduced to a few miserable rags; and she lent me some money and introduced me to the west end merchant with whom I am at present in business. *She* didnt leave me to die like a dog without giving me a thought."

"How could I tell what was happening?" pleaded Fanny, sobbing.

"Of course not. Besides, what was it to you? I suppose you were comfortable enough in your warm drawing room, talking to Hickson."

"I'm very sorry I ever saw Mr Hickson. Why didnt you write?"

"No: I'm not chicken enough for that. And what could you have done if I had written?"

"I dont know. I'm sure I would have done something. At any rate, it would have prevented me from being happy while you were starving."

"It doesnt matter, though" said Fenwick gloomily. "I'll settle myself quick enough now. Let us talk about something else. It's a fine sort of evening, isnt it?"

Fanny sniffed; and they walked for some distance in silence. Then, with a fresh flow of tears, she said, "I suppose we had better part. But dont say it was my fault."

"Fan" said Fenwick solemnly: "do you love me still, or do you not?"

"I vowed to do so; and I have always kept my vows."

"Then" said he, dropping his tragic tone rather too suddenly, "you may as well kiss me."

Fanny blushed. "In the middle of the Park on Sunday, with all the people about!" said she. "What would they think?"

"There arent any people hereabouts" said Fenwick, kissing her. But Fanny did not enjoy public endearments. She felt only incommoded and disreputable; and she insisted on returning to the scene of the meeting. Suddenly Fenwick nudged her with his elbow and whispered, "Come along; and dont look round."

Fanny at once did what she had been warned not to do, and saw a man standing with folded arms behind a tree, looking at the remnant of the prayer meeting.

"Fraser, thats Mr Davis."

"Hush" whispered Fenwick impatiently, "I know. Come on. Dont let him see us."

"Look at his clothes. Look at his face. Oh, Fraser, do you think we ought to speak to him?"

"Whats the good of speaking to him? Dash it, cant you come on?"

The angry sibilation of Mr Fenwick's whisper reached Davis's ear. He looked quickly round like a man whom circumstances had made sensitive to whispers, and saw Fanny gazing at him. He approached her, and said, in a hollow voice:

"You are surprised to see me here, Miss Watkins, skulking like an outcast where I was once the observed of all observers."

"How d'e do?" said Fenwick distantly, but uneasily; for Davis overawed him.

"You are still in your place amongst the elect?" said the preacher.

"I have attended the meetings ever since" said Fanny. "I hope you are quite well, Mr Davis."

"Ha! Oh yes, I am very well, *very* well indeed."

Fenwick turned pale; and his lips dried as he met the glittering eye of the ex-preacher, whose laugh was followed by a rattling cough which terrified Miss Watkins. "Fan" he whispered: "come along. By George, he may be mad for all we know."

But Fanny was afraid for her former apostle, not of him. From her remembrance of his disease she could surmise why his face was almost fleshless, and his color a ghastly brown, with a spot of scarlet on each cheek. His eyes had always been brilliant, though less unpleasantly so than at present. It was the absence of the happy assurance which his conviction of spiritual safety had formerly given him that troubled her most. He was impressive still; but his impressiveness was now theatrical, and seemed to her diabolical. She noted also his chin, unshaven for a week, his scornful expression, and his shabby clothes, which last, chosen as they were with theatrical taste, he still carried so as to make them become him.

"You may see" he said, "how well I am. It is long since Death first laid a hold of me, and he is tightening his grip at last."

"I hope not" faltered Fanny. "Surely you have no reason to fear it. You—"

Her voice failed her as Davis, without a sign of the old ecstasy which she had hoped to call into his eyes, folded his arms, and said:

"It was easy to give to religion the credit of my happiness, when I was happy. Ive been listening to Larkins here today unbeknown to him. He's happy. He's in love with himself as I was once with *my*self. It's a passion that theres no disappointments in. But let Larkins, if he has that much man in him, fall in love with somebody else, and then look to his religion for comfort, and to his prayers for satisfaction. Dont he wish he may get it? I'm not a religious man; and yet I'll die as game as any of em; though while I say it, I'm nearer face to face with it than Larkins, who talks of it so glib, and dont believe that he's within forty year of it. Youre astonished to hear me talk like that, Miss Watkins. Well, it's no wonder. Larkins and the rest are great men now; but they never have the public that I had when I played with em."

"Oh Mr Davis, think of yourself. Youre wandering in your mind: I know you must be. You that once moved all our hearts so, dont have us to think that your soul could ever be in danger—"

"Dont go near the lunatic, Fanny" whispered Fenwick, catching her arm as she advanced a step.

"My soul!" cried Davis. "I am very willing to put it up for auction at the next meeting if I can get my price for it. I dont ask much. I'll name a woman; and for five minutes' talk with her, aye, for her address, or even the mere sight of her, I'll sell myself, body and soul."

"No, no: you dont know what youre saying" interrupted Fanny, beginning to share her lover's fears.

"Better than ever I did when I spoke to you afore" said Davis. "I told you then about religion. I tell you now that theres no such a thing as religion. Theres nothing but destiny. Do you think I dont see its finger plain in my meeting you here this night? Do you think I dont see it in my meeting him here with you? [He darted his finger towards Fraser Fenwick, who recoiled.] Do you think it didnt come clear into my mind that night when I went to the house where she lived, and found it being pulled down, and the young gentleman scholar that first brought me to the room where she was, and that used to take her to the museums and explain the pictures to her—little knowing how near I was to them—come there too on the same errand? Well for him he was the sort he was; or I would have strangled him as soon as looked at him."

"I told you he was mad" whispered Fenwick.

"Heres how the destiny is in you being here. It was you, Miss Watkins, that sent me to reclaim your cousin. In reclaiming him I lost myself; for it was in his very lodging house I met her. It was all arranged before I was born, and before you was born, that I should take to religion to the express end that I might be sent to that house. It was ordained that you should take to it too, that you might send me; and not, as you think in your foolishness, that your soul may be saved. It was predestinated that your cousin there should take to evil ways and need me to pluck him from the burning in order that I might fall into the fire myself. And whatever the hend may be, I'm free of it; for thats predestinated too; and not all the wisdom of the world nor the prayers of the elect can avail against it one jot or tittle."

"I am afraid we must be getting home" said Fenwick, attempting an abject blandness, but hardly able to keep his voice from quavering. "Some day we shall have the pleasure of seeing you again."

"How do we know?" said Davis. "We shall meet if we are destined to."

"Yes" said Fenwick. "It's Fate, you know. Good evening."

"Ha! Good evening" said Davis, with a contemptuous glance which indicated his appreciation of the other's anxiety to get rid of him. But Fanny drew a tract from her pocket, and tendered it to him, saying,

"Excuse my taking the liberty, Mr Davis; but here is a copy of the first little book you ever gave me. It did me so much good that I have carried it about ever since to distribute to others. I know I make very bold in offering it to you; but I dont know how else to try and prevent you hardening your heart."

"No" said Davis, his manner much softened, and a smile,

melancholy, but genuine, appearing on his countenance. "I thank you sincerely; but I have had to do with tracts in a professional capacity, as I may say; and I know their vanity. I am sorry I'm shocking you; but, you may believe me, only for a different way of talking, I am the same man I was before, or at any rate, the remains of him. Farewell!" He lifted his hat; replaced it; and stalked away through the trees.

"There!" said Fenwick triumphantly. "So much for your religious chaps! I never set up to be a saint; but I dont think I ever came so low as that, with all my backslidings. I'll back a gentleman against a ranting revivalist any day in the week. I hope youll cut it and go to church respectably like everybody else, now."

"It's too dreadful to think about" said Fanny tearfully. "Do you think he really meant it?"

"Come on; and dont make a fool of yourself over the fellow" said Fenwick. "Why the dickens should he say it if he didnt meant it?"

Miss Watkins looked wistfully at him for a moment, missing something in him which she felt still smouldered in Davis. It was now urgently necessary for her to go citywards, as it was Mrs Watkins's custom to make her daughter account for any prolongation of her absence from home, with the result that systematic deception of her mother, when it did not involve a downright lie, and sometimes when it did, was the only sin which Fanny had hardened herself to commit with scruple, except on Sundays. On this occasion, however, she was relieved by the generosity of Fenwick, who hailed a cab, in which they drove to Broad Street: Fanny being afraid to approach nearer to her home in the forbidden company of her lover. The novelty of riding in a hansom, the exciting risk of being discovered by her parents, and the charm of her cousin's society, softened the sombre impression which Davis had made upon her; whilst Fenwick, who had accepted in good faith the honorary title of Captain conferred on him by the cab driver, was so happy that he invented an aristocratic garden party at Richmond, in which he placed himself as the most admired object, and described the whole to her at great length. She listened eagerly until the cab stopped, when she saw Mr. and Mrs Watkins, stationed just within the gates of the Liverpool Street railway terminus, gazing with stern surprise at her as she alighted with the assistance of Fraser Fenwick's hand.

"Now, Fan. Eyes right if you dont want to get run over" said Fenwick, rejoining her after paying the cabman, and not perceiving the reason of her sudden halt in the centre of the carriage way.

"This is nice conduct, Miss" said Mrs Watkins harshly."Come here and walk home with your parents this instant."

Fenwick was devoid of courage but not of impudence. For the first time since his childhood, he neither owed his uncle money nor intended to borrow any from him. He liked to assert his independence when he had the opportunity; and Mr Watkins was not sufficiently venerable to frighten him into forgoing the present one. So he winked reassuringly at Fanny; raised his hat; and said:

"How d'e do, Aunt Flossy?" Then he seized Mr Watkins's hand and added, "How is every inch of you, old buck?"

Mr Watkins started; glanced at his nephew's face; and gazed at his waistcoat, without abashing him in the least.

"Well" said he, speaking through his shut teeth, as his habit was, "you have a nerve! I see by your clothes and your cheek that youve made a pot on something."

"We'll take a turn together; and I'll tell you all about it. Whatll you drink?"

"Drink! Me drink! Give yourself no more of your airs with me, my lad; for I'm too old a man to be took with them."

"Who is it that youre speaking to, Tom?" said Mrs Watkins, affecting surprise. "Dont let me see you turn your head again, Miss, until you are locked in your own room at home."

"Let her alone, Flossy" said Mr Watkins. "Fraser is going to walk a bit with us."

"You can keep him to yourself then" said Mrs Watkins. "I am not going to walk in the face of day—much less Sunday—in company with a thief."

"Hush, mamma" said Fanny sharply. "You shouldnt talk like that."

"I'll let you know whether you will teach me how I should talk" said Mrs Watkins, so fiercely that Fanny recoiled, expecting a blow.

"Flossy!" interposed Mr Watkins warningly.

Mrs Watkins checked herself; muttered something about spoiling the girl; bade her daughter come home without further delay; and walked on sulkily. Her husband waited until she had gone some distance, and then followed with Fenwick.

"Since when" said he, "'ave you been able to go about in ansom cabs, and dress yourself like a gentleman?"

"Pshaw! ever so long. Lady Geraldine stood to me like a brick. So long as a fellow can get round the women, he need want for nothing."

"Lady Geraldine! Why, she came around to me, and told me to have nothink more to say to you, and to keep Fanny from you until you came with a character from 'er."

"Yes. She got an idea that it would keep me steadier if I knew that the lift she gave me was the last chance I could look for anywhere. She told me she'd tell you so; but hang me if I thought she would have taken the trouble to do it!" He added a version of his rescue by Lady Geraldine, sparing his own dignity as much as he could without straining his uncle's credulity, and adding that he was now employed as shopman by a fancy stationer in Mayfair.

"Of course" said he, "it's a great thing for the fellow to have a gentleman to attend the sort of people that come into his shop."

"No doubt" sneered Mr Watkins. "And now that you are at the door, you can come upstairs if you care to face Flossy. I'll back you up."

"Another time. It's rather late just now. By the bye, dont let her drop too hard into Fanny on my account. I made her come with me. Good night!"

Mr Watkins parted from him with regret; for he had calculated on his presence to divert the wrath of his wife, who, though in the last resort she submitted to him, did it under so perceptible a protest that her submission created as much discomfort as her contumacy could have done. When he entered the drawing room, she was sitting alone at the table with a book beside her. It was the autobiography of a popular preacher, who had detailed therein so many atrocities committed by him whilst in a state of reprobation, that the volume was as interesting to Mrs Watkins as the Illustrated Police News, which she did not consider proper reading on Sundays.

"Wheres Fanny?" said Mr Watkins, looking round the apartment.

"In her room, and as stubborn as your wicked indulgence could make her. Perhaps yòud like her brought down, and apologized to."

"Steady, Flossy, steady. You know I never interfere with your management of her beyond that I wont have her beat; but I had just as soon she warnt too much bullied."

"Yes; and see what has come of your notions! Driving about the public streets with that young scamp, and then rebuking me before him."

"Theres no such harm in it. You cant expect a grown-up girl to go your way like a baby or a tame cat."

"If you think my way is not fit for your daughter to go, you can take charge of her yourself" said Mrs Watkins sullenly.

"No: I'll stick to our contract, Flossy. I know that my own beginnings were not such as fitted me to set up for rearing a young girl; and Ive always owned to it. I wont interfere."

"But you do interfere. What hold have I over the girl if you wont let me punish her? She knows it well too, and minds what I say to her no more than if I was a post."

"Thats not true, Flossy. Theres not a more dutiful girl in the parish; and I often wonder how she stands your nagging as quiet as she does. I suppose you think nobody is to have a temper except yourself. I was drove to the turf because I wouldnt take as much from my father as Fanny takes from you every day that a tin tack goes wrong in the house."

"You always encourage her, and take her part against me. Only for you I would have chastised the stubborn spirit out of her when she was young enough; and—"

"Only for me" interrupted Mr Watkins, turning on her with a fierce and sneering countenance, "you would have played the very devil, and either broken the child's spirit or forced her on to the streets."

Mrs Watkins quailed, but replied sharply, "Hoity, toity! I was well beaten myself; and I'm thankful for it now."

"Thats a lie that you have persuaded yourself into, to justify yourself now that you can take it out in licking your own child. I was licked too, morning, noon, and night; and I know what it done for me, as well as I see what it done for you. I wont have Fanny's life made hard because you come of a family well known for their temper. She shall take her fling if she likes. She's old enough to have it, and good enough to be trusted with it."

"My family was as good as yours."

"They couldn't well ha been worse; bar Annie, that was Fraser's mother" said Watkins candidly.

"And they were content to go by what they found in their Bibles; and thats 'Spare the rod, and spoil the child.'"

"Ah! Perhaps youll tell us who says that in the Bible."

"Solomon" she answered vehemently.

"Ah!" repeated her husband. "Perhaps youll tell us what sort of fist Solomon made of bringing up his own son."

Mrs Watkins was silent.

"Ive never heard it read how Rehoboam went to the bad" he continued, "without thinking of how *I* went to the bad, and how my father licked me."

"I'm glad you think yourself wiser than Solomon."

"I'm not saying against his being a wise man; but if I was to follow his example in everything, maybe youd be the first person concerned to stop me."

"I dont want to hear any of your wicked talk" said Mrs Watkins, rising.

"You shall hear as much as I like. Whoever else you may ride roughshod over, you ought to know by this time that I mean to have my way when I'm bent on it."

Mrs Watkins bit her lips; twisted her watch chain about her finger for a minute; and then left the room. Her husband listened for the noise made by the door as she closed it behind her.

"Lord forbid she should bang it!" he thought. But she shut it quietly. "Humph!" he added: "Ive landed safe on this event, anyhow."

# CHAPTER IV

On Saturday afternoon, Mrs Summers was knitting by the open windows of her sitting room, enjoying the heat and brightness of the weather, when her servant announced Mr Scott.

"Mr Scott!" said Mrs Summers, surprised. "Something about the pictures the master sent down last week, I suppose. Oh dear! theyre all in the smoking room, where theres no light."

"I dont think so, maam" said the servant: "I asked him to go into the music room: but he stayed in the hall, and gave me to understand that he was come to pay you a visit."

Mrs Summers hesitated. She recollected the artist's civility to her at Easter; but she thought that the servant could hardly be right. In any case, she considered, there could be no impropriety in receiving him where she was; so she bade the maid shew him in. His embarrassed manner as he entered increased her doubt. When they had exchanged greetings, she coughed, and said she supposed that he had seen Mr Grosvenor recently.

"No" said Scott: "I have seen him only once since I left, and that only for a moment. A— The fact is, I have come down to speak on some private business to you, if you will be good enough to interest yourself so far in me."

"I am sure— Anything I can do— Most happy—" Mrs Summers cleared her throat, and added, "What did you wish to speak about, Mr Scott?"

"I thought that perhaps your niece might have told you."

"Harriet!" said Mrs Summers, changing color.

"Some time ago" said Scott deliberately, "I asked her to marry me. It occurred to me that she might just have mentioned it to you."

"Not a word" replied Mrs Summers, staring at him. "And you mean to say, Mr Scott, that Harriet is engaged to you?"

"No. She wouldnt have me."

"What!"

"She refused me; but I am not going to take that refusal. Now in order to propose to her, I had to waylay her on the road from

Richmond. That, I am afraid, was not the proper way to approach her. Still, I had no other opportunity of meeting her. You know that men are in a hurry about such things; and I am sure you will excuse me for not speaking to you first."

"Your feelings are very honorable to you, Mr Scott."

"And now, I want you to sanction my addresses to your niece, and to give me an opportunity of asking her to change her mind."

Mrs Summers tried to assume a becoming composure. "I am really so taken aback by this" said she, "that I scarcely know what to think. I need not say that I have no objection to you, very far from it indeed, Mr Scott. Your offer is a better one than Harriet could ever have in reason hoped for. At the same time, though I say it, she would make a fit wife for the highest nobleman in the land; for, let alone her steadiness and thrift, it would surprise you to hear her speak about pictures out of the books she has read. She can talk to any French person in their own language; and you know what her manners and appearance are. Her conduct is all that it should be to gratify the strictest: indeed, if she has a fault, it is that she is too sensible for her age—she is a few years younger than yourself, Mr Scott. But to tell you the truth, she is very independent; and I am afraid I would have little influence over her once her mind was made up on any subject. Still—"

"I dont mean that you should try to persuade her" said Scott hastily: "I think it would be much better not. But may I rely on your approval?"

"You may indeed. Yet perhaps Harriet acted for the best. Although she is, as I say, fit for any station, the time might come when you would fancy some—some unsuitability."

"The only objection to that is that I have thought it out and made up my mind about it" said Scott, with a trace of his characteristic impatience. "I suppose there is not a marriageable woman in the world with reference to whom some unpleasant possibility might not be set up."

"No doubt you are very right, Mr Scott" said Mrs Summers; "and since you say you have considered over it, it must be left to Harriet to decide."

"Then I may take it that there was no reason, except her own fancy, for refusing me. No other engagement, or anything of that sort?"

"Oh dear no. Not the least in the world. You mustnt suffer yourself to be discouraged at the first attempt, Mr Scott. You couldnt expect a girl of nice feelings to say yes offhand, could you now?"

Scott did not answer. He began to think that Mrs Summers was a fool.

"Of course you wouldnt think of Harriet continuing in business?"

"Certainly not. That reminds me to ask whether she has any other relatives interested in her. I believe her parents are dead. May I ask whether she has any regularly constituted guardian— beside yourself, I mean?"

"Not a soul. Myself and a friend of mine—a worthy lady, but not related to us—have been her only guardians since her father died and left her as he said—and I hope it's no lack of respect to the dead to say that he had a wicked tongue—better able to take care of any dozen matrons in Scotland than they were to take care of her. She was the best of daughters to him; but he put some whims into her head which might make anybody, not knowing her well, think her a little strange in her opinions. But she will get out of all that when she is settled; and I know you are too sensible a gentleman to set any store by a few foolish expressions which she just repeats as she heard them from her father. Poor orphan! her mother died in her confinement."

"Harriet is a Presbyterian, I presume?"

Mrs Summers coughed, and answered in a lower voice, "Her mother, my sister, belonged to the Church of England. My poor father was churchwarden at Nottingham, where my grandfather had been mayor. We were brought up to a higher station than it was our lot to fill. It would be too sad to tell you all our troubles, Mr Scott; how our home was broken up by Hatty running away and making a Scotch marriage with Mr Russell; how my father died when his affairs were in confusion, and left us on the world;

and how I came to be here with young Harriet. But it was the Scotch marriage that began it all, though it was small blame to poor Hatty that she listened to Joe Russell; for he could have talked any one out of their five senses."

"Did he turn out badly?"

"Well, I cannot say that he did. He was very kind to Hatty. But Lord bless us, he was a dreadful man."

"But how? If he treated his wife well, and was so agreeable, why do you call him dreadful?"

"I dont mean in worldly ways. But he believed in nothing."

"Oh! Is that all?"

"Quite enough, I think" said Mrs Summers gravely. "I am sorry to say he spoke his mind too freely before Harriet; and it is in that way that she sometimes talks thoughtlessly, as young people will. I thought it right to mention it to you, and to assure you that she knows her duty none the worse for it."

"No doubt" said Scott. "Is it long since her father died?"

"More than five years. He died in Scotland, where he had followed the profession of a land surveyor."

Scott laughed as he recollected how she had told him at their first meeting that she could draw maps.

"He was also connected with the government" continued Mrs Summers, "under the Commissioners of Inland Revenue. He was considered very clever."

"Do you think, Mrs Summers" said the artist, "that I could see Miss Russell tonight?"

The housekeeper considered how she should answer. Harriet might not be pleased if she consented; and Scott would be displeased if she refused. He was at that moment looking straight at her, waiting for a reply. There was a pause. Then a shadow was cast through the window; and Harriet stepped into the room from the grass without. Mrs Summers was confounded: Scott, who stood up hastily and scowled, as his habit was when he was ill-at-ease, felt scarcely more collected. Harriet greeted the artist as if his presence were the most ordinary event in the world, and closed and laid aside her parasol with composure. As the weather was very warm, she had discarded her black costume, and made for herself a dress of grey alpaca, which material, being then out of fashion, recommended itself no less by its novelty to the observant artist, than by its usefulness to the dressmaker herself.

"It was so hot, aunt, that I was tempted to give myself a quarter holiday" said she, as she sat down. "So I shut up my shop at half-past three."

"How can you speak in that way?" said Mrs Summers. "One would think you sat all day behind a counter, and sold ribbons."

"It is not the counter that makes the shop" said Harriet quaintly. Mrs Summers trifled uneasily with her spectacles. It disappointed her to see Harriet becoming, as she thought, vulgar, when she wanted her to appear at her best.

"The vicar's wife called on me this morning, and paid me for her dolman" said Harriet, after a pause. "She was greatly pleased with it, and promised to recommend me to her friends. She is a very nice old lady, and chats in a very friendly way, in spite of her grand appearance. But a still greater piece of news is that I have got a new customer: no less a person than Lady Pentry's maid, who wants a complete garden-party costume."

"Yes, yes, Harriet" said Mrs Summers; "but perhaps your business affairs are not very interesting to Mr Scott."

"On the contrary" said the artist, reddening.

"Who do you think I got a letter from on Thursday?" continued Miss Russell, disregarding her aunt: "a letter that had been sent from my old lodgings in Islington to nearly all the Miss Russells in London before it reached me?"

"I'm sure I cannot tell" said Mrs Summers.

"From Mrs Samson, who used to be so kind to me at Little Kinross. She has sold her public house to an American, who has turned it into a great *café*. I am sorry for the old place; for I believe I have run barefoot into the little private bar a thousand times to see my father. I knew all the regular frequenters perfectly well; and I remember I often used to stand on the table and sing songs for them when I was little. It was in that way that I charmed Mr Grubb, the tobacconist, who left me fifty pounds in his will. My poor father used to be proud of shewing his cronies how clever I was. Mrs Samson regrets him still, and says in four different parts of her letter, that there never was a gauger like him, and that she could not get on with the next one they appointed at all. Please excuse my rambling in this way, Mr Scott. The letter has set my mind running on the people amongst whom I have passed nearly all my life, and on the scenes where I met them."

"You may well apologize, Harriet" said Mrs Summers, ill-humoredly. "I wonder at you."

"Anything that concerns Miss Russell, interests me" said Scott. Harriet made him a curtsey, and sat in silence, at her ease, and unreasonably happy. Scott, also silent, was not at his ease, and was but disturbedly happy. Mrs Summers was silent, but neither happy nor at her ease; for she wanted to leave them alone together, and could not think of a plausible pretext for doing so. A bee flew in through the window; buzzed about the cut flowers which stood in a glass dish on the table; and flew away again.

"What a lovely day!" said Mrs Summers.

"Yes" said Scott.

"I am glad it is so hot" said Harriet. "What is called seasonable weather is good for trade."

Mrs Summers looked at her reproachfully. Another and longer silence ensued. It was broken by a knock at the door.

"Come in" cried Mrs Summers. A servant entered.

"Some ladies and gentlemen with an order to see the house" said the servant.

Harriet's expression became resolute. Scott's fingers moved to a grasping position. Mrs Summers, after an apology, and some remarks on the worry of being disturbed constantly by sightseers, left the room. Then Harriet turned attentively towards the artist, without any pretence of being unaware that his business at Perspective was with her, and waited for him to speak. He cleared his throat and began stiffly.

"I have come down here today because I felt that at our last interview I altogether failed to express the depth of my feelings on the subject which we discussed, and because I fear that I most unintentionally gave you the impression that I had not sufficiently considered the practical aspect of the step I was taking. Perhaps, also, a certain abruptness of manner which is one of my infirmities may have displeased you. As to that, my only defence is that I am an artist, and not a man of the world. I have called on Mrs Summers and explained my object to her, feeling that I could not again resort to my former plan of meeting you without still further prejudicing myself in your esteem. You have insisted on some social disparity which you fancy exists between us so much that I feel that the tumult of my feelings may expose me to the suspicion of being deficient in respect for you. I am resolved that there shall be no misconception now; and though I am conscious of expressing myself very lamely—"

"On the contrary, Mr Scott, you are making quite a speech."

The artist, completely deflated, looked at her for a moment in a red fury. Then he thrust his hands into his pockets; walked to the window; leaned against the shutter, and said:

"I beg your pardon. I deeply regret to have been so tedious."

"Not at all" said Harriet gently. "Why are you so determined to misunderstand me?"

"I! It is you who persistently misconstrue every word I say. Even if you had the common amiability to listen to me, you would not have the heart to appreciate what I mean. As well talk to the wall as to a woman."

"I am very sorry" said Harriet humbly.

"You must excuse me for saying what I think, Miss Russell; but I am a bad hand at dissimulation. And there is an end even to my patience."

"Yes."

Mr Scott looked at her angrily, and went back to his chair, with assumed carelessness, whilst she sat with her hands folded in her lap, and her calm eyes turned contentedly towards the scene without. As he tried to think of a sarcastic remark, he suddenly recollected how he had often reproached himself for his petulance at their previous interview, and made good resolutions to be wonderfully tender and courteous next time.

"You understand that I wish to renew my offer, do you not?" he said, hesitating. "What answer?" He paused.

"Did I not answer you clearly the last time?" said Harriet, a wistful tone coming into her voice in spite of her.

"I wont take that answer" said he vehemently, rising. "Do you suppose you can refuse a man in that cool fashion? Why should you refuse me? I have earned some right to be considered. I have worked hard at my art, and succeeded at it. I have never harmed anybody; and I owe no man any debt except debts of kindness. I am well off; and I have only one wish, one necessity left, and that is you. Am I to let myself be ruined by your caprice? Surely you are not heartless enough to refuse me for no reason whatsoever?"

"You must know as well as I do that you are not talking sense" said Harriet quietly. "Reason or no reason, I am not bound to marry you, although you seem to have persuaded yourself that I am."

" I have persuaded myself of nothing of the sort. I know you are not bound. I wish you were."

"You made out that my refusal was heartless. You surely cannot expect me to give up my liberty of choice because, through no fault of mine, it may bring you some disappointment."

"Some disappointment! In Heaven's name, have you any power of reasoning? What can be more heartless than to make a man whose only crime has been love for you, miserable for life? What more atrocious than to destroy the career of an artist in its very outset? You propose to do both deliberately; and then you say it is not your fault. Of course it is your fault if you can help doing it."

"But how can I help it?" said Harriet, too inexperienced not to be distressed by his vehemence, and almost losing her self-possession.

"How! You ask me how. You know as well as I do. You can help it by marrying me."

"But if I do not wish to marry you?"

"You might, for once, think of something besides yourself. It is always the same with women. They profess to be devotion and self-sacrifice incarnate. In reality they are utterly selfish."

"Mr Scott" said Harriet, rising, "I cannot think that you are jesting with me. But, if I must say it, you are talking such non-sense that I could not take your proposal seriously if I were ever so well inclined to." And she made a step towards the door.

"Can you not wait and hear what I have to say? Dont lose your temper."

This was too much for Harriet's forbearance. She gave him a look of reproach, and went resolutely towards the door. Scott placed himself before it. Any sort of coercion was, to Harriet's temperament, an outrage. Her expression became ominous.

"One moment" pleaded Scott. "I beg your pardon. I am so much crazed that I dont know whether I am talking sensibly or politely, or not."

"Please leave me at liberty to go or stay as I please."

"I will not. I am resolved not to go back today with one word unsaid."

Harriet looked at him. He returned the look in a manner which shewed that he had no intention of moving from the door. He was nervous and muscular, but small. To her strength, activity, and indifference to the superiority of his sex in combat, many a hardy urchin at Little Kinross could have testified; and Scott, as she drew a deep breath and went back to her chair, where she sat down with no more decided expression than one of sorely tried patience, little knew that her last thought before doing so had been a regret that she could not with dignity obey her impulse to give him a shaking and throw him away from the door as she had once, when only thirteen years old, thrown a cowboy of fifteen, who had tried to shut her into a field with a bull reputed to be mad. She had not been in love with the cowboy, whose head she had subsequently knocked against the gate; and she was in love with the artist. Nevertheless her fingers had tingled as she looked at him with the gate adventure in her mind.

"I ask you" said he, approaching her, "to consider seriously what I have said to you. Do not treat it flippantly, or decide hastily on a matter which is everything in the world to me. And above all, do not keep me in this state of suspense. Tell me at once whether I may regard myself as a man with a settled and happy future."

"I will tell you nothing at all."

The artist was alarmed. "Why?" said he, raising his eyebrows.

"Because a child may lead a horse to the water, but ten men cannot make him drink."

"Eh?" said Scott. Waiting in vain for an explanation, he added, "What on earth has that got to do with it?"

"You have forced me to listen to you. You cannot force me to answer you."

"I hope I have not offended you" said he, with awkward humility.

"You have left nothing unsaid or undone that could offend me."

"But on my honor, the offensive part of what I said was exactly the part I did not mean. I expressed myself badly—"

"It seemed to me, Mr Scott" interrupted Harriet, "that it was the part you did mean. While you are artificial, delivering prepared speeches and following a set design of making yourself agreeable, you are polite enough. But when you forget your design and fall into your natural manner, you try my patience almost more than I can endure for an hour. Do you think I could endure it for a lifetime?"

"I would not cause you an instant's pain for all the world. It was sheer stupidity, nothing else. Why did you not tell me that I was making a fool of myself? I would have waited for a year sooner than have annoyed you."

"When I made you understand it in the plainest manner, you forced me to put up with as much further annoyance as it suited you to inflict, by violence."

"You quite mistake me. I only wished to prevent you from acting hastily." Harriet shook her head. "You could have gone out through the window." The tightening of her lips warned him that this was too silly; and he pleaded, "It was a mere impulse, an instinctive movement on my part."

"That is precisely why I disliked it" said Harriet. "Studied actions sometimes do injustice to their authors, who may have planned them in defiance of their better sense. Instinctive actions are involuntary revelations of the real nature from which they spring." This was a verbatim quotation from Smith.

"I can only apologize" said Scott, sitting down crestfallen. "If you would only give me the right to speak to you as I feel, you would have no more reason to complain of my running into the other extreme through the pain of excessive self-constraint." He brightened a little when he had said this, and looked inquiringly at her; but she did not heed him. She was going once more through a calculation which had occupied her often during the previous fortnight. Whether was it better to become a wealthy and independent tradeswoman without any friends save those of Mrs Froster's rank, or wife, housekeeper, and nursery maid to a young artist who was very fond of her, who would introduce her to society in which, as she thought, her higher qualities would not be lost, nor her personal graces cost more circumspection to guard than they were worth, and whose fortunes she was confident of being able to further by her shrewdness sufficiently to allow her to share them without any sense of dependence.

"Mr Scott" she said, answering his last remark after a pause: "have you considered that if you marry a dressmaker, your friends, whether you like it or not, will say that you have married beneath you? And have you thought of me not only as I am at this moment, but as a constant associate, who will grow old, and from whom there will be no release?"

"I have thought it all out thoroughly. I assure you it is not my character to act without reflection."

Harriet relapsed into meditation, and seemed troubled.

"You are hesitating" said Scott, rising, and holding his chair with one hand as if that alone prevented him from running towards her. "You would not have asked me those questions if you did not mean—Do you really mean *yes*?"

Seeing that he was only waiting for her assent to seize her in his arms and kiss her, she moved her chair a few inches back with a feeling approaching to aversion. It seemed to her bad enough to become a man's property, without being pounced upon the instant the bargain was concluded.

"I will become your wife on two conditions—"

"Granted!" cried Scott, letting the chair loose, and advancing.

"Stop" said Harriet determinedly. "The two conditions are: first, that our marriage is not to be a religious ceremony."

"I would have proposed it myself; but I thought no woman would forgo the dressing and so forth at a wedding."

"Second: that, while I will undertake to consider what is due to your position as far as I can, you will not expect me to behave badly to such of my friends as are not ladies nor gentlemen."

"Of course not. And now?"

"And now" said Harriet, holding out her hand in the hope of modifying the impending caress, "we are agreed. I accept."

He caught her hand, and, stooping, kissed her with as much ardor as a gentleman, however short his stature, can, when standing, display in saluting a lady who is sitting, without losing his balance. Then he knelt on one knee beside her chair, put his arm about her waist, and pressed her shoulder to his chest, looking eagerly into her eyes all the while. But the charm did not work. Harriet endured it for more than half a minute. Then she gently disengaged herself, and said, softening the request by speaking in her sweetest tone,

"Stop. Sit down. Marriage is a very serious thing. I cant play with you now."

Scott, heavily discomfited, was yet glad to obey, not merely because his position was hurting his knee, but because he suddenly saw that his conduct was unbecoming, and that she was more serious about him than he had yet been about her. He drew a chair near but not close to her, and sat on it in silence. Before either spoke, Mrs Summers returned. Seeing them sitting silent and apparently desponding, she feared that she had come too soon, and halted in obvious embarrassment.

"Aunt" said Harriet gravely: "you will be glad to hear that I have arranged to marry Mr Scott."

"Indeed! Dear me! That will be very nice" said Mrs Summers. A pause followed this faltering congratulation. "I think we had better have some tea" she added then. Whilst she was preparing the table, Harriet went into the garden, where the artist immediately joined her.

"I wish you would go now" she said.

"Why?"

"Because I have taken a great step today; and until I am alone and quite at rest, I shall feel as if I were carrying a burden. Dont you understand?"

The artist now did understand. "I am a wretched animal" he said; "but I understand. Artists understand love better than marriage; but I am capable of learning. From you."

Harriet smiled quite radiantly.

"I will come tomorrow, early in the afternoon?" said he inquiringly. She nodded assent. Then he took his hat, and bade Mrs Summers farewell, to her surprise and relief.

"Good evening, dearest" said he, rejoining her in the garden, and taking her hand.

"Good evening, Cyril" she replied, with another smile. So he kissed her, solemnly and childishly.

# CHAPTER V

ONE afternoon in June, Lady Geraldine Porter sat in her drawing room with the blinds down. Out of doors the flagged pavement glared in the sun; and the passers-by kept the shady side of the street. At five minutes past four Ernest came noisily into the room, perspiring.

"Awfully hot" said he, dropping with a bounce into an easy chair. Lady Geraldine looked reproachfully at him.

"Ive come to keep you company" he added with a grin. "I know you are always glad to see me."

"Then be pleased to sit down quietly" said Lady Geraldine. "Your boorish manners and wearisome conversation may be your misfortune. Your habit of destroying every chair you sit in is your fault."

The next arrival was Hawkshaw, who looked almost cool.

"How shockingly warm!" said he as he sat down, his attitude languid towards the weather, attentive towards his hostess.

"What frightful heat!" said Isabella Woodward, coming in soon after the poet. "I have just left Clytie in the carriage on her way to Victoria to meet papa; and I believe she will get sunstroke, or perhaps freckles, which would be still worse."

They then considered whether that day or the preceding Tuesday had been the warmest of the season, and discussed summer garments, summer beverages, hydrophobia and the reason why so many people had already left town.

"By the way" said Lady Geraldine, addressing Hawkshaw, "I saw your friend Mr Scott the other day gazing at some furniture in a shop window. A young man so employed is always an object of suspicion to me."

"You would suspect him still more" replied Hawkshaw, "had you—like me—had the privilege of accompanying him in a walk through the suburbs. At every house which bears a bill on the window, he stops; stares; vacillates; and finally passes on with visible reluctance."

"He has just finished a wonderful picture" said Ernest. "A glorious work. He has been offered a signed blank cheque for it, to fill up himself, you know, with whatever amount he likes; yet he is not satisfied. I am not at liberty to say who made the offer."

"Pray" said Isabella, "is Mr Scott going to be married, or is he not? I am quite tired of hearing rumors about him."

"As I am the only friend in his confidence, I am really not in a position to say" said Hawkshaw, smiling significantly.

"Then he *is* going to be married, because if he were not you could have no possible reason for leaving the report uncontradicted" said Lady Geraldine. "There, Mr Hawkshaw! you have an excuse now for telling us about it, which I believe is all you have been waiting for."

Hawkshaw smiled on his hostess, and said, "I have recently had the pleasure of an introduction to a young lady in whom my unfortunate friend takes a strong interest. If he be indeed bent on marriage, she will probably be his accomplice on the occasion."

"Come, Mr Hawkshaw" said Lady Geraldine. "You have betrayed him. Spare our curiosity these 'ifs.' "

"She is wonderfully charming, is she not?" said Isabella.

"I should, if I consulted my own wishes, evade your question" replied Hawkshaw. "But Lady Geraldine *will* have it out of me. Candidly then, she is the most unpleasant woman I have ever had the misfortune to meet."

"Dear me!" said Lady Geraldine. "Then is the description you gave me ever so long ago, on the authority of Mr Woodward's secretary, a mere romance; or is it the same lady?"

"The same lady unquestionably" said Hawkshaw. "But the excellent Mr Smith is peculiar in his taste. Perhaps he is rather young, and not looking at it from our social angle, quite. No wonder poor Cyril suffers from chronic depression!"

"But what is she like?" said Isabella. "Is she bad looking? You surely did not expect style from her."

"Well, really" said Hawkshaw, "I cannot deny that she is handsome in her way. Still, beauty is dependent on associations. When I was a boy, I thought a ship of war, one of our old wooden ones,

the most beautiful object in the world. I think so still, as far as in-
animate things are concerned. Grace, grandeur, strength, and a
vigilant power within needing only provocation to devastate like
a whirlwind, all combine to make it at once admirable, beautiful,
terrible. But fancy a woman so endowed! Would you find the
same charm in her that you found in the great vessel? Can you
apply the description?"

"Perfectly" said Ernest gravely.

"Not in the least" said Lady Geraldine emphatically.

"I scarcely know how to describe her" said Hawkshaw. "She is
handsome; her individuality is above such a vulgarism as *style*;
and her understanding is distressingly acute. Her occasional affectation of simplicity is so exquisitely perfect that I confess it would
have imposed on me had it been consistent with her shrewdness
and self-command. But she is made of steel, with a heart of snow,
triply Scotch, the idealization of matter-of-fact, the sepulchre of
emotion, the shrine and sanctuary of canniness. Poor Cyril is her
puppet. She knows every note in his gamut; and no sooner does a
question rise between them than she consummately unravels it pat
to her own desire, and he submits, enraptured at her genius."

"Poor Mr Scott!" said Isabella. "I felt pretty sure that he was being trapped when he mentioned that she had refused him at first."

"The infinitude of purpose in this woman" continued Hawkshaw soaringly, conscious that Ernest was drinking in his words
to intoxication, "is not more significant of her than the utter dearth
and oblivion of passion. She is the very sublime of sordid. Now
Cyril, though not free from the brutality of the craftsman, derives
his inspiration from the true fount of idealism, the antique myth.
His sympathy with nature in her veiled aspect, when all her out-
lines are dim, and impression takes the place of perception, is
apparent in the eternal fog, mist, and storm with which he trans-
mutes canvas into nature and thought. In such a mind, the collision with everything most foreign to it, combined and clothed
with a certain measure of beauty and a subtle portion of grace,
must necessarily produce a bewilderment amounting almost to
spell. The mirage is dazzling. The man, unboundedly fertile in

himself, does not feel the aridity of the desert in which he has pitched his tent, because the insidious drain of the thirsty stone breast has not had time to make itself perceived. But what he will do when the illusion vanishes, and the sucking sand exhausts him, I shudder to think."

Ernest uttered a reverent murmur, like the response to a Litany.

"If they quarrel, they can separate, as every one else does nowadays" said Lady Geraldine, unimpressed and impatient. "Is she a nice woman? Presentable, I mean?"

"I confess that amidst the larger impressions I received, I had almost forgotten her manners. As far as my humble judgment in such profound issues can be relied on, she is presentable. These Scotch people are never uneducated as all classes in England are, more or less. Oh yes: she is presentable. I verily believe she would hold her own unabashed at a feast of the gods."

"In short, she behaves like a lady."

"No. There is no point of comparison. But she is original; and that saves every situation."

"Pray have compassion on my limited intelligence, Mr Hawkshaw. If she were sitting in the room with us at present, would she be dowdy, or awkward? Would she make Mr Scott ridiculous and make the rest of us uncomfortable if I invited them both?"

"Decidedly not, within middle class limits. And after all, Cyril is middle class. That is our tragedy: we artists. We are unique and beyond class; but we all have middle class relatives, especially wives."

"There is no difficulty about wives" said Lady Geraldine. "They are necessary and wholesome appendages to their talented husbands, who would be disreputable without them. But young ladies who are merely engaged cannot be politely invited without their mothers or whoever chaperons them. Mrs Summers is the chaperon in this case. I have not the slightest objection to her on her own account; but she is so well known that her appearance here would have to be explained; and perhaps Mr Scott would not be quite so heroic as to relish that."

"You are lost in the benighted aristocracy of this land" said

Hawkshaw gallantly. "You should be president of a republic of intellect."

"You are so wonderfully courageous, Lady Geraldine" said Isabella. "I envy you the independence with which you defy the prejudices of society. You will have to put 'No dresses made by Miss Russell of Richmond admitted' in the corner of your cards. Consider how she would feel among her former customers."

"I shall simplify the matter by not sending people of that way of thinking any cards at all" replied Lady Geraldine. "I have no sympathy with such nonsense; and I am exclusive enough not to care for the society of people who cannot afford to share my indifference. Besides, how are we to be entertained? The old practice of living on the contemplation of our own privileges is as obsolete as six o'clock dinners in Bloomsbury. We must have clever people to talk to us. Now, real cleverness is only to be found in people who depend on it for their living. Nothing else seems able to knock it into men. Look at the wonderful creatures you meet at Halkett Grosvenor's! How many of them, do you think, would care to bring their relatives with them, or to publish the domestic arrangements of the first thirty years of their lives? Yet they are the only people worth the trouble of meeting."

"They are so fond of consoling themselves for their touch of secondrateness on that ground that it is a pity they cannot hear you say so" said Hawkshaw. "But how does it apply to Cyril's canny but not coruscating betrothed?"

"Simply to shew you that if she be really clever, presentable, and respectable, it will not matter one jot what she may have been. If she married an ordinary man, the case would be different. But Mr Scott is an aesthetic pet. He is not expected to act like ordinary mortals; and his wife will be all the more interesting if she was a Highland lassie, or a colleen, or something romantic. Consequently I am not more courageous than others in taking her up: I am only farther-sighted. In a few years every one of her husband's set will have done the same."

"I do not think she will ever get into the very best society" said Isabella.

"That opens the question of which society is the best" replied Lady Geraldine. "There is—so they all say, at least—an inaccessible circle of awful people, the true cream of humanity, expensive, impervious to light, indigestible, stagnant, and uppermost, just as cream ought to be. But it is as impossible to live amongst such people as it would be for the Queen to have her crown continually on her head. Even I, who for my husband's sake have to dine drearily with them twice in the season or so, scarcely know whether their very existence be not a myth, like Mr Hawkshaw's favorite pagan deities. I know very well that when I recoil into common sense life, I invite lots of people merely because they can talk well, or sing anyway, or what not. So long as nobody talks about them, I ask no questions, and am grateful to them for saving me the expense of professional entertainers, to whom I object, as they destroy the social character of my gatherings, and make any house a mere theatre. For instance, for my last afternoon this season, I have had to engage a professional chorus of sixteen individuals for whose competence and respectability the agent who supplies me with such things pledges his honor. The result is that I am pestered for invitations by people whom I neither know nor care to know, although there will not be room for all my personal friends unless I throw open the kitchen."

"The chorus, I presume, is for my benefit" said Hawkshaw.

"I do not know, I assure you" said Lady Geraldine. "You have been so kind as to propose to recite your translation of some Greek play—you need not tell me the name: I should forget it immediately—and it appears that you are to be interrupted occasionally by a chorus. The arrangement is incomprehensible to me; but I do as I am told in the matter, about which, although I anticipate the greatest pleasure from your recitation, I understand absolutely nothing. Philistine as I am, I enjoy aestheticism after a fashion; and I am always glad to have at least one meeting every season devoted to it; although it is not often that so eminent an exponent as you deigns to assure my success."

"You are very good" said Hawkshaw. "It is unfortunate that we have had to retain an old version for the choruses. It was manufactured for the music, which, it appears, does not suit my lines. I spoke to Burton, who is going to work up the choir, about altering the music, as I suppose it could easily be adapted to my rhythms; but like all musicians, he is conservatism personified, and evidently considers the music the principal feature in the affair. So I left matters as they were."

"Whose music is it?" said Isabella.

"I dont know" replied Hawkshaw. "Mozart or Verdi, or some such hackneyed composer."

"Mendelssohn, I think" said Ernest. "Burton is strong on Mendelssohn."

"Very possibly" said Hawkshaw, rising to take his leave. "I have no doubt one man can do that sort of thing as well as another." He then withdrew with Ernest, who never missed a chance of being seen in Piccadilly with a fashionable man of letters. When they were gone, Lady Geraldine sighed with relief, and said,

"I could endure the stuff which Mr Hawkshaw talks so glibly every day, provided he would always carry Ernest away with him. My nephew's three o'clock visits commonly terminate at seven when I dine out; otherwise not until midnight. How is Mr Woodward? He does not seem to be half so busy as he used to be."

"That is because he has got a secretary."

"Oh! The amiable young man who told you all about the future Mrs Scott?"

"Yes. He has the study nearly all to himself now; for papa has become so lazy since he found that Mr Smith could do all his business better than he could himself, that he only goes down for a minute to sign his letters, and to do any of the family correspondence that does not fall to my lot. He actually makes Mr Smith open all the letters. The other day, happening to go in, I found him grinning over a long bill of Madame Lesparre's for my clothes and things. He told me he had instructions to pay it, if I would be good enough to check it."

"Still, if he was going to pay it—!"

"Just so. I checked it like a lamb. He is very useful, because nothing would be done now without him. Clytie calls him The Drugget. He doesnt mind. He cares for nothing but using long words. 'My one technical accomplishment' he says, 'is a laboriously acquired discrimination in carpets, cloths, and patent flooring stuffs.' He buys them for us. He puts his finger on a roll of oilcloth and says, 'For nearly three years I kept the ledgers of the man who introduced that detestable pattern into England.' Clytie thinks he is too stupid to know when she makes fun of him; but he knows perfectly well. I think he is a good young man, who reads a chapter of the Bible every night before going to bed. Although I must say he is very nice, considering."

"Considering what?"

"Well, his position and antecedents, of course. It is a relief to find that at least he never was a shopman."

"Nonsense! I cannot understand how you Irish people are so far behind your time in that respect. If I were an Irishman, I would be an ardent republican. I would wear red caps, and keep a stand of pikes in my pantry. Yet you are worse than the Hindoos in your devotion to caste. What a pity it is that your culture is not equal to your brains!"

"How about the English, whose brains are not equal to their culture? But dont fancy that I am disposed to defend my country. I hate Ireland. It is the slowest, furthest behind its time, dowdiest, and most detestably snobbish place on the surface of the earth. Papa wants me to go to Dublin this winter. But I wont. I feel that we are in the middle of a great Art movement; and I cannot live without art and artists: life without them is brutality, as somebody says. The Dublin mob of successful tradesmen, lawyers and doctors, with their eternal silly-clever gabbling persiflage, all of it ill natured—no: never! I would rather spend my life in the most out-of-the-way village on the continent than in that horrible house of ours in Pembroke Road."

"Dear me! I get on very well with Irish people."

"You are English. My father says that you attribute to us all the romantic virtues of schoolboys—in which we are remarkably deficient—to excuse yourselves from treating us as responsible people."

"Miss Woodward's carriage" said a servant, entering.

"That means that Clytie and Mr Woodward dont intend to honor me with a call" said Lady Geraldine. "Goodbye!"

"Papa is tired after his journey from Brighton" said Isabella. "Besides, he will have all the letters of the last three days to go over with Mr Smith after dinner; and whenever he has any such prospect he firmly believes that he has not an instant to spare. Goodbye, dear Lady Geraldine."

That evening was one of the few which Isabella passed in her father's house during the season. She was in low spirits; and she sat for a long time, thinking of Lady Geraldine's intention of countenancing Cyril Scott's bride.

It was her custom, when suffering from nervous disturbance, to seek relief in two ways. When depressed, she cried, and drank strong tea. When irritated, she stamped at intervals, and vehemently ejaculated "Damn!" In both cases the remedy predisposed her to give way more readily to the next attack. At present, neither of these resources was convenient; for she was seated on a balcony formed by the roof of the porch, and could be seen through the window by her father and Smith, who were seated at a table in the back drawing room. Mr Woodward was unusually busy in consequence of having received a petition which his constituents wished him to present. Also, as he made it a rule to speak in parliament at least once every session, he had requested Smith to examine a blue-book with a view to the compilation of a harangue long enough to fill at least a column of the local Irish newspaper.

"I think weve settled all the letters now" said he, yawning.

Smith assented, seeing that his employer was pleading for a postponement of further work.

"Have you had time to skim over that blue-book since?" said Mr Woodward, broaching the subject unwillingly.

"I read it through carefully—"

"Blood an' 'ouns!" ejaculated Mr Woodward, "you dont mean to say you read it all?"

"I did; and I think I have extracted all that is necessary."

"I'd rather you read it than I. I wonder what that petition is about. Have you read *it?*"

"I have." Mr Woodward looked at him with admiration. "But I dont very clearly understand it. Some man named Magrath—"

"Magra" said Mr Woodward, correcting him.

"—Magra" resumed Smith, "shot a bailiff because some estate was striped, whatever that means; and he was sent to penal servitude. The petition is for his release, on the ground that he was provoked; that the bailiff's mother could well afford to lose her son; and other reasons which seem to be quite irrelevant."

"What a pack of fools they are! They know as well as I do that the petition is all stuff. Pack it back to them; and tell them not to bother me. I remember Magrath's father in the days of the Shanavests; and a bitter bad one he was. Well, well! Is there anything else to be done?"

"Unless you would like to dictate your speech to me."

"Just write it out yourself: I can look over it when youre done. Theyll like your long words and your literary style." Smith blushed. "Youll find last year's in that old newspaper that I had in my hand a minute ago—Lord knows where it's gone to now! That will give you the hang of it. All you have to do is to fill it up with this year's names and figures, and just alter it enough to save appearances. Anything will do for the fools to see in the paper. I wont read half of it: I'll just say whatever comes into my head."

"But" said Smith, alarmed, "will it not be a different Act of Parliament, or a new measure of some kind, that you will speak about?"

"Not a bit of it. It's just the same every year. When we go into supply, I get up and move ten or twenty thousand pounds off the vote for the constabulary. All I want is a few new figures to shew that theyre not wanted, and that theyre only a lot of idle blackguards stealing about the roads in the quietest country in the world; though God knows what we should do without them! Do you think you can manage it for me?"

"I will try."

"Thats right. And now, I'm so tired and knocked up by travelling, and driving, and writing, and one thing or another, that I think I'll be off to bed."

"Then perhaps I had better take the speech home with me and work at it there."

"Oh no. Sit where you are. Nobody'll say a word to you for the next two hours. Only dont overdo it. Too much writing and blue-book reading has shaken many a man's health. So away with you the minute you feel tired. Heigho! Goodnight."

Smith bade him goodnight. Mr Woodward yawned; rubbed his eyes; and went into the front room.

"Bella, my dear" said he: "I hope youre not catching cold there."

She shook her head without turning to him.

"You havnt got the toothache, I hope?"

"No" said she, rousing herself. "What put that into your head? Are you going to bed?"

"Yes. I am tired and—Goodnight!"

"Goodnight!" said she, kissing him, and feeling inclined to cry as he patted her paternally. When he was gone, she looked into the room, and saw the secretary seated in the light of a reading lamp at a distant table, writing, deleting, and cogitating alternately. At his first revision of the printed speech of the previous year he reduced it by more than three-quarters, in which state it appeared to such advantage that he resolved to submit it to Mr Woodward in the hope that he would prefer conciseness and elegance to verbose obscurity. Lest, however, he might appear to have grudged the toil of preparing a long speech, he paraphrased the original in full, remodelling the ornamental portion of it to his own taste, and introducing a quotation from Thomas Moore. Thus he was enabled to offer his employer a speech after both fashions; and in the upshot Mr Woodward delivered the condensed one in committee of supply, and sent the other to the local paper, perceiving in both a fresh proof of the capacity of his secretary.

Smith was commencing this task when Isabella turned wearily from the deepening shadows on the sheds, glass-houses, and unfinished buildings of the Exhibition site. She crossed the front room listlessly, and stopped at the side of the table opposite to that at which the secretary was writing. He looked up; noted her drawn face and dull eyes; guessed her state of mind; and expressed a hope that he was not in the way.

"Oh dear, no" she replied, dropping into an easy-chair.

"The sight of anybody writing is almost as annoying as that of two persons whispering. It is a communication of ideas in which the spectator has no part" said Smith.

Isabella was too moody to relish the secretary's inveterate sententiousness. She made no reply; and he resumed his work silently.

"How I envy you!" said she, after watching him for some time. "You can work."

"I *have* to work" replied Smith; "and when a thing, no matter how good it may be, becomes compulsory, it ceases to be a luxury. I, on the contrary, envy you because you can work and choose your work. It is a grand thing to be able to say 'I *can* work.' There is somewhat less credit in saying 'I *must* work.' "

"That is all very fine. But people never do work unless they are forced to."

"So much the worse for them; for if they have any brains they are always in the blues."

"And that, Heaven knows, is punishment enough."

"It is probably the only really terrible affliction which excites derision instead of sympathy; except, perhaps, sea-sickness. Work is the only thing for it."

"Why is it that though it is so much pleasanter to work than to be idle, yet people do idle?"

"For exactly the same reason that although it is much pleasanter to be able to speak German than not, few Englishmen do speak it. It is not at all pleasant to learn. It is just as necessary to learn how to work as to learn how to do anything else; and the apprenticeship is so irksome that people would rather endure idleness than face it."

"But the preparation is work too; and I thought all work was pleasant when the habit of working was formed."

"I doubt that. There is no such thing really as idleness; for the idle people are often the busiest; but they are unsatisfied. I suppose work in the sense we mean is sustained and intelligently directed effort resulting in the production or attainment of some worthy end. No doubt Shakespear revelled in the power of writing plays to an extent which overpaid him for the drudgery of inking them down; but he probably took as little pleasure in his copybook and English grammar as any other schoolboy."

"Then I wish I had learned to work."

"So you can. You can paint."

"I can *not* paint, Mr Smith; and you know that perfectly well."

Smith had heard of the uncertainty of Miss Woodward's temper; but this was his first glimpse of it in action.

"All artists despair of perfection" said he.

"Thank you for the sarcasm."

"I assure you I did not mean it that way. After all, if you are resolved never to paint until you are perfect in it—a point which no man ever yet believed himself to have reached—you will be like your countryman who would not go into the water until he could swim."

"It is of no use: I have had a professional opinion on the subject. Mr Scott told me I could not paint, and that I never should. I know perfectly well that I am good for nothing."

"To believe that you are good for nothing is the first step towards becoming so" said Smith, improving the occasion as usual.

"I wish I were dead: if there were only an easy way of dying."

"I assure you there are many easy ways" said Smith gravely. "If you really wish to kill yourself, I am sure I can find out the best way. I will get some books on toxicology at South Kensington, and look up the subject for you."

"Thank you. When I am in a hurry to die, I will find out a way for myself. Ugh! It's not right to talk in that way, Mr Smith."

Smith grinned. "Do you remember the fable of death and the woodman?" said he.

"Pray do not talk about death" she said, with a shiver.

"I beg your pardon for thoughtlessly following up the subject" said Smith, proud of his indifference to the terror which was so grim to her. "I am so accustomed to think of the subject that I am apt to forget that it is less familiar to others."

This confirmed Isabella's impression that the secretary was religious. "I suppose the fear of death is natural to every one" she said; "but it has no more terror for a Catholic than for any one else."

"I do not doubt it" replied Smith, surprised by this unexpected application of his remark.

"So far from it" continued she, looking at him as if defying him to contradict her, "Catholicism is the only religion which gives you assurance for the future life. It does not leave you on your deathbed in a vague uncertainty, as Protestantism does. You can expiate your sins, and be assured of happiness at last without any dreadful alternative of everlasting torment."

"That depends on the value of the assurance" said Smith, too young and too militantly sceptical to leave the point unobjected to. "Besides, you have the certainty of purgatorial torment; and as, if a man believes anything on his deathbed, it is not that he is bad enough to go to hell, why, I should imagine that a Protestant takes his chance rather more comfortably."

"We are not to believe or disbelieve things according as they seem comfortable to us or not."

"Very true" replied Smith, prudently returning to his work.

Miss Woodward looked at him with dissatisfaction; for she preferred dogmatic contradiction to an assent which evidently belied the conviction of her opponent. Forgetting that Smith was an Englishman, she felt sure that he was at that moment enjoying the consciousness of superiority with which an Irish Protestant contemplates Roman Catholicism.

"It is a pity" said she sourly, "that so many people mistake bigotry for religion."

"There is no real difference" said Smith. "The only man in The Pilgrim's Progress who is not a bigot is Mr Worldly Wiseman. I would not give a halfpenny for the faith of a votary who would not cut off the whole human race if it differed from him."

"Then I am thankful to know that your power falls short of your will. I should be sorry to be as pious as you are. But since I changed my own belief I have begun to see that the Protestants are really the bigots. When I believed what I was taught in my childhood, I used to fancy that Catholics were all wicked persecutors; that to confute them, it was only necessary to open a Bible; that Queen Elizabeth and Lady Jane Grey were in the habit of silencing cardinals with their arguments; and many other things equally opposed to the truth. I know better now; but my experience ought to be a warning to those who are too confident in their own opinions."

"Have you ever applied it to your present opinions, Miss Woodward?"

"There is no need, because my present opinions have the sanction of God's Church. Besides, I have shewn, by renouncing the errors I was bred in, that I am not swayed by prejudice."

"Then you think that a false religion is like measles or scarlatina: that no one is likely to catch it twice?"

"My religion is not false" said Isabella indignantly. "Pray speak for your own, of which you may possibly know something."

"Excuse me. I have no desire to obtrude the fact on any to whom it may be a matter of indifference; but it is due to myself to disclaim most emphatically the influence of any religion whatsoever."

"You dont mean to say that you are an atheist" said Isabella, with sudden interest and a complete change of tone.

"Atheist is a bad counter for interpreting between us; for it probably conveys an entirely different impression to each of us. Further it implies affirmation. My position is one of pure negation. I am an Agnostic." He felt like Professor Tyndall or Mr Huxley as he spoke.

# IMMATURITY

"How strange! I did not think you went so much into society. I suppose you write for the magazines."

"I do neither. What a curious association of ideas!"

"Well, no man who goes in for being aesthetic ever does believe anything nowadays. Lots of strong-minded women do the same. It is really very dreadful when one thinks seriously about it. For my own part I think the intense devotion of the Byzantine painters far more beautiful."

"It is valuable and interesting now because it is happily extinct. But it must have been a very lamentable obstacle in the eyes of such of its thoughtful contemporaries as were impatient for the advance of civilization."

"Extinct! Why, I think Mr Donovan Browne's pictures overflow with it."

"On the contrary" said Smith, rising and putting away his papers: "they dont contain one scrap of it. Angelico and Filippo Lippi and the rest of them painted as if they were sent on earth to glorify God. Mr Donovan Browne paints as if he were self-dedicated to the task of painting beautiful pictures, or, in other words, of ennobling his fellow-creatures; and if we were not tired of the part of his genius which belongs to our own age, and blind to that which belongs to the infinite epoch of the highest art, we should draw a triumphant contrast instead of an apologetic comparison between him and an admirable but obsolete school which owed its concentration to mental narrowness."

Hawkshaw himself could scarcely have surpassed this. Isabella stared. Smith bade her goodnight, and made haste to go, lest he should spoil the effect of his eloquence by subsequent triviality.

# CHAPTER VI

AT noon on the following day, a party of excursionists, passing Richmond on their way to Hampton Court Palace by steamer, made themselves merry at a man who was reclining on some cushions in the stern of a boat sculled by a young woman in a dress of striped calico and a huge straw hat without any trimming. She handled the sculls skilfully, keeping within the shadow of the bank, but apparently indifferent to the heat of the noonday sun.

"Thats right, old chap. Take care of yourself" shouted a man from the steamer.

"Hev a piller" cried another, throwing out a crumpled paper bag.

A groan followed these witticisms. The rower checked the boat until it was tossing in the steamer's wake. The man scowled at his deriders, and turned again to his shipmate, at whose face he had been gazing before the passage of the steamer. Seeing her smile at the ridicule to which her exertions had exposed him, he shifted himself uneasily, and laughed.

"It is impossible to appreciate a cockney" said he, "except when he is in the country, making holiday. Canals ought to be made for them, if they must go a-sailing. They dont appreciate scenery; and they interfere with the artist's business."

"They appreciate it, in their way, just as much as you do. There: the wash of her paddles is just catching us, and you will get splashed. I told you so" she added, with a laugh, as a few drops fell on his face and provoked him to an exclamation of impatience. Then she bent to her oars again; and the boat went on so suddenly that her companion fell supine on the cushions.

"I wish youd let me pull" said he, when he had recovered himself.

"I hate to sit idle and let another person do for me what I can do better for myself."

"So do I."

"So cannot you."

"No doubt you can manage a boat better than anybody, and could teach Noah navigation. But I would *like* to row."

"You only think it. It is never a pleasure to do what we cannot do well. You would enjoy it about as much as I would painting a picture. However, you shall have one oar at least when we come back against the tide."

"I wish you would come and sit here, and let the boat go wherever it pleases. I have something to say to you."

"No. I am not going to loll about in this weather. Let us talk as we are." She sent the boat a little further from the bank, steadied it, and said, "Go on."

"I want to know when we are to be married" said he. "Betrothal may be the sweetest time to most people; but it is only a period of oppression to me. You wont let me give you presents, or spend half my leisure time with you. Every feeling which comes more from the heart than from the head is 'nonsense' according to you. I am afraid to behave as if I cared a jot for you, lest you should think me a fool, or make me feel like one. You seem to take more interest in business and external matters than in our closest personal concerns."

"Poor Cyril!"

"Yes; but I want to know how soon I am to cease being poor Cyril. I do not see any reason why we should not get married at once."

"Nor do I."

"Well" said he, lifting himself on his elbows; "but are you ready?"

"I have been quite ready since last Tuesday."

"And why on earth did you not tell me so?"

"I did not wish to hurry you." He made a gesture of impatience.

"I was only waiting to complete the transfer of my business to two very good workwomen who were associated with me in London, and who wanted to enter into partnership with me here. They gave me two hundred pounds for assigning them the lease; and I have handed them over the stock for the sake of old acquaintance, and so got rid of the whole concern. When you consider that I did not invest a hundred and thirty pounds in the business; that I made from three to as much as fifteen per cent while I carried it on; and that the making of the connection was a mere stroke of luck, I think I have done very well."

"I am glad you have got rid of it; though, for the matter of that, I could have given you two hundred pounds and saved you all the bother. However, now that your three per cents and eight per cents are off your mind for good, how soon, seriously, may I arrange to be married?"

"Seriously, I am ready when you are ready. Dont upset the boat, please."

"I am ready to pull ashore and go into the first church or registrar's we meet."

"I should not mind; but you will have to provide a license and a ring. It would be as well, too, to have some idea of what we are going to do when we *are* married."

"I suppose we shall go off somewhere. Where would you like to go?"

"To Jerusalem."

"And Madagascar?"

"I am in earnest. I want to see Italy, where Vasari's painters lived. I want to see Palestine; and I would rather have all my gadding about over before we settle down in a house of our own. The variety of travelling will help you to get used to me. If we went to some stupid place you would soon be tired of me."

"Never. Remember that I have all my love-making to do yet; for you have defrauded me of the rights of courtship. Let us go to a quiet place just for a little."

"Remember the fate of Mr Vesey. But, Cyril, lad: have you any plans of your own?"

"No. I was thinking that perhaps you would like to go to Scotland."

"What part of Scotland?"

"I dont exactly know. I suppose St Andrews, or Edinburgh, or

Glasgow, or— Are there any other places in Scotland?"

"One or two others. Now, will you listen to my plan? It is an expensive and a troublesome one."

"Hang the expense! What is it?"

"Go tomorrow to wherever the proper place is; and get a license for the nearest date you possibly can. Not one of those expensive special licenses, though: there is no use in wasting fifty pounds to save a fortnight. Then—when we are married, I mean—to please you, we will go to some country place for a fortnight. By that time you will be in as great a hurry to come back as you are now to go. Dont interrupt me. We will stay in London as long as is necessary to prepare for travelling; and then we will go as far round the world as we can afford time and money for: that is, if you can work in foreign countries; for if it would interrupt your career, it must all be given up."

"Not a bit. We will see everything together; and I shall have a holiday for the first time these ten years. There is plenty for me to pick up wherever there is a cloud and a sun in the sky; so it will not really be lost time. Not, mind you, that I believe a man need go further in London than the nearest unfashionable square to find something just as well worth painting, and just as hard to paint, as the bay of Naples, or a sunset at Damascus that could be worked up with a sixpenny bottle of magenta dye. Nor, as an artist, can I stand as much picture gallery as most tourists can. However, I defy any country on earth not to teach me something; and I defy all the world to weary me when you are by my side."

Harriet dipped her oars, and pulled a vigorous stroke. Then she said,

"I half doubt whether I am not doing you an injury in marrying you. You talk as though you had never seen married people in your life."

"I never have seen such a couple as I have determined that we shall be. Why are you so resolved on our being unhappy?"

"I have no intention of being unhappy. But there are different kinds of happiness. We are very happy now, roaming idly about the river on a lovely summer day—at least, I am happy. Still, would a life of this kind be bearable, much less delightful?"

"What is the use of bothering ourselves about it when there is no chance of our spending our life like this? No matter what happens, if I have only your sympathy, we will walk hand in hand—"

"Yes, I know. I hope we will. Well" she continued, more gaily: "is my plan a good one?"

"Capital. We will talk it over as soon as I find out about the license."

"Aye: you always put off business to some other time. However, I am as little disposed to trouble about it today as you are; but then I have earned the right to be lazy. All my baggage is ready, and my affairs in order. Aunt Angel will keep what little unportable property I possess until we have a house of our own. At what time is Mr Hawkshaw to be here?"

"Half-past three, he said."

"Then get up and unship that big oar; and we will pull back to the bridge" said Harriet, laying aside the sculls. "I am going to be stroke; so you must pass me; and pray do not capsize the boat, as you will if you attempt any nonsense."

Scott stood up; set the boat rocking; and reeled to the place assigned to him, without giving his betrothed anything more tender than a blow on the shoulder from his knee. When she had satisfied him that the injury was not of a fatal nature (for in spite of the solidity of the impact he felt as though he had trod on a butterfly), they pulled briskly towards the bridge, and were presently hailed by Hawkshaw, who descended to the riverside and embarked with less than his usual languid grace of movement. Dexterity in the management of boats was not one of the accomplishments which the poet and the artist had acquired in the days of their early intimacy.

"Allow me to take your place, Miss Russell" said Hawkshaw.

"Thank you" said Harriet, "I will keep my place until we get up to a less crowded spot."

"I dare not gainsay you" said Hawkshaw, shrugging his shoulders; "but it is irksome to sit inactive and see you tugging at the oar."

"It is still more irksome to swim in your clothes" said Harriet. "Now, Cyril: pull hard; and put us out into the tide."

Scott put forth all his strength, and splashed his companions a good deal. The poet opened Miss Russell's sunshade; placed it betwixt himself and the blade of his friend's oar; and reposed on the cushions until the boat was again in solitary waters away from the town. Then they pulled in to the bank; laid by their oars; and entered into conversation.

"The bliss of gliding along, abandoned to your care, in such a scene as this, is one of those sensations which only a poet can understand" said Hawkshaw. "You do everything so consummately, Miss Russell."

"It is well we have a poet here to enjoy it" replied Harriet. "It would be a pity to throw away such a sensation."

"Hawkshaw" said Scott; "Harriet and I are going to be married tomorrow."

"Tomorrow!"

"As soon as we can" said Scott. "So you may hold yourself in readiness to officiate as witness, or father, or best man, or whatever your function may be."

"I am ready, aye ready. If I may ask, what are your subsequent arrangements?"

Scott acquainted him with the plan which Harriet had proposed.

"You will be in town during the last week of July?" said Hawkshaw.

"I suppose so" said Scott.

"Then you must give me one of your wedding cards to send to some one."

"A card!" said Scott doubtfully. "Shall we get cards printed, Harriet?"

"Certainly not, as far as I am concerned" said Harriet.

"For whom do you want cards?" said Scott.

"I will tell you" replied Hawkshaw. "On the afternoon of the twenty-eighth, our robustly minded friend Lady Geraldine Porter will hold her last reception of this season. On that occasion, your unworthy servant will entertain the company by reading his latest production, a translation from the Greek. There will be some singing as well. Grosvenor will be there—and everybody else."

"What has that to do with us?" said Scott. "Apart from wishing success to your translation, of course."

"Be good enough to hear me out. The At Home lacks a factor essential to its completeness; and if I can put Lady Geraldine in a position to supply it, I shall engage her everlasting gratitude. The one thing needful is—"

"Myself, I suppose" said Scott, looking indignantly at Hawkshaw.

"Ha! ha! ha! No. Lady Geraldine will content herself modestly with the better half of so illustrious a man. In a word, she has set her heart on the distinction of being the first to welcome Mrs Cyril Scott; and if you both run away without making a sign, she will hardly know how to do it."

Scott looked inquiringly at Harriet.

"I hope that does not mean to go to the house of a lady who never saw me, merely because her friends want to stare at me" said Harriet, troubled.

"My dear Miss Russell" said Hawkshaw: "the truth is the truth. You will be stared at, and hard stared at, as long as there is taste in man or envy in woman [Harriet shook her head impatiently]. Lady Geraldine, as you say, has never seen you; therefore the only sentiment directly personal to yourself which she can possibly feel is one of curiosity. But her disposition towards you as the wife of Cyril, in whom she takes quite a motherly interest [Scott repudiated this with a toss of his head], is kindly in the extreme. You must distinguish between Lady Geraldine's invitation and an attempt to secure your services for the gratification of social inquisitiveness. She is not your friend; but she invites you in order that you may become her friend. If she does so, I am very sensible that she will receive a boon more enviable than it is in her power to confer; and thus your pride need not hesitate to accept a distinction which your compliance will prodigally overpay."

"Believe me, Mr Hawkshaw" said Harriet, "you derive far more pleasure from your own skill in composing pretty phrases than from any gratification which they are likely to afford to me. I had hoped to be able to defer my first plunge, or rather my first soar, into society until our return from the continent; but I would make up my mind to go if I could feel quite sure that I might not do Cyril more harm by going than by staying away."

"Please yourself" said Scott. "I am not in the least dependent on society. If it came to such a push, I can do without society more easily than it can do without me. Humph! Artists, whatever their faults may be, are not to be had by the dozen at the nearest tailor's."

"Ajax raging amongst the sheep, as usual" said Hawkshaw. "I am quite sure—setting aside as too absurd for contradiction the possibility of your presence doing Cyril any harm—that your staying away would be attributed to his fear of society."

"Worse than that" said Harriet, speaking just in time to avert an expression of defiance from Scott, "I might fancy that fear, or at least, some want of resolution, had influenced me. We had better go."

"Then let it be understood most distinctly" said Scott, "that I go because Harriet wishes, and not because I care one snap of my fingers for society, or any of its surmises, or attributions, or interferences in the concerns of others."

"It shall be set forth in a neat handbill, and distributed amongst the guests" replied Hawkshaw.

"Go to the devil" said Scott, turning angrily away. Then, ashamed of the disrespect for Harriet's presence implied by his swearing, he added, "I beg your pardon, Harriet; but that—that *ass* would provoke anybody."

"You hear how he abuses his best friends, Miss Russell" said Hawkshaw. "May I take it then that you will go?"

"Are we expected to bind ourselves body and soul to Lady—?"

"Yes" said Harriet, interrupting Cyril: "we will go if she does not think better of inviting us."

"I undertake that she will not" said Hawkshaw. "By the way, Cyril, who will be at the wedding besides myself?"

"Nobody that I know of" replied Cyril, looking inquiringly at Harriet. Hawkshaw noticed that he answered no question without making this mute reference.

"What? None of your family?"

"Most decidedly not" said Scott. "I dont want to be bothered with a pack of women who would want to dress, and eat, and make the whole affair uncomfortable by being strangers to Harriet. She will see quite enough of them afterwards. We have arranged to have only yourself."

"But one witness will not be enough" said Hawkshaw. "What about Mrs Summers?"

"I had rather she did not come" said Harriet; "but if she wishes to, it would be wrong to make the least objection; so we had better count on her. If she is content to stay at home, and another person is necessary, I know a Mr Smith who would be sure to come. I do not know whether he is old enough to be a witness; but I would be glad to have him in any case. He is the only person in England with whom I am on terms that would justify me in asking for such an accommodation; and indeed I am so far indebted to him that I think I ought to pay him the compliment—such as it is—of letting him know how I have cast my lot."

"You never told me anything about him before" said Scott.

"You would scarcely take as much interest in him as he took in me" said Harriet. "Very likely you have seen him, Mr Hawkshaw. He is secretary to your friend Mr Woodward."

"Isabella's father!" exclaimed Scott.

"You never told me about Isabella before" said Harriet.

"Pshaw!" said Scott. "I think I know the man you mean. You remember" continued he, turning to Hawkshaw: "there was a reedy looking young fellow sitting at the table the morning I met you at Queen's Gate."

"That is he" said Hawkshaw. "He was talking that morning, and was coming out rather when you came in and stopped him."

"May I ask him to come?" said Harriet.

"Certainly, if you wish" said Cyril.

"Then" said Harriet, "we have arranged all our business matters; and we had better be getting back. Dinner will be ready at half-past five."

"Had I a less imperious hostess" said Hawkshaw rhythmically, "I would plead to be allowed to lie here as long as the sun should sustain itself above the horizon."

"I am sorry to disturb you, and still more so to shock you" said Harriet; "but your imperious hostess has rowed a good deal, and is exceedingly hungry."

"Enough: you are the mistress, not the slave of human prejudices. You impart a touch of romance even to hunger. But I move on one condition only. You must let me take your oar."

"Very well" said Harriet reluctantly. "You two shall row me home. I hope we may arrive in safety."

"With such a freight" replied Hawkshaw, "we can fail only through excess of care." He rose as he spoke, and cautiously changed places with Harriet, who reclined on the cushions whilst the two young men sent the boat through the water zigzag: Cyril splashing whilst Hawkshaw handled his oar warily, with the air of a man engaged in a difficult matter, and resolved not to make a false step.

"This is a much handsomer vessel than the one we hired last day" said he, when he had grown sufficiently accustomed to his work to speak. "Did you get it at the same place?"

"It is not hired" said Scott. "It is one of Grosvenor's. I told him last week that I was in the habit of coming down here; and he offered me the run of his boathouse."

"Yes" said Harriet; "and Cyril came down the next day and insisted on taking out one of the two gondolas that are there."

"A gondola!" said Hawkshaw. "Why didnt you bring it out today?"

"You will not catch me in it again" said Scott. "Everybody stares at it; nobody can row it; and out of the two in the boathouse, one is so rotten that it would snap across if you got into it, and the other leaks like a sieve."

"The usual fate of such notions" said Hawkshaw. "Where is the boathouse?"

"In the grounds" said Scott. "Pull away."

They were now traversing that part of the river which adjoined Perspective Park. Ahead was a rectangular stone building into which the water flowed through a wooden gate.

"This must be the scene of your adventure with Isabella Woodward" said Hawkshaw. "She tells it very well, too."

"I dont know what you are talking about" said Scott. "What adventure?"

"According to her account" said Hawkshaw, "you were strolling along the river's margin in sweet communion with her, when you slipped; sent her flying in the midst of a cloud of her own sketches into the wood; and went backwards yourself head over heels into the water."

"Cyril, Cyril!" cried Harriet: "you are drenching me. Do put in your oar properly."

"What outrageous lies that woman tells!" said Cyril. "No such thing ever happened. I was standing over there one evening, when she came out of the wood; and I believe I knocked down her sketchbook by accident. That was all. I wish people would not be always coupling her name with mine; as if we were anything more than the merest of acquaintances. She had the audacity to show me some miserable sketches—Hallo! Weve shot past the boathouse. We will have to turn."

"So we have" said Harriet. "Stop pulling, Mr Hawkshaw. Drop your oar into the water and hold it there steadily; and do you, Cyril, pull as hard as you can."

When Hawkshaw opposed the blade of his oar to the water, he was surprised to find the handle recoil upon his chest; travel upwards until it obtained a purchase against his chin; and roll him backwards over the thwart into the well of the boat, where he lay gasping for breath. At the same moment, Scott, making a vigorous stroke, failed to reach the water with his oar, which skimmed along the surface and sent him heels over head into a position similar to that of his friend, whose downfall, however, was neither so sudden nor so violent. Harriet, quickly placing a hand on each gunwale of the boat, prevented it from capsizing, but was unable to catch either of the oars, which floated past her down the stream. Presently the artist, with his face red, and his hair disordered, rose, followed more deliberately by Hawkshaw, who was pale, breathless, partly discomfited and partly amused by the mishap.

"What the mischief did you do that for?" said Scott.

"My dear fellow, do not add unjust reproach to the physical anguish of a misfortune which I am so far from being responsible for, that I do not even comprehend its nature. My oar became possessed of a demon."

Harriet was laughing so that the boat shook.

"I am glad to have amused you" said Scott. "Where are the oars, I wonder?"

"Somewhere in the neighbourhood of Teddington, by this time" replied Hawkshaw.

"Humph! This is a nice thing. Grosvenor's oars are lost; and I have a lump on the back of my head as big as an egg."

"And—not to mention that all the salient portions of my person are severely abraded—I am, I feel sure, a study in black and blue."

"Serve you right for your stupidity. What on earth made you do it?"

"I know what my oar—or rather Grosvenor's oar—" said Hawkshaw, glancing down the river, "did; but for the life of me I cannot understand how you were involved in my fate."

"Oh, dear! dear!" said Harriet. "Pray excuse me, Mr Hawkshaw: I could not help laughing. Cyril's tumble was his own fault. He caught a crab."

"How can you talk such nonsense?" said Scott. "Is it likely that I could catch a crab after rowing all day? I am not such an idiot as that. It was Hawkshaw who made some confounded mistake and came flying all over the boat."

"Never mind him, Mr Hawkshaw. But we must start at once after the oars if we mean to overtake them. I will take the sculls;

and you can both rest yourselves. Now pray dont delay. You ought both to be ashamed to offer to supply my place after what has passed."

"I feel that deeply" said Hawkshaw, crawling to the stern. "Do as you will, Miss Russell. I had rather write an epic than row another mile tonight."

"Harriet" said Scott sternly: "sit down. I will row."

"Cyril" said Hawkshaw: "dont be such an old fool. If you lose our last pair of oars, which you will, if, as is most probable, you catch another crab, we shall drift up and down with the tides until the crack of doom."

"I am not jesting now" said Cyril. "I have decided to row."

An angry feeling came to Harriet at his tone. When she had suppressed it, she sat down on the thwart just quitted by the poet, and said,

"Cyril: are you annoyed?"

"He has got a bump on his admired head, poor fellow" said Hawkshaw from behind them.

Scott looked angrily down, irresolutely up at her face, and then alternately from right to left with a shamefaced laugh. At length he caught her hand; squeezed it; kissed it; and went to the stern, where he threw himself down beside Hawkshaw, whilst Harriet unshipped the sculls and rowed swiftly down the stream. They watched in silence for the missing oars, and soon saw one entangled in the weeds near the bank. Shortly afterwards they overtook the other; captured it; and returned against the stream, keeping close to the margin, and picking up the one which they had observed before, as they passed.

At dinner, Hawkshaw gave Mrs Summers a fanciful account of the accident.

"Lord ha mercy!" said Mrs Summers. "It's a wonder you were not all drowned. And what would I have done if the oars had been lost?"

"By a judicious parade of our corpses" said Hawkshaw, "you might have diverted general attention to the lesser calamity."

"Goodness forbid! I wonder at you, Mr Hawkshaw, to speak,

283

even in jest, as if two oars were of more importance than the lives of three fellow creatures, let alone my own niece."

"You are very right" said Hawkshaw. "It was an unbecoming remark; and I am ashamed of my thoughtlessness."

After dinner, they discussed the best means of travelling; and the two men related their experiences of continental sightseeing until the hour arrived for their departure. Harriet walked with Scott to the gate. Hawkshaw purposely lingered to say a few words to Mrs Summers about her potted flowers, of which he was qualified to speak: several of his shorter poems being little more than rhythmical lists of garden-produce.

"Cyril" said Harriet, as they crossed the lawn: "tell me the truth about Lady Geraldine Porter's house. Ought I to go there?"

"Why not?"

"Well, in travelling about, we shall meet people; and I may have some opportunities of becoming used to society. Do you think you would feel more at ease if I put off going about with you until then?"

"Put all that out of your head" said Cyril, to whom the sensation of reassuring Harriet was agreeably novel. "If you dont value my opinion, you may be quite sure that Hawkshaw would not be eager to get the credit of your appearance unless he thought you beyond criticism, as I do. He is a dandy, and may be relied on in such matters. He studies to conciliate society, which is more than I have ever thought worth my while."

"Mr Hawkshaw is not too refined to make fun of Aunt Angel to her face; and I am not afraid of any society which is satisfied with him. But I am not sure that the habit of conciliating other people does not give him the advantage of you sometimes."

"You mean that I am more selfish than he?" said Scott, reddening.

"Not in large matters" said Harriet gravely. "I should be sorry to compare him to you seriously. But do you know that he is a great deal more good-humored than you, and more sensible in putting up with the little annoyances which happen to everybody occasionally?"

"I know I made a fool of myself for a moment in the boat. It is not pleasant to be conscious of having done that, as I too often am. But you must make some allowance for the misfortune of being an artist. It is all very well for Hawkshaw, who turns out cheap wares by priming himself up now and then for a desperate fit of working, and gets credit for it all the moment it is before the public, to take things easily. It is different with me; for I have drudged year after year until I have very little patience left for anything but work. If it was easy work, that could be dashed off by the help of a few tricks in a fit of enthusiasm, like his poetry, a man might keep his nerves robust at it. But it is the holding on day after day only a hair's breadth from failure, and putting on every touch with his heart in his mouth, that makes a painter sensitive; and that is the way I work even still; for no matter how sure I am of my hand—and I have paid the price for becoming a tolerable workman—something new is always turning up, and always will, unless I take to cobbling up the same trick over and over again like Vesey, which I hope never to do. Being a master in my trade means being an apprentice for life, bothered by the remarks, and impertinences, and lies of critics and snobs, whom, despicable as they are, one cant ignore, knowing how easily they might blunder on some truth. When you have stared for six months at a piece of canvas, you see it so differently from other people that you are ready to believe anybody's eyesight sooner than your own. With all this strain to be endured, a very small addition makes a great difference; and, besides, it brings about a habit of calculating on a sure reward for patience, which makes the gratuitous worries of commonplace life doubly unendurable. Just think of all this when you see me irritated for a moment by some trifle; and above all, remember that it is this very sensitiveness which makes sympathy so indescribably precious to an artist.

Harriet looked thoughtfully at the ground, and said nothing. Scott, having made that kind of speech which makes its author feel ridiculous when it fails to make an impression, glanced at her with disappointment. At last he said,

"Has it ever occurred to you that sympathy is just as real a necessity to a man as money, or clothes, or properly cooked dinners?"

"I think that this necessity for sympathy is a very bad fashion, and nothing but a fashion. I believe that people nowadays are proud of being pettish, and think it a great thing to say that they are hard to please; that they cant bear this, and cant endure that; that they are misunderstood—"

"I was not talking about mere humbug."

"I am not sure of that."

"What are you not sure of?"

"I do not mean that the feelings you have described are not real; but if you are proud of being easily annoyed, or feel a bit less obliged to bear your share of everyday drawbacks than ordinary people, I think that *that* is what you call humbug."

"Indeed? Then you suppose that an artist's feelings are as blunt as those of a stockbroker?"

"I dont see why a stockbroker should not have feelings like an artist; although he has to learn to keep them to himself, and to know his place in the world. But in any case, if an artist is superior in feeling, he ought to be just as superior in self-control?"

"You seem to know a great deal about artists."

"As far as I have read about them, they seem to have tempers the same as ordinary men. I suppose when a painter finds himself impatient he says 'This is the sensitiveness of an artist.' And when he is in a good humor he thinks it is something special to himself too."

Scott did not answer her. When they approached the gate, he turned and saw Hawkshaw following them at some distance, putting on his gloves leisurely.

"Come on, cant you?" shouted the artist. "We shall lose the train."

Hawkshaw looked up in surprise; took out his watch; shook his head; and did not hurry himself.

"Fancy" said he, when he joined them, "leaving this charming spot, and its more charming associations, with any but the lingering steps of regret."

"Good night" said Scott, taking Harriet's hand with formal courtesy.

"Good night" said she, looking at his face. At this moment, she suddenly thought of his somersault in the boat, and smiled. He, unwilling to be charmed, turned away towards the gate; and Hawkshaw enjoyed the remainder of the smile.

"Adieu, Miss Russell" said he, delicately squeezing her hand. "This day shall be consecrated in my memory as an idyll." He always pronounced idyll with a short *i* because it was more useful so for rhyming to fiddle, middle, and riddle.

He followed Scott to the gate, thanking Miss Gwendoline with so much urbanity as she held it open for him that she had a pleasant revery about him afterwards. "For" she thought, "if that Scotchwoman, who is only the housekeeper's niece, and as hard as nails into the bargain, can catch an artist, why should not I have just as good a chance with a poet?"

"My dear Cyril" said Hawkshaw, when he overtook his friend, "I recant. She is altogether charming. When I said she had no softness, no feeling, no sympathy, I blasphemed. Beneath the veil of her incomparable originality, she is made up of all three."

"I am glad you have found it out. I wish I could."

"Oho! Sits the wind in that quarter?" Receiving no answer, he continued, "At any rate, we have succeeded in penetrating her former baffling impassibility. Heavens! how she laughed when we came to grief on the river!"

"Humph!"

"What a reproof to human vanity! I really believed that the boat received its volition from us, up to the moment when the Thames asserted its supremacy beneath my chin. I know I shall feel quite upset tomorrow in consequence of it. I envy you your insensibility, my friend. You craftsmen, who drudge away day after day until effort becomes your routine. brutalize yourselves for everything else but your work. You catch a crab; flare up into a rage; and feel the mishap in the essentially vulgar manner of a common boatman. But I, who never worked steadily in my life, and am a creature of impressions, am sensitive enough to feel such a dislocation in a day's poem for a whole week."

Scott looked up as though to make some hasty reply, but checked himself.

"And why so dull?" said Hawkshaw.

"Dont bother me."

"Poor wretch! I had forgot your imminent nuptials. No wonder you are sad. No matter. Take heart, my friend. You are not married yet."

"I am as good as married. She has sold her business, and committed me to her irrevocably."

"You dont say so! She must be fond of you. I did not think she was the woman to trust her livelihood to the promise of a mortal man until she had him padlocked for life. Happy Cyril!"

"The trust is the padlock, as you would see if you had any common sense. However, there is no use in talking about it now. Whether I am making a fool of myself or not, I am in for it. Let me hear no more of the subject."

Hawkshaw raised his eyebrows; pursed his lips; and gave a whistle which descended a major ninth in pitch before it ceased. Then he shrugged his shoulders; and the two friends walked to the train without exchanging another word.

# CHAPTER VII

In the forenoon of the first of July, Scott and Hawkshaw, strolling together along the arrival platform of Waterloo Terminus, were joined by Smith.

"Ah! our friend Mr Smith!" said Hawkshaw, lightly shaking the secretary's hand.

"How dye do?" said Scott, who did not seem at his ease. However, he shook hands with friendly vigor.

"We are all in good time" said Smith. "There are more than ten minutes to spare yet."

All three looked at their watches.

"It is one of those occasions" said Hawkshaw, "on which the consequences of being late are so unspeakable that even the strongest minds rush into the opposite extreme and come too soon. Mr Scott and I have been perambulating this secluded end of the platform for the last eight minutes. May I suggest our continuing to do so until the train comes in."

As they walked to and fro as far as possible from the expectant luggage trucks, porters, cabmen, and postal officials, Hawkshaw and Smith chatted; and Scott occasionally laughed, and affected carelessness for a moment, after which he put his fingers into the pocket of his waistcoat to reassure himself that some object therein had been neither lost nor forgotten. When the hour at which the train was due had passed, they stood on the edge of the platform, and looked up the line in silence; Smith envying the careless gaiety assumed by Hawkshaw, and the latter, though conscious of the success of his own dissimulation, equally envying the apparent imperturbability of Smith. At length the last few belated porters ran across the line and scrambled upon the platform just in time to escape the buffers of the engine; Scott felt in his pocket for the last time; the train stopped; and Harriet alighted. She shook hands with Smith; and then all four smiled at one another.

"What about your luggage?" said Smith.

"It has all been sent on to St Pancras, thank you" said Harriet.

"Well" said Scott: "I suppose we had better take a four-wheeler to the—"

"To the scene of action" suggested Hawkshaw.

"It will save time to go in two hansoms" said Smith. "I will call them."

"Our friend unexpectedly proves to be a man of action and resource" said Hawkshaw. "I feel angry with myself for not forestalling his happy thought."

The rattling of the cabs prevented further conversation until they reached the Strand, where an accident had interrupted the traffic.

"What are they all stopping for?" said Harriet.

"A block, I suppose" said Scott. "They seem quite content to stay here all day, too. I wish all the drivers in the street were going to be married."

"I should say most of them are married already, to judge by their faces." Cyril looked at her, and then at the surrounding drivers, who did not look happy. Few drivers do, in a block. The traffic was presently resumed; and Scott said nothing more, but mused as they went on. Harriet also was thoughtful. They had been bound to one another for some weeks; and, though they had derived much pleasure from the union, the bond had chafed them more than once. The artist, because he had not been prepared for this, and the dressmaker, because she had been prepared for it, felt despondent as they prepared to make their covenant irrevocable.

When the block occurred, Hawkshaw, in the other hansom, asked Smith whether the Woodwards were quite well.

"Pleasant people, are they not?" said he, leaning lazily back against the cushions.

"Yes" said Smith.

"Very charming girl, Miss Woodward, is she not?" said Hawkshaw, watching the secretary.

"Which Miss Woodward do you mean?"

"Eh?"

"No doubt you refer to Miss Isabella?"

"No doubt I do. However, it is obvious from what you say that you have never thought about her one way or the other."

Smith resolved to defeat the poet. "My remarks are not to be depended on" he said. "Something odd about your question induced me to parry it: for what reason, I do not know—probably because the fact of a man thinking about a young lady at all is usually construed as an indication of romantic regard. She seems to me to be rather interesting to study, but decidedly too frivolous to admire."

Shortly afterwards the two cabs stopped at the office of a registrar, before whom Cyril Scott and Harriet Russell contracted with one another to become man and wife. During the formalities of the very simple but quite impressive civil marriage ceremony, the bride maintained her ordinary composure. Scott was hasty and nervous in his manner, and disconcerted by the compassionate interest with which the registrar seemed to regard him. He attempted to take possession of Harriet's marriage lines, and was put completely out of countenance when the registrar baffled him. He was further taken aback on being told that the contract was complete before he had removed the ring from his waistcoat pocket. The registrar then informed him that the rite of putting on the ring, though unnecessary, might be performed for the entertainment of his friends; and Harriet received the symbol of the estate into which she had entered before Smith and Hawkshaw, who conducted themselves with becoming gravity during the transaction. This done, they took leave of the registrar; re-entered the cabs; and drove to St Pancras. On the way thither, no remarks were made in either conveyance other than might have passed between distant acquaintances. The newly married couple were to go to York that day, and continue their journey to Scotland next morning. They had sent their luggage before them; and when Cyril had reclaimed a travelling bag at the parcel office, and secured an empty carriage, nothing remained to be done until the departure of the train, before which about ten minutes remained to them for congratulation and farewell. Scott turned from his wife to his friend.

"Well" he said: "I will see you before we go abroad."

"Yes" said Hawkshaw: "it will break my fall from friend of the man to friend of the family."

"Stuff! Seriously, my marriage need not make the slightest difference in our relations."

"My dear fellow: it need not; but it will. It always does. A year ago I was next to your manly heart, over my regard for which I vainly try to appear unsentimental at the present juncture. Already I am next but one. In a year, I may at best be next but two. And so on."

"Why dont you get married yourself?"

"That would be burning the candle of friendship at both ends. I prefer to wait and watch the results of the experiment on you. Besides, you must remember that I cannot roll in guineas as you can."

"You can if you work hard enough."

"Do not obtrude the spectre Drudgery on me at such a moment as this. I may work when you go—or perhaps drink would console me better; for I am convinced that I am still young enough to leave this platform with the most desolate sensations."

"What ever you do, dont drink."

"Brandy is absolutely necessary to make my ideas flow. I know what that shake of your head means; but they are capital ideas, I assure you. Better live ten years drunk and write a hundred poems, than sixty years sober and compile soullessly for the publishers. I sacrifice myself to art."

"You will never persuade me that a man can work better drunk than sober. However, there is no use going over the old argument again."

"Not the slightest. Let us eat and drink—especially the latter—for tomorrow we die."

In the meantime, Harriet and Smith conversed also.

"I hope" said he, "that you will not put the past so completely away from you as not to remember our old studies when you are amongst a French-speaking people, or wandering in the flesh through those galleries of Italy which we used to visit cheaply in imagination."

"I am sure I shall enjoy myself very much. When I become weary of idly looking at all the shows, I shall find plenty of occupation in the worries of travelling: luggage, lodgings, and such things. I look forward especially to the pictures."

"Yes. It will be better than South Kensington by gaslight, and Saturday afternoon at the National Gallery. Mr Scott will discuss the pictures with you much better than I used to."

"I doubt whether he will listen to my opinions with as much patience. I shall owe my capacity for enjoying my travels to you."

"I fear that when you see the works we used to read of, and enter into the society of men of the stamp of those who wrote of them, I shall fall back into a very insignificant place. I can only console myself with the reflection that though we lose our respect for our earliest guardians and instructors as we grow up, we sometimes retain our regard for them."

"Perhaps, Mr. Smith, you may take the opportunity to grow up simultaneously with me, and keep your start in the race. It is as easy to stand up and push as to sit down and mope."

"That depends on one's constitution. I have no aptitude for pushing, and would only make a fool of myself if I tried it. I know your opinion of me well enough; but I can only go on in my own way."

"It is a very bad way, if it turns your education and cleverness to no account. Pray excuse me for lecturing you."

"Take your seats, please" cried the guard.

Scott shook hands cordially with Smith; fervently with Hawkshaw.

"Goodbye, my dear fellow" said the poet, controlling his voice with difficulty. "This ends the first act of us; and we shall be devilishly old and sordid before the second is over." Scott shook his head, and said nothing.

"Goodbye, Mrs Scott" said Smith.

"Goodbye" said Harriet, laughing at the first mention of her new name. Bidding the two men farewell gaily, she entered the carriage, followed by her husband, who presently appeared at the window in a travelling cap. The three men looked as cheerful as possible, and glanced along the platform at the subsiding hustle as the last passenger took his place and the last door was slammed. Then the guard gave the signal; and the train rolled away: Hawkshaw flourishing his glove in response to the waving cap of the bridegroom.

When the train was out of sight, Smith turned to his companion with a triumphant consciousness of his own unabated spirits, and of the weakness of the cynic and fine gentleman, whose eyes were wet.

"Mr Hawkshaw" said he: "I feel sure that you would prefer to digest this scene alone. Good morning. You will pardon my abruptness, I hope."

"Certainly" said Hawkshaw coldly. "Good morning."

In the afternoon, Smith went to South Kensington, to the gardens of the Horticultural Society,[1] for which Mr Woodward, who was a fellow, had given him an admission. Here he wiled away the time by watching the game of lawn tennis, which was being played at every available spot in the gardens by parties of ladies and gentlemen. At one of the nets there Miss Woodward, her sister Clytie, and Ernest were among the players.

Smith turned back to avoid passing them, and strolled away to another part of the grounds. In a few minutes he heard a footstep behind him. Turning, he saw Isabella approaching him, racket in hand.

"Why did you run away from us?" she said, looking, not at him, but at the grass on her right-hand side.

"I was not quite sure that you regarded my right to approach your party as a matter of course."

"What nonsense!"

"You are very kind; but I think your sister is just a little intolerant of that unfortunate carpet sinister on my escutcheon."

"Clytie can scarcely pretend to be fastidious when she accepts the attentions of such an idiot as Ernest Porter. By the way, I

[1] Now replaced by the Imperial Institute and the Natural History Museum.

thought you had gone out of town today."

"I! No."

"Papa mentioned that you had gone off somewhere; and that gave me the idea that you were in the country."

"I got his permission to leave before he came down this morning, as I had an early appointment. I was at a wedding."

"Not your own, I presume. You look much too happy."

"Not my own, I am glad to say, Miss Woodward; but that of a friend of mine to—I believe—a friend of yours."

"And are they really married?"

"Then you knew all about it. I thought it was to be kept a dead secret until this afternoon."

"I knew, when you mentioned a wedding, whose it must be. Pray tell me what it was like. Ladies, you know, are always curious about such things."

"And gentlemen, unfortunately, never can describe them properly. You can picture the uninteresting figures of the bridegroom, Mr Hawkshaw, and myself. We were the only persons present beside Miss Russell, as she was then. We met her at Waterloo; bowled off to a registrar's in a couple of cabs; got married—that is, she did; went straight to St Pancras; and parted: the principals going off to Scotland together, and the witnesses creeping back to their bachelordom severally."

"I hope the bride looked charming. Let us walk about a little."

"I omitted a description of her dress from sheer ignorance. She looked very well, and wore a plain travelling dress of some kind."

"Did you or Mr Hawkshaw drive in her cab to the registrar's?"

"What a question, Miss Woodward! Mr Scott drove with her, of course."

"She must be a very queer woman to drive to her wedding in the same vehicle as her bridgeroom. And had she no lady with her?"

"No. Her aunt is not active enough for such flying expeditions; and she pleaded illness and her fear of the heat. In reality I suspect she looks on the civil contract as a heathen rite, which she would have compromised her faith by attending. She also wished to keep a friend, whom Miss Russell declined to ask, in countenance by staying at home with her."

"I fancy her people must be glad to get rid of her, or they would scarcely treat her in that way."

"Wait until you see her, Miss Woodward. At present you have quite a false impression of her."

"So you think, Mr Smith. But I know what women are."

"I assure you you are mistaken. Mrs Scott cannot be imagined. She is unique."

"Yes, yes. I am sick of hearing of her virtues. Mr Hawkshaw talks as if she were the only woman in London. Poor girl, her glamor will wear off soon enough. I presume she will make an attempt to get into society."

"I do not know."

"If so, I pity her. She will only get snubbed for her pains. However, perhaps her fibre is coarse enough to stand snubbing. I wonder how Mr Scott will like it though. He is excessively sensitive; and I believe it will kill him, or drive him mad. But indeed he must be mad already. He might have married *so* well."

"I doubt if he could have done better than he has done."

"Oh, you dont know how popular he was. He might have had almost anybody for the asking. How can men do such insane things? Money, birth, an appreciation which he will seek in vain from a common nature, all thrown away for a mere fancy. His frankness has ruined him. Any woman who was not troubled with too much self-respect could have twisted him round her finger; and no doubt this Miss Russell saw her chance and made the most of it. Not that I blame her. She was quite right—from her point of view. Ah! I envy people who know the world and have no scruples."

Smith said nothing.

"His career is ended now, of course."

"How so?"

"He has thrown himself away; and society will throw him away too."

"Perhaps Mr Scott's experience of society may have led him to believe that it had nothing to offer him which he cared for so much as the privilege of marrying the person he liked best."

"The person he liked best! The idea of a man entrapped by a cunning workgirl, trying to figure as an independent chooser after his own taste! We shall see, when he wakes from his dream."

"You must remember that he had seen a great many women who never worked. It is possible that on deliberately comparing the results of frivolity with those of labor, he may—being a working man himself—have greatly preferred the latter."

"That may be fine philosophy; but it is not the common sense of society."

"The common sense of society may be an admirable guide to the common forms of society; but it is not applicable to such a very uncommon transaction as the choice of a wife is to each individual."

Isabella uttered an exclamation of impatience. "There is no use in talking to a man on such subjects" said she. "They never can understand anything that is under their noses."

Smith thought that she must be sincerely convinced of this to display her feelings as she was doing at present. "Allow me to carry that racket for you" said he, awkwardly trying to change the subject.

"Thank you; but I prefer to have something in my hand" she replied, restlessly swinging it to and fro as she walked. A pause followed, during which she looked doubtfully at his face twice.

"I hope you do not suppose that I have any personal objection to Mr Scott's marriage" said she, at last. "Men are always fishing for motives."

"I conclude that you take an interest in Mr Scott, and are sorry to believe—however erroneously—that he has made a false step."

"But you are quite mistaken. I do *not* take an interest in Mr. Scott. His fate is a matter of the most profound indifference to me."

"You surely do yourself an injustice, Miss Woodward. A young and handsome man of genius must inspire some interest in all cultivated minds."

"But I was speaking of personal interest."

"Oh! you mean that you were not in love with him?"

"No, not exactly that—How absurd you are, Mr Smith! How old is Mrs Scott, if I may ask without incurring a suspicion of jealousy?"

"I do not remember exactly; although I have heard her mention her age. My impression is that she is twenty-four or twenty-five."

"So old? She acknowledges twenty-four?" Isabella was twenty-four, and spoke of herself as an old woman whenever she told her acquaintances that she was twenty-one.

"She is probably younger than she looks" said Smith. "Her style is not girlish, but essentially womanlike. Her matured self-possession is one of her charms."

"So you have implied several times. You should have worn a green scarf this morning. I am beginning to think that you did not come out of your acquaintance with her quite unscathed."

"I do not think I have ever been in love. But I have no doubt that I would have fallen into it headlong with her if she had permitted me. I am glad now that she did not. After all, it would have been ridiculous, since I am so much younger than she."

As he was speaking, they came within view of the tennis net which Isabella had left. Clytie had been joined by some gentlemen. Isabella raised her hand to her head to assure herself that her hair was neat and to readjust her hat. Smith noted these circumstances.

"I find that my time is spent" said he, looking at his watch. "I must go home."

"You wont join us?"

"I cannot."

Miss Woodward ran off to the tennis ground, and arrived there with sparkling eyes, affecting exhaustion. Smith left the gardens.

## CHAPTER VIII

LADY GERALDINE PORTER'S friends assembled at Wilton Place on the afternoon of the 28th July, to hear Mr Patrick Hawkshaw recite his new translation of a Greek tragedy, with music by Mendelssohn.

Smith arrived punctually at four o'clock, and saluted Lady Geraldine with stolidity, the effect of fright induced by his inexperience of the forms of society. He owed his invitation, which had been sent him through Mr Woodward, to his fame as a witness of the romantic wedding, and to the hostess's conclusion that an honor conferred on him would please the bride. His presence was acknowledged with a nod by Hawkshaw, who was dressed in a long black coat, dove-colored trousers, primrose gloves, and a bronze-hued scarf, fastened by a brooch representing a small green beetle with red eyes. Except that his manner was more effusive than usual, he did not seem discomposed by the imminence of a task the mere imagination of having to accomplish which made Smith's knees knock together. Isabella arrived at a quarter past four. She wore a black straw hat with a crimson ostrich feather and an unusually wide brim, lined with white silk, the radiating pleats of which made a halo about her face. Her dress was of black silk, trimmed with gold braid, and decorated with bows of rich crimson. It was tied back to define her shape, and was made with sleeves and skirt short enough to show her high kid boots and black gloves, the latter reaching to the elbow, and having three fine lines of crimson thread on the back of the hand. In color the costume reminded Smith of that worn by the enemy of man on the operatic stage. The opposite extreme of taste was represented by a young lady with a short fuzzy crop of auburn hair, and only one visible garment, which was of a leaden color, and clung to her like an old-fashioned bathing gown fresh from the ocean. She kept her eyes wide open; moved slowly; and looked sad. Smith discovered subsequently that she was a sister of Scott, and a person of lively and agreeable humor, as he might have surmised at once had he recollected how little disposition those to whom grief is a reality feel to turn it to account in fashion or play.

The room soon became crowded. A servant made his way to the reading desk and placed upon it a portfolio of green velvet, from which some pages of manuscript protruded. Mr Burton appeared at the piano, and, finding himself stared at, turned over the pages of the score with a critical air. Then there entered a file of eight females, two middle-aged and stout, four old and shrivelled, one young and pretty, and one doubtful as to both years and charms. They placed themselves on the chairs behind the reading desk; four sopranos to the left, and four contraltos to the right. They were followed by an equal number of men, of whom some were meek and close-shaven, and others coarse and moustached. They seated themselves behind their female colleagues; four tenors to the left, and four basses to the right. Among the latter was one with long black hair, prominent features, and a ghastly appearance, painful to see because the man was young and well built. When he had taken his place, he scanned the audience with a haughty expression, assumed to conceal the embarrassment caused by his unfamiliar surroundings. Smith, recognizing him, turned his face away in order to avoid being seen by him. Isabella was watching the door; and the secretary saw her pass from eager curiosity to impatience as guest after guest arrived. Presently Mr Burton raised the top of the grand pianoforte, and cut off the view of the door hitherto enjoyed by the choristers on the right. Then Ernest appeared, jerking his thumb over his shoulder towards the staircase, and implying generally by his expression and demeanour that some notable arrival was imminent. A half silence followed, during which those who had not noticed Ernest's antics heard their own voices so distinctly that they also became silent, and turned round just in time to see Scott as he entered, ruddy with sunburn and confusion, accompanied by Harriet and a small party who had joined them in the hall and on the stairs. Those who did not understand the interest of the occasion appealed for information to their neighbors. Guests near the door pushed forward and stood on tiptoe.

Others, more remote, even stood on chairs to see what the rest were staring at. There was a trace of anxiety in Harriet's expression; and she blushed a little as she responded to Lady Geraldine's warm greeting. Isabella looked at her for a long time, and then turned slowly towards Scott. But she could see no sign of disappointment or disillusion in his vigorously happy face. He seemed to feel ridiculous in public as a newly married man; but he submitted with good humor to much hand-shaking, and was evidently pleased by the cordiality of his welcome. Lady Geraldine was delighted with Harriet, whose appearance not only dispelled all her misgivings, but surpassed the favorable expectations which she had founded on the reports of Hawkshaw.

Seeing the poet excite general envy by hastening to pay his respects to Mrs Scott, Smith resolved to follow his example. He accordingly left the corner to which he had retired, and made his way towards a sofa near the door on which Harriet was seated; but before he reached it, Burton, who was becoming impatient, struck some chords on the pianoforte; and the audience, bating their voices, returned to their chairs. Smith took the nearest vacant seat. Isabella had placed herself on the sofa: Ernest and Miss Scott being between her and Harriet. Scott, always restless in society, particularly during musical performances, stood among a group of men close to the door, where his retreat was open to solitude and sleep in the other reception rooms.

Hawkshaw now advanced to the rostrum. On it were a reading desk, an armchair, and a small table with a croft of water and a tumbler. The poet took his handkerchief from his pocket and laid it at hand on the table; poured out some water; pulled off his gloves; opened his manuscript; and flirted a few leaves before arranging it for use. He then said that he proposed to himself the honor of introducing an unworthy struggle of his to interpret betwixt his hearers and a master mind of Hellas whose gigantic shadow illumined all subsequent dramatic poetry. The poetic intellect, he added, would not mistake this graphic paradox for what is called a bull. A brief criticism of Greek literature followed; and he concluded by promising that Mr Burton and the

choir would enable students of the collision of diverse tempera-
ments to analyse the mode in which the graceful Jew had illustrated in his own divine art the inspirations of the rugged Titan
of antique song. As Hawkshaw sank into his chair and seemed
lost in thought, the music began. It was new to the choir, who
had been selected less for their voices and appearance than for
their proficiency in reading at sight, and was indifferently executed. Hawkshaw, who had privately complained of the excision
of some of his most passionate lines by Lady Geraldine on the
ground that they were not fit to be read in a respectable house,
so puzzled his hearers by compound adjectives that they were
divided between admiration for his genius and regret that they
had been induced to listen to him.

Meanwhile, the principal bass singer was attracting general
attention. His coarse, tremulous voice, wrecked by ill-usage and
imitation of the common manner of Italian operatic singing, had
a rattling sound as he forced it into prominence above all the rest,
which made nervous listeners shudder. He inflated his lungs twice
as often as his colleagues, who were themselves not very skilful
in the art of husbanding their breath; and in the intervals occupied
by the recitation he was covered with perspiration and seemed to
suffer from successive extremes of heat and cold. Yet, whether
sitting or singing, he posed himself defiantly, as though challeng-
ing a comparison of his person with that of Hawkshaw, whose
slight figure, refined affectation, and voice no more than ordinarily resonant, he apparently despised. When he first stood up
and became visible to those near the door, Smith saw Harriet
recognize him, and lean back so as to be screened from the platform by her sister-in-law. Ernest relieved the tedium of listening
by burlesquing his peculiarities in pantomime for the amusement
of Isabella, who vainly strove to abash her entertainer by the
severity of her expression. Lady Geraldine sat close by, sternly
watching her nephew, and hoping that she was exceptional in
her want of relish for Attic tragedy.

At last Hawkshaw closed his manuscript; thanked the audience
for their sympathy; and descended from the platform amidst ap-

plause. A general rising followed. Young ladies dressed like Miss Scott shook the poet's hand. Young men with long hair patted him on the back. A few persons thanked Mr Burton for the exquisite music, but were stolidly received by him. Scott, and others who had spent the past hour downstairs, reappeared and declared themselves enraptured by the performance. Smith remained in his place until the choristers rose to leave the room, when he made his way to Harriet, and stood before her so as to screen her from persons passing out. This stratagem succeeded: Davis neither identified Smith's back nor saw through it, but strode out with an imitation of his old elastic gait, which he was compelled to drop as he descended the stairs holding the balustrade.

"Thank you" said Harriet, as she gave Smith her hand. "That was very thoughtful and clever of you."

To be complimented on his address was novel and pleasant to Smith. "The unfortunate wretch must be dying" said he. "I hope you enjoyed your stay in Scotland?"

"Much better than I expected. We tramped about a good deal for the first week. Then we settled in a very pretty cottage on a dairy farm; and I tried to make Cyril paint, quite uselessly. When he was not sitting in a swing that hung in the garden, watching me at work with a trowel, we were haymaking, driving cows, splashing the milk by way of churning, and behaving altogether in a very nonsensical way. I had no idea that Cyril was such a boy; and I certainly would not have believed that I could be still such a girl."

"It was quite romantic."

"Yes; and, as you know, I am not in the least romantic."

"That confirms what you used to say, that romantic people have not sense enough to be really happy."

"What heresy do I hear Mr Smith utter?" said Isabella, taking the opportunity afforded by the rising of Ernest and Miss Scott to move towards Harriet.

"I was merely quoting" said Smith; "so you must not hold me responsible."

Harriet restrained an impulse to turn round too quickly to her

303

neighbor. She raised her eyes without any appearance of special interest. She looked at the large hat, the tight dress, and the long gloves, and never again credited Miss Woodward with any attraction for her husband. Isabella, conscious of this survey, reciprocated it, hoping to find some disadvantage which distance had hitherto concealed. She discovered that Harriet's holiday had left her a little freckled, and that her boots, square-toed and large enough for her feet, were unfashionable. At this moment Scott came up, and, greeting Smith, failed to notice the presence of Isabella.

"You have forgotten me, I suppose" said she in a low voice, as the artist stood before her, grinning at Smith with much less reserve than he had used in his bachelor days.

"I beg your pardon" said he, looking round, and taking her proffered hand. She looked up at him for a moment with a smile which conveyed a tender reproach. He immediately dropped her hand.

"You look very happy" she said sadly, but still smiling.

"Well, I suppose I do" said he bluntly. "Why should I not? How is your father?"

"He is as well as usual."

"How are you?" Isabella was about to imply that she had not long to live, and did not care how soon she died, when he continued, "But you need not tell me. You look the perfection of health and—and beauty." This was the first compliment he had ever paid her; and he jibbed at it quite obviously.

"Go on" said she, casting away her prudence at a sudden impulse: "you need not fear misconstruction now." He laughed, and said,

"No. You see the advantage of being a married man."

"I see the change."

"Then you think I am changed?" said he, with awkward jocularity.

"You seem to be less oppressed by a sense of your aesthetic dignity than you used to be."

"How so?"

"You are actually condescending to something like good humor. I should have liked extremely to see you driving cows or sitting in a swing."

"Humph!" said Scott, with his old petulance. "You think that art and artificiality are one and the same thing; and you think it ridiculous for me to enjoy myself naturally."

"I think nothing of the sort. You are as touchy as ever."

"I touchy!" exclaimed Scott, too amazed to be indignant.

"I long to be in the country myself, far from all this heartless society, and in daily contact with Nature."

"In that hat?" said Scott, looking at it dubiously.

Isabella, now seriously annoyed, replied sharply, "Pray, Mr Scott, are you laughing at my dress?"

"Not at all. I am admiring it. It is highly original."

"Another change effected by matrimony! You used not to know whether one had a dress on at all or not. No doubt you have had your attention drawn to the subject since you entered the domestic state.'

Scott's color deepened; and he looked fiercely at her to discover by her face whether she had intended an allusion to his wife's former calling. She looked back at him smiling, with her lips apart and her teeth closed. Fortunately Hawkshaw joined them at that moment, and changed the subject.

Meanwhile Lady Geraldine was on the landing, remonstrating with a man attired, notwithstanding the season, in a brown overcoat with an Astrakhan collar. His moustache was waxed at the ends; and he shrugged his shoulders in deprecation like a Neapolitan. But his accent was British: his foreign air had been acquired in Leicester Square.

"Who is he, and what is the matter with him?" said Lady Geraldine.

"Signor Cartouche" the man was beginning, drawing back his elbows and turning up his gloved palms, when Lady Geraldine interrupted him imperiously.

"How dare you send a person named Cartouche into my house?"

"What could I do, madame? I could not send you artists. You wanted good readers; and it is well known that he who learns music by note ceases to be *artiste*. The greatest Italian singers—"

"Nonsense. I know nothing about artists: I asked you for respectable-looking people."

"But, madame, upon my honor Signor Cartouche is most respectable. He has been a public speaker, a preacher. His health is unfortunately shattered; but he reads music excellently; and those who can do so are so hard to get now, with both opera houses open, and rehearsals daily at each, that I could not have replaced him in London. Besides, he has a magnificent voice."

"It is quite useless to tell me about magnificent voices. I dont understand music. But I understand common sense; and I know that his appearance is shocking, his behavior obtrusive, and his voice much too loud for my drawing room. He has drunk a quantity of claret cup in the dining room; and he is now excited and very unpleasant."

"I am deeply sorry, madame. I shall never engage him again."

"I do not wish to ruin the unfortunate man" said Lady Geraldine, startled. "But I beg you will get him out of the house at once."

"He shall leave instantly" said the agent.

"So much the better!" said Lady Geraldine. "Except for him, I'm perfectly satisfied with your arrangements. Good evening." She turned from him to enter the drawing room, when she was confronted by Ernest.

"Where are the Scotts?" said she. "I want them to come downstairs."

"Go in to Mrs Scott, and you will see no end of a lark" said Ernest. "She and old Musgrave are having a pitched battle with Hawkshaw and Bella Woodward about poetry and painting and the deuce knows what not. Musgrave is pumping Mrs S.; and she is coming out stunningly. Listen to the row theyre making."

Lady Geraldine listened, and heard the resounding tones of Musgrave above the chatter of the other speakers.

"You havnt a word to say, Mr Hawkshaw. You are floored. Mrs Scott is quite right; and you havnt a leg to stand on. Come down with me, maam; and let us refresh ourselves. Lots of prog in the dining room."

Harriet descended the stairs with Musgrave, followed by Hawkshaw and Isabella. Lady Geraldine came down with them. When they reached the hall an unusual stillness in the adjoining room, broken only by a few footsteps, and the voice of a man speaking with subdued tone and soothing emphasis, caused Lady Geraldine to stop and look inquiringly at Hawkshaw.

Musgrave, unheeding, walked in with Harriet, and found himself in a lane which the company had formed, coming towards him through which was Davis, his eyes brighter than before, his cheeks flushed, and his arm interlaced with that of the agent, who was coaxing him from the room.

"Come, come, Cartouche" said the agent. "Theres a good fellow. You are a little upset with the afternoon's work."

"I tell you" said Davis scornfully, "I am as well as any man here. I can speak as well—or better—than any man here. Any man here—"

"Yes" said the agent. "I know youre quite well. I want to say something to you outside. Just two words on important business. As a gentleman, you will oblige me. Come, Cartouche! As a gentleman."

"I am no gentleman" said Davis, wrenching himself free from the other. "I tell you all" he continued, turning to those around him with a gesture of admonition, "that there is a day coming when your fine coats, and your high titles, and your easy manners will stand to avail you nothing. I tell you there is a day coming when your costly wines and your pampering victuals will turn to dust between your teeth like them apples that grows by the Dead Sea, where the cities stood that thought as little what was going to overtake them as perhaps you do now. I see in your faces like a glass the destiny that you think to avoid. But you cannot. You cannot. I tell you that no man can turn away the fate thats fixed for him. You may look for sympathy when your hearts are

crushed, but you wont find it. Youll find your friends took up
with their own troubles, and ready to turn on you, and to make
light of you."

"Pray let me get away, Mr Musgrave" said Harriet. "I do not
wish to meet that man."

"Dont be afraid" said Musgrave. "He will do you no harm, I'll
engage."

"I am not afraid" said Harriet; "but—" she did not finish her
sentence; for Davis, who had paused to scan the faces about him,
suddenly recognized her. Smith, who had entered the room a
minute before, stepped irresolutely forward, fearful of some out-
burst from the preacher. Davis saw him, and looked with astonishment from one to the other. During the pause which followed,
Grosvenor and a party of men came in with Scott, who, observing
his wife in the vicinity of a madman, as Davis appeared to be,
placed himself beside her.

"Dear me, where are the servants?" said Lady Geraldine.
"He must be put out."

At this, Grosvenor and a few others came about Davis. He,
burning hot, and evidently passing through one of his transient
attacks of weakness, took no notice of them, but continued to
stare at Harriet with an expression so wretched that his assailants
were at once emboldened and disarmed.

"Now look here, you know, my friend" said Grosvenor: "you
must go. You have no right to behave in this way." So saying, he
took Davis gently by the arm and urged him insinuatingly
towards the door.

"Come!" said a gentleman, whose sharp manner and formal
dress marked him as a military officer. "Off with you, my man."
And he grasped the singer's arm. Davis instantly freed himself
with a violence that cleared a space about him.

"Scott" said Musgrave: "take this lady away. Our friend looks
rather like a case of fever. I'll look after him myself."

At this suggestion, Grosvenor turned pale and retreated. The
officer checked himself in the act of renewing his operation against
the preacher. Davis, who had been endeavoring to steady his

shivering lips, cast a look of defiance at them, and recovered his self-command after a giddy struggle.

"Nobody here need fear that I am going to disgrace them" said he. "But let nobody think that they are going to disgrace me by putting me out like a dog. I have been belittled and set aside for fine gentlemen; but I should like to see the gentleman that would put me out of this room before I chose to go, as broken as I am. I have made as good men as any here come crying to me by the strength of my voice and the power of the spirit that was in me; and thats more than I have seen done today by college taught men with the dead languages at their backs. I done it because it was my destiny to do it; and I speak of it, not in vanity, but to shew them that despise me that they do it not from my lowness or their highness, but because it is my fate to be despised, just as it was my fate to be respected and looked up to before that fate come upon me, more than the proud lady of this house herself."

Ernest uttered a low chuckling laugh and whispered "He's gloriously drunk."

"The laughter of fools" said Davis, hearing him and regarding him sternly, "is just like the crackling of thorns under a pot. It flashes up with a noise and a smoke, and then vanishes like the fleecy cloud in yon heaven. But dont go away this night and think scorn of my words, saying to one another 'Oh! he's drunk.' No! It was not drink that brought me down. I am not drunk now, nor ever was, nor ever will be; and some day, when your hour comes, it will be brought home to every one of you how I am right. Mind, to every one of you. It wont be kept back from you because you are rich and can keep silk curtains between you and the poor in the streets. Silk curtains wont keep out your fate. I could tell you a story of a person that thought he could, and found out his mistake. Aye, you may murmur. You are not willing to hear *me*, though you could sit and listen for an hour to the finicking poetry of one of your own sort."

Smith listened uneasily to this harangue. He felt that both Harriet and Lady Geraldine must be regarding with contempt his want of courage and address in not interfering, forgetting that his fellow-guests were at an equal disadvantage. A sense of responsibility was instinctive in him. Accordingly, he stepped to the side of Davis, and said in a low voice, which was nevertheless distinctly heard in the general hush,

"Excuse me for taking the privilege of an old acquaintance, Mr Davis. I am going now; and you will greatly oblige me by coming with me. I should like to say a few words to you alone, if you will be so good."

"Sir" said Davis haughtily, and yet a little abashed, "I thank you. I took notice of you before, and of others; but I did not come here to cut at them that might consider my acquaintance a disgrace by pretending to know them in this company. Bear me witness that I did not intrude myself upon you or on any one."

"I should have had no such feeling" said Smith, offering his arm, and feeling wretchedly confused by the publicity of his situation, though he seemed commandingly self-possessed.

"I do not deny that you have always been the gentleman, Mr Smith; and our destinies has been the same in their turning point, I believe. I go with joy at the asking of one, where I would not budge at the bidding of ten." He took Smith's arm as he spoke, and walked out of the room with as much dignity as that uncomfortable connection admitted of. All present watched him as he went; but, save for a glance at Harriet, which dropped at once before her resolute eyes, he looked at no one. Until the door was heard to close, there was perfect silence. Then there was a din of conversation.

"Poor fellow!" said Musgrave. "Theres not much of him left. I have a great mind to go after him and give him a letter for the Brompton Hospital."

"Indeed you will do nothing of the sort, Tom" said Mrs Musgrave. "Let him go in peace, now that he *has* gone; and let us be thankful that we are rid of him."

"Oh, that blessed Mr Smith!" said Lady Geraldine to Grosvenor. "Well may the Woodwards cherish him. I hope he will not catch fever from that miserable creature."

"It's all right" said Grosvenor. "The agent says it is only consumption."

"Harriet" said Cyril, who stood near with his wife: "if you dont relax you will break. It's all over: he's gone. I believe you frightened the wits out of the fellow by your face."

"I hope nobody noticed me" said Harriet, in a low voice. "That man was a preacher once; and he wanted me to marry him."

"What!" said Scott, astonished, and not pleased. "He knows you, then?"

"I think it must have been the sight of me that made him so strange. Only for Mr Smith, he would have recognized me upstairs. It is very extraordinary that I should meet him here."

"I hope we may meet no more of your acquaintances" said Cyril, rather sulkily.

"You need not fear" said Harriet gravely. "He is the only one of them I am either likely or loth to see again."

Scott realized, too late as usual, that his remark had not been a happy one. Whilst he was trying to devise some tender atonement, Lady Geraldine took Harriet away to the table. Presently he heard the voice of Musgrave behind him.

"Hallo, Master Scott! So you have been getting married, eh?"

"I have" said Scott, giving his hand with a smile.

"And how do you like it, so far?"

"Better than I expected."

"Thats right: thats right. Hush! Do you see that lovely creature standing near the table? You walked off with her a minute ago from me."

"What of her?" said Scott, surprised.

"You should have married her. She has more sense in her bustle than all the other women here have in their bonnets. Watch her. She knows how to walk. I want you to tell me who she is. I suppose you know her."

"Not very well. I have only been married to her for a fortnight."

"Ha! ha! ha!" roared Musgrave, shaking his hand a second

time: "you couldnt have done better. I did not give you credit for so much sense; and I gave her credit for more. She's thrown away on you."

From that time until her departure, Harriet was being talked of by nearly all who were not actually talking to her. The men praised her unanimously; though a few added that they had rather she was Scott's wife than theirs, as she seemed very well qualified to take care of herself, meaning, and of her husband also. Of the women, some allowed that she was unobjectionable, but protested against the admiration of the males as uncalled for. Others said that she was very nice and well behaved, quite wonderfully so in fact, considering what she was. A third said that people might talk as they liked about a real lady being always well dressed, but that a dressmaker who knew her business would always know where to go, what to get, and how much to give for it better than anybody else. A fourth, that it was doubtless their own want of taste, but they were utterly unable to see anything in the woman. A fifth praised her more than the men; called her sweet, pretty, and innocent looking; and would listen to nothing in her disfavor. The rest shook their heads when appealed to, and said that Mrs Scott was a clever woman who knew perfectly well what she was about. On the whole, as the men admired her, and the women did not feel sure that they had any advantage of her, Harriet had no reason to be dissatisfied with her reception. But she was wearied by the constant circumspection which she had had to maintain, and she said to her husband as they drove through Mayfair to the hotel at which they were staying,

"Lady Geraldine is very nice; but I wonder what pleasure she finds in letting all those people treat her house as their own, talking about nothing, and going home again without having done themselves any good. I saw several persons who did not hear Mr Hawkshaw read at all. I must say I think it is a stupid way of killing time. The only interesting person I met was that big man with the loud voice; and his wife apologized to me afterwards because he was not the same as all the others. She seemed quite ashamed of him."

"They are stupid affairs" said Scott, who was also fatigued; "but you will get used to them."

"I wonder why I should be at the trouble of getting used to an unpleasant thing which is of no value to me. However, I suppose it is useful to you to know people. You are forgetting that we have to call for the visiting cards?"

"No" said Scott: "the place is at the next corner." He caused the cab to be stopped at a stationer's shop, and went in, leaving Harriet without. The cards were handed to him by an insolently civil young man, who thanked him, and inquired whether he could do anything else for him. Scott, recollecting that he wanted pens, asked the young man for some.

"Certainly. These [producing some gold nibs about a sixteenth of an inch broad at the operative end] are favorites with the best people. Many ladies have recommended them highly to me. Sixpence a dozen."

Scott rejected the broad nibs, and was in consequence suspected of being a clerk. Nevertheless, as he left the shop, the young man accompanied him civilly to the door, curious as to the lady in the cab, whom he had no sooner seen than he was astonished, and stood motionless in the doorway until the vehicle disappeared.

"Married, by George!" he ejaculated, as he returned to the counter. "Mrs Cyril Scott, and no address. The husband's card without a Mister on it, short and sweet. It's plain that he's no gentleman in spite of his cheek, or he would know better than that. Do you know" he added, addressing his principal, "who Mr Cyril Scott is?"

"Do you mean the artist?"

"Thats the man" replied the shopman. "I could see that he was only a professional."

Harriet, as her husband rejoined her in the cab, remembered that she had told him at Lady Geraldine's that he had no unpleasant encounters to fear from any one but Davis, and thought it strange that the trivial incident of the card purchasing should have followed to remind her that she was prone to forget, but unlikely

313

to be forgotten. Nevertheless as she had never admitted Fraser Fenwick to her acquaintance, she did not think it necessary to explain to Cyril that the shopman who had just served him was a person familiar with her former circumstances, and, like the preacher, an old admirer.

# CHAPTER IX

WHEN he left the house in Wilton Place, Davis, with his arm still linked in that of the secretary, on whom he frequently leaned heavily, took his way in silence to Wilton Crescent and thence across Grosvenor Place into the Green Park, where he seated himself as if his strength was exhausted. After a fit of coughing, he gasped for a few moments, and turned to Smith, saying,

"I met her at last. Do you see the hand of Destiny there?"

"It was a singular coincidence, no doubt."

"It was no coincidence. Dont deceive yourself with words. It was the destiny pursuing me all through. I know what beliefs are; for Ive held em, and been filled full of em. But give me the belief that everything that happens goes to confirm the truth of, before them that throws you back on your faith ten times in a minute. When you knew me first, Mr Smith, there were moments when I found it hard to believe. I said many a time, 'Lord: help thou mine unbelief.' At last, when I put together all the things that happened to me, and saw how wonderfully one thing came out of another, I began to see that what I had took for the dispensations of Providence, was the workings of an immutable destiny. When I turned to my Bible, I was amazed at my own blindness; for there was Fate proclaimed in every line of it! Prophecies of the doom that was coming to the people surely, no matter what they might do to escape it; men raised up and preserved through dangers for the work appointed to them; other ones plunging in wickedness and despair that was foretold of them years afore they come into the world; the high cast down, and the lowly exalted; what do they teach you? What does the two men ploughing in the field, and the two women grinding at the mill, teach you? Why should one of them be taken and the other left? Why shouldnt the other be taken and the one left? Not from any fault or doing of theirs; but because it was their destiny. I laugh now when I see Larkins and his like trying to change it, when they are only being drove along by their own appointed lot. But it is not many men in whose affairs the finger of fate shews itself so plain as it has in mine. Think of what has happened this day! It was you led me to her at first. It is you that has just led me from her at last. And how did that come about? Did we arrange it between ourselves? Was our meeting in the house of a great lady a thing that might happen any day? When I crept round the other Sunday night to take a look at the meetings where I used to preach, who did I see standing before me? Young Fenwick, who was led to drink in order that I might go to my doom through him. And what brought him there? Did he know I was to be there? Would such a reprobate have gone amongst prayer meetings of his own accord? Why did he select that night of all nights in the year to do what he never done before? Look at myself! Why did I leave the preaching to sing in a chorus? I thought I did it of my free will. I know now that I did it to the end that I might be brought into that house when she was there. And why was she, who was born no more than the equal of the servants that waited on her today, brought amongst the high and mighty? I might go on asking you questions until the last trumpet, and you couldnt answer one of them except by Destiny; and that answers them all. It is my fate, and your fate, and her fate, and his fate."

"*His* fate? Do you know Mr Scott, then?"

"I mean the young man: Fenwick I think his name was. Who else are you thinking of? Who else is entangled in it?"

"Of course you cannot know" said Smith, angry with himself for having mentioned the name. "Perhaps I had better tell you that it is hopeless to trouble yourself further about her. She is married."

"To a gentleman?"

"To a gentleman."

"Why? To raise her up as I was beat down. To carry out the fate that was through it all. I never thought for an instant to have her after I saw what she was, and how little she could value a true man. There was a time when I expected to hear of her marriage every day; and I used to feel that I could almost kill the man, whoever he was; for I saw plain enough that *you* had no chance of her.

But now the news of it only settles my mind. It was she that first made me rebel again' my death; and it is she that makes me care no more for it at present than I do for them that tried to lay hands upon me to put me out of that house. You see how it works round in that too."

"But excuse me, Mr Davis. Of course I cannot prove to you that what has happened was not destined to happen; but—"

"No" said Davis steadfastly; "nor all the wisdom of the Chaldeans cant either."

"Just so. But what on earth use is such a belief? It simply amounts to saying that whatever is, is. It is a great deal easier to say, I am alive, I have been disappointed, I have got a new hat, or I have broken my leg, than, It was ordained that I should live, My fate was disappointment, I was destined to get a new hat, or It was the destiny of that piece of orange peel to lie where it did that I might slip on it and break my leg. The two forms amount to exactly the same thing."

Davis shook his head and smiled. "Wait" said he. "It will be brought home to you some day; and then you can explain it away with your blind human reason, if you like."

"But it seems to me that you have acquired the habit of persuading yourself that your own ideas are supernatural revelations, and believing in them accordingly. You used to have exactly the same conviction of the dispensing power of Providence that you have now of the existence of irrevocable decrees of Fate."

"Indeed!" said Davis calmly. "And what is Providence but the name under which we disguise Fate? People pray to Providence. Do their prayers ever change it? Not a bit. They pray for a thing. If it is their lot to get it, they would get it if they never said a prayer. But they would rather think—poor worms!—that Fate was set aside at their request. Similarly, if they dont get it, they persuade themselves that they are better without it; and so they cheat themselves into thinking that they can change the unchangeable."

"Well, well, there is no use in arguing about what can be neither proved nor disproved, particularly as it would be perfectly valueless in either case. You have got yourself into a meta-physical mess; and, cheap and common as it is, nothing but your own sound sense will ever get you out of it."

"Common men and cheap livers have as good a right to the truth as the richest in the land."

"You quite misunderstand the sense in which I used the words" said Smith. "You ought to give me credit for not meaning to be personal. I am as poor a man as you, and not in the least remarkable, as you are."

Davis looked at him doubtfully for a moment, and then proffered his hand. Smith took it, but seized the opportunity to rise and construe the salute as a farewell.

"A word before we part, sir" said Davis, clinging to his hand. "You will bear witness that I scorned to speak to her before her grand friends today."

"Most willingly" said Smith. "You shewed the greatest delicacy."

Davis squeezed his hand. "Used she ever to speak about me to you: well or ill?"

"I do not remember" said Smith, embarrassed. "In fact, I am sure she never spoke about you to me. She is naturally very reserved. Goodbye."

The preacher relinquished his grasp of Smith with reluctance, and watched him walk into Piccadilly and disappear. He sat for a long time after this looking listlessly at the ground, at intervals raising his head and gazing at the descending sun with vague bitterness. He had not dined; but his disease had reached a stage at which eating is a trouble. Occasionally, as a fit of weakness came upon him, and left him shuddering, he felt a pang as the prospect of death returned to him, and he found nobody at hand to whom he could boast of it. At such moments he felt that it was miserable to be friendless, and reproached Smith for deserting him. Nevertheless, he still looked on the end of his decline as remote. He had been told once by a doctor that he would probably last another year; and this, instead of impressing him with the imminence of dissolution, had given him a habit of regarding it as an event which would happen in a short time, but not immediately.

When the sun went down, he had fallen into a sleep, the deepest he had enjoyed for a long time. He was disturbed by a light in his eyes and a hand roughly shaking his shoulder.

"All out" said a policeman. "Closing time."

Davis looked sleepily around. It was dark; and the lamps were lighted in Piccadilly. Seeing the policeman waiting for him to move, he rose reluctantly, and turned away, wondering whether a bribe would have secured him the privilege of lying there undisturbed until morning.

"Now then" said the policeman: "you cant get out that way. You must go by the turnstile."

Davis obeyed; and the constable followed him until he was satisfied of the loiterer's ability to walk home. The night was warm and the streets were crowded as he started towards Lambeth, where he lodged. For some time he maintained a fair speed, and strode with some of his old vigor. But his exhilaration was followed by a feverish attack of weakness. His drowsiness returned; and he no longer observed the passers-by, so that he felt like a man walking through an uninhabited plain in a dream. In this condition he made his way to the river, walking steadily with the sense, familiar to tired pedestrians, that if he halted to rest for a moment he would be unable to resume his journey.

On Westminster Bridge, the side walk is separated from the carriage way by a kennel of iron, the edge of which rises for some inches above the level of the road, and serves to overthrow wayfarers whose attention is engaged by the traffic which they are hastening from the midst of, or preparing to pass through.[1] After nightfall, when the obstruction is invisible because of the darkness, these accidents are common, and are indeed inevitable by passengers who cross the street at that place, and have not been apprised of the danger by previous experience. As Davis approached, a party of three students were conversing with two young women. Scarcely conscious of their presence, and fearful

[1] This mantrap no longer exists.

of becoming giddy if he should swerve from his straight course, the preacher came against the woman who stood nearest to the kennel, and was immediately requited by a violent thrust from her elbow which sent him staggering towards the roadway, where, tripped by the iron edge, he fell supine on the stones. A shout of laughter from the students, mingled with threats and abuse from the woman, followed, but ceased as the party, seeing their victim unable to rise, made off amongst the crowd. Davis made an effort to get up. He sank back with the conviction that he would never rise again. A knot of people soon collected about him and gazed at him with interest. One man stirred the recumbent figure with his foot, and, not eliciting any sign from it thereby, went on his way. Then a couple of policemen came.

"Whats this?" said one of them.

"'E f'yoll over the ken'l an 'e cawnt git ap" said a boy.

"Come!" said the policeman, stooping to shake Davis by the shoulder, and detecting the odor of Lady Geraldine's claret cup. "Up with you."

"It's all right" said Davis faintly and lazily. "Let me alone. I had rather lie here. I cant walk."

"Oh, cant you though" said the policeman. "Perhaps you think youre going to be carried." So saying, with the assistance of his comrade, he hauled the preacher upright. "On with you" he continued, giving him a shake: "you can walk well enough if you like."

"What right have you to put your hand on me?" said Davis, roused by the violence with which he had been lifted.

"Now, none of your nonsense, or it will be the worse for you" said the policeman sternly.

Davis looked angrily at them for a moment; but his ideas of what had happened were so confused that he submitted, preferring to go wherever they chose to lead him rather than make the effort of shaping any further remonstrance. Still, he did not like the men's hands upon him. For some yards he walked steadily. Then he reeled, and attempted to lean against one of the policemen, who repulsed him by a rough shake, concluding with a push.

Davis broke away from the constable; turned round; and struck him in the face. He hardly knew what followed. Giddy and almost suffocated, he felt that he was being dragged along, that the policemen's knuckles were bruising his neck and their fingers gripping and twisting his arms. After a time he recovered himself a little, and found that he was standing in a police station, his coat split and covered with dust, his hat crushed out of shape, and an inspector taking a charge of drunkenness and assault against him from the mouth of an angry policeman with a discolored eye. Presently his name and address were required.

"I am not drunk" said he. "My name is St John Davis. I demand that a doctor be sent for, to certify that I am ill and not drunk. I want to be let lie down somewhere." When he had said this, his attention wandered, and he heeded nothing more until he was moved forward again. "I know the law as well as you do" he said then. "I have a right to speak in this park; and I dare you to prevent me. You tried to shut it up once; and the railings come down for it." There was a laugh at this; and he was led to a cell without further ceremony.

"I am not drunk: I am seriously ill" he protested, as he stumbled in.

"Youll be better in the morning" said a policeman jocosely, shutting the door.

In the morning. however, Mr Davis was dead.

# BOOK THE FOURTH
## FLIRTATION

# CHAPTER I

DURING the autumn, the house in Queen's Gate was tenanted by a police constable and his wife. Mr Woodward was in Ireland with his constituents. Miss Woodward was at Rosstrevor, her sister in Dublin. The secretary had been invited to consider himself at liberty until their return; but he had not left London: the trouble and expense of holiday making being more terrifying to his shyness and inexperience than the prospect of change of air was attractive. He continued to call daily at Queen's Gate, where he forwarded the few letters which came; borrowed such of his master's books as he cared to read; and occasionally looked through the albums, at photographs of Isabella with swings, Japanese umbrellas, hammocks, sea coasts, and snowstorms. The rest of his time he spent in walking, reading (for which, however, he found his taste declining), and reviewing his attempts at poetry: the last with more success than in the Islington days, since when he had become less sentimental and more critical. Soon, fearful of deteriorating through idleness, he began to meditate a change in his mode of life. He reflected that he might at any time lose his place through the death or caprice of his employer, and that a private secretaryship might then prove a bad recommendation to another clerkship. He therefore, after some deliberation, and searching of official reports, determined to obtain a nomination from Mr Woodward, and present himself before the Civil Service Commissioners for examination in the subjects deemed necessary to a clerk in the department of science and art at South Kensington. With this view, he brought his school-books to light one evening; and when he had spent nearly an hour thinking of the scenes which their appearance, their print, and the odour of their leaves recalled, he began to store his memory with geographical names, definitions of simooms and spoondrift, and operations in decimal fractions. As his experience at Figgis and Weaver's ledgers had qualified him to accomplish feats of compound addition with ease, and as his tuition of

Harriet had grounded him in French, the only foreign language required, he soon saw no reason to doubt that, if he obtained the nomination, he could succeed in the competition. He yet resolved to obtain the advice of an expert as to the best method of preparation, and accordingly he answered the advertisement of a Mr Sadler, whose business it was to fit candidates for the task of satisfying or overreaching the professors appointed to examine them. This gentleman recommended Smith to study nightly with him at his house in Tavistock Square for three months. Smith, in reply, asked his terms for a fortnight. Mr Sadler, whilst assuring him that the matter would end in his completing a month at the loss of a guinea, agreed to accept three pounds, ten shillings, and sixpence. Smith paid him that amount, and early in September went for the first time to Tavistock Square.

He was asked by Mr Sadler into a large parlor, which had not been painted or papered for many years, but had been splashed with ink every working day during the same period. The uncurtained window was obscured by a perforated zinc blind, and by dirt. The furniture consisted of two wooden presses, a long deal table, and a number of chairs, plain wood, cane bottomed, or stuffed, all more or less battered, burst through, or ragged. Seated at the table were several youths who scribbled on sheets of paper, and looked at open volumes with a dazed expression, which, with their frowsy condition of hair and clothing, suggested to Smith strong tea, late hours, and weakened perception. When he entered with Mr Sadler, the noise of voices subsided; and one young gentleman, whose arm was reared for the purpose of hurling a lump of bread, pretended to scratch his cheek. When a place had been found for the new-comer, and a task devised to test his powers of spelling and composition, the grinder (so Mr Sadler was technically described) took his seat before a desk at the end of the table and resumed his duties, which at present concerned four pupils who were construing Horace. One of these was a sprucely-dressed youth, supercilious in manner, who confidently offered wrong solutions of every difficulty propounded by Sadler, and never admitted his error when it was pointed out.

Two others were pleasant fellows, apparently superior to the rest in intelligence, but incorrigibly remiss in their studies. A pale young gentleman with a greatcoat and woollen muffler, who sat next Smith, informed him that he was on sick leave from a government office. Smith, desiring to be agreeable, expressed his sympathy and his desire to know whether leave was easily obtained in public departments. The young gentleman replied that as the government office in question was built over a drain, more than half the staff were usually incapacitated by typhoid fever, and that his main object in seeking an appointment elsewhere was to save his life. He was of opinion that Mr Sadler's professional merits were quite up to the average. This reassured Smith, whose confidence in the grinder had been shaken by the other students denouncing him as a humbug whenever he left the room.

At the end of an hour, Smith, accustomed to lonely independence, began to feel ill at ease in his state of tutelage amongst youths fresh from school or college. He whiled away the rest of the time by the help of a report which contained particulars of previous examinations for the post for which he intended to compete, thinking that if he had purchased it beforehand, he might have saved his three and a half guineas.

"Well, Smith" said Sadler, stretching himself and yawning, as the new student prepared to leave, "how are you getting on, eh?"

"I have not done very much tonight."

"No, I dont think you have" said the grinder drily. "You know you will have to depend on yourself to get through. I cant make you work. I can only tell you what to work at."

"That is very true. I have been looking over the papers and I dont feel particularly anxious about my success. If there were any test of my ability involved, I might feel doubtful. As it is, if I can manage to remember a few names and rules until the examination is over, I shall be safe."

"Indeed" said Mr Sadler sarcastically.

"Well" said Smith, nettled at his manner, "what does any examination test besides memory?"

327

"You cant pass in English composition and mathematics by dint of memory alone. But you mistake the point. The question is not whether the system is perfect, but whether you can propose a better one. Would you have us go back to patronage?"

"There were *some* clever men under that system, at any rate" said Smith spitefully.

"Well" said Sadler, yawning again, "if you dont like the system, you can let it alone. Nobody wants to force you into the government service; and I presume you dont expect to be taken in at your own wish for nothing."

"Of course not" said Smith. "Goodnight!"

"Goodnight" said Sadler. "Tomorrow at seven sharp. Dont be late."

Smith did not reply.

"To think of my having wasted nearly four pounds on that idiot!" said he to himself as he walked to Gower Street station. Then he thought of the things he could have bought for that sum. "This much is certain" he concluded. "I am not going to drag out these calm autumn evenings in yonder sordid den."

In spite of this declaration, he went the next night, lest he should have to reproach himself with peevish haste subsequently. But this second trial proved less tolerable than the first; and at the end of an hour he pleaded business, and left: Mr Sadler acquiescing rather sulkily. He never went again, nor did he write to apologize, feeling that unless he told a lie, silence was likely to be less offensive than explanation. Sadler did not trouble him with inquiries. On the first evening of his pupil's absence, he said "Where is Smith?" On the second, he said "What on earth can have become of Smith?" On the third, "It is a very queer thing of Smith not to send word of what he means." On the fourth, he remarked to the students that he thought Smith's behavior very impertinent, but that he should not bother himself one way or the other about him. Finally, he forgot him.

One morning Smith found at Queen's Gate a letter addressed to himself in a strange handwriting, with the postmark "Warrenpoint," a place of which he had never heard. He turned the envelope over with misgiving; then opened it, and took out four sheets of paper, the first of which was headed "Carlingford House, Rosstrevor." It was evidently from Isabella. He replaced the sheets in the envelope; mounted to the drawing room; looked through the album; and walked to Kensington Gardens, where he took a chair in the sunshine, and read:

"Dear Mr Smith—You are astonished, I know, at my writing to you, are not you; but I must unburden my overwrought feelings to somebody. Besides, I am really fond of writing to anybody whom I can rely on to understand me.—

[Smith looked from the letter to the tops of the trees, and grinned.]

"—You can form no conception of what a *beastly* place this is. (I know perfectly well that it is wrong for ladies to underline their letters; but no epithet would express what I feel about Rosstrevor without some special emphasis. It really is most beastly). In the first place, no Englishman can possibly imagine how thoroughly detestable these north of Ireland people are. They are not Irish at all; only a sort of mongrel Scotch, and they spend their leisure in fighting and chalking up shocking things on the walls about King William or the Pope, according to their opinions. They are ill-mannered, thrifty, tasteless, false, and ferocious. I admit that they are clean; but I would much rather be amongst my dirty, genial, picturesque, good-for-nothing countrymen of the South.

"Carlingford Lough is a great long bay with a narrow neck, and is surrounded by mountains, most of which have large rocks on the top which the people tell you were thrown across from the opposite sides by giants related to Fin McCoul, if you ever heard of *him*. As you stand in Warrenpoint, which is at the landward end of the lough, and look out towards the sea, Rosstrevor is on your left a mile or two along the shore, and Greenore is further away on your right. We went to Greenore the other day by steamer from Warrenpoint; and it turned out to be nothing but a sandbank, with a railway station, a gasworks, and a coastguard depot built on it. People make excursions to it as they might to Hampton Court, and come back disgusted at having seen nothing. It is the greatest imposture I know of in the way of sightseeing, except Shanklin Chine; and even that affords some gratification to unfortunate Englishmen (I hope you wont think me very personal) who have never been in the Dargle, and therefore cannot be expected to know the difference between a ditch and a real glen.

"Another treat was a visit inland to Bessbrook, the model village; where the inhabitants neither swear nor get drunk, and look as if they would like very much to do both. This place would really and truly make Mr Ruskin cry if he saw it, it is so excessively ugly. It is nothing but a gigantic factory overshadowing a few hideous grey streets where the operatives live. In the grounds of the factory there is the basin of the waterworks. In order to make it look as like a lake as possible, they keep a swan there, which I am sure passes its time in regretting that it cannot drown itself. I refused to be shewn through the factory; and we all came away out of temper. The worst of Bessbrook is that you never suspect its existence as you go along the innocent country road until you turn a corner, and are barely warned of civilization by seeing a lamp-post when the place envelops you in its barren greyness and dashes your spirits for the remainder of the day. The nearest town to us here is Newry, an unspeakably dismal hole. It is threaded by a canal, a river, and two branches of railway, and they seem like forty when you take a walk through the town and meet a bridge or a level crossing at every few yards. If you can imagine a bundle of mill chimneys, some markets, and crowds of cattle straying amongst them, all stuck at a bottom of a dark valley, you will have Newry to the life. Blackwall is quite Parisian by comparison. Rosstrevor itself is undeniably pretty; but it is monotonous, and life here is oppressively slow. Culture is as little understood as it is everywhere in Ireland; the natives look shocked when I speak of the theatre; and an attempt at artistic dressing sets all the heads in the place shaking portentously. I could find it in my heart to rail at my native land for ever; but out of consideration for your feelings, I forbear. The only sensible institution in the emerald isle is absenteeism.

"I have just had a letter from Miss Scott. She says that her sister-in-law wrote to her from Rome a few days ago, and that the happy couple are very well, except that the bridegroom has been severely bitten by mosquitoes. How savage he must have been! The bride is, of course, accustomed to roughing it, and is still delighted with the novelty of her position.

"I have no more news to tell you. I wish I had, as much for my own sake as for yours; but here discussion is confined to the murders and riots which at times cast a gleam of excitement on our social communion. It is really surprising that life can be so dull, when popular feeling is so explosive.

"I want you to do me a little favor,—

["I thought as much" said Smith].

"—but a very particular one. At least, it is not exactly a particular one; but I would rather not entrust it to any person who might talk about it. I want you to go to the left hand top drawer of my dressing table, and take out a purple morocco case which you will find, I think, lying in a corner amongst a lot of hairpins. At any rate it is the only case in the drawer, so you cannot mistake it. If you will slip the enclosed note into the little pocket in the lining of the lid, and leave it at once with Mr Hawkshaw, at No. 16B Ladbroke Grove, Notting Hill, you will render me an inestimable service, and shew yourself a true friend. I do not know what you will think of this request; but there is nothing really strange in it. Mr Hawkshaw wants the case immediately; and I have no other means of returning it to him, except through you.

"I fear I have been terribly prolix; but it is a wet day, and I have nothing to do but write. I suppose you have heard from papa, and know as much about him as I do. Clytie is making a small sensation in Dublin—not a very difficult thing to do there. Let me see—No, there is nothing more to say, rain or no rain. So believe me, dear Mr Smith, sincerely yours,

ISABELLA WOODWARD.

331

"P.S.—Of course you will not mention anything to anybody. I should be plagued with no end of questions."

Smith read the last part of the letter again.

"The question is" he thought, "will there be any breach of faith towards Woodward in acting as his daughter's go-between; for the affair must be an intrigue of some sort, or why should she make a secret of it?"

As he returned to Queen's Gate, he considered whether the explanation in the letter might be the true one. There was no reason why Isabella should not have borrowed a morocco case from the poet, or why he should not suddenly have occasion for it. Nor did any way of restoring it appear feasible except the one she had adopted. "After all" he concluded, "I cannot refuse without insulting her; so I have no choice but to obey. I wish she had applied to anybody else, confound her."

When he reached the house, he learned that the Irish post had arrived during his absence, bringing for him an envelope and a packet. The packet was a cardboard box containing jeweller's cotton and a key. Enclosed in the envelope was a tiny note unaddressed, but wrapped in a scrap of paper on which Miss Woodward had written "Patrick Hawkshaw Esq., 16B Ladbroke Grove. By favor of Robert Smith Esq." Smith took the key, and asked the caretaker which was the prettiest lady's bedroom in the house. She replied suspiciously that she did not know. Smith went upstairs feeling like an inexperienced thief.

The first room he entered appeared to be the one he was seeking; for a crucifix stood on the mantelpiece; and an autotype reproduction of Lionardo's Monna Lisa hung above it, apparently selected, in the absence of a Madonna, as the nearest substitute. Smith examined the furniture of the apartment, luxurious in comparison to the garrets of Islington and Chelsea. He raised the blinds, and admired his image at full length in the mirror panels of the wardrobe. He smelt at the cut glass bottles on the table, and opened the little boxes beneath the toilet glass, in which he found two curl papers, a discarded powder puff, a broken earring, a patent remedy for corns, and a quantity of hair combings. Then he tried the key in the left hand top drawer of the table, and found the morocco case among the hairpins, as Isabella had described. He relocked the drawer, and carried the case downstairs to the study, where he opened it in order to put in the note. It contained a brooch and a pair of earrings with pendants of cumbrous shape, minutely worked in tarnished gold after a design which reminded him of the works of an old verge watch which he had seen with his grandfather. They were set with diamonds, some of which were as large as peppercorns; and Smith perceived that if the stones were genuine, the contents of the case must be valuable. It occurred to him that if the articles were the property, not of Hawkshaw or Miss Woodward, but of his employer, he would be implicated in a theft. However, as he felt no right to assume that Isabella was capable of robbing her father, he put the morocco case in his pocket, started towards Notting Hill, and resolved to trust to chance that the affair might turn out harmlessly.

It was not yet eleven o'clock in the forenoon when he reached Ladbroke Grove; and the servant who opened the door of No. 16B told him that Mr Hawkshaw was in bed. Smith sent in his name, and alleged particular business. He was then ushered into the front parlor, where the table was prepared for breakfast, and the folding door stood partly open, revealing a bedchamber, whence the poet presently invited him to enter. He accordingly passed through the door and discovered Hawkshaw in bed, with a small table beside him on which were some bottles of soda water, one of brandy, and a tumbler.

"Good morning, Mr Smith" said he, raising his dishevelled head lazily from the pillow. "You must excuse me. I wish you all imaginable health, wealth, and wisdom; but for my own part I go to bed so late that if I rose early I should be nodding all day afterwards. Have you breakfasted?"

"Thank you: I breakfasted three hours ago."

"Bless me! Such is the power of poetry. Dr Watts was the greatest of the master singers. Have some brandy and soda?

No? Happy man, fortified by the calm shadow of Temperance. Pray sit down."

Smith, ill at ease, sat down near the bed. Hawkshaw wondered what the particular business was. Both meditated on the power that each possessed of disconcerting the other.

"I have called on you in consequence of receiving a letter this morning from Miss Woodward" said Smith.

A fancy that the visit might have been prompted by jealousy came to Hawkshaw. "She told you, doubtless" said he, "that I have been staying at Rosstrevor—a barbaric watering place in the north of Ireland—for the last three weeks. I only arrived here the day before yesterday after an execrable passage *via* Greenore and Holyhead."

"Not a word of it."

"Singular!" said Hawkshaw, with a smile. "As we were the only rational beings in the place, we were thrown entirely upon one another for company. Either Miss Woodward is the most forgetful of mortals or you have unaccountably failed to engage her confidence."

"On the contrary, I have engaged rather more of it than I care for."

Hawkshaw's bantering manner changed to one of suspicion. "Which means?"—said he, coldly.

"Which means this" replied Smith, exhibiting the morocco case.

Hawkshaw looked at it. "This is dramatic, Mr Smith" said he, staring at him with an amused air; "but, like many dramatic points, quite incomprehensible."

"You dont understand, then?" said Smith, perceiving that Miss Woodward's explanation was false.

"Unless it is a case of pistols, which I hope for the credit of your common sense it is not, I certainly dont" replied the poet, becoming paler.

"Pistols!" repeated Smith, also losing color, and confounded by the remark, to the relevance of which he had no clue.

"In short, Mr Smith, what the deuce do you mean?"

"Miss Woodward—"

"No matter about Miss Woodward, if you please. Confine the conversation to ourselves."

"I dont understand you" said Smith, indignant at this interruption; "but I will send Miss Woodward that answer if you like." As he spoke, he rose as though to leave the room.

"One moment" said Hawkshaw. "I see we are at cross purposes in some way. Sit down and enlighten me, I beg of you."

"Miss Woodward has written to me to *return* you this case. I have taken it out of a drawer in Mr Woodward's house during the absence of the family; and I have discovered that its contents are valuable. Her letter, which professed to exhaust all the news of her visit to Rosstrevor, mentioned nothing about your stay there. It also described this case as having to be returned to you, whereas it now appears that you never saw it before. Excuse my saying so, but I can see that you are at a loss to understand the affair. So am I. Here is the case. You will find a note in the lining, where I was directed to place it."

Hawkshaw took the case; looked blankly for a moment at the jewels; and opened the note. It was brief; and when he had read it, he blushed, and looked irresolutely from the paper to the diamonds, and from them to Smith, whose eye he sought to avoid by turning on his pillow and feigning to read the note again. Then he said uneasily,

"Thank you, thank you. It is all right."

"And now, Mr Hawkshaw" said Smith, "would you mind giving me a receipt for those jewels."

"But why? Were you instructed to obtain documentary evidence of my receiving them?"

"No. I ask of my own accord. I think you will admit that my position in the matter is very unpleasant; and as a man of business I desire to supplement my documentary authority for taking a lot of diamonds out of a drawer in an empty house, by similar evidence of my having disposed of them honestly."

"But do you think any question can arise?" said Hawkshaw anxiously.

"I know nothing whatever about it. When I hold your receipt, I will be in a position to prove that I have done what I was asked to do. Without it, it can be shewn that I got the diamonds, and I cannot shew that I have given them up."

"But I can prove it. Surely you do not doubt my honor."

"Suppose you lost the jewels, and died the day after" said Smith, in the matter-of-fact tone in which Figgis and Weaver's clerks had been accustomed to propound similar dilemmas to customers who stood on their honor.

"True" said Hawkshaw ironically. "You are indeed a thorough man of business; and your reasons for desiring a receipt are unimpeachable. But the reasons why I should give it are not equally clear. Suppose—to adopt your own hypothetical style of argument—you were to sell my receipt to the highest bidder as soon as you had obtained it! The proceeding would be quite that of a man of business. Holding a marketable commodity, what more natural than to put it up to auction?"

"How do you mean?" said Smith, understanding him, but affecting bewilderment to cloak his agitation. "What pecuniary value could attach itself to such a receipt."

"No thank you, Mr Smith" said Hawkshaw, turning on his back, and smiling coolly from his pillow: "I am not a business man, and I object to be cross-examined. In fine, I am inexpressibly indebted to you for so kindly fulfilling your mistress's commission; and I most positively decline to give you any written acknowledgment whatever, as I by no means recognize you as having any concern with the transaction at all, more than a postman has with the contents of the letters which he delivers."

"Even a postman demands a receipt for a registered letter."

"Ingeniously put" said Hawkshaw, perceiving with satisfaction that the secretary had lost his presence of mind; "but I do not intend to argue my foregone conclusion. As our present humors seem to have missed that degree of congeniality which is necessary to agreeable intercourse, perhaps you will not deem me inhospitable if I suggest that we should now part with expressions of mutual esteem."

"No; because I do not esteem you. I shall inform Miss Woodward that I gave you the jewels, and failed to obtain any acknowledgment beyond an involuntary blush."

Hawkshaw's face changed for an instant; and Smith, adding "Good morning" walked out, feeling that he had struck the last and hardest blow. As he went through Notting Hill Gate on his way back, he cursed the poet's insolence, and thought that he would like to thrash him if only he knew how.

From this frame of mind, when he returned to Queen's Gate, he sought relief in writing an account of what had happened to Isabella; but by the time he had finished, his equanimity was partly restored; and on reading what he had written, he found his aggravation so apparent in it, that he tore it up, and composed a second and more dignified letter. Then, having despatched his missive and the key to Ireland, he went home to study and think of his adventure alternately during the rest of the evening.

# CHAPTER II

CARLINGFORD HOUSE, Rosstrevor, stood on a sloping ground between the high road from which the traveller could look down on the roof, and the sea, which washed the rocky foot of the garden. In this garden sat Isabella, alone, and provided with materials for sketching. It was noonday, and there was a haze of sunlight through which distant objects appeared to tremble, and sounds to travel undiminished from the further shore of the Lough. Notwithstanding her preparations, she was not painting, but reclining on a shawl which she had spread on the grass beneath an old carriage umbrella which served as a tent. A letter lay unopened on the shawl beside her. Another, which ran as follows, was in her hand.

16B LADBROKE GROVE.
*27th September.*

"*Ma belle* Belle—You are as generous as you are beautiful. How shall I say in prose what I dare not hope to sing in poetry? Alas, my dear love, queen of the isles of coral, witch of Atlas, and benignant goddess enshrined in the very innermost niche of my heart of hearts, my pen is stricken lame with the load of gratitude which I would fain impose on it. Plain language is too cold, and hyperbole too artificial to express the deep but willing humiliation, the pure rapture which your sublime act has caused me. Ah my love, you give with bounteous hands, and I kiss them both across St George's Channel. * * * * * Let these stars stand for what I mean, but cannot write. You have saved me from exile and beggary.

"And now let me say, dear one, that I can by no means abuse your munificence so far as to make away with your pretty inheritance. I fear I make but a poor figure in not returning it forthwith, and deeming myself boundlessly rich in possessing the heart that proffered it. But the fact is, my dear Isabella, that there is such a thing in the world as honesty—though I had well-nigh forgotten everything but love. My debts are just debts; and it would be a pride very unworthy of your elect that would prompt me to abscond and rob my creditors sooner than borrow a jewel from your white neck, which needs no adornment save its own loveliness.—

[Isabella paused to reflect and began to look discontented.]

"—In a word, I will not sell the brilliants, but will raise sufficient money on them to stave off my immediate difficulties, and to give me time to finish my book and hand it over to the publishers. Of course I can expect nothing for it, as I have mortgaged it so heavily to them that I am half afraid its sale will barely recoup them. That done, I will work as never man worked before, get out another volume, and make Simonton produce a drama which I have already planned, keeping your image before me whenever I am tempted to flag. Thus I shall redeem your ornaments, hang them upon you in triumph, and—who knows? —perhaps say, 'I am rich and famous, and need wait no longer to claim your hand.' Meanwhile, Heaven knows I shall need encouragement. I shall have to live like a hermit, and to drudge at that bitter toil, reviewing. Fame is a leaden-footed jade. I asked Tabuteau, my publisher, for another advance last week, and was fool enough to let drop a word about my growing reputation. He retorted, with that pleasure in 'taking down' sensitive men which distinguishes the whole tribe of business people, that my reputation had established itself so well in my clique that no doubt it would spread over the four mile radius in the course of some years. I had to laugh; for I owed the brute money. Judge how much reason I have to love you, who have opened a golden door of escape for me from this slavery.

"Talking of men of business reminds me, incredible as it may well seem, that I have something to scold you about. How could you be so rash as to entrust such a delicate matter to your father's secretary? I have always mistrusted him; and he discharged his commission in a manner which fully confirmed my suspicions. He had the audacity not only to demand a written acknowledgment from me *for his own satisfaction*, but, on my refusal, to

339

suggest very directly that I stood towards you in the relation of a receiver to a thief. Eventually I told him to be off; and I would have done so sooner had I not been in bed at the time, and consequently not in a position to risk any dispute with him. Were I alone concerned, I should be simply amused; but I confess it irritates me to hear your name bandied by this ill-bred young precisian. Pray write to him at once insisting on his returning your letter of instructions, as I am quite sure he is capable of making use of it either to extort money from you or to curry favor with your father by betraying you. Your gift was profaned by the touch of this detestable emissary. Beware always of Christian young men who affect straightforwardness of speech. Smith is a bad imitation of the very worst points of his friend Mrs Scott, with the addition of sundry vices peculiar to himself. But enough of him. He has no business in our world. It is fortunate that he knows nobody.

"When, in the name of that eternity which every minute of separation contains, may I hope to see you again? Surely you do not want to stay in Ulster for ever. There are plenty of people in London already. I more than suspect that half our acquaintances have never been out of it. Grosvenor is at Milan, but intends to spend the winter at Perspective. Lady Geraldine is where she ought to stay always—managing her dairy farm in Devonshire. I have not heard from Cyril Scott since he went away; however, there is nothing strange in that, as I know he would rather paint thirty pictures than write three lines. This is all my stock of gossip.

"I see by my watch that I must bring this letter to a close, if I am to save the post. Again and again let me thank you and bless you; though these sentiments, genuine as they are, are only overgrowths of my love, and of my pride in having such a noble lover. I am almost tempted to envy the humble swain who covers his distant mistress with kisses by a simple stenography of crisscrosses. Nathless I hope to do so in delirious actuality very soon. Till then, think at least once a day of Yours for ever

PATRICK HAWKSHAW."

"Humph!" said Miss Woodward, looking at the letter critically: for she had received many love letters. "Rather overdone. If he means it, what a weak wretch he must be; and what a fool I was to throw away my diamonds on him! I wonder how much they are worth. Mamma used to say five hundred pounds; but that is nonsense. Let us see what the detestable emissary's version of the affair is. I wish I had seen them fighting—the fools!"

300 Queen's Gate, Kensington.
*27th September.*

"Dear Miss Woodward—I received your letter this morning, and immediately delivered the case to Mr Hawkshaw at his apartments in Ladbroke Grove, as requested. I return the key by this post.

"I think it right to tell you that when I discovered the value of the contents of the case, and perceived from Mr Hawkshaw's manner that he had never either seen them or expected to receive them, I exceeded your instructions so far as to ask him for a written acknowledgment of their receipt. I am bound to say that I did not do this in your interest (though it occurred to me afterwards that had I made the demand on your behalf, it might have been more plausible and effectual) but solely in order to be able to prove, in case any question should arise, that I had disposed honestly of these valuable jewels, which I had taken in the absence of the family from a house which I was privileged to enter. I fear you will be offended by my doubts; but the peculiarity of my position, the knowledge that ladies sometimes do foolish and impulsive things with the best intentions, and the fact that the caretaker evidently suspected me of a felonious design when I asked for your room, all combined to make me feel so uncomfortable, that I thought the precaution of asking for the receipt would be an excusable piece of officiousness. However, my demand was useless; for Mr Hawkshaw positively refused to accede to it; and a ridiculous scene ensued: he sarcastically taxing me with a scheme to obtain 'documentary evidence' to put up to auction, and I expressing my suspicions of his reasons for rebuffing me. Eventually he politely turned me out; and I left in a revengeful humor which I poured out in a letter to you, which I have just torn up. I mention this that you may know the terms on which I stand with Mr Hawkshaw, in case you should require any further service from me in connection with him. Pray understand that I will gladly undertake any such service: what I mean is, that he might object to hold any communication with me.

"I hope you will excuse my troubling you at such length about a difficulty which is probably only interesting to myself. I am sorry your stay at Rosstrevor is less entertaining to you than your description of it was to me. Mr Woodward has not given me any intimation of his return as yet. I am, dear Miss Woodward, Yours faithfully,                               ROBERT SMITH."

Hawkshaw's correspondence with Isabella had arisen in this way. At the close of the London season, being threatened with bankruptcy, and unable to obtain further advances from his publishers, it had occurred to him that if he became engaged to the daughter of a wealthy member of parliament, his creditors would be content to wait, and even to let him enlarge his indebtedness in the hope of getting paid out of her dowry. Though adverse to matrimony, he felt sure that he would enter into it eventually, as others had done who objected to it as much as he. He did not love Miss Woodward; but she was the only eligible young lady whom he was likely to win; for the fashionable world sought after him as an agreeable guest and distinguished poet, not as a possible husband for its daughters. He relied on her notoriety as a flirt, and on the seclusion of Rosstrevor to save him, should he fail, from being reputed a matrimonial adventurer. Accordingly, he packed some volumes of poetry in his portmanteau; borrowed as many five pound notes as he could; and crossed the Irish Channel to the County Down, where he met Isabella. In a few days he confessed that he had followed her purposely, and then, after many unnecessarily clandestine meetings, and walks on the shore by moonlight, he declared his suit. She, after saying that it could never be, permitted him to clasp her to his breast and kiss her. Both agreed that their love should remain a secret until he was in a position to marry her; but Hawkshaw, having his own purpose in view, and no faith in her discretion, at once took steps to spread the news of his engagement in London. Soon after, growing tired of Rosstrevor and Isabella, he told her that he must return to his literary work in London. She was not sorry to hear it, and appointed a farewell interview, at which she tore herself from him in such hysterical agony, that he for the first time felt proud of the passion he had inspired, and sure of its reality.

In London he found a number of bills awaiting him. These, and seasickness, made him so wretched that he wrote an account of the expatriation and beggary impending over him to Isabella. She, believing herself capable of noble actions, and longing to perform them, resolved to give him a set of diamonds bequeathed to her by her mother, which, as they were in old-fashioned settings, she seldom wore. The satisfaction of this impulse did not gratify her for long. She had hardly written to Smith when she began to doubt whether Hawkshaw's ruin and her own heroism were not shams. When she received his letter, which she thought greedy in its acceptance, and fulsome in its thanks, she grudged her diamonds to him; despised him for taking them; and began a new romance, based on respect for virtue. The figure to which she now attributed all the qualities most opposed to those of Hawkshaw was that of her father's decorous and reserved secretary. Before sunset she had imagined a phantom Smith, above all earthly passions and associations, and was abasing herself before it, and longing to lean on it for support, or by some act of self-abnegation to win its respect.

The same evening she went for the first time to the Roman Catholic church at Warrenpoint, pursuing her fancies, as she went, to the point of being repudiated by Smith, and subsequently exciting his remorse by dying in his arms. In the church she remained in prayer until she noticed that there was a priest in attendance to receive confessions, and incidentally to provide her with an audience. She seized the opportunity to give a bad account of herself in general, and a harmless one in particular, to a good-natured gentleman who was old enough to have learned manners at Salamanca instead of Latin at Maynooth, and who was not inclined to be severe with a young creature evidently suffering from low spirits even though he understood her case much better than she did herself. Isabella returned to Rosstrevor comforted, but a little disappointed that her sins had been made light of.

# CHAPTER III

ON Michaelmas night Mrs Watkins, having provided a goose, and appointed seven o'clock instead of half-past two for dinner, entertained Mr Larkins and Mr Fenwick at Bishopsgate Street. She had invited the treasurer because she hoped that he would marry Fanny. Mr Watkins had desired Fenwick's presence on the ground that now that his sister's child was behaving himself, he could see no use in keeping up a coolness with the poor lad. Mrs Watkins had complied because even she believed that her nephew was distinguished by an exceptional gentility of manner which was likely to make Larkins think well of her social position.

The dinner proceeded pleasantly. Larkins, who had spent a fortnight in Boulogne, gave an account of the language, manners, and institutions of the French nation. Fanny was happy because her lover was at last reconciled to her family. Her parents were busy carving and listening to Larkins. Fraser Fenwick, who had never been in France, pretended to wonder how any interest could attach to such a familiar resort as Boulogne. When the remnant of the goose was removed, the company were cheerful; but after the plum pudding they felt unwell; and Larkins's conversation, which had taken a religious tone after his refusal of a third portion, ceased altogether as the servant discomposedly collected the plates.

"Selina" said Mrs Watkins, "take off the crumbs before you put the dessert on the table."

"Yes'm" said Selina, retiring to the sideboard for a tray and brush, with which she swept the crumbs into Mr Larkins's lap, rapped his knuckles, and cleared a little space in front of him. Having thus done honor to the stranger, she was about to withdraw.

"Selina" said Mrs Watkins. "Go all round the table."

"Yes'm" said Selina, resuming her task. Another silence followed, during which Mrs Watkins looked downwards as if returning thanks, and her guests affected unconcern. Selina finished her

345

sweeping opposite Fenwick, who pointed out a single small crumb which she had overlooked, and privily seized her sleeve betwixt his finger and thumb, so that when she reached forth her brush towards the crumb, her elbow was unexpectedly jerked back, and the contents of the tray scattered.

"Thatll do, Selina" said Mrs Watkins, looking sternly at her nephew, who presented an impassive profile to her, and winked with the other at Selina. The dessert was then put upon the table. It consisted of a decanter of sherry, one of port, a glass dish of almonds and raisins, a green plate containing apples, and a yellow earthenware vase filled with pears and oranges. There was also a kettle mounted on a hot brick, and a black bottle.

"Mr Larkins?" said the hostess.

"Cold water for me, if you please, Mrs Watkins" said the treasurer firmly.

"Oh, dont say that."

"I'm greatly tempted" replied the teetotaller with a smile. "But Ive found a certain resistance works, where I can draw as much strength against temptation as I want, and no rates to pay."

"Well, this is a great disappointment" said Mrs Watkins. "Wouldnt you try some wine?" Larkins shook his head. "Is there nothing at all I can get you?"

"I'll take some fruit" said he. "I think the natural juice of the fruit as it was given to us, worth all the fermented spirits in the world. I know youll give me a cup of tea by an' bye."

"That I will" said she. "Fanny, hand Mr Larkins the ammins an' raisins. Fraser: I believe you never touch anything now."

"Very seldom" said Fenwick, looking at the bottle.

"Youre much better without it. Tom?"

"Cant you give the lad a drop to drink?" said Mr Watkins in a low voice, which Larkins pretended not to hear.

"I assure you I wouldnt touch a drop. I'd rather not" said Fenwick.

"Tom?" inquired Mrs Watkins again.

"No" said Mr Watkins shortly.

Mrs Watkins looked irresolutely at Fenwick. He was preparing an orange for Fanny. She looked at her husband; but he would not look at her.

"Fanny, my girl" said Mr Watkins, "would you like to drink anything?"

"No thank you, father" replied Fanny, too much afraid of her mother to accept the offer.

"By the bye" said Fenwick, "what has become of that pal of yours, Larkins? the dark fellow who used to preach so thunderingly: Davis, or whatever his name was?"

"Hush-sh-sh" said Mrs Watkins.

"Oh Mr Fenwick" said Larkins, "how little we think of what we're saying when we talk lightly about God's creatures!"

"Whats wrong with him?"

"I hope nothing is wrong with him" said Larkins. "I hope and trust that there is nothing wrong with him."

"Where is he?"

"No mortal can tell" said Larkins solemnly. "He has gone up, I hope."

"Gone up!" repeated Fenwick. "I never knew he was in business for himself. Why should you hope that he is broke? I thought you were very thick with him."

"He's not thinking of bankruptcy, man" said Mr Watkins. "Davis is dead."

"You dont mean to say he has kicked the bucket?" exclaimed Fenwick.

"Thats a nice expression to use before a minister of the gospel, in the presence of death almost" said Mrs Watkins.

"Davis wont quarrel with the word, anyhow, Aunt Flossy" said Fenwick.

"Shame!" said Mrs Watkins, "shame on you, Fraser."

"His death was an awful lesson, Mr Fenwick" said Larkins. "Nothing ever shocked a conviction of the instability of human life into me, as much as the news of his sad end did. He had a bold, powerful mind. He could reason with the greatest scholars, and put them down like children. He never thought of himself. He had such a gift of preaching as none of us never had, Mr Fenwick, no, not one. He would have moved the very stones if theyd 'a had ears to hear him. And look what it all come to in the end. There he lies in the dust of the earth, after dying, as one may say, in a common gaol. And here am I carrying on his work, and standing in the very shoes I once thought myself unworthy to loosen."

"He always seemed to be in a queer state of health" said Fenwick. "I wonder was he at all mad."

"I hope he may have been" said Larkins, shaking his head. "I hope so."

"Well, blow me if I understand you" said Fraser. "Why do you hope it?"

"I'll tell you why" said Mr Watkins, impatiently. "Because he died much as you may die if you take to your old ways again. He was found drunk on Wes'minister Bridge shovin women off the pathway; and when the police laid hold of him, he fought till his clothes was torn to atoms. When they got him to the station, they left him alone in a cell; and when they went to look after him at three in the morning, he was dead. No one would ha' knowed him only for me bein by chance run in for the coroner's jury, and identifyin him. It turned out that he had taken to singing and went by the name of Cartouche for a year past. The doctor said that he couldnt have lived another month, he was so far gone in decline, and that he had used himself up all at once in the fight with the police. One of them give evidence there, an' he had as pretty a black eye as ever I seen. It come out through a man that keeps a singing shop, that used to keep Davis on hire for parties and theatres like as you would a pianner or a quadrille band, that he had been employed on the day of his death in a baronet's house in Wilton Place, where he went on outrageous. And to shew how things come about, Fraser, whose house do you think it was? Lady Geraldine Porter's!"

"How very extraordinary!" said Fenwick, pulling his moustache, and addressing Larkins. "It happens that Lady Geraldine Porter is an intimate friend of mine."

Larkins, instead of forming a high opinion of Mr Fenwick's consequence, formed a low one of Lady Geraldine's.

"The end was" continued Mr Watkins, "that the jury brought in death from natural causes accelerated by a drinking fit, or words to that effect. They said that the policeman with the black eye ought to get something out of the poor box or somewhere. It was the doctor that put them on to that. The notion of a man getting a lick with a month's stamina condensed into it tickled them; but the coroner didnt seem to look at it in that light. Leastways he gev him nothing."

"Perhaps" said Fenwick, "if Davis had kept himself quiet at home, and not been so jolly certain that he was better than everybody else, he might have died in his bed, like a gentleman."

"I am sure" said Fanny, betraying a disposition to cry, "that the police told lies and ill-treated him. I am certain I would a great deal rather believe Mr Davis than a policeman, or Lady Geraldine Porter either."

"Hold your tongue, Fanny" said Mrs Watkins sharply. "It doesnt become you to take Mr Davis's part as you always do."

"I dont see why I shouldnt take his part, if nobody else will" retorted Fanny. "It was you yourself that first told me to respect him."

"Not, mind you" said Mr Watkins, interposing quickly to save his daughter from rebuke, "but what Fanny may partly be right. A policeman likes his little bit of authority, and can be rough with his ands as well as any other man."

"It matters little now what any earthly tribunal may think of him" said Larkins. "When I reflect on his awful fate, I says to myself, How can I be thankful enough that it didnt fall on me? For I am no better of my own strength than he. I'm not strong, as he was. I'm not swift, as he was. But the battle was not to him after all; and why not? Because that which cannot err says that the race shall not be to the swift nor the battle to the strong. That which cannot err says that the mighty shall be cast down; that the first shall be last, and the last first. Thats the way faith comforts the weak. When we see the rich and the great of this world thinking little of us, and setting us aside, and passing us on the way to the vain eminences that they prize, what consoles us? Why, the word of God consoles us; for it tells us that those same people, those very proud ones that are trampling on us, will one day be set beneath our feet and put to nought, whilst we are reigning in bliss for ever and ever. It may look unlikely, but it will come. Our enemies may have as little thought of them promises as that poor man of whom we have been speaking had of his downfall; but they will be made our footstool unless they come over to us in time."

"I wonder have *you* nothing to answer for" said Fanny suddenly, as Larkins paused to take breath.

"Hear hear!" cried Fenwick, hammering the table with the handle of his knife.

"Fan, my girl" said Mr Watkins, whilst his wife sat amazed at her daughter's audacity, "that aint polite."

"Fanny" said Mrs Watkins, recovering herself; "leave the room."

"Oh no, maam. Not on my account" remonstrated Larkins. "Let the young lady stay—as a favor to me."

"Favor to you, indeed!" said Fanny, who had turned red at her mother's command. "I dont need to be begged off by you as if I was a child." Then she burst into tears and rose to leave the room.

"Come back and sit down, miss, this instant" said Mrs Watkins sternly.

Fanny went out and shut the door with such violence that the tea-tray rattled on the sideboard.

"She's her mother's daughter! Eh, Larkins?" said Mr Watkins, with a grin.

"I should be sorry to say so, sir. The young lady's nerves is upset by what we have been talking of: a shocking and an awful subject, Mrs Watkins; and I hope youll excuse her hastiness on that account."

"Not at all a proper subject to discuss before ladies" said Fenwick. "Miss Watkins was quite right to leave the room."

"Indeed!" said Mrs Watkins. "Perhaps you had better keep your opinions until they are asked for."

"You might do worse than take your Aunt Flossy's advice, Fraser" said Mr Watkins.

"I am ashamed that a child of mine should conduct herself so in your presence, Mr Larkins; but what can I do when her father is resolved to spoil her?"

"Well, well, we must make allowances" said Larkins. "I hope Miss W. will come down to tea and restore the happiness of the table."

"If wickedness and obstinacy are all the qualities she intends to make us happy with, she had better stay where she is" said Mrs Watkins. "She shall not enter this room again until she apologizes to you for her rudeness."

"No, no" said Larkins reprovingly. "Excuse me, but if the young lady has committed an offence—and which of us has not backslided some time or another?—it is not from me that she must ask pardon. I couldnt set myself up to that hithe; for what is the likes of me? Nor I cant allow you to set me up."

"Youre too meek, Mr Larkins" said Mrs Watkins. "She needs to be humbled."

"So do we all" replied Larkins. "But it isnt for us to humble one another, or to bow down before one another."

Mrs Watkins bit her lip, and did not reply.

"Fraser" said Mr Watkins, "do you just slip upstairs and coax Fanny to come down to tea."

"I hope youre not going to send the young man into your daughter's bedroom, Mr Watkins."

Her husband's brow lowered as she addressed him by his surname. "Come" said he, "there has been unpleasantness enough over this. If she wont come down for Fraser, she wont for any one else; so he had better go; and let us hear no more nonsense about her bedroom."

"There is no need" persisted Mrs Watkins, reddening, "I will send Selina with word from me that she is to come down at once."

"Yes; and she'll come too, very likely! Larkins: youll excuse our making you uncomfortable by our little squall. We'll drop the subject now, and be sociable. Away with you, Fraser; and tell her there'll be no more about it, but just to come back as if nothing had happened."

Fenwick left the room. Presently he returned, looking alarmed.

A thrill of apprehension seized Mrs Watkins. Larkins, anticipating some excitement, looked with curiosity at Fenwick. The host alone controlled himself.

"Well? What is it? Out with it" said he.

"She's gone."

"Gone!" said Mr Watkins. "Where to?"

"I dont know. I looked first in her room, and then downstairs. Selina heard her go out some time ago."

"Are you sure, Fraser?" said Mrs Watkins, trembling.

"You neednt flatter yourself that there is any error about it, Aunt Flossy" said Fenwick. "She was quite right not to stand it too; if you want to know my opinion."

"Just sit down and keep yourself quiet" said Mr Watkins. "Larkins, I wont be away long; and the missus will take care of you until I come back. You neednt mention what has occurred to any one, if you dont like." He left the room, and presently the house door was heard to shut softly behind him.

"She'll come back in a few minutes, I'm certain" said Larkins consolingly. "Only a little huff, thats all."

"But she may be in the house. That Selina would say anything, Mr Larkins: *would* you mind my going and seeing for myself?" said Mrs Watkins.

"You may save yourself the trouble; for I tell you she's gone" said Fenwick, sitting down. But Larkins begged his hostess to act just as if she had no guest to consider; and she went away to search and call about the house.

"Old cat!" said Fenwick, when he was alone with Larkins. "If I were Watkins, I would knock sense into her quick enough."

"Let us not be uncharitable, sir. Doubtless she is a little hasty."

"Hasty be damned! She's always the same—enough to drive

352

anybody out of their wits. She thinks she's an angel as long as she keeps the ten commandments. I wish there was an eleventh against domineering savages. She honors her father and mother because theyre dead—her mother was an old hen like herself—and she takes jolly good care, by bullying them, that her children shall honor her while she's alive."

"I fear, Mr Fenwick, that you have not thought about the real eleventh commandment."

"Oh, bother the real eleventh commandment! It's like the one unpardonable sin, which means whatever you happen to be preaching against."

Larkins, about to reply, was interrupted by the return of Mrs Watkins, whose expression shewed that her search had been futile. She said nothing, but rang for the kettle; and a comfortless meal followed. Larkins tried to console her, but finding himself contradicted by Fenwick whenever he spoke, he relapsed into silence, which was disturbed only by Mrs Watkins starting, and the two men looking at one another, when any noise on the stair, or footstep arrested in the street opposite the house, attracted their attention.

At last Mr Watkins returned and asked for some tea, disregarding his wife's anxious looks. When he had been supplied he glanced round the table in his furtive manner, and said,

"It's all right. She's gone to her aunt Virginia's."

"How do you know, Tom?"

"How do I know? Easy enough. The policeman seen her turn down towards Liverpool Street. I suspected what she was up to then, and right enough, when I asked at the station, she had just taken a ticket for Leytonstone. Strahan sold it to her. So she's safe enough. The change of air will do her good. Give me another piece o' bread, and Larkins another cup o' tea, will you, Flossy?"

Now that her fears were dispelled Mrs Watkins gave way to resentment, and declared that her daughter might stay where she had made her bed; for that she should never set foot in Bishopsgate Street again.

"P'raps she doesnt intend to" said Fenwick.

An angry reply was averted by Larkins, who rose to take his leave, protesting that he had spent a very pleasant evening, and expressing a hope that Miss Watkins would soon follow the example of the repentant prodigal.

"Tom" said Mrs Watkins uneasily, when he was gone. "I think somebody ought to go after that girl tonight."

"I will go with pleasure" said her nephew.

"And pray why should *you* go?" said Mrs Watkins, resuming her hard manner.

"I dont know but what Fraser Fen'ick mightnt be the best one to go after all" said Mr Watkins. "Fan'll be all for obstinacy if I go; and youll be all for obstinacy if you go; but she can ease her mind by complaining to Fraser; and he can call in on his way back and tell us if she's all right."

"Have your own way" said Mrs Watkins sulkily. "If rebellious children are to be considered before every one else, I wash my hands of it."

"It's half-past eight" said Mr Watkins, "so if you mean to get to Leytonstone and back tonight, Fraser, you had better start. The last train back starts at ten minutes past eleven. Youll catch the quarter to nine at Fenchurch Street, if you hurry. Here! I had better settle your fare, as youre goin on my business."

"Excuse me. It is quite unnecessary."

"Well" said Mr Watkins, pocketing his money, "no one can quarrel with you for being a gentleman as long as you are willing to pay for it. Just tap at the shop door when you come back, and I'll let you in. I'm going to sit up and look over my books."

"All right" said Fenwick. "I suppose I will not see you again, Aunt Flossy." He advanced to shake hands with her as he spoke.

"Goodnight" said Mrs Watkins, folding her hands in her lap.

Fenwick checked himself, made her a bow, and withdrew.

The host and his wife, left alone together, did not care to begin a conversation which would, they knew, end in a dispute. When the silence became embarrassing, and Mr Watkins felt that she could not hold her tongue much longer, he went downstairs to the shop, whilst she remained to superintend the removal of the tea-things, and to while away Fenwick's absence by knitting. For three hours she sat defending her anger against her remorse, which was reinforced by thoughts of railway accidents, young women decoyed from uncomfortable homes, destinations never reached, misplaced confidences, murders, and all the dangers of a wicked city, until a noise below, and a subdued sound of voices, announced the return of her nephew. A period of suspense followed. Then she heard the two men moving, as though their interview were at an end. She listened for the noise of the house door closing on Fenwick. Instead of it she heard a scream like that of a woman in extreme terror. Mrs Watkins shuddered and ran out, almost sick with fear. On the stairs, about eight steps above the level of the hall, she found Selina, half laughing, half whimpering.

"Please'm" gasped Selina, "it was Mr Fenwick. I was comink up to bed in the dark, and e come out of the shop without me seeing him or knowing he was there; and e puts is and through the banisters and ketches me suddingly by the hankle. I thort I should ha' died."

"And why werent you in bed long ago?"

Selina wiped her mouth with her apron apologetically.

"Nice conduct, to scream that way in the middle of the night. You ought to be ashamed of yourself. I have been watching your behavior with Mr Fenwick, Selina, and the next time I see any such scandalous nonsense, out you go. Get to bed; and dont think of making your late hours an excuse for not having the kitchen fire lighted in the morning, as you did last Monday."

Selina went to bed abashed; and her mistress descended to the shop, where Mr Watkins was putting away his books.

"What was that, Flossy?" said he. "Fraser larking with Selina, I suppose, as usual."

"Yes, the hussy!"

"I wish he'd let the girl alone."

"It is her own fault. You may be sure he would respect her if she respected herself."

"Ah! It dont answer to have servants that are too particular

355

about respecting themselves. They are mostly full of cheek. And it aint in Fraser to respect anything, not even *him*self."

"What news did he bring, Tom?"

"She's safe enough at her aunt Virginia's."

"Humph!" said Mrs Watkins, hiding her relief. "And when is she going to condescend to come back?"

"She wont hear of coming back at present. Being riled, she says she'll never come back. However, that was to be expected. It was Larkins triumphing like over Davis that made her angry. The fact is, Flossy, she was sweet on that chap. Dont you remember how she took on about him when we gev him the go-by?"

"But that was ever so long ago."

"Aye; but the inquest revived it. I always thought, when you wanted to take his photograph out of the halbum to burn, and couldnt find it, that she ad it id somewhere. However, she wont break her eart about him; and as Virginia's agreed to keep her for the present, theres no more to be said until matters cool down."

"Virginia is ready to take her part against me, of course."

Mr Watkins made no reply, but put out the gas, chained the door, and went to bed.

# CHAPTER IV

In October, Smith had to superintend certain preparations for the reception of the family at Queen's Gate. These were carried out by an Irishwoman named Mrs Daly, who had been attached to the late Mrs Woodward, and, since her death, had acted as servant, housekeeper, nurse, and, on emergencies, chaperon to her daughters. Every morning Smith read to her the instructions written to him by Mr Woodward and Isabella. For such of these as were dictated by economy, Mrs Daly invented explanations intended to reassure Smith of the wealth and great consequence of the family; and he soon began to look upon her as a tedious person who had an exaggerated opinion of his credulity. She was quite illiterate, and often told the secretary that she never could read handwriting. Nevertheless he found that she could always identify the writer of a letter by looking at the superscription.

One day Smith told her that Mr Woodward travelling north, and Isabella travelling south, had rejoined Clytie in Dublin, and that the entire family were at that moment crossing the channel.

"The carriage is to be at Euston at half-past six" said Smith. "Miss Isabella says you had better leave the breakfast room carpet as it was before, and put the rug with the hole in it under the black cabinet in the drawing room."

"Throth it's them that *has* the money that grudges it" said Mrs Daly. "She thinks things good enough for London that she wouldnt let into the pigstye of the house at home. An' is Corny comin wid him, sir?"

"I suppose so. The letter doesnt mention."

"Poor lad! The say never agreed wid him" said Mrs Daly, sighing.

Next morning, when Smith arrived at Queen's Gate, Mr Woodward was in bed. There were but few letters to be attended to; and in half an hour the secretary was idle. A little later Hamlet appeared, looking ill and fatigued.

"Well, Cornelius" said Smith cheerfully. "So you have come back. How are you?"

"Och, I'm nearly kilt."

"Rough passage?"

"Savin your presence, sir—"

"Cornelius" interrupted a voice from the doorway, "the master wants his hot water."

"Yes, Miss Bella" said Hamlet submissively, and withdrew.

Isabella had apparently escaped seasickness; for she looked well. Smith, who had not seen her since she had been toiling through the pleasures of the London season, felt as though she had brought into the room some of the marine freshness of Carlingford Lough. He had never seen her eyes so bright, or her smile so natural. She advanced and shook his hand without speaking.

"I hope you had a pleasant voyage" said Smith, conscious of a partly pleasant internal disturbance, and not venturing to meet her gaze.

"It was very rough; but I am a good sailor, so papa and I escaped. You must not broach the subject to Clytie, though; and as for poor Cornelius!—but you have seen *him*."

"Your stay by the sea has evidently benefited you."

"Yes: I suppose it has. Rosstrevor is such a darling place."

"Why, I thought you were heartily sick of it. Are you not glad to be in London again?"

"Glad! I think London a detestable place. After the mountains, the sea, and the beautiful fresh air, it seems intolerable to breathe in this prison of a city. However, here I am; and here I must stay. But I did not come down to talk about myself. How can I thank you sufficiently for the service you have rendered me about those miserable diamonds?"

"Really, Miss Woodward, you have already thanked me by letter very much more than I at all deserve. You made me feel quite mean, when I thought of the smallness of the service, and the caution with which I undertook it."

"How noble of you to think so!"

"Nonsense!" said Smith abruptly.

Isabella saw that she had miscalculated his appetite for flattery. "Of course" she said, with her habitual air of discontent, "you thought the transaction strange, and not very respectable."

"I certainly thought it strange; but that was all."

"I was weak enough to pretend in my letter to you that I was only returning the jewels. You *must* have felt very little respect for me when you found out—as you explained to me— that I had been telling you a lie."

"But it did not seem to me that you were bound to confide in me. I accepted it as a conventional excuse, like the 'not at home' formula for 'I dont want to see you.' I understood your account to mean, similarly, 'I dont want to tell you.' "

"You are really very matter-of-fact, Mr Smith. You rub the gloss off everything."

"I am sorry for that. Matter-of-fact people are a great nuisance, and always will be, so long as they are in the minority."

"Brukhusht is ready, Miss Bella" said Hamlet, calling through the door.

"Very well" she replied. Then, turning to Smith, she said, "I must go now. I know that my secret is safe in your keeping. Once more, thanks. Farewell."

"One word" said Smith. "What on earth does he mean by 'brukhusht'?"

"Breakfast, of course" said Isabella. "Oh, you *English*man!" With this apostrophe, and a mocking grimace, she ran away through the corridor.

"Very engaging" said Smith. "Fancy an antelope in high-heeled shoes!" Nevertheless the ridicule in this speech, expressed at her expense, was felt at his own; for he was beginning to experience feelings towards Isabella which reminded him of those with which Mademoiselle Sangallo had formerly inspired him.

Mr Woodward did not appear in the study that day until twelve o'clock, when he entered with a portmanteau containing nearly all the letters which had been forwarded to him during his absence. They were in the same state of confusion that had involved all his correspondence before the appointment of Smith, who perceived how vain was the hope that his chance of a nomination for the civil service might be unobstructed, thanks to the system he had introduced, by any further necessity for his services at Queen's Gate. Three o'clock struck before the letters were put in order, and the neglected replies despatched.

"Now, sir" said Smith, "I think everything is settled."

"Why, what the gallows have you done with all the letters that were in the portmanteau?" said Mr Woodward, who supposed that little more than the ordinary morning's work had been accomplished.

"They are all disposed of."

"Bedad, Smith, I dont know how I should get on without you. Youre a great fellow."

"It is a mere trick of routine. Any clerk could do as much, and probably for less money."

"Then why didnt they turn up when I wanted them?" said Mr Woodward good-humoredly.

Smith resolved to defer his request, and took his leave. In the hall he found Hawkshaw in conference with the footman. The poet looked at him as he passed out without making any sign of recognition. Smith, who had been about to bow, checked himself and affected abstraction until he reached the street.

Meanwhile, Hawkshaw, having ascertained from the servant that Miss Woodward was alone, prepared himself for a scene. She was sitting near the window when he entered the drawing room; and the first thing he noticed was that she had on a dress with a row of conical buttons down the front, which she had worn the last time he had embraced her. Remembering that on that occasion his breast had been dotted by small, painful contusions, he resolved to content himself with a kiss. But she, without rising, held out her hand and coldly bid him good day.

"Clytie is in bed, and papa is in the study" said she; "so I am left alone to encounter any visitor whose evil star may lead him hither. It is by mere chance that you find us here at all; for we only arrived from Ireland last night."

Hawkshaw was surprised; but he determined to learn her intention at once. "Isabel" said he: "have you forgotten what passed between us at our last meeting?"

"Doubtless something of a very affecting description. I really forget."

"By Heaven!" cried Hawkshaw, "if this is not mere coquetry, it is the most heartless perfidy that ever woman's brain conceived."

"Mr Hawkshaw!" remonstrated Isabella, quailing a little.

"I know not what suspicion is beginning to dawn on me" said Hawkshaw, striking his forehead, and walking quickly to and fro through the room. "The lures with which you drew me on—the jewels—the gradual withdrawal of confidence and warmth afterwards—your silence for the last fortnight—the trivial excuse that your packing left you no time—pshaw! I see the infernal plot in all its black atrocity; and it has succeeded but too well; for my honor is lost. But at least tell me what was your motive in this. Was it revenge for some fancied wrong; or was it the mere delight in ruin which women have cherished since the serpent poisoned their first mother?"

"I dont know what you are speaking of. *I* draw you on! What a coward you must be to make such an insinuation!"

"A coward! I should indeed be one, were I to suffer myself to be put to silence by such an answer. Call me a fool if you will; for, after devoting all that was in me to singing the snares of your sex, I have walked open-eyed into the trap myself. Well, enjoy your triumph. The bird of paradise has netted the fowler. What does it matter how the victim feels?"

"If you have anything to accuse me of" said Isabella angrily, "say what it is, and stop talking *rubbish*."

"I accuse you" said Hawkshaw, confronting her, "of having entrapped me by false pretences, by lies smiled, sighed, acted, and conveyed in clinging of arms and pressure of hands, into an obligation which I am by your worse than infernal treachery bound in honor to repay at the very moment when you know I can as easily grasp the stars as make good a single stiver of it. I accuse you of having planned this from the outset in order that I should not escape as an unfortunate man, but drink to its dregs the bitter cup of a dishonored caitiff."

"I never asked you to pay me. I dont want you to pay me. It is you who have broken your promise. Why, I have received, and can shew, fifty letters of congratulation with which I have been persecuted since you so busily spread the news of our engagement."

"Aye: you have my weaknesses ready to cast in my teeth, no doubt. I suppose I did give utterance to what my heart was so full with. I am glad, however, that you admit our engagement."

"I do not. I defy you to quote a single promise of mine."

"I shall not attempt to; for I know that you guarded your tongue, and lied dumbly. I thought as little of watching your calculated words, as I did that your hired messenger, in his coarse attempt at treachery, was merely acting by your instructions."

"What an infamous suggestion! I think that common gratitude might have induced you to spare me it."

Hawkshaw changed his manner, and bowed humbly. "Yes" said he, "I forgot. Thank you for reminding me of it I have accepted your bounty. I thought for a moment that I was a man, and so transgressed."

"I did not mean that: at least, you irritated me into meaning it for an instant. You are perfectly welcome to the jewels; and I do not consider that you are under any compliment to me, as you did not ask for them. But as you took them—and were glad enough to get them, I believe—you have no right to accuse me of plots, and lies, and treachery, and the rest of your insinuations, which are neither manly nor polite."

"And are you indeed so ingenuous as to believe that a man smarting under such injuries as mine will observe the conventions of society? No, Miss Woodward, they were made for lesser occasions. But one thing at least you cannot deny. You wish to jilt me. At Rosstrevor you permitted me to address you in a manner which implied either that you looked upon me as your affianced husband, or that you are accustomed to carry flirtation to a point of which modest women stop short. Which of these views am I to accept?"

Isabella hesitated. Hawkshaw was now talking sense. "I am not going to discuss the modesty of my conduct with you" she said.

"You are right" he replied. "We will then take the first alternative. When I left Ireland, we were engaged. When you meet me again, you ignore this, and treat me as a mere acquaintance."

"Well" said Isabella impatiently, "did you expect that I would jump up and hug you the very moment you appeared at the door? Perhaps you are disappointed because I was not in the balcony waving kisses to you as you came along the street."

"Such a course would not have been more extreme than the one you took" said Hawkshaw, a little taken aback.

"You overwhelmed me with a torrent of invective the moment you came in."

"Do you mean that I have been too hasty?"

"I think that 'hasty' is a very mild term to apply to your language and conduct during the last five minutes."

"You must consider how deeply I feel on the subject" said Hawkshaw, puzzled, and seeing a necessity for caution arise out of his former precipitation. "Think what it would cost me to lose you!"

She sat down, looked through the window, and closed her lips.

"Isabella" said he: "you are keeping me in suspense. What am I to infer from your coldness?"

She still looked away from him, and said nothing.

"Isabella" said Hawkshaw, with emotion, coming close to her chair, "dearest Isab—"

"Mr Hawkshaw" said she, interrupting him, "we will, if you please, revert to the terms of our former acquaintanceship. You will excuse my saying that you have shewn yourself to me today in a perfectly new light: one that has convinced me that neither your happiness nor my own would be furthered by prosecuting the foolish vein of sentiment into which we unfortunately allowed ourselves to fall at Rosstrevor."

"Miss Woodward" said Hawkshaw, with dignity: "you have outwitted me. Let it be as you say. After what has passed, it could not possibly be otherwise. I am confident that I have dealt with you honorably in this matter. I leave you with a sore heart, but with a sound conscience. Good evening."

"Before you go" said Isabella, "let me tell you that your suspicions with regard to my hiring Mr Smith and giving him instructions are entirely unfounded; and that I believe the soreness of your heart will trouble you as little as the soundness of your conscience."

"Your genius for repartee is native" said Hawkshaw, bowing. "I will not venture a contest in lists where my English honesty of purpose would avail me nothing."

"Nothing, indeed" retorted Isabella, "because it is too transparent."

"Good evening, Miss Woodward."

"Good evening" said Isabella scornfully, and rang the bell.

Hawkshaw retired. The footman, scanning his dress and deportment, felt that such a man, though a poet, was above criticism. Yet, particular as he was about the propriety of his demeanor in public, Hawkshaw entered a public house in High Street and drank some brandy and water. Then he strolled along Kensington Palace Gardens, meditating on the change in his circumstances. The loss of Isabella's person did not cause him any regret; but he knew that she would now contradict the report of her engagement to him, which had hitherto postponed the day of reckoning with his creditors, who had more confidence in his plausible manners than in his literary ability. He was therefore in danger of bankruptcy, from which he shrank, as he was unaccustomed to it. He was also troubled by his obligation respecting the jewels, which he had pledged for forty-five pounds. With part of this sum he had satisfied the claims of those tradesmen whose business it was to supply daily needed things, a discontinuance of which was incompatible with existence. The rest he was spending fast on gloves, cabs, and flowers. The amount which remained to him was far below that which, with any addition which he could borrow, would suffice to redeem the diamonds. Otherwise he would have made an effort to return them to Isabella; for this debt was the only one of which he felt ashamed.

Suddenly he conceived an idea. Was it not the privilege of a poet to convert his misfortunes into money? One follower of his school, an admired poet and respected man, having had the good fortune to lose through death a wife with whom he had lived on disagreeable terms, had versified his bereavement in a poem which affected all who read it, and greatly advanced the reputation of the writer, who enjoyed, to boot, the sarcasm on his true relations with the deceased which the lament conveyed to his private mind. Worse rhymesters than Hawkshaw had done the same thing on less occasion than the breaking of a heart by a woman's treachery: a description which Isabella's conduct would bear in poetry. Hawkshaw hailed a passing cab; drove to Ladbroke Grove; drank more brandy; and before midnight finished an alliterative poem which placed his conduct in such a light that he went to bed over-come with sympathy for himself.

# CHAPTER V

ONE morning Mr Woodward found among his letters a package addressed in the handwriting of his sister-in-law, Mrs Foley.

"What the mischief has Kate sent me?" said he, taking it up and endeavoring to extricate the enclosure. "'Tch! How has she managed to stick it together? Here" he cried impatiently, throwing the packet across the table to Smith: "open it if you can. If you cant, pitch the damned thing into the fire. Serve her right for gumming and swaddling a letter like that."

Smith opened the packet, and took out a small volume bound in a black kid cover bearing neither ornament nor inscription, and lined with white silk. The leaves were of rough, heavy paper with untrimmed edges. On every page the blank margin at each side occupied as much space as the letterpress itself.

"Whats the name of it?" said Mr Woodward.

Smith opened the title-page, and immediately chuckled.

"Well?" said Mr Woodward. "Let us hear the fun."

"I beg your pardon" said Smith. "I really dont know what made me laugh. This is A Song of Bent Branch and Broken Laurel. By Patrick Hawkshaw, author of Wheat Sheaves, Hamlet, or a Second Book of Revelations, and other travail. Fourteenth impression. *Now there was, not far from the place where they lay, a castle, called Doubting Castle, the owner whereof was Giant Despair; and it was in his grounds they were now sleeping.* London: Tabuteau Brothers, Paternoster Row. *N.B.*—The circulation of this book is restricted to the friends of the writer, without whose authorization no person will be supplied with a copy. As the object of publication is not to profit by the curiosity of the public at large, the price of each signed and numbered copy has been fixed at two guineas. The type will be dispersed after the hundredth impression."

"Two hundred guineas!" exclaimed Mr Woodward, taking the book from Smith, and looking at it with wonder. "He might have gilt the edges of it for the money, instead of making a compliment of not even cutting them. I wonder does Kate think I am going to read this. I dont think she would have the face to ask me to take a copy at two guineas. Humph! Humph! Listen to the fellow.

> My traitress did inherit from her sires
> The mocking gleam of its marmoreal fires—

His verses are like himself. I must read her letter, and see what she means by sending me such rubbish. Perhaps it's for Isabella; though I dont know why she should send it to me, if so. Bent Branch and Broken Laurel! This is worse than the tracts her aunt used to send me every month for the poor children."

Whilst Mr Woodward was opening and reading his sister-in-law's letter, Smith turned over the pages of the book, and endeavored to gather the sense of it from reading lines here and there throughout it. He was interrupted by his employer.

"Smith" said Mr Woodward hurriedly: "just let me look at that book for a moment. Thank you. You might write, now that your hand is in, to Fagan, and tell him that I wont have the Morriseys coming to the gap for their turf; and to put a charge of shot into young Shea if he sees him snatching at the other side of the river, and cant get at him any other way."

Smith obeyed. Mr Woodward took the book; made a pretence of referring to a page; and laid it down close by so that his hand rested on it. He then resumed his perusal of the letter, repeatedly scratching his head, and muttering to himself. The secretary observed him with some apprehension; for, seeing that he was forbidden to meddle further with the book, it occurred to him that his employer had made some discovery with reference to Hawkshaw.

"Smith" said Mr Woodward, when he had finished reading the letter, and had twisted it about in his hands for some minutes: "would you give that bell a touch for me?"

The secretary rang; and Hamlet presently answered.

"Didje ring, sir?"

"Is Miss Isabella in the house?"

"I don know, sir" said Cornelius cheerfully. "But sure I can go an' look. Shall I tell her to come t'ye?"

"Go and find out where she is; and come and tell me; and hold your tongue; and be quick" said Mr Woodward sternly.

Hamlet disappeared, and presently returned to say that Isabella was alone in the breakfast parlor. Mr Woodward left the room, taking the book and the letter with him.

"Whats the matter wood him this mornin, that he's in such a tare about?" said Cornelius to Smith.

"Probably some business that only concerns himself."

"It consarns Miss Bella, I'll bet. He looks as if he was goin hot foot to the brukhusht parlor to comb her hair the wrong way for her. Much good may it do him too, the poor owl' man. He'll go in an' shplutther at her like a proud paycock; an' the next minit she'll be his darlint child that nothin's too expinsive to put on the back iv. She gev a skin jacket to Mrs Daly's niece over in Ireland that she didnt wear a dozen times, afther payin a power o' money for it."

"Mrs Daly's niece is your sister, I suppose?"

"God forbid—that I maytnt sin! She's my cousin."

"I am right, at any rate, in supposing that Mrs Daly is your aunt?"

"Yis, sir, an' a cute owl' wan she is."

Smith was relieved from the presence of the valet by the bell; and soon after, having finished his work, he resolved to go home, as there was no sign of Mr Woodward's return. Seeing Mrs Daly in the conservatory as he went out into the corridor, he hastened away, fearing that she might engage him in conversation; but before he reached the hall, she called his name in a loud whisper. He stopped, and resigned himself to listen again to the Irish brogue, which he detested. But she only took a little note from her apron; thrust it hard into the hollow of his hand with her brown finger; winked with a vivacity extraordinary at her age; and retired quickly without speaking. Smith looked after her in astonishment, and then opened the note.

"Dear Mr Smith—Please meet me in the Hort. Gardens today at half-past four, near where we were playing tennis when you were there before. I am in dreadful trouble. Do not fail, or you will ruin me. Tear this up.                I. W."

Smith laughed at this note, but remembered with uneasiness his part in the diamond transaction, which he felt sure was now discovered by Mr Woodward. He waited for the appointed time with impatience; and it wanted three minutes of the first quarter of the hour when he entered the Horticultural Gardens. The third quarter was striking when Isabella appeared, panting and apologizing for the delay.

"I was detained by papa" said she. "I had to go with him to the railway; and I am supposed to be paying visits now. Clytie will probably find out that I am doing nothing of the sort. But that is a minor evil. I have come to you for assistance. Everything is discovered."

"But I dont understand" said Smith.

"I mean about the jewels. Mr Hawkshaw, in order to revenge himself on me, has had the meanness to publish the whole story in a poem which has fallen into my aunt's hands. She sent it to papa this morning with a long letter in which she tells him that everybody is talking of me, and that all sorts of stories are being circulated about the diamonds. It was only yesterday that some stupid creature told my aunt that I was the real 'Isabel,' and that all the silly talk about its being the countess of this, and the duchess of that, and the princess of the other was nonsense. And now papa wants to see my jewels. What am I to do, to prevent the whole miserable truth from coming out?"

"You forget that I dont know what the truth is. Let me remind you that I am not in your confidence further than the bare fetching and carrying of your ornaments implies. Do not unintentionally let me into a secret by concluding too hastily that I know it already."

"But I want you to advise me what to do."

"Then you must tell me what you have done, Miss Woodward."

"I thought you knew all about it. It is so very obvious. But men

369

never see anything. I suppose I must tell you, although you will think my confession a foolish one. Well, Mr Hawkshaw told me he was on the brink of ruin; and, like an idiot, I gave him my diamonds to sell and save himself with."

"That was very generous of you. He must be a great rascal if he has abused your kindness."

"But it wasnt so much gen— Besides, he tries to make out that I was engaged to him."

"I do not see how that alters the case. Were you really engaged to him?"

"No" said Isabella, looking straight into the eyes of her interlocutor, as she always did when she told a lie.

"What is the difficulty then?"

"The difficulty! Why, I must prevent papa from finding out that I gave away mamma's jewels to Mr Hawkshaw, whom he cannot bear. Just imagine what he and everybody else would think of such a thing!"

"I dont see it."

"Then you dont know what people are. Pray dont be stupid— I mean, at least, dont be impracticable. I have a plan which you must assist me to carry out. Promise me that you will."

"I would like to know what your plan is, before I promise" said Smith, his caution roused by her coaxing tone.

"Anybody would promise then. A friend ought to know beforehand whether he means to help or not."

"I am willing to assist you; but I will not commit myself to a plan; because as yet I see no necessity for one."

"Well then, this is it. I must get back the diamonds at all hazards. I want you to go to Mr Hawkshaw, and find out from him what he has done with them. I know he must have sold or pawned them; and when I know where they are I will manage to get them back by buying or redeeming them."

"But think of what it will cost you! Such gems would not be resold by a dealer except at a great price; and even to redeem them would require more money than you could afford—at least, unless you have large resources."

"Do you think they would want so much? The things are very old-fashioned."

"Diamonds are never old-fashioned."

"But I have a lot of things that I dont want; and Mrs Daly can raise money on them for me."

"Would it be wise to trust to a servant?"

"Oh, Mrs Daly knows all about it. She has often got money for me before."

Smith stared. "Supposing even that you get the jewels" said he, "what good will that do you?"

"It will make everything smooth by a plan I have arranged. The moment I get them, I will send them to Mrs Daly's niece, who has charge of our house in Ireland. Then she will send them back to papa."

"Well?"

"Well! that will bear out what I said. What a thorough Englishman you are, Mr Smith!"

"Excuse me. No doubt I am very slow; for I am still utterly at a loss. What did you say, that this plan will bear out?"

"Papa asked me for the diamonds this morning. Of course I had to tell him that I had left them at home: that is, in Ireland."

Smith recoiled, and regarded her with surprise and disapprobation. She looked at him anxiously, and added, apologetically, "What else could I do?"

"I must say, Miss Woodward" said Smith, "that I understand your plan less than ever. Why you should condescend to deny any act to your father is best known to yourself; but when the act is one of which you have every reason to be proud; and when its concealment involves loss of money, the wholesale corruption of your servants, and a web of useless deception, your plan seems to me the most inconceivable of follies."

Isabella bit her lip, and stood divided betwixt disappointment, shame, and wounded pride. "Then you will not help me. Is that what you mean?" she said.

"I will certainly not help you to be unworthy of yourself."

"It is very easy for you, who are independent and have

nothing to fear, to preach" she said, angrily; "but you dont understand my position. In the world, one must consider what is expedient. I cannot see that I am behaving so very wickedly after all. The jewels were mine; and I had a perfect right to do as I pleased with them. And I am only trying to spare papa a great deal of annoyance, which I would needlessly inflict by telling him the truth."

"He would much rather you inflicted such a paltry annoyance, than deceive him; conspire with his servants against him; and destroy all his confidence in you and his pleasure in your company."

"That is mere sophistry, Mr Smith. How can he lose confidence in me when he will never know that I have deceived him?"

"How long is he likely to remain ignorant of a secret which will be known to Mrs Daly, to Hawkshaw, who publishes poems about it, to Mrs Daly's niece, and probably to several others?"

"Mrs Daly and Lizzie can be trusted implicitly."

"And the others? Hawkshaw, for instance?"

"But what am I to do?" said Isabella, almost in tears. "What is the use of arguing when I have already told a story? I cannot go back."

"It is much better to go back than to go forward according to your plan."

"I wish I had never seen the diamonds" cried Isabella. Then she stamped on the gravel, and added, in an audible whisper, "Damn them!"

Smith started. A young lady who could not reason, and whose ideas of right and wrong arose accidentally from personal considerations, was to him a commonplace. But a young lady who told deliberate lies, who pawned her clothes by the hands of her servant, and who cursed, shocked him.

"I cannot too strongly advise you" he said, "to tell Mr Woodward what has become of the jewels. If it will feel awkward to add that when he took you by surprise this morning, you made an excuse on the spur of the moment to save him some annoyance, you must bear it as a penance for having told him what was not true."

"Yes" said Isabella, brightening, "I begin to think you are right. If I put it in that way, he could not be very angry, could he?"

"It is not a question of putting it this way or that way" said Smith intolerantly. "I only suggested what I supposed to be the truth."

"Of course. But do you think he will be disgusted with me? I know you think I am as bad as I can be; but really and truly I could not bear to have papa turn against me."

"On the contrary, I shall not be surprised if he conceives a higher opinion of your candor than if you had told him at first; and he will certainly not reproach you half so much about the diamonds, his attention will be so occupied with your confession."

"Then perhaps it will have been all for the best that I did not tell him."

Smith looked serious.

"I feel that I must do as you say" she said, after a pause; "but I shall be dreadfully afraid to tell him, I dont know how to set about it."

"I am glad you are convinced. Now that you have discarded your plan, I may say, without seeming to tempt you to abandon a low course for a low motive, that I believe you could not possibly have succeeded in it."

"Do you think not?"

"I am sure of it. Even if you had been able to obtain sufficient money, which I greatly doubt, the delay would have betrayed you, if Hawkshaw had not anticipated it by doing so himself."

"Perhaps so. Indeed, I am sure you are right. It is a consolation, when one has to give up a plan, to know that it would have been no use."

"I am greatly afraid, Miss Woodward, that, after all, you have rejected it chiefly on account of its inexpediency. Why not choose on the merit of the alternatives?"

"There is no harm in convincing oneself that the right course is always the most expedient, is there?"

"No" said Smith, checking himself as he became conscious of congratulating himself on his superior virtue; "and now that I think of it, I am not quite sure that I have any other reason for recommending rigid honesty, than my conviction of its superlative expediency."

"I think not" said she, with envious sadness. "I believe you love honesty for its own sake."

"Precisely. Only I cannot exactly make out what its own sake means."

"It means its own sake I suppose" said Isabella, with some impatience. "Dear me, how long we have been talking! It is past five. I must go."

"You are quite resolved to adopt the right course, Miss Woodward?"

"Oh yes. I think so."

"You think so?"

"Well then, I *will*. At least I am almost certain that I will."

"Excuse me. But I wish you would arrive at a perfect certainty before we part."

Miss Woodward hesitated. "There is no use in affecting an indomitable virtue, Mr Smith" said she; "for I am wretchedly afraid to tell papa; and I know that all my courage will vanish when the hour arrives."

"I always thought Mr Woodward the most indulgent of fathers. If he is, surely it is very ungrateful to shrink from him in terror."

"But that is the very thing that frightens me. Dont you see that it makes any deceit so much blacker? If he were a harsh, cross man, as some fathers are, it would be a pleasure to defy and outwit him. As it is, he will think me ungrateful for telling him a story, and mean for coming to make a virtue of necessity by confessing what I could no longer hide. I wish he could in some way be made aware of the plan I have sacrificed. He would know then that I could have imposed on him if I had chosen to, and that my confession was made voluntarily because I could not bear to deceive him."

"It is useless to advise you" cried Smith, with unconcealed disgust. "Women have no moral sense."

"Dont be in such a hurry to think ill of me, Mr Smith. I havnt said that I wont tell papa the truth. I fully intend to tell him."

"Do; and you will have no reason to care what anyone thinks of you, inasmuch as you will have satisfied the demands of your own self-respect."

Isabella was twisting her finger in her belt, and looking uneasily at the ground, at the buildings, and at Smith by turns. "I suppose" she said, "there is no chance of Mr Hawkshaw having the jewels still in his hands. It is barely possible that he might not have sold them."

"It is possible; but it is not very probable. Besides, that does not alter the case."

"No. Of course not." For some moments Isabella stood silent, still fingering her belt. Then she said, "I think I will go over to the Oratory, and speak to Father Ignatius. He will tell me what to do."

"What on earth is the good of going to a priest? a man whose professional prejudices and seclusion from the world render him the worst possible adviser! Besides, a priest, no matter how well-intentioned he may be, refers all ethical questions to a false basis, and gets all his notions of right and wrong more or less perverted."

"I wonder at you, Mr Smith. You are the last person I should have expected to find subject to such absurd prejudices."

"Granted then, that Father Ignatius is informed with eternal wisdom, what can he tell you beyond what you know already in this matter? You surely dont expect that he will tell you that it is right to lie to your father."

"No, I suppose not" said Isabella, evidently struck by this argument. "But then there can be no harm in going to him."

"There can be no good in it either. He will only set you a

penance for what you have already done."

"He will do that in any case the next time I confess to him; and I fear he will set me a heavier one for listening to you on the subject of our holy religion."

"At all events, you can scarcely help getting the impression that no matter how badly you act, you have a ready way of getting rid of the responsibility by compounding for an absolution."

"Please stop, Mr Smith. I cannot hear you on that subject."

"In short, then" said Smith, "I am opposed to your going to the Oratory, because I have learned by experience that people never resort to religion in practical matters except when they require an excuse for a wrong action. What is falsely called a narrow and recondite path is in reality a broad and obvious, though little frequented thoroughfare; but, like any other road, it can be seen only in the open air, and not inside a church."

"That may be true of other Churches, but not of the true one. There! please do not speak about it any more. It is too late to go to the Oratory now; and I am going out after dinner; so you may set your mind at rest about Father Ignatius. I must run home as hard as I can. Goodbye."

"I conclude that the whole matter will be settled before to-morrow."

Miss Woodward nodded, and ran away. Smith strode home, excited by his hatred of religion, puffed up by the success of his legitimate priggishness, and amusing himself with visions of destroyed Churches and confuted priests.

# CHAPTER VI

NEXT morning, Smith awaited the appearance of Mr Woodward in some trepidation, knowing that his advice to Isabella, if carried out, might cause his dismissal.

"Good morning" said he, as Mr Woodward entered.

"Morning" growled Mr Woodward.

"Good!" thought Smith. "She has had the grace to tell him, after all."

Nothing further was said until the usual business of the morning had been disposed of, when Mr Woodward, looking hard at his secretary, and frowning, although his nostrils twitched a little as if he were amused, addressed him in a stern tone.

"Youre a nice young vagabone to leave in charge of a house, arnt you?"

Not knowing how to reply, Smith said nothing, and smiled.

"What are you grinning at?"

Smith looked serious for a moment, and then smiled again.

"Well?" said Mr Woodward.

"My only breach of trust, if it was one" said Smith, "was undertaken with great misgiving. But I dont see how I could have refused to undertake it."

"Couldnt you have written straight off to me, and told me what was going on?"

"I did not know what was going on, Mr Woodward. I dont think you would have thought better of me, had I turned informer on the strength of a suspicion which I had no business to entertain."

"Humph! You have been advising Bella about her conduct towards me too, eh?"

"Miss Woodward was so much at a loss yesterday, that she appealed to me, as I was the only person who knew of the affair."

"Does she usually go to you for advice?"

"No" said Smith, blushing.

"I'll engage she'd rather go to her holy fathers in the Bromp-

377

ton Road" said Mr Woodward, who was a good Protestant after the Irish fashion. "No wonder, for the poor child to get confused in her principles with their images and candles and confessions! I believe they teach her that it's her duty to tell me lies because my father was head of an Orange Lodge."

Smith did not feel bound to defend the Roman or any other Church.

"Take my advice, Smith" said Mr Woodward, dropping his grumbling tone, and speaking gravely and gently; "and whenever you see a girl carrying on such transactions as this one that you got mixed up in, be sure she is making a fool of herself; and dont stop to stand upon your honor, but either tell her parents, or put the life across in her by pretending that youre going to do it. If you dont like to do that, keep out of her affairs altogether. And now, since you were so active in helping Bella to give away her diamonds, I want to know whether you are as ready to help me to get them back again."

"I am as ready, and far more willing, sir."

"Then I wish you would call on that robber, and find out what he has done with them."

Smith now related what had passed between himself and the poet during the interview at Ladbroke Grove, and also how they had since cut one another; adding, that he feared that if he attempted to communicate personally with Hawkshaw, he would be refused admittance at the door of his house.

"I wish you had wrung his neck" said Mr Woodward. "I dont want to hold any discourse whatever with him myself; so I have written to him to say that I will send you tomorrow for the diamonds if he will undertake to recover them within that time. I enclosed him a cheque for fifty pounds to redeem them; for I suppose he has pledged them. To make all sure, I told him if that was not enough, to write at once to me for the balance. So that is how the matter stands at present."

"I will go to him tomorrow, then."

"I am not sure that I was wise to trust him with the cheque" said Mr Woodward, scratching his head; "but I suppose it cant be helped. Egad, it's a thundering heap of money to fling away for nothing, bad scran to him and it! Come in there!"

"Misther Hawkshaw, sir" said Hamlet, opening the door.

"Hold on a bit" cried Mr Woodward, springing up hastily: "dont let him—"

He was interrupted by the entrance of Hawkshaw. "I will not detain you more than five minutes, if you will allow me that short time" said the poet, with graceful deference to Mr Woodward's age. "Perhaps I had better not open my business until we are in private."

"My young friend here is well acquainted with the only business that we are likely to transact" replied Mr Woodward. "Sit down."

Smith handed a chair to Hawkshaw.

"Mr Woodward" said the poet: "allow me to hand you back this cheque for fifty pounds, for my acceptance of which, you relied on considerations which I declare emphatically that I have never given you the least reason to believe me capable of entertaining. Allow me also to return you these jewels. In taking them as I did, I acted foolishly, no doubt. I had to choose between embracing a gift which was, I thought, a token of the purest and noblest sympathy, and sacrificing it to the weak rebellion of my own personal vanity and a base fear of the ignoble misconstruction of others. I made my election like a poet, not like a man of the world. I hope it is unnecessary to add that these gems have never left my possession until this moment. I renounce them now because I can no longer look forward to hanging them about the neck of my wife, a triumphant vindication of my disinterestedness, and an eloquent memorial of my love."

Smith was seized with remorse. He began to fear that he had been unjust to Hawkshaw.

"You have acted properly in restoring the jewels" said Mr Woodward gravely, "whatever you may have done in taking them."

"My own sense of honor is at rest on both points" replied Hawkshaw; "and, that being so, I should perhaps regard any ulterior sentiment as a weakness. Yet I should have thought that the fact of my returning the gems would suffice to disarm suspicion."

"I have no desire to discuss the question" said Mr Woodward. "I am obliged to you for bringing me my daughter's diamonds."

"I cannot say" said Hawkshaw, rising, "that you have convinced me of the sincerity of your sense of obligation."

"Why, blood an' ouns, man" exclaimed Mr Woodward, suddenly abandoning his dignified deportment, "do you expect me to be obliged to you for making my daughter the talk of the town, at two guineas a head? Do you think to downface me that you didn't redeem those diamonds from the pawnbroker yesterday, with the money your scandalous book has put into your pocket?"

"I am not surprised at your misunderstanding me" said Hawkshaw calmly.

"Arnt you? Well, *I* am surprised at your thinking I have so little sense as to be bamboozled at my age by such excuses. Bella sent you about your business the very day after we came back from Ireland. And how long have we been here? More than a month; and yet you only bring back the diamonds today, and then not before you were asked."

Hawkshaw bowed; took his hat; and went towards the door.

"Ring the bell, if you please, Smith" said Mr Woodward, exasperated by the suavity of the poet. "You may think yourself lucky that you live where and when you do, Mr Hawkshaw. In my time a young man would have shot himself sooner than take presents from a woman; and so saved some one else the trouble of shooting him afterwards."

"A bad argument, believe me" said Hawkshaw. "Good morning." He went out, attended by Hamlet, who, having arrived in time to hear his master's last words, scowled at the poet as he accompanied him to the door, and slammed it on his heels the instant they were past the threshold.

"It's an argument that would shut *you* up effectually, anyhow" muttered Mr Woodward, as Hawkshaw disappeared. "Eh, Smith?"

"It is an argument with which he would have an equal chance of shutting his opponent up. The wrong man gets hit sometimes."

"Indeed! Well, praps youre right. Youre wise for your age. However, argument or no argument, I'm glad that I have the jewels back, to say nothing of the fifty pounds. The beggar must have made a mint of money out of that book, or he would never have given up the cheque."

"Then you do not think he was at all influenced by the sentiments he claims?"

"Psha! What a fool he is!" By this Mr Woodward meant that Hawkshaw was no fool. "Praps by dint of repeating all that string of balderdash, and writing and rhyming it, he may very nearly believe it himself in the end. It's his business to twist common sense, and to justify the wicked for reward, as Isaiah says. Eh, doesnt he? 'Woe unto them that call evil good, and good evil; that put darkness for light, and light for darkness; that put bitter for sweet, and sweet for bitter.' I think thats the passage, eh?"

"So much the worse for the poets!"

"Just what I was going to say; so you have a wish, and I wish you may get it too. Heigho! Are there any more letters to be attended to?"

No further allusion was made to the diamonds; although an occasional chuckle from Mr Woodward shewed that he was pleased with himself for having spoken his mind to Hawkshaw. But the secretary thought that the behavior of the poet had been superior in dignity during the latter part of the interview.

As Smith was crossing Cromwell Road on his way home, an open carriage passed him, in which sat Isabella and Mrs Daly, who had been converted by a black silk dress and bonnet into an imitation of a reduced gentlewoman. On seeing him, Isabella caused the carriage to be stopped. He accordingly went to the door of the vehicle, beneath the rug of which he espied a quantity of firewood in little bundles, and several brown paper parcels.

"We have been at high mass" said Isabella. "This is one of our holy days."

Smith looked at the firewood, wondering whether it could be consecrated for some rite with which he was unacquainted.

"No" said Isabella: "we did not get that at the Oratory, Mr Smith. Mrs Daly has been marketing at the co-operative stores. I want to ask you whether you are a judge of india-rubber plants?"

"What is an india-rubber plant?"

"Oh, you know them very well. Those big green things."

"All the few plants I know are green."

"Are they indeed? I am going today to Parson's nursery in the King's Road, to buy some plants. I shall be alone—except Mrs Daly, of course. If you can be there at three, you can help me to select the plants; and I can tell you some news meanwhile. Can you come?"

"With pleasure. At three?"

"At three, yes" replied Isabella, and directed the coachman to drive on, which he did with that pretence of not hearing the order, and acting of his own accord, which is affected in his profession.

"Thats a simple poor craycher" observed Mrs Daly compassionately, as they drove away. "He's a bit of a sawney, I think."

"So much the better" said Isabella. "I have had enough of the other kind. It is a comfort to have found a really *good* man at last."

"Musha, an' d'ye call that a man? Sure what is he, more than a young lad about the house, runnin to post letthers an' the like for the masther? I'd have you remember, Miss Bella, that he's not your aiqual."

"Dont bother me, Essie" was the only reply.

At three o'clock, Smith met the carriage at the gate of the florist's in the King's Road, and entered the nursery with Isabella, leaving Mrs Daly to make excursions to and fro in the neighborhood for the benefit of the horses. The business of purchasing the india-rubber plant was soon despatched. The gardener, a hard-featured Scotchman of forty years, admired Miss Woodward's dark eyes, and improved her bargain by so liberal a gift of flowers, that Smith felt bound to give him a gratuity. After this, no objection was made when Isabella asked leave to walk through the conservatories for the purpose of seeing the orchids; and she was soon alone with the secretary in a damp atmosphere of earthy fragrance, where the thermometer marked eighty degrees, and blossoms of a variety of delicate hues and fantastic shapes sprang from suspended strips of board.

"I suppose you know that I told papa" she said.

"Yes. I inferred as much from what he said this morning. Have you heard of Mr Hawkshaw's visit?"

"I did; but I want to hear about it from you. Papa did not give me any particulars: he only gave me the jewels, and told me that the robber, as he calls Mr Hawkshaw, had contrived to redeem them out of what he made by that odious book."

Smith told her what had passed between the poet and Mr Woodward. When he had finished, she said,

"I am delighted that papa let him know how vile his conduct was. I only wish I could have told him my own opinion. But that is the misfortune of belonging to my sex. Rebuke, no matter how just it may be, always sounds like ballyragging from the lips of a woman."

"It does not sound dignified, even from a man, Miss Woodward" moralized Smith.

"Yes; but a man is quite different. He has no need to care. However, I must not forget that I have to thank you for saving me from involving myself in a dreadful mess, and forfeiting my father's esteem and my own, for ever. He was not in the least angry with me, although he absolutely raged against Hawkshaw. He did not offer me the shadow of a reproach: indeed, I think his chief feeling about me was anxiety lest I should begin to cry like an idiot, which I very nearly did. What you said was quite true. It was an unworthy thing of me to be afraid of him; and it only shews what cowards guilt, or at least folly, makes us."

"I am glad the fair course has vindicated its expediency. And now, if it would not be too inquisitive, may I ask you the meaning of something you mentioned last night, which I did not quite undertstand?"

"Pray do not hesitate to ask me anything."

"I want to know, then, what motive Mr Hawkshaw had for the revenge to which you attribute his publication of the poem. Surely he is not bad enough to injure you for behaving generously to him."

"I dont know what motive he could have had; except that a coldness sprang up between us when I came back from Rosstrevor."

"A coldness?"

"The fact is, Mr Smith, we were so much together at Rosstrevor that he fancied I cared more for him than I really did; and when, after our return, I disabused him of that idea, he walked out of the house in a huff. A man never forgives a hurt to his vanity."

Smith pulled his whisker reflectively, but said nothing. Isabella suddenly became passionate, and added, "It is an infamous lie of his that I led him on. His book is full of it; and he had the meanness to say it to my face that day."

"Never mind" said Smith soothingly. "Nobody will believe a rejected suitor."

"Wont they indeed? People are so bad themselves, that it is just the sort of odious insinuation that everybody will believe."

"Even so, the best way to discredit him is to take no notice of him. What does it matter what people think about it?"

"That is all very fine, Mr Smith; but what is the use of denying oneself the pleasure of behaving recklessly if one gets no credit for it?"

"If you think it a pleasure, why, of course, none at all."

"Mr Smith" said Isabella, after a pause: "do you really believe that virtue is its own reward in this world?"

"If it were not" he replied promptly, "it would be vice."

"That is nonsense, you know."

"Then you can fall back on your reward in the next world" said Smith, with a sceptical grin. "Be virtuous, or you will go to hell."

"Hush, pray" she said, shuddering. "I wish you would find something more comfortable to talk of than religion."

"This compartment is the hottest we have been in yet. I feel quite limp. Shall we return to the fernery?"

"By all means. I feel as though I were having a Turkish bath with my clothes on. Ugh! How bleak it is in here, by contrast!"

In the places through which they had just passed, they had occasionally met a gardener, or been warned of his presence by the splashing of water from a hose. In the fernery they were quite alone.

"What a maze of green!" Isabella exclaimed, looking round. "Can you believe that we are in the King's Road and not in paradise?"

"Rather an artificial paradise" said Smith, missing the lead she was offering him.

"Rather an artificial Adam, you mean."

Smith blushed, conscious that had she substituted Eve for Adam, her words would have expressed his own thought.

"Why artificial?" said he.

"You are so matter-of-fact. Do you ever read poetry? What books do you like best—next to the proverbs of Solomon, I mean?"

"The maxims of La Rochefoucauld" replied Smith.

"Oh yes. Joking apart, his epigrams are so delightful that one does not mind their being so false, and wrong, and meretricious. Meretriciously brilliant, I think, describes La Rochefoucauld exactly. But it was not that kind of writing I spoke of just now. Do you care for poetry?"

"I do not read it very often; so I suppose I do not care for it."

"When you do read it, who is your favorite poet?"

"Shelley."

"Oh! Yes, of course. I always thought Shelley a little old-fashioned; and there are so many of his poems which it is not right to read."

"Too irreligious?"

"Oh dear, no! I am not in the least prejudiced; and one is accustomed to that sort of thing in poetry. But I think it is possible for a poet to be too imaginative. Shelley's sensuality marred everything he wrote."

Smith stared at her without attempting to reply.

"I suppose you have never attempted to write?" she said.

"I blush to say that I belong to the ridiculous race of amateur poets."

"Oh!" cried Isabella, clasping her hands, "*do* shew me something that you have written."

"Pardon me; but I have not yet fallen to the depth of carrying my effusions about in my pocket to be recited on the slightest provocation."

"Promise to let me see at least one of them."

"Really, I have made a resolution never to hand about my efforts to be admired. I have nothing to gain by it except a sense of absurdity and some insincere praise."

"No matter. I have something to gain, as I have a strong desire to see these poems which you keep hidden. I will tell you exactly what I think of them, I assure you."

"Well" said Smith, forgetting what she had said of Shelley, "I yield. You must remember that they are all fugitive pieces. Most of them were composed in one night, and have not been as conscientiously polished as they should be, however little they deserve it. I stipulate that they are not to be shewn to anyone else."

"I would not think of shewing them without your permission."

"Then I will bring them to you some day; and I will be glad to hear your opinion of them."

"Very well. Mind, you have promised! What o'clock is it?"

"It is just four."

"Gracious! We have been here an hour. Mrs Daly will be so angry. Let us go at once."

Smith took leave of Isabella without a suspicion that she considered him almost a saint because he had not behaved in the fernery as Hawkshaw would have done.

"Only think, Essie!" she said, as they drove away. "We lost ourselves in the greenhouses, and were trying to get out for ever so long before we could find anybody to shew us the way."

"Ye'd betther be very careful, Miss Bella" said Mrs Daly querulously; "or ye'll lose yourself where itll take more than an owl' Scotch garner to set you to rights."

"Hold your tongue, Essie; and dont be impertinent."

"Yes" said Mrs Daly, letting fall a few tears: "thats always the way. When youre in any divilment or disthress its Essie here, and Essie there, and Essie th'other plaise. An' now I'm to be kept waitin in the cowld for an hour, and not open me mouth. No matther. Youll be rid o' me some day, plaze God."

"Come, Essie" said Isabella, half impatient, half coaxing: "dont be an old ass. You know I hate being bothered with sermons. You mustnt let the coachman hear you crying."

Mrs Daly sniffed, but remonstrated no further with her mistress, who was meditating on the probability of some of Smith's sonnets having been inspired by herself, and wondering whether the vanity of Hawkshaw was not common, in greater or less degree, to every member of his sex.

That evening in his rooms in Danvers Street, Smith examined a book in which were four copies of all his compositions, and considered whether he should entrust it to Isabella, or transcribe the best poems for her on separate sheets. The latter course, he thought, would deprive him of the credit of his fertility; would be very troublesome; and, as his favorite works might be those least adapted to her fancy, might prove a means of withholding from her the only examples to which she was capable of doing justice. He incurred no risk by sending the book except that of its loss, which, he persuaded himself, in revenge for the vanity implied by his anxiety about the impression its contents were likely to make, was no great matter. To make it the more imposing, he copied in all the scraps of rhyme he could find, separating each

by a row of stars, and heading them Fragments. Searching for
more of these among some old papers, he found a poem entitled
Lines to a Southern Passion Flower. He felt ashamed as he recalled the infatuation which had led him to write it. On reading
it, he found to his surprise that it was superior to the sonnets
which he had just revised, having been written warmly about a
woman, instead of coldly about an abstraction. He immediately
copied the lines into his book; and although during this process
they seemed to lose much of their glow, he flattered himself that
they would be better appreciated by Isabella than they had been
by Harriet.

# CHAPTER VII

One morning, a month after Miss Watkins had left her father's house, Fraser Fenwick stood before the door of Sir John Porter's mansion in Wilton Place, considering whether he would announce his presence by a hard pull at the servants' bell, or a gentle one at the visitors'. Having taken the latter course, he was confronted by an elderly man dressed in a black coat and pepper-and-salt trousers, who looked at him with an air of reserve, and waited silently for an explanation of his appearance at half-past eleven in the forenoon.

"Will you tell Lady Porter that Mr—that Fraser Fenwick would be very much obliged if she would see him for a moment?"

"Is it business?"

"It's private business" said Fenwick. Then, fearing that offence might be taken at the implied rebuff, he assumed a genial manner, and added, "It's partly private pleasure as well. You tell her my name, and itll be all right. Fraser Fenwick's the ticket, old man."

"You had better stand in on the mat" said the man. "I'll see whether I can disturb her with your message at this hour, since you wont send up word of your business." With these words, he glanced round the hall to assure himself that no portable articles of value lay within reach of the visitor, and went to the presence of Lady Geraldine, to whom he apologetically notified the desire of Mr Fenwick.

"Is he respectably dressed?" said Lady Geraldine.

"Yes, my lady" said the man reluctantly.

"Is he sober?"

"I did not detect the sign of liquor on him, my lady. I only had a word with him at the door."

"Does he look as if he had been behaving himself well lately?"

"Beg your ladyship's pardon?"

"Never mind. He may come up."

Lady Geraldine found an occasional interview with Fenwick

amusing; although he never came except when he was in trouble. She now put on an expression of vigilant severity, and seated herself in an easy chair near the window. Meanwhile Fenwick, having received the servant's curt "This way" with a sudden access of haughtiness, was mounting the stairs, his courage sinking as his body rose step by step. He flinched as the door was flung open for him contemptuously.

"Come in" cried Lady Geraldine sharply. Fraser trembled and went in.

"Well, Fraser, I am glad to see by your appearance that you have been doing well" she said, convinced by his visit that he had been doing the reverse.

"Thank you, Lady Joldie, I believe I have got rid of all my wild oats at last. I had my salary increased to thirty shillings a week the other day. I think I have deserved your recommendation this time."

Lady Geraldine felt ashamed of the feeling of disappointment which his reply caused her. "I hope so" she said. "Did you come for nothing else than to tell me about your salary?"

"I am sorry to intrude—" began Fenwick, reddening.

"Dont take up my words like that. I have no objection to your coming whenever you have anything to say that redounds to your credit. But I am sure you want something; for you would not be here if you could help it, I know."

"I assure you, Lady Joldie, that I would rather be with you, even as a servant, than with anyone else; only I fear that the less you see of me, the better you are pleased. I look on you as my mother."

"Then you take a liberty, a very great liberty. For the future, have the goodness to look on me as a much more distant relative in no way responsible for your actions, or liable to be discredited by your education."

"It is presumpshus, no doubt" said Fenwick, who had been a skilful coaxer in his childhood; "but what with your goodness and my loneliness—"

"Fraser" interrupted Lady Geraldine: "since you have given

up drinking, your displays of sentiment have lost the plausibility they used to derive from your faith in them. Your nerves are too healthy at present to leave you any chance of affecting me. What did you come for?"

"I did not come exactly—" A pause.

"Yes, Fraser? You were saying that you did not come exactly. I think you had better add some explanatory remarks."

"I am afraid you wont approve of what I am going to do."

"Most likely not."

"I—I am going to be married."

"What! You!" said Lady Geraldine, looking at him sternly. "And who is the wretched woman?"

"She doesnt think herself wretched."

"Indeed! What is *your* opinion?"

Fenwick fidgeted with his hat and said nothing.

"Well? You have not told me who she is."

"It is Fanny Watkins, my cousin."

"Oh! I thought she had given you up."

"We were estranged for a time, Lady Joldie. But she has quarrelled with her family; and as our engagement had been renewed in secret a little while before, I felt bound to offer to marry her at once, as a gen— I mean, I felt bound in honor."

"The foolish girl! And so, because she is out with her family, she is going to marry you to spite them."

"No. We were engaged long before the row took place."

"And did her parents approve of the engagement?"

"I dont know whether Uncle Tom did or not. Her mother didnt; but she never approves of anything except what she plans herself, or what somebody else disapproves of. It is through her that Fanny had to run away from home."

"To run away!"

"Only to her aunt's. I was sent after her, and it was then that we agreed to wait no longer, but to make her independent at once."

"Independent! Eighty pounds a year is a pretty independence for the daughter of a well-to-do tradesman. She thinks she is securing her liberty, I suppose, poor little fool! What do you expect me to do to abet you in this pretty business, pray?"

"Well, Lady Joldie, I would like Uncle Tom to be reconciled to the match. He is such a good man of business that he might help me along in many ways. Besides, Fanny is sentimental about him; though she is only too glad to be rid of her mother. If you would be so very kind—you never deserted me when I was in worse straits before—I think he would listen to you."

"I hope he will" said Lady Geraldine energetically. "If I have an opportunity of speaking to him, I will tell him to bring his daughter home and lock her up until she is old enough to take proper care of herself."

"But she loves me. Really and truly she does" said Fenwick, taken aback.

"Nonsense! Love *you*! How long do you think she would love you on eighty pounds a year? How long would you love her, with her appetite and her house, perhaps her children too, running away with your money about six times as fast as you could make it?"

"We have been calculating; and we dont think it would be so little, after all."

"You are a pretty pair of calculators. Do you remember how you got on when you had half as much more, and no one beside yourself to provide for?"

"I'm sure I could have kept a wife on half what I wasted then, Lady Joldie. You dont know Fanny. She is a very good house-keeper. She couldnt be otherwise, having lived so long with her mother, who counts every coal that is put on the kitchen fire."

"That shews how much you know about it, Fraser. There are never two good housekeepers in the same house. Daughters of such women as your aunt never know the value of money; for they are never allowed to handle it."

"If we were reconciled to Uncle Tom, there would be no fear. I know lots of clerks who support large families on a pound a week."

"Do you know any of their wives?"

"Well, I know that they have wives. I have spoken to some of them."

"And were they all satisfied with their wisdom in marrying clerks with a pound a week?"

"They didnt seem to mind."

"Stuff! They did not tell *you* what they thought of themselves, no doubt. Once for all, Fraser, you have no business to marry; and your cousin is only in a pet. If you bring her here, I will try to bring her to her senses. I will even call on her, if she is within my reach; but instead of advising her to marry you, I will tell her to go home and wait until she has a little more experience."

"I had rather you didnt do that, Lady Joldie."

"I am sure I do not care what you had or had not rather. You are just as foolish as she, and would be just as unhappy afterwards. In about six months you would be consoling yourself with all your old vices."

"Never. I will work my fingers to the bone first."

"What good will that do, if nobody will pay you for your work? Most people are willing to work; but the will is of no use, unless there is a way too."

"Where theres a will, theres a way."

"May I ask" said Lady Geraldine, irritated, "whether you think you reminded me of that proverb, or I you?"

"Or you me?" said Fenwick, confused.

"Oh, I have no patience with you, Fraser. You are very stupid." Here the butler came to the door. "Well, what is it?"

"A person, my lady—a man—Thomas Watkins, he says, wishes to be allowed to speak to your ladyship."

Fenwick whistled with surprise. "Is there anybody with him?" he said.

The butler looked respectfully towards his mistress, ignoring Fenwick.

"Shew him up" said Lady Geraldine.

"Therell be a precious row now" said Fenwick, when the servant went out. "Wont you take my part, Lady Joldie?"

Lady Geraldine answered him with a frown. Then Mr Wat-

kins entered; made a bow; and stood near the door, restlessly
scanning every object which was not far above the level of the
floor. For some moments he attached no meaning to anything
that he saw. He was wishing that he could explain his business
from behind the counter of his own shop, instead of on the thick
carpet of a mansion in Wilton Place, the very air in which
seemed to him as though it needed to be breathed according to
forms of which he knew nothing.

"Good morning, Mr Watkins" said Lady Geraldine affably.

"Good morning to your ladyship" returned the purveyor in
guarded tones, with another bow.

"Sit down" said Lady Geraldine. "Fraser: hand your uncle a
chair." Mr Watkins looked up quickly, and stared at his nephew.

"How d'ye do, uncle?" said Fenwick, presenting a chair and
winking at him.

"Your family are quite well, I hope" said Lady Geraldine.

"Quite well, I thank your ladyship. I hope your ladyship is the
same."

"Thank you, Mr Watkins: I am very well. I have just learned
from Fraser that you have had some domestic trouble in which
he is concerned."

"Yes, my lady. I come to speak about that, if it would not be
looked upon as a hintrusion. I am well aware that nothing but
your ladyship's goodness would lead you to mix yourself up in
such affairs at all."

"Pray do not speak of intrusion, Mr Watkins. You are quite
welcome."

"I thank your ladyship. My daughter is a good girl; but she
does not like to be drove too hard; and she has had a little fit of
temper, as young girls will. Now, I make bold to say that Fanny
has as good a chance of settling herself well in the world as any
young woman in her position should desire; and I would wish
her to wait a while, and see whether she might not do better than
what she wants to do at present. Not that I deny your countenance being a great recommendation to Fraser; but wheres the
need for hurry? When she's twenty-one she can marry who she

likes; and *his* means'll be none the worse for a year or two of waiting. If your ladyship is friendly to Fraser, I dont wish to thwart you; but I have my wishes and dooties as a parent to think of; and I want to do the best I can for my girl."

"Then, Mr Watkins, you will certainly not marry her to that scapegrace. You must not think that I approve of this match. I was just telling Fraser what I thought of it when you came in; and if you think that your daughter will listen to me (although I have very little hope of that) I will speak to her with the greatest pleasure, and try to dissuade her from such a mad act."

"I dont see why she's to be called mad" remonstrated Fenwick.

"Fraser" interrupted Lady Geraldine sharply: "sit down." Fenwick, who had hitherto stood, obeyed. "Now hold your tongue until I give you leave to speak."

Mr Watkins, feeling bound to second Lady Geraldine, looked reproachfully at his nephew, who, after a momentary impulse of rebellion, submitted with a grin.

"I am greatly beholden to your ladyship for thinking of Fanny, and taking my part" said the purveyor. "It's more than I could have expected."

"But recollect that I can do very little if these children are obstinate. Fraser is independent of me; and even were he not so, I have no reason to believe that any earthly consideration could restrain him from acting foolishly. Nothing will teach your daughter but experience. However, I suppose you can forbid her as long as she is under age."

"She's very obstinate" said Watkins, despondingly. "We cant keep her under lock and key; and a girl that has run away once might do it again in a worse way. And I dont know that I have a right to go again' her if her heart is set on Fraser. I'm afraid she will never be comfortable at home, after what has passed. I thought perhaps your ladyship might have managed it, effectual and quiet, by telling Fraser you wouldnt have it."

"I have told him so already. But if you cannot compel your daughter, how can I compel Fraser, who is nothing to me except a periodic nuisance?"

"You promised to stand by me if I behaved myself" pleaded Fenwick; "and so I have. I have a right to get married, havnt I?"

"No" said Lady Geraldine: "certainly not. A man without means has no right even to think of marriage."

"But I *have* means. It will be time enough to abuse me when I let my wife starve. Being married will make me work, and keep me steady. Hang it all, I am not such an out-and-out ruffian as you seem to think."

"Steady, Fraser: steady" said Mr Watkins.

"It's all very well to talk of being steady; but I get no more credit for being steady than for being the other thing. A worm will turn if you walk too much on him."

"Pray do not become obstreperous, Fraser" said Lady Geraldine. "Had you not better take the opportunity of telling Mr Watkins what you can do for his daughter if he gives her to you?"

"Aye" said Mr Watkins, suddenly bristling. "Why did you go and wheedle Fanny behind my back, instead of coming to me fair and open, and asking whether I'd back you in it?"

"Because I knew you wouldnt back me in it" said Fenwick; "and because it was no use to speak to you until I had Fanny's consent."

"And when you had it, why didnt you come then?"

"I was going to. I came here this morning to ask Lady Gerald-ine to help me to bring you round to it."

"That is so" said Lady Geraldine, in answer to an inquiring look from Mr Watkins.

"And for all I have got by the move" continued Fenwick bitterly, "I might as well have stayed at home."

"That aint a very grateful way of expressing yourself before her ladyship, Fraser."

This rebuke only elicited from Fenwick a petulant sniff, which, because it recalled to Lady Geraldine the manners of his spoiled but pretty childhood, wrought more with her in his favor than his former submission.

"Mr Watkins" said she: "I dare not advise you to listen to

Fraser. He has been a very bad boy indeed until six months ago. Since that, he has got on very creditably. He once had a knack of engaging the interest of people who employed him; but by dint of invariably abusing their kindness, and destroying his appearance by bad habits and bad associations, he has now nothing to depend on but such encouragement as he may earn by hard work. Of late he has behaved himself irreproachably; and perhaps, as he says, a settled home would make his reformation permanent. But I am afraid he could not get on at first without some help from you."

"I tell your ladyship the truth. I am not bent again' Fraser personally at all. When poor Annie, his mother, was nurse in your own family, I wont say but what I was in a worse way of life myself than ever he was. Annie never gave me up when all the rest did; and theres no denyin that it was marriage that settled me. Therefore Ive had thoughts that much the same thing might happen to Fraser. But your ladyship sees, heres the difficulty. Whatever else I may have been, I was sharp; and my sharpness stood to me when I took to business. Now, Fraser aint sharp. With all his tossin and gamblin, an' bettin, he never learned how to put on his coin. He'd spend as much money to be seen in a ensom keb, to save carryin a parcel, or to make a shopgirl think he was a hofficer in the Guards, as a real sharp man would have kept goin for a year on. The very way people petted him shewed that they looked on him as no more than a child. Only for that I might take him into my business—"

"And live with Aunt Flossy!" interrupted Fenwick. "Not if I know it."

"There!" said Mr Watkins sulkily. "Whats the use of doin anything for him? He hasnt even sense enough to listen to the whole of a good offer."

"I didnt know you were making me an offer" said Fenwick. "I thought you were excusing yourself from making one on the ground that I am a fool."

Lady Geraldine's bosom heaved. Mr Watkins noticed it, and understood that his hostess was repressing a yawn.

"We have taken up enough of her ladyship's time" said he. "Once for all, Fraser Fen'ick, if I see my way to giving you a good chance, are you too much of a gentleman to sell eggs and bacon across a counter for your living?"

"Not if I can make more by it than I do now by selling stationery, and if I can live where I like."

"Then just step downstairs and wait for me in the street. I would be glad to say a word in private to her ladyship consarnin what I intend to propose. That is, with her ladyship's leave."

"I shall be very glad" said Lady Geraldine. "Good morning, Fraser."

"Good morning" said Fenwick, and retired a little sulkily.

"I was thinking, your ladyship" said the purveyor, rising, and speaking in a respectful tone of confidence, "of putting Fraser in a branch establishment that I ope to hopen shortly here in the west end. His manners would suit it well, whereas theyd be lost in Bishopsgate. If Fanny is determined to have him, why, I must only make the best of a bad job, and give him as good a chance as I can. Suppose this come about, would your ladyship be inclined to stand by him by giving the place your custom?"

"Certainly not. Do you think I will throw over my old tradesmen who have served me well for Fraser, who never served anybody well?"

"Thats right, your ladyship; and I wish all customers was so honorable and considerate. Well, you done all you could for the lad; and now I'll do all I reasonably can for him: that is, if Fanny is bound to take him. I dont doubt but if he keeps steady, he will make a connection."

"I hope so" said Lady Geraldine doubtfully.

"I wish your ladyship good morning" said Mr Watkins, bowing.

"Good morning, Mr Watkins" said she sweetly, and sighed with relief when she was left alone. The purveyor too, when he stood once more on the pavement where his rights were equal to those of any other Briton, breathed more freely, and resolved never again to seek the company of those who considered themselves his betters, however affable they might be, or however their greatness might serve for a bulwark to the constitution of his country.

In the afternoon Lady Geraldine had another early visitor: Ernest. "I had hoped" she said, with undisguised dismay at his appearance, "that you were safe at Richmond for a month at least."

"I am not going to stay at Grosvenor's. I could not be bothered wasting my time amongst such a lot."

"That means that you are not wanted there. I am very sorry to hear it, as it has left you at liberty to come to me—your usual refuge when no one else will endure you."

"I know you are always glad to see me."

"Indeed! At present I should feel really grateful to you if you would go away."

Ernest grinned, and sat down. "I just thought I would tell you the news" he said. "I loafed down to Perspective last Sunday just to see what was going on."

"Was there anything or anybody in particular to be heard or seen—besides yourself, of course?"

"I should think so. There was Hawkshaw, who is *the* sensation at present. His get-up is something to see, I can tell you."

"It always was something to see."

"Yes; but the man is broken: you would not know him, poor chap! no more arty ties and all that. He has set up a suit of dead black, long skirts, broad collars, and a black stock. His coat and his head look as if a brush hadnt touched them for six weeks. No gloves; and for all that you can see of his cuffs, he might as well have no shirt. He is a regular scarecrow; and he has turned miser as well: travels third class; walks long distances; and comes into a drawing room with boots on as big as gas meters, all spattered with mud."

"In short, takes as many liberties with society as if he were really a man of genius."

"So he is, you know" said Ernest. "They say that in spite of all he could do to prevent it, he made a lot of money off that book of his. Not that it's of much use to him; for he looks twenty years older than before it came out."

"Charging two guineas a copy, and masquerading in disreputable clothes by way of advertising it, is a very curious way of trying to keep down the profits of a book."

"It's not two guineas now. The demand was so great that he was forced to consent to a cheap edition. But you never admit that a poet may have such a thing as a heart. I suppose you would like him to dress himself splendidly with nothing but gall within."

"How eloquent! I hope you are not going to cry, Ernest."

"It's no laughing matter. I know for a fact that he told Parry, the editor of The Republic of Arts, the true story of The Bent Branch. They were alone together in the office in the Strand. Parry, who is no chicken either, couldnt speak; but he stooped down; kissed Hawkshaw's hand; and cried like a child."

"I hope that is not true; because it is a little too disgusting to amuse me. Such maudlin imbecility is beneath even a man. No one would dream of attributing it to a woman, bad as we are. Now I beg you will not pretend that you can understand and sympathize with the sorrows of Mr Hawkshaw. You play the buffoon passably; but if you were wise you would never pose as a man of feeling."

"I should be a precious fool if I expected any appreciation of a poet's sensitiveness from you" said Ernest sulkily.

"Then spare me Mr Hawkshaw's broken heart; and tell me what his book is about, according to the latest version. I know already that it is not worth reading. Margaret Scott insisted on lending it to me; and I gave it up at the fourth page."

"The greatest poem of the century! But look here: have you got the book still?"

"No: I gave it back the day after I got it."

"You were awfully lucky; for it's very hard to lay hands on a copy. I wonder would Meg Scott lend it to me."

"I perceive that you have not read the greatest poem of the century."

"Well; but of course I have an idea of what it is. Would you mind asking her for it again? I want to read it awfully."

"I would mind very much."

"But why?"

"Because I never lend books that are not my own to young gentlemen who only return them when they are absolutely forced to, after keeping them for a year and treating them very badly."

"All right. All right. You neednt make such a fuss about it. I can get it by the dozen from other people whenever I want it. Being here, I just thought that you might have it convenient."

"I quite understand. And now, what is the latest gossip about it? At first the perfidious female who is so incomprehensibly mixed up with the betrayed poet and with a precious stone of some sort, was said to be a princess. Then she was a duchess, then an actress. What is she at present?"

"Pshaw!" said Ernest: "everybody knows that it is Belle Woodward."

"Yes; but what did Belle Woodward do?"

"Well, that is rather a delicate question, you know. You wont repeat what I tell you, will you?"

"Not for the world. Probably I shall not even believe it."

"Joking apart, I would not for a thousand pounds have it known that *I* said anything about it. Of course you know that Belle was madly in love with Cyril Scott."

"I do not. But if necessary to your tale, I can assume it."

"There is no mistake about it. She was nearly wild when he threw her over. Well, she made a vow that she would revenge herself by making a man suffer as much as she had suffered; and to make sure that Scott should know of it, she selected his nearest friend as the proper fellow to go for. Poor Hawkshaw met her at Rosstrevor, and walked into the trap with his eyes shut. There is no use in telling you how such a man could love when he went in for it."

"Not the least."

"At all events, he *did* fall in love with her; and they became engaged. Rosstrevor, it appears, is a moonlight sort of place, with the sea and so forth; and he used to walk with her at night about the cliffs and make plans for their future happiness: never dream-

ing, of course, that it was all a game of hers. At last he had to
come away to London; and he gave her, as a pledge of his love,
the sonnet that he has now published in the book. You saw it, I
suppose. It is called Sinfonia."

"What is the meaning of that?"

"Oh—it is—er—well, I suppose it is the name of some goddess. However, it does not matter. She gave him a heap of diamonds as *her* pledge, worth about forty thousand pounds, knowing that he had come to desperate grief through money losses,
and thinking that it would be a torture to him to have such a
mine of wealth in his hands and not be able to touch a halfpenny
to save himself from starving. Before she came back she wrote
no end of letters picturing the joys of their meeting, and working his feelings up to a fearful pitch. She came. They met."

"Good."

"I wish you wouldnt interrupt me. It's very clever, you know,
Aunt Joldie; but it's scarcely worth your while to come it over
*me.*"

"Pray go on. You left off at a most exciting place, like a penny
number."

"Ha! ha! ha!" roared Ernest, unexpectedly tickled by this
witticism. "Ho! ho! Oh, pon my oath! Ha! Well, I'll be damned!"

"Ernest!" cried Lady Geraldine: "behave yourself. Do you
consider that a string of oaths is the natural utterance of an
English gentleman?"

"No, I dont. But if you upset a fellow with your jokes, he must
let out somehow."

"Very well. Now that you have let out, as you call it, perhaps
you will finish your story. You were saying that they met."

"Theres nothing more to tell. She pretended she scarcely knew
him; pitched the sonnet in his face; and left him nearly mad. He
would have died only for the relief of writing the book. He sent
her back the diamonds, of course. His whole life is blasted; but
still, as far as money goes, the affair has been a great piece of luck
for him."

"So it seems. I must say that Belle's version of the story is more plausible than yours."

"What does she say?"

"Simply that Mr Hawkshaw told her such a piteous tale of poverty at Rosstrevor that she was foolish enough to give him some jewels which had been left to her mother. He pawned them, and then spread a report that she had engaged herself to him. After that, she refused to receive any visits from him; and he immediately brought out this book. She then told her father about the business; and he made Mr Hawkshaw give up the diamonds, offering him at the same time the money to redeem them. However, thanks to the sale of the book, the offer was not accepted; and Mr Hawkshaw saved his credit at the eleventh hour by restoring the jewels at his own expense."

"Thats the Woodwards' story. He never pawned them. They were a love token."

"If so, they would scarcely have been sent through Mr Woodward's secretary, as I believe they were. And if they were not pawned, they would have been returned the moment Belle broke with him, instead of being kept until they were asked for, and until he had the means to redeem them. Belle has common sense on her side this time. He has nothing but a parcel of poetic nonsense that contradicts itself; and I think he displayed extreme meanness in taking the girl's diamonds in the first instance, and absolute rascality in dragging the affair before society for the sake of filling his pockets afterwards."

"I am sorry I cant agree with you" said Ernest, rising, and buttoning his coat.

"Going, Ernest?"

"Yes."

"I shall not see you for some time, I suppose."

"Possibly not."

"Offended?"

"Not at all. It is not worth my while to be offended. Good morning."

"Good morning" said Lady Geraldine. "Really" she added, to herself, when he was gone, "I think I prefer Fraser."

# CHAPTER VIII

Smith brought his book of poems to Queen's Gate; but it lay in his drawer in the study for a week before. On Isabella's reminding him of his promise, he produced it with an affectation of having forgotten it.

"You must promise not to let these destroy the cordiality of our present relations" he said. "Rhyme is the only vent for that tendency to make a fool of himself which man is ashamed to indulge in ordinary conversation."

"Never cry stinking fish, as papa says" replied Isabella. Smith thought this rather coarse. However, he had to hand over the poems, which Isabella said she was sure were perfectly beautiful.

In the following night, the weather, which had been cold and dry, became warm and damp; and when the morning came, Smith, with parched eyes, and no power to pronounce nasal consonants, learnt that Miss Woodward was in bed in consequence of a bad cold.

"Faith, sir" said Hamlet, "I see youre dearly as bad as beself. The basther's id a harrid state, God bless hib. It's a bortial dap tlibate, is th' Igglish."

During the next three days, Isabella kept her bed; and her father, Smith, and Cornelius plied their handkerchiefs. On the fourth, Mr Woodward said to his secretary,

"Heres a letter from Stannard, who was to have spoken on the Irish Land Bill tonight about some special grievance his constituents have. He has to go off unexpectedly to Plymouth to look after his son, who has hurt himself on board ship there; and now he wants me to put the question for him. He says I know all about the subject, and can deal with it better than he could. And sure I know no more about it than the babe unborn; only the other evening, when he talked to me for half an hour about the Ulster tenant right, I looked wise, and told him he was the only man in the House that knew the right end of a lease from the wrong one. And now all the thanks I get is this job. Will you just look over his letter and see whether you can make anything of his figures and dates, while I write to him? Anyhow, it cant be helped. I'm sorry the poor lad has hurt himself."

Smith took the letter, which he perceived would require some study. He therefore asked whether he might take the letter home and study it at leisure.

"That would be the best thing to do" said Mr Woodward. "Could you drop in a little before nine, and tell me anything you can make out of Stannard's rigmarole?"

At the appointed hour Smith returned to Queen's Gate. It was a wet night; and when he had taken off his overcoat and goloshes, he was invited to ascend to the drawing room, where he found his employer sitting before a blazing fire.

"Only for Stannard" said Mr Woodward, "the House might go whistle for me this night. Sit down; and tell me the news."

Smith sat down and communicated the result of his researches to Mr Woodward. He then rang the bell. Hamlet, in a swallow-tailed coat and a crimson waistcoat, answered it.

"Get me a cab" said Mr Woodward.

"Wh' then" remonstrated Cornelius, "youre not goin out in the pours o' rain, wud a cold on you, are you?"

"Go and do what youre bid, you scoundrel; and hold your tongue."

"An where d'ye think I can get a cab at this hour, when there isnt one in the town but whats engaged?" Here Mr Woodward, suddenly scraping his chair violently along the carpet, seemed about to rise and commit murder. Hamlet fled, and soon came back to say the cab was at the door.

"You neednt stir until it clears up a bit, Smith" said Mr Woodward, as he went out. "Be the bye, theres a letter on the chimneypiece from that jobmaster in the Old Brompton Road. I wish youd look over it, and call on him on your way in tomorrow."

Smith, left alone in the drawing room, warmed himself on the hearthrug, and read the jobmaster's letter. Presently Isabella, with a work basket and a book in her hands, came into the room. She seated herself, with the languor of convalescence, in the easy chair vacated by her father, and stretched out her hand to Smith without saying a word. He had scarcely touched it when she drew it back again into her lap.

"I hope you are much better" said he, vaguely alarmed.

"Thank you. I do not feel very strong; but I suppose I am getting well."

"Terrific weather" said Smith, after listening for a moment to the plash of the rain on the balcony without.

Isabella reclined in her chair, and looked at him with a smile, in which some gentle irony was visible. "Yes" she said. "Is it not? Heigho!" As she spoke, she made her eyes large and lustrous; and Smith, more uneasy than before, felt warned to go home. Nevertheless, as the book she had in her basket was his own, he resolved to wait a little longer.

"Allow me to make a confession, Miss Woodward" said he, jocularly assuming a grave demeanor. Her smile vanished, and she made a gesture in deprecation. "Ever since you came into the room, I have been deeply conscious of the fact that you have read, or are reading, my poems."

"Oh, Mr Smith, what folly!"

"I assure you I am perfectly in earnest."

"Hush. You do not know me. You do not know yourself. Blind that I was, not to have thought of this before!"

Smith felt the roots of his hair stir; and his knees became weak.

"The question is" said he, in an unsteady voice, which, with his paleness, belied the affected jauntiness of his manner, "what do you think of the poems now?"

"Come!" she said soothingly, perceiving his agitation, but mistaking the cause of it: "sit down, and let us talk calmly. I know I can trust you to be patient, and look the truth steadfastly in the face." She was touched; for she had never seen such genuine emotion exhibited by a lover before.

Smith was glad to sit down; for he could hardly stand. The chair she pointed to was a small one close to her own. As he seated himself he drew it still closer to her, because he knew that she expected him to do so. Also, because his sense of humor was mixing oddly with his alarm at finding that his actions were somehow escaping his own control.

"Am I to understand" said he cautiously, "that my presumptuous attempts at poesy have—have annoyed you?"

"No. They have pained me for your sake; but they have not annoyed me. They have taught me the heroism of your conduct."

"I do not exactly understand. I am not conscious of having acted heroically."

"You make light of it. But believe me, I am not insensible to the fidelity with which you, without one word of remonstrance, carried my jewels to that wretched man. No wonder you spoke bitterly to him, and sought to protect me from him. I know now why you strove so bravely to save me from acting unworthily, and in the same breath demanded whether I was affianced to your rival. You knew me better at such moments than you did when you were alone penning these rhapsodies about my poor face. Stop: dont say anything more of that. Not even a woman's vanity could believe these lines deserved. Do you think I do not know what I am better than you? I, who have spent years before the mirror! Trust me, I could laugh at all this about a southern passion flower, did I not know how thoroughly you felt what you wrote."

Smith looked into her eyes with wonder, and observed, for the first time, that her eyes and hair were dark, like those of the dancer.

"You see" she continued, "that I speak to you with perfect candor. To avoid every false and conventional mannerism that the world might deem suited to the occasion, is the least tribute I can pay to the truth. But let us forget all this hopeless folly. Do not press me to answer you. Let us be friends, near friends, brother and sister if you will."

"Miss Woodward" said Smith, feeling that his position was becoming too serious to justify further deception: "I am very sorry that you should have so completely misunderstood my poetry. I dare not stand on any further ceremony. The fact is, I neither feel towards you as a brother nor do I desire that you should regard me as one."

Isabella sighed and smiled sadly at one stroke. Then she said, "Well, well, be it as you will, Robert." (Smith jumped.) "I have no hope to give you, scarcely any heart. When next I plight my troth, it shall be as the spouse of Christ. The cloister is more peaceful; and it cannot be less happy than the world."

Smith, dumbfoundered, had not the heart to persist in his elucidation. He resolved to temporize. "You must not think of such a life as that" said he. "It is bad enough to be unhappy, without being useless as well. Indeed, the two states cannot exist in perfection without one another."

She shook her head, and said, "I will never engage myself again."

"Then you have been engaged before?—but of course I have no right to ask."

"Do not be jealous, my friend. It was long ago, or at least it seems so. I was only a child. I must have been very young, for I was able to love, and to weep when I was betrayed."

"What! Were you betrayed?"

"Aye" said she, clasping her hands in her lap, and looking into the fire. "Not in any improper sense, of course; but he was faithless; and I was foolish enough to be surprised—hurt, even. Yet you see I survive, perhaps to love again and be again betrayed."

"I hope not" said Smith gravely.

Affected suddenly by the contrast between this simple remark, and the passionate disclaimer which she had intended to provoke, she turned towards him with beaming eyes and parted lips, laying her hand lightly on his arm.

"Is there then" she said, "a steadfast and abiding love to be hoped for amidst the ruins of so many other selfish and transient ones?"

"Experience alone can test the worth of any love" said Smith, striving to retain his clearness of mind beneath her touch.

"You are right. Ah, I am so tired of boasters, who value a woman's heart at a few false oaths!"

A pause followed, during which both looked at the fire.

"How is it all to end?" she said then, growing a little impatient of his scrupulously modest demeanor. "Have you thought of that?"

"There is little use in thinking of it" he replied. "The facts will not change. It is impossible for me to aspire to the part of a lover. Five-sevenths of my income depend on Mr Woodward. I am not insane enough to contemplate asking a woman to share the sum of forty pounds a year with me. I have for some time been waiting for a favorable opportunity to obtain from your father a nomination for a public office; but after what has passed, I feel that to do so would be almost treacherous."

"That is so like a man, Robert. You carry conscientiousness to the most fanciful extremes. And it is so delightfully characteristic of you to talk about five-sevenths by way of making love. But we shall not be lovers yet. Listen to me. Will you be content to be my friend?"

"I suppose I must" said Smith, with a smile.

"Do not assent so grudgingly. Consider what a beautiful bond friendship is. It is unconventional: it is unselfish. Let it be an interchange of holy offices. You can keep me in the straight path by the influence of your great-hearted integrity. I can offer a woman's sympathy; and that, worthless though it may be, was never yet a little thing in the eyes of a man."

"It will assuredly never be such in mine" said Smith gallantly. "I fear that the profit of the bargain will all be to me, and the disappointments to you."

"I will take my chance of that" she replied. "Indeed I wish it were true; for I know too well how weak a friend you have gained, and how little you are likely to preserve any regard for her."

"Let us hope then, since we are both prepared for disappointment, that we may be thoroughly disappointed. For my part, except as regards my being of use to you, I am very hopeful."

"Well, I permit you to hope" she said, involuntarily allowing an arch glance to escape through her studiedly sad expression.

"Oh, bother!" she added, rising. "Somebody is coming. Dont let Clytie find you here."

Smith rose hastily, prepared and very willing to go.

"Let us shake hands on our bargain" said Isabella, in an indescribable voice, losing all control over the roguish caprice of her eyes. Smith, hopelessly confused, could remember nothing but the gallant convention that a man who loses the chance of kissing a pretty woman is a fool. He took her hand; threw his left arm round her; kissed her twice; and ran out of the room. As he passed through the hall, he was in such a hurry to escape, that after clapping on his hat, he snatched his overcoat and goloshes, and fled into the night without waiting to put them on, slamming the door behind him. He was soon checked by the rain, which descended on him so copiously, that he had to retreat beneath the shelter of the portico next door, and put on his waterproofs.

"Ha! ha!" he chuckled, as he emerged a second time: "that was not so bad for a respectable young man like Smith. He is a gayer dog than people think."

In the Fulham Road, he saw a hoarding covered with posters, some hanging in drenched rags, and others, more recently attached, glistening with rain in the light of a street lamp. The weather was of that kind in which passers by, hurrying to shelter, do not halt to read placards; but Smith, seeing on a yellow sheet a picture of an ocean steamer and the word Australia in large letters, stopped and read it attentively. He learned that he could be transported to the antipodes of Queen's Gate for as little as fifteen guineas, or as much as seventy. His tastes led him to prefer the luxury to be secured by the larger sum: his resources fell short of the outfit and capital with which it would be necessary to supplement the smaller. He wondered whether, if he mentioned that he had inadvertently become engaged to Isabella, Mr Woodward would supply him with means to emigrate, or merely put him out of the house. A sense of dampness at the wrists and elbows soon warned him to stand no longer in the rain.

When he was seated in dry clothes before his fire in Danvers Street, the recollection of his interview with Miss Woodward humiliated him. Yet it made him laugh and behave ridiculously. He pulled his slight moustache; went to the mirror; and gazed at the face which had won a woman's admiration. He tried to imagine himself married. Isabella in a decorated apartment, with her pretty costumes and expressive eyes, was an attractive figure; but Isabella always, Isabella everywhere, inevitable, the first face to be seen in the morning, the last at night, Isabella in sickness or trouble, in a bad temper, in curl papers, at meals, Isabella old and decaying, Isabella a mother or a housekeeper, dragging the chain of union even more wearily than her husband! Smith shook his head.

"And yet I do not feel safe from her" he said to himself. "The least worthy women are the least consistent; and she might take it into her head to achieve a triumph of constancy to her present lowly lover that nothing but a honeymoon could explode. I wish I had burnt those cursed poems. I have acted like a scoundrel, or, what is the same thing, like a fool. Well, what is done cannot be undone. With which sententious remark, I, Don Juan Lothario Smith, will to bed, to bed, to bed."

## CHAPTER IX

ONE morning at half-past five o'clock, Smith, finding himself awake, and likely to remain so, was seized with an appetite for adventure. He resolved to take an early walk, and see how Chelsea looked at dawn, this being as much of an adventure as a man in his position can afford. In winter, such a project must be executed suddenly or not at all; and he sprang out of bed and pulled on his trousers before he had time to dwell on the cold, the certainty of being overcome with sleep at breakfast time, and the hunger which attacks the unaccustomed early riser. He dressed himself as carefully as for an afternoon promenade; stole downstairs; unchained the door quietly; and went out into Danvers Street, which had never seemed less cheerful to him than it did now in the half light of the morning.

Starting at a brisk pace to warm himself, Smith went along the embankment, whence he saw the river and Cheyne Walk grey and deserted. He quitted the river at Chelsea Bridge, and went through Sloane Street to the Brompton Road, by which he reached the South Kensington Museum. Here, looking at his watch, he found that it was only twenty minutes past six. Being by the time warm, and rid of the uncomfortable sensations with which he had set out, he abated his speed, and amused himself by watching the few persons who were going to the Oratory to attend the first mass there, much as *they* might have watched a company of pilgrims approaching a Buddhist shrine. Whilst he was thus occupied, a young lady, warmly clad in a sealskin coat and muff, came by. She looked at him, and stopped.

"Miss Woodward!"

"Robert!"

"Lucky I spoke first, or I should have had to say Isabella" thought Smith. Then he said, "This is a strange hour for you to be abroad."

"How did you find out that I intended to come? I did not mention it to a soul."

"To tell you the truth, my presence here is purely accidental. I have been out walking since before six. May I ask where you are going at such an unearthly hour?"

"I am going to mass at the Oratory" said Isabella gravely. "I hope I am not late." She looked at her watch. "Oh no: there is plenty of time: it does not begin until half-past six."

"Dont go in at all. Let us take a walk."

She shook her head, and said, "I should not have expected bad advice from you, of all people."

"Still less, of all people, should I have expected you to refuse it" said Smith, who was in the flippant and sarcastic humor proper to an adventurer.

Isabella stared at him. "What is *that* for?" said she.

"Nothing" he replied. "Only an impulse to say something ill natured. Well, are you determined to go in to that—that ecstasy shop."

"I am. Will you come in with me? If you do not, I shall think it is because you are afraid of the influence you scoff at."

"Will the ceremony last long?"

"Only half an hour. Do come in. It will not harm you to try once."

"Very well. I will go; although I doubt whether it is quite fair; for curiosity is my sole motive—apart, of course, from the pleasure of accompanying you."

"Never mind the motive. Come to scoff: you may remain to pray."

Smith looked at the Oratory clock. The half hour was close at hand; so they went together to the doors: she leading the way confidently, he following nervously, his face solemn.

"You must tell me what to do" he whispered, as they entered the porch. "I am utterly ignorant of the ritual."

"Hush! You have only to take off your hat."

Smith obeyed, and pushed open the door, making a wry face at the odor of stale incense, which was to him the very smell of superstition. However, he followed Miss Woodward to her seat with the reverent demeanor which those who are unaccustomed to churches maintain in them, feeling some of the exhilaration of a successful comedian as he did so. His companion, glancing at him occasionally, fancied that the rites of her church were making an impression on him. But he was far too Philistine and Protestant in his little culture to be impressed by low mass. He was accessible to books, but not to spectacle. Not a word passed between them until they had left the church and were once more in the road without. Then he drew a deep breath, and said,

"May I ask how often you have witnessed the performance at which we have just assisted?"

"Thous—hundreds of times, at least."

"Oh! Then you are so used to it that you dont mind it. For my part, I cannot conceive any rational being consenting to endure it twice."

"I thought you liked it" said Isabella. "You are a dreadful hypocrite."

"True. But hypocrisy is the penalty I had to pay for going where I had no business. I had no choice, in good taste, between looking as I did not feel, and walking out. I wonder at any one of your culture patronizing such a stupid business."

"Is it quite in good taste to attack the most precious convictions of others, merely because they do not happen to agree with your own?"

"Every man who entertains a belief, or a disbelief, has a right to become a propagandist, both for the sake of testing himself and enlightening others. At the same time, as I have had enough of religion during the past half hour to last me for a year, and not half enough of you to last me for a day, I would much rather you talked about yourself."

"You are in a very unusual vein this morning, I think. Satire and compliment are not usually near your lips. The only news I have to tell you about myself is that I am going away."

"Indeed" said Smith, forgetfully displaying more complacency than concern. "Where are you going to? and how soon will you be back?"

"You would have me believe that you care greatly, I suppose."

"I would have you believe that I am at least not wholly indifferent."

"I *do* believe it then; though I suppose I shall be sorry for it, like all other women. Well, I am going with my aunt Mrs Foley to a house in Derbyshire, where there is to be no end of rich and stupid people, and not one conversable person among them all."

"Then why go?"

"I have been invited; and I must go. Besides, at this season it is absurd to be in London when one can help it. And papa would like me to go. In short, I dont know why I am going; but I *am.*"

"I hope you will enjoy yourself."

"There is not the slightest chance of my doing any such thing. The host is an old Indian; and the house is always full of old Indians: yellow creatures, who eat curry and chutney, and entertain you by telling you the Hindoo for every sentence you utter. I feel ashamed of having a complexion or a liver among them."

"When do you start?"

"Today, at twelve o'clock."

"So suddenly!"

"Yes. Is it not?"

"And shall I not see you again?" said Smith gravely.

"Why, I intend to come back, do I not?" she replied merrily. "You have survived a fortnight without seeing me; and when we do meet, you do not always behave yourself."

"How soon will you be back?" said Smith, still gravely.

"I do not know. I may be away until January if I am asked to spend Christmas in the country."

"I expect by that time to be a civil servant, and also to be entirely forgotten by you."

"Are you going to leave papa?"

"Yes."

"And you believe that my memory is as short as my eyesight? I have more reason to fear being forgotten than you, if I may measure your constancy by your warmth. But I must give you my address. I shall expect you to write to me."

"Impossible. I could not write to you whilst awaiting a favor from your father, knowing how he would disapprove of it. Besides, you could not write to me—at least I presume you would not care to adopt the questionable practice of writing clandestinely to a man."

"Of course not" said Isabella, with a slight blush, looking at the pavement to prevent herself from betraying, by a stupended stare, her amazement at the morality of this inconceivable young man.

"So that I would not even know whether my letters were agreeable to you. Indeed, you will see on reflection that receiving letters would be as bad as answering them. Neither of us would feel our hands clean in the transaction. I think we had better not write except when we have something special to say."

"I suppose you are right" said Isabella, giving him up as altogether beyond her, and raising her eyes to his with an odd mixture of ridicule and admiration. "You are such a monster of propriety that I should be afraid to write to you even if there were none of the objections you have mentioned. Here we are at the Albert Hall. I wonder your principles did not restrain you from bringing me the longest way home."

"I am not wholly adamantine. I conclude, from your stopping, that I am not to come any further with you."

"I think you had better not."

"And I am not to see you for three months; perhaps never."

"Not for three whole months."

Smith looked along the street in both directions, and saw that there were some workmen, milkmen, and newspaper boys in sight. When he turned again towards Isabella, she had retreated beneath the portico of the Albert Hall.

"So the word is farewell" said he, following her.

"The word" she replied, without affectation, "is farewell."

"Once more then, permit me to misbehave myself." He quickly gave her a kiss; and the whoop of a neighboring milkman seemed to deride him for it. He released her, and looked apprehensively around. Isabella hastened away towards Queens

Gate. Before she disappeared, she turned and waved her hand. He lifted his hat in acknowledgment, and went his way, enjoying the prospect of a long respite from further lovemaking, and very far from realizing the ineptitude with which he had conducted it.

When he reached his lodging, he found a note asking him not to come that day to Queen's Gate until half-past twelve, as Mr Woodward expected to be engaged in family matters during the forenoon. After breakfast, he had a fancy to spend a morning in the city, where he had not been since Harriet Russell's wedding. He accordingly went by steamer to London Bridge, and after sauntering for some time, he entered the Liverpool Street railway terminus to buy a newspaper. As he passed through one of the booking offices, his attention was attracted by a group near the fire. Foremost among them, and bearing himself in such a manner that it was impossible to say whether his intention was self-assertive or apologetic, was Fraser Fenwick, attired in a glossy hat, blue frock coat adorned with a flower, white waistcoat, lavender gloves, patent leather boots, and trousers of small black and white check. His companions were unknown to Smith, who was so surprised at the improvement in the garb and features of his former fellow lodger, that he looked at him a second time in order to be sure of his identity, and in so doing was recognized by him. Smith took off his hat, in deference to a tall woman of determined aspect who was of the party. Fenwick, surprised, but gratified, returned the salute, considering that Smith's appearance was gentlemanly enough to impress the others favorably. Smith then passed on to the platform, but was overtaken by Fenwick.

"How d'ye do?" said Fraser, proffering his hand.

"Thank you, I am quite well" replied Smith, taking it.

"Haw! Thats right. What do you think I'm up to today?"

"I should say you are going to a wedding, at least."

"I should say so too, by George. Turned off before twelve, sir. Love, honor, and obey, or cherish, or whatever it is."

"Then it is yourself."

"Myself, sure enough. A fellow must shake down some day. Lady Geraldine Porter, a great friend of my poor mother's, set her heart on making a match for me. So here I am, noosed at last."

"I wish you all possible happiness, Mr Fenwick."

"You are a free man still, aint you?"

"Yes" said Smith, smiling, but with a qualm at the thought of Isabella.

"I'll tell you what" said Fenwick. "Come down and see me executed. It is only as far as Leytonstone; and there will be a good breakfast. I will answer for everybody being delighted to see you."

"I should like to, very much; but I am due at Kensington at twelve, so you must take the will for the deed."

"I should have liked you to be there. Between ourselves, all this ceremony and speechmaking is a nervous business; and a fellow needs to be backed up. However, if you cant come, of course—"

"I really can not. I must be off as it is. Once more, allow me to congratulate you. A pleasant honeymoon. Goodbye."

Smith returned by rail to the west end, and reached Queen's Gate at half-past twelve. As he ascended the steps, a carriage arrived opposite the house, with Clytie. He returned, and opened the door for her.

"Good morning" said she, jumping out. "I have just packed off Bella to the north. You will feel quite lonely now, Mr Smith."

"Why so?" said Smith, who had learned to defend himself against the banter which Clytie habitually practised on him, by affecting slowness of comprehension.

"However" she continued, ignoring the question, "you will be all the more inspired. Really, Mr Smith, you cant think how I cried over some of your poems."

"My poems! Where did you see them?"

"Why, they have been kicking about the house everywhere for the last month."

"Pray put them in the fire when next you find them. It is a pity to have the house encumbered by rubbish, particularly rubbish that kicks."

"Oh, that would be too bad. Guess my favorite poem."

"I dare not. But I am flattered to hear that you have a favorite."

"Do you know the little one called The Arabian Knight?"

"Yes. And do you prefer that?"

"Well, it disappointed me at first. I expected to find a story about men on magic carpets flying about in the air."

"Thank you; but I had enough of carpets when I was in the city. I was in the carpet line there, you know."

It was evident that Smith was neither ashamed of the city nor without a certain satisfaction in having left it for the west end. It was also evident that his only feeling for Clytie was one of good-humored superiority. She hated him extremely, and relieved her feelings by ringing the bell violently. Then Hamlet appeared, scowling.

"Do you know how long I have been standing here?" demanded Clytie.

"Ye'd betther ax the good-lookin bosthoon you keep to open the doore" replied Cornelius sulkily.

Smith passed on, being in a hurry to indulge his indignation in private against Isabella's careless treatment of his poems. Finding the study unoccupied, he sat down, and with a sudden revulsion against his recent dallying resolved to tell Isabella unequivocally at their next meeting that his heart was not touched by her, and never had been, if the event of his leaving Mr Woodward's employment did not avert that encounter for ever.

\*    \*    \*    \*    \*

Some months later, Smith, seated at nine o'clock in the evening in his lodging, received the following letter.

"BANGALORE, DERBYSHIRE,
*4th January* 1880.

"Dear Smith—I have just received your letter, and am exceedingly gratified by the news of your success in the examination. I have no doubt, if you continue the same steady fellow I have always known you, that you will make a first-rate position for yourself in your new office. As we are going off today to see the

Peak, I have only time to send you a few lines; but I hope you will call on me occasionally and let me know how you are getting on. At present I am rather at a loss without you, as I am a little be-hindhand with my letters. I am so pressed for time here that they accumulate in heaps. I shall see about advertizing as soon as I come back. I anticipate a busy month in consequence of my daughter Isabella's marriage early in March with a gentleman whom she met here: a Mr Saunders, who has lately returned from India. I had a touch of bronchitis last week, but I am well now, and, on the whole, have had no reason to complain during my stay. Faithfully yrs                    FOLEY WOODWARD."

Mrs Tilly, entering the room at this moment, with the small tray which she usually left with her lodger before retiring to rest, recoiled, fearing that she was alone with a lunatic. Smith, who had heeded neither her knock nor her entrance, was standing with his back towards her. In his hand was a letter, with which he made a sweep through the air, throwing back his head at the same time, and uttering a hoarse whispered sound. This performance he re-peated twice, and then, turning, saw Mrs Tilly on the threshold, the tray jingling in her hands, and her face pale with doubt.

"I beg your pardon" said he: "I did not hear you come in. The fact is, I have just received such good news in this letter that I was giving three cheers under my breath. I had no other means of giving vent to my feelings without disturbing the neighbors."

# EPILOGUE

ONE evening Smith left his lodging in Thurloe Square, South Kensington (it felt like Belgrave or Grosvenor Square to him), and, as the moon was full and the weather fine for walking, turned towards Putney. Here he crossed the bridge, pausing on it solemnly to admire the moonlit river, and proceeded to a picturesque house not far from the Surrey shore. On inquiring for Mrs Scott, he was ushered into a room on the ground floor, where he found Harriet, little altered in appearance by the lapse of years and change of circumstances: indeed, to a superficial observer, not changed at all. With her was a boy, with features which were a snubbish reproduction of her own on a small scale, and an impudent expression which burlesqued the old petulance of Cyril Scott. He was protesting that he would not go to bed until the return of his father; and in this too, he displayed a combination of impetuosity and obstinacy which shewed that he had inherited qualities from each of his parents.

"I am in a difficulty with the boy" said Harriet, seizing her unruly offspring's head, and rolling it to and fro against her bosom, where, in an attempt to coax her, he had unwarily placed it. "Cyril, he says, promised him that he should be put to bed by Mattie; and Mattie is at the Crystal Palace looking at the fireworks. It is very unfair of Henry; because when he was taken to the fireworks, Mattie went to bed without complaining."

"Better let him alone until he gets sleepy, and then he will be glad to go" said Smith.

"You do not suppose anything would induce him to confess sleepiness, I hope. Why wont you go to bed, Henry?"

Henry explained generally that going to bed was a cod, and particularly that he wanted Mr Smith to see his picture. Upon this point they based a compromise, by the terms of which Smith was to see the picture, and Henry, having ascertained his opinion of it, was to retire without further demur.

"Here!" said Harriet, producing a board on which the child

had plastered the brightest colors in his father's paint-box: "this is Henry's representation of the fireworks he saw, painted in emulation of Cyril's Fata Morgana."

"Tell him what Mrs Duncan said" cried Henry.

"Mrs Duncan said that she thought this by far the more sensible picture of the two. Henry was much more pleased by the remark than his father."

"It is first rate, very fine indeed" said Smith. The painter looked at him sceptically, as children do when they are put off, but not deceived, with compliments.

"Now, Henry!" said Harriet.

"I suppose Ive got to go" said Henry, thrusting his hands into his pockets with a shew of indifference. "I'm not going to walk, though. I want to be carried."

"Shall I carry you?" said Smith.

"No" said Henry. "I want Mamma to carry me. Besides, I'm too big for *you*."

"Do you remember your father telling you not to make me lift you?" said Harriet.

"Never you mind. I'll make it all square with the governor. Come on! Stop" he added, as Harriet was about to lay hands on him: "bar games. Promise that you wont tickle—ah!"

The stipulation ended in a shriek of laughter, as Harriet bore him off in her arms with an ease which proved that she had lost none of her former strength.

Quarter of an hour later, Harriet returned and found her visitor looking meditatively at the ceiling.

"A penny for your thoughts" she said, in her Scotch accent.

"I was just recalling an old idea of mine that of all children, yours would run the least risk of being spoiled."

"I used to think so myself, too. But, after all, what could you expect from us? Cyril was a spoiled child, and is so still, in some ways. I was a spoiled child too: at least, my father never crossed me in anything. If Henry turns out as well as Cyril, I shall be very well satisfied with him; so I am not afraid to spoil him a little. Cyril spoils Mattie on the same principle, or perhaps because it is the only method of education that comes naturally to him. They are both, in their different ways, very precocious, very bold, and prodigiously selfish, as all healthy children of their age ought to be; but they are much funnier and better able to shift for themselves than if they were kept down. In the end they are most likely less troublesome as well. I hate to see children, or indeed anybody, *afraid*."

"No doubt you are right. I remember how I secretly hated the solemn humbug my parents used to pour forth on me, when they were seized with an attack of duty."

"You were a very strange boy when I first knew you. That is, if you were ever really a boy at all."

"I dont think I ever was" said Smith. "I never felt like one. And I certainly did not consider myself one when I met you."

"That is the puzzle about you" said Harriet. "You are not a boy; and you are not grown-up. Some day you will get away from your books and come to know the world and get properly set. But just now there is no doing anything with you. You are just a bad case of immaturity."

"I never could feel grown-up; and I believe you were born grown-up. I am afraid I am incurable."

"Time will cure you. I am curious to see what you will be at forty."

"Married, perhaps. But I cant feel marriageable. And I doubt if I ever shall. Is marriage really a success?"

"What is the use of asking that? What else is there to do if you are to have a decent home? But it is not fit for some people; and some people are not fit for it. And the right couples dont often find one another as Cyril and I did. The routine for most is, one year of trying to persuade themselves that they are happy, six months of doubt, and eighteen months of conviction that the marriage is a miserable mistake. Then they get tired of bothering themselves over it, and settle down into domestic commonplace, quite disenchanted, but not tragically unhappy. Of course, children make a great difference; but most people get quite tired of them, just as the children themselves do with a plaything when its novelty wears off."

"It doesnt seem to have anything to do with me" said Smith. "It may be all right; but if it did not exist I should never dream of inventing it. Goodnight."

"Will you not wait for Cyril, and take some supper?"

"No, thank you. I intend to walk back to Thurloe Square; and it will take me until bedtime to do that."

"Well, as you please. You know you have only your own inclination to consult here."

"On the contrary, I have my habits. If I were to follow my inclination I would stay here for a week at least. Goodnight."

"Goodnight."

As Smith recrossed the bridge, he stopped and stood in one of the recesses to meditate on his immaturity, and to look upon the beauty of the still expanses of white moonlight and black shadow which lay before him. At last he shook his head negatively, and went home.

THE END